BIRTHRIGHT

OF

SCARS

RISING

LAURISA
BRANDT

Cover Design by: Franziska Stern - www.coverdungeon.com

Interior Design by: Laurisa Brandt

Illustrated by: Laurisa Brandt

Printed in United States of America by Amber Gryphon Press

Identifiers: ISBN: 979-8-9867207-0-8 (paperback) | 979-8-9867207-2-2 (eBook)

For Beck and Paige, who deserved more than one season.
Disrel admires your spunk.

For my hero and husband,
who hopes I can make back the money I put into publishing this book,
and who thinks I will wait to break even on that investment
before publishing my next book.

CONTENT ADVISORY

While this adventure contains many heartwarming moments of sunshine and friendship, some readers may find certain scenes or chapters to be upsetting or triggering. This story contains scenes of genocide, racism, sexual assault, murder, and torture. These subjects, when handled more seriously (as I feel they ought to be) will inherently be more graphic and detailed. I made my best effort to portray these elements delicately yet honestly, to write this story the way the characters told it to me. None of this exists for gratification.

This story is about a true, enduring, selfless love, the light shining in a dark, deadly world. Just as I have taken care when showing the depravity of human nature, I have also taken care in showing various expressions of love through this colorful cast of characters.

It is my hope that you, dear, courageous reader, will emerge from the last page of this story, a person more full of love, light, and compassion. Thank you for trusting me with your time.

p.s. ~ To my friends and family who dared to come this far: forget it's me. You've been warned.

PRONUNCIATION GUIDE

Cinnabar — SIHN-aa-BaaR

Disrel — diz-REL

Doni — don-EE

Jadkwe — yahd-kway. A foreign country known for its blue sand desserts

Koti — koh-TEE

Kyreasheluhn — KIER-Eash-EL-uhn

Mored — MOHR-red

Phaedra — FAY-DRah

Tygo — TEE-Go

Ulyia — yoo-LEE-uh

liddicoatite — lid-ih-coat-ite. A rare form of tourmaline that has a trigonal-ditrigonal pyramidal shape.

netyardot — net-YAR-doh. Non-ferrous magnetism with a strong repulsion to various other elements. Controllable when combined with a corestone, which provides the pull/attraction, creating a positive-negative effect.

Pyron (modern) / Pyre-eluhn {antiquated} — PI-run, *less commonly,* PEER-ron from antiquated PEER-ay-EL-uhn.

Pyrelux — PEER-eh-luks

QAV-X — khavh-ex. Qorzanopteryx Assault Vehicle — model Xyraxaryx

qorzan — kor-zuhn

skyn — skin. A nonflammable, cut-resistant fabric that is spun from stone. Also a one-piece garment or accessory garment made from this material.

Skynhound — skin-hound

Thelis — THEL-lis

wind — invisible forces present between stones that generate force, energy, attraction, and repulsion. Some stones generate only a positive or negative wind and would appear non-magnetic until brought into the presence of a compatible stone. Some types of wind will flow through nonpermeable barriers, such as steel or paper, while others are blocked or diluted by the same barriers.

EUCLASE

DOLOM

SELEN

PYRON

TOURMAL

GULF
of
TOURMAL

0 25 50   100   150   200
Miles

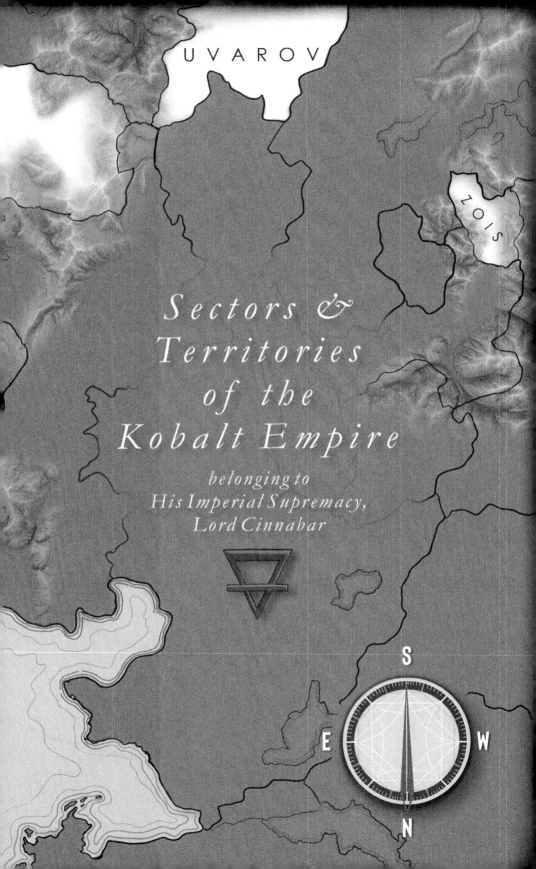

UVAROV

ZOIS

Sectors &
Territories
of the
Kobalt Empire

*belonging to
His Imperial Supremacy,
Lord Cinnabar*

S

E

W

N

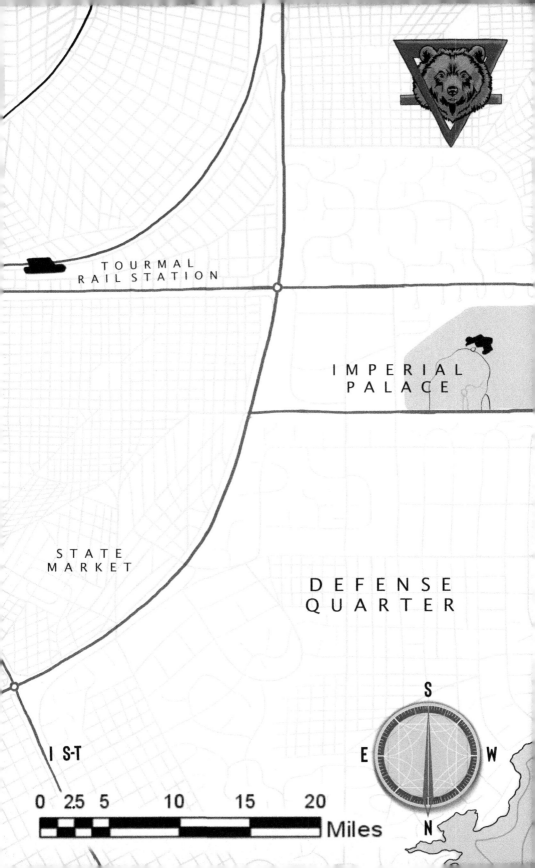

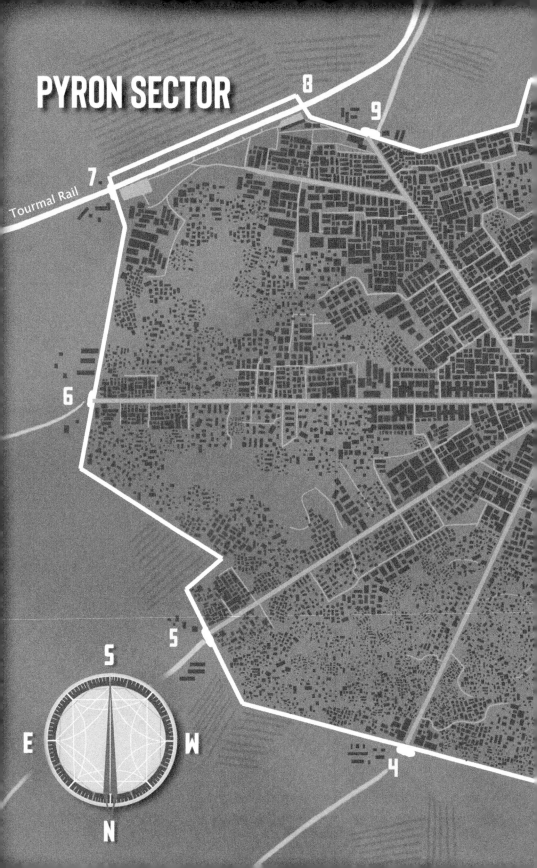

PYRON SECTOR

Tourmal Rail

PROLOGUE

Disrel threw himself at Father, kicking and swinging his fists. Father swept one long arm around him, dragging him to the floor and tickling his stomach. Disrel squealed and writhed and strained to keep his eyes open, but there was nothing he could do. The muscles and veins in Father's lean arms rippled as he dug his fingers into Disrel's ribs and stomach. Father was as strong as qorzan steel, his arms like stone.

"No, stop! Mercy! Please, stop!" Disrel laughed breathlessly and withered under the painful shocks that ripped through his sides. When would this torture end?

His younger sister, Solla, threw herself onto Father's back and wrapped her arms around his neck. Father reared back with a roar. He clawed Solla off his neck and rolled her onto the floor, pushing his face against her, pretending to eat her like a wild bear.

"Now I've got you, little girl! Nom, num, nom, num!"

Solla shrieked and gripped Father's braided black hair in her little hands. She stamped at his chest with her bare feet.

"D'rel! D'rel!" Her cry for help was cut short by spastic laughter.

Disrel clamored up on all fours, huffing and puffing. His own single braid whipped around his face. It was the braid of a warrior, a protector. He could win this. With a battle cry, he stabbed an invisible knife into Father's side.

Father reared back, grabbing him around the neck as he fell and rolled over him. Disrel stabbed again and again at the bear's stomach while Solla rushed in, but Father pulled her underneath him and laid her next to her brother.

"Now, I have you both for my supper." Father squeezed them together against his chest and planted kisses on their cheeks.

"I can't breathe. I can't breathe," Disrel panted. His head pounded from exertion and he wriggled until Father released him.

Father sat back. "Alright. That's enough, you two."

Solla squealed from her position on her back and kicked her legs.

Father swatted her on the bottom. "Time to sleep."

Solla picked herself up and trotted a half circle around Father. "Be a bear again. Eat me."

"This bear is full. He can't eat any more little girls tonight."

Disrel thought about how strong and deep Father's voice was. One day, he would grow into a man just like Father. But since he'd just turned nine, that was still a long way off. He sat back, catching his breath, unsure if he had won or lost the fight. His cheeks ached from smiling. Any day that ended like this was a perfect day. He loved wrestling with Father, and hearing Solla's laugh as she screamed for him to come save her. She was four now.

"Eat me." Solla ran up against Father's chest and planted her fists.

Father collected her like an infant and arrested her hands in his mighty palm. "You need to sleep so you're strong enough to fight bears tomorrow, little tigress."

"No." Solla wriggled.

"Yes." Father buried his mouth against her chubby neck and snarled. She let loose another happy squeal.

Disrel crawled over to the mattress in the corner of the room. It had been a long, good day. Any day that Father came home from work was a good day. Any day he returned with food was an even better one. And the days when he wrestled with them on the floor were the best of all days—the best that could be had since Mother had been killed a year ago in the marketplace. A sable cut her throat because she resisted arrest, trying to get home with medicine for Solla. Disrel had seen it happen, had run home and told Father. There were many bad days after that one, especially for Father. And since then, Disrel and Solla had to stay hidden while Father was at work. It was lonely and frightening, not knowing when Father would come home or if he would bring food—even though he did more often than not.

Father turned down the light of the stone lamp in the corner of the room and crawled onto the mattress. He pulled Solla and Disrel close and wrapped their blue blanket around the three of them, tucking it under Solla's chin and planting a kiss on her forehead. Disrel felt the muscles in Father's arm around him. He was sure Father could fight and kill a real bear if he ever had to.

Solla snuggled into Father's side. "Tell me a story."

"Very well," Father laughed and lifted his eyes to the stained, sagging ceiling where he always looked when searching for a story. Then he looked down at Solla. "Many sunrises ago, a little girl was playing by the seashore."

"Make it a warrior's tale," Disrel said.

Father glanced over. "And a strong young boy was sailing in a boat he had built."

"And food," Solla added. "All kinds of food."

"And the boy's boat was full of every kind of wonderful food. There were pies and racks of ribs and big beautiful bananas and melons."

"I want cloud candy," Solla grinned.

"And there were baskets of cloud candy."

Some minutes later, Solla's eyes drooped, and Father brought the story to a close with a mighty yawn. Disrel often pondered the stories Father told in the lingering silence that followed, but his heart was burning with a question.

"Father?"

"Yes, my son."

"When will Solla and I be able to go outside in the sun again?"

Father sighed softly and hugged Disrel more tightly. His mouth was drawn with sadness. "I don't know."

"Why can't we play with the neighbor children while you're at work? They're Pyrons just like we are."

Father looked at him. "You might say the wrong thing, and then the soldiers will come and kill us."

"Why don't our neighbors dread saying the wrong things like we do?"

Father hesitated. "My son, we are not—"

Voices echoed through the thin walls of the apartment. Big booming voices, and pounding.

Father scrambled up and turned on the lamp. He ran to the door and pressed his ear up against a crack in the jam. Disrel sat up and listened.

"Open the door!" the voices demanded in between bursts of drumming. Other commands were muffled and jumbled, but they were coming closer. The walls shook.

Solla pulled the blanket over her head and whimpered. Disrel's heart raced. Would the soldiers knock on their door too? What did they want?

Father rushed back over to the bed, his face hard and his movements tense. "Not a sound! Just like we practiced. Come."

He hurried them over to a metal container tucked next to a can of trash and picked up the lid. Disrel jumped into the dark cavity. It was barely large enough to hold him and Solla. He felt like he had grown since the last time he'd crawled inside.

Father's voice strained with fear. "Don't come out, no matter what happens." He picked Solla up and planted a kiss on her cheek. "Can you be very quiet for Father, my little sunshine? You must be very good for Brother. That's my brave tigress. You're strong. You're not afraid of anything. Not bears or soldiers."

Solla whined and scrubbed the back of her hand across her groggy eyes. She hated being in the dark box even when Disrel sat with her and tried to make a game of it.

The warped, metal door to their tiny apartment rang brilliantly under the soldiers' deafening blows. Father squeezed her to his chest before setting her down on Disrel's lap.

"I love you both very much. Disrel, remember this: Never forsake the way of Pyron. My greatest desire is that you live free. That's how we were created to be, and no other way is worth living."

Disrel hugged his little sister and wrapped his hand around her mouth, stifling her whimpers. Why was Father talking like this? He would always be around to remind them, to show them the way of Pyron, wouldn't he? Father's terror-stricken face hovered over the open container a moment, and his deep, dark eyes bent with love.

Disrel's throat was dry with fear. He had so many questions, but all he could do was nod. The lid came down hard, enveloping him and his sister in a vat of darkness. *Whump.* Something heavy landed on the lid of the chest. Disrel pressed his face up to a rusty pinhole in the side of the container. Father paced the room, combing his tumbling black locks fitfully, his elbows and shoulders high. Would the soldiers search the room? Would they notice the chest, the only piece of furniture in the one-room apartment? Would they look at the disheveled mattress in the corner and suspect that three bodies had only just been warming it?

The door snapped back against the wall under a deluge of men in armored unitards, perfectly molded to their hulking figures. They carried long poles, crowned with curved blades that could both slice and impale, and their transparent catlike eyes were darkened by the sheets of tinted glass that rimmed their helmets. A pair of crimson boots thumped across the sagging floor, echoing the authority and power of Imperial Sables, women so tough and cruel that they could overpower a grown man and laugh while he struggled in his blood.

"Couldn't you hear us knocking?" The sable's goosebill nose leveled with Father's and her icy gaze frosted right through her visor. The Kobalt language was a sawtooth blade, grinding and vengeful, devoid of blessings and praise. "Where is the renegade? Why is he always coming through this neighborhood?"

Father held his chin even with the sable's. "I wouldn't know him if I met him, miss."

"You've seen his wanted poster."

"I've seen his mask on your wanted posters."

The sable cuffed Father to the ground with one chop of her arm, and her gloved hand jerked his head up by his braid.

Disrel shook but kept a hand clamped firmly over Solla's mouth. She squirmed and arched, unable to comprehend the danger. He wrapped his feet around her legs to keep her from kicking the sides of the container. His heart raced as the sable's pitched interrogation reverberated through the metal chest.

"It will be alright, little sister. It will be alright." He pressed his lips to Solla's ear, hoping the soldiers would ask their questions and move on. They had been looking for the renegade for months and didn't always make arrests.

Father did his best to answer the sable's pointed questions with his limited Kobalt tongue. "I haven't seen anyone or anything suspicious in this neighborhood."

Her weapon collided with Father's head. "Liar!"

He crumpled forward on the floor and Disrel's heart stopped.

"Everything and everyone in this sector is suspicious. That is why we are here—to quench this rebellion." Her lithe shadow turned to her troops. "Arrest and interrogate this man further. He knows exactly where the renegade is hiding."

Disrel's cheeks burned and he choked back tears as the sables scraped Father off the floor and carried him from the room in cuffs. He wanted to leap from hiding and throw them all off the balcony. But he was only half the length of their spears, and even Father, as strong as he was, could do nothing.

The soldiers trickled back through the doorway and the sable commander's frigid eyes scoured the empty room. With a discontented turn of her head, she swept from the apartment, slamming the door behind her. The door ground back open on its broken hinges with a moan. Disrel's hand fell from Solla's shriveled face.

She sputtered and kicked. "Father. I want Father."

Disrel rubbed his watering eyes and sniffed. The words *it will be alright* kept falling short of his lips. It was a lie. Others in their neighborhood who had been arrested for interrogation had never come back. Would they take Father to prison? To a sector far away? His chest cramped and an aching lump swelled in his throat. Without Father, he and Solla were utterly alone in a hostile world. They were strays.

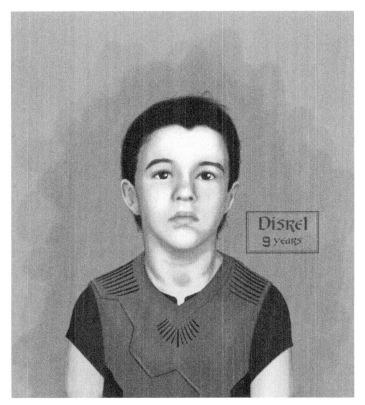

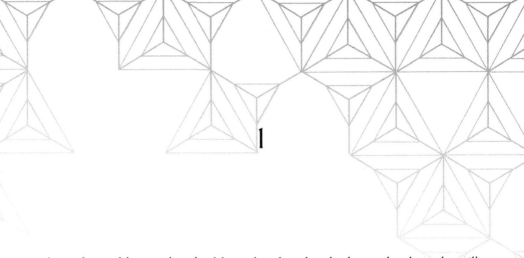

1

T he problem with a dead legend is that there's always the threat he will resurrect, and any time he does will be inconvenient for those in power.

Fifteen years after the military shot the renegade down into Tourmal Bay and a fisherman pulled up his helmet, nobody spoke of him—at least, not in public. And the state wrote one new restriction against Pyrons into law each day.

Disrel plucked a pamphlet out of a trash bin and brushed an orange peel off its cover. He leaned back against his favorite lamppost, thumbing through the pages while garbled conversations between buyers and sellers droned in the bustling marketplace around him. He inhaled deeply, savoring the warm notes of butter, vanilla, and cinnamon. No other lamppost offered such a clear view of the market's busiest intersection—or stood as close to the baker's oven—as this one. A patron sank his teeth into a steaming roll, and Disrel swallowed back a wave of saliva, his tongue tormented by the pleasure in the patron's smile. Maybe one day he could afford to treat himself to one of those.

Disrel observed the sea of shoppers around him and the eclectic display of fashion. Even the common man's attire—close-fitting, one-piece garments that covered from neck to wrist to ankle, were rich with color and texture. But a recently published law required that Pyrons wear white, simply to make them more obtrusive than they already were. Like all Pyrons, Disrel was lean, dark-eyed, and suspicious. He knew his potential, and he knew the only thing that held a patrolman's eye longer than a thieving stray was a loitering Pyron male.

Loaded pushcarts rumbled over the pavement. Money jangled in open hands and on tabletops. The distinct thumping of combat boots and weaponry rattled from behind.

"You! Pyron! Buy what you need and get moving."

Disrel turned smoothly to face the soldier. The steel-blue eyes of the Kobalt patrolman challenged him from behind the tinted helmet visor. A curved glaive menaced from its haft in the soldier's grip, its frosted qorzan steel edges haloed by the golden hour light. Disrel sauntered off through the crowd and eyed the wares he passed with casual interest, knowing the soldier would watch him for several minutes. He enjoyed making them feel vigilant while strays made off with food behind their backs.

The patrolman moved on. Disrel circled around the market block and settled back up against his lamppost. He flicked the pamphlet up in front of his chin and resumed being suspicious. A pile of rotting juri fruit now crowned the top of the garbage bin, their bright yellow guts oozing through the cracks in their swollen peels. Disrel's eyes watered at their sharp, tangy odor, and he pivoted around the lamppost. A grating voice pitched above the market cacophony, drawing his gaze to the source.

"It's the law. No ID, no sale." A grocer pulled her loaves of bread back into her booth and away from her customer.

A young woman leaned across the counter, hands outstretched, fingers clutching two dark tokens. Her curly, black locks shook around her temples. "My child and I haven't eaten in days. Two chips is two chips."

"Spend them elsewhere. We only accept empire-authorized credits. Next customer."

The ragged girl followed the vendor doggedly around the table, sunken cheeks pressed to the light, her shimmering white garment swinging around her body. "Akkoni, please! We went to primary school together, remember? We played together after hours every day! I never dreamed I'd have to beg for my bread. You know we've been pressed out of our trades."

Akkoni bagged the next customer's goods and accepted the payment.

"Please!" The little Pyron pushed in front of the customer and locked eyes with the grocer.

"I don't know you, woman. Vex me and I'll call for soldiers!"

The haggard woman withdrew in defeat, clutching the two chips tightly in her thin, pasty hands. Her snowy garment glistened regally with flecks of gold. It was a spotless token of her indigenous heritage. Her famished eyes ransacked the loaded bars on every side, tables of fruit ripening in the sun, crimson cuts of fresh meat stacked on cold marble slabs in the shade. Her nose flared at the barrels of coarse spices being sifted by other shoppers. She placed one of her frail hands under her stomach, revealing the peculiar roundness of pregnancy.

For a moment, she reminded Disrel of Mother and the time they'd come to this market to find medicine for Solla. Mother had stood just like that, hand under her stomach, hungry, but thinking only of her children. Had she not been pregnant, she might've outrun the sable that killed her.

The tips of the woman's fingers were stained and blistered, probably from digging through pounds of alley rubbish to find those two chips in hopes of exchanging them for some pastries for her child. But few would ever be caught exchanging goods with a stray Pyron, even this late in the day. Once word got around, it attracted more strays, and that made respectable customers uncomfortable. And that was bad for business.

The woman rounded the corner of the booth where the baker was stacking fresh loaves. He gave her a nod, but only to let her know that he saw her and not to try to take one. She retreated against the tent cover, and the blithe rhythms of a flute and drum wafted over the marketplace. The minstrel's tunes were a soulful language to all strays. It told them where the soldiers were and how many there were at any given time. But this woman was deafened to everything but her own hunger. Disrel paced, hoping to draw attention to himself before a patrolman noticed her.

The little Pyron's ravenous, midnight eyes swept the market, then lit upon Akkoni, back turned to serve another customer. Then the baker bent over, sliding lumps of dough into the brick ovens. In one swift motion, the stray dropped her two chips on the table, lifted a steaming, braided round up to her chest, and plowed into the crowd.

Akkoni threw herself against the table. "Stop her! Pyron thief!"

The boom from the minstrel's bass drum shook the spice mounds into puddles. The stray danced through the marketplace like a wild roe, white garment streaming in ribbons from her ankles.

A soldier turned his polearm horizontally, checking her path. His lips warped and his eyes blazed. "Another street rat stealing food."

"I paid for it!" The woman shielded the bread against her breasts as though it were a suckling child. Her raven curls whirled as she turned, and a second soldier scooted up behind her.

Disrel picked up a cracking juri fruit and bounced it lightly in his palm. It jiggled like a cup of pudding. Three more strays would eat tonight. This was for Mother.

The soldiers pressed their poles around the woman's neck and chest.

"The Tourmaline lady said you're stealing it. So who am I to believe? A stray ashrat or a citizen trying to sell her wares?"

Disrel cast, and the brilliant lemony pulp splattered across the soldier's visor. He plowed away from the lamppost and into the stream of people.

"There's another one!" The soldiers barked and pursued him. A third soldier left his post and blocked Disrel's path with his polearm, squaring his armored hips and shoulders.

"Stand down! We have the authority to kill anyone who interferes with an arrest."

Disrel grabbed the haft and swung underneath the soldier's elbow, throwing him down and sprinting on. The others rushed in with glaives lowered. Disrel hauled around a corner and slapped his hand on a garbage barrel, strewing its putrid contents into the street. A rush of sewage rolled across the soldiers' boots and they stumbled through the refuse as Disrel darted nimbly back and forth through the sea of bodies like a white rabbit fleeing foxes.

The soldiers beat the crowd with their staves until the sea parted before them. Disrel flew, arms and legs pumping madly, darting left and jumping right. He vaulted a melon cart and slid around the corner of a permanent stone booth, the soles of his boots hissing across the slick surface. He skimmed over the pavement and tumbled off a retaining wall into the woven ceiling of a pergola in the plaza below. The ropes jolted his fall, and his arms and legs spidered the air while the ground rocked below. The soldiers trotted down the steps to the market's lower level, weapons dancing in their fists, eyes glinting with wrath for their netted prey. Disrel grunted and wriggled in his snare; he was meat for the butcher. A netted sparrow. Helpless. Waiting for the soldiers to drive their black qorzan steel through his stomach and drain his blood into the gutters, drop his entrails on the pavement for the dogs. Beads of sweat wept over his temples, and his breath roared through his throat. Passersby pointed and snickered.

The lieutenant's lip curled upward as he menaced him with his polearm. Disrel kicked at the weapon with his free foot, but the momentum only spun his vulnerable backside to the patrolmen.

The other soldier drew his knife and caught Disrel's leg under his arm.

"How should we truss this one?" He tugged at the hanging ropes, sliding one across Disrel's back and under his elbows.

"Upside down. Like pork on a spit."

The soldiers cinched the ropes, hanging him from his elbows and ankles, stomach down. The lieutenant lifted his rust-colored combat boot against his knee, gingerly stripped a piece of garbage off the sole, and transferred it almost affectionately onto Disrel's face. He wiped the fingers of his glove on Disrel's shoulder. The putrid stench seared Disrel's nose, and his stomach twisted. He gagged and shook the garbage from his cheek.

"Ashrats don't like garbage?" The soldier got down in his face, showering him with spit. "How come I always find you digging in it?"

Disrel glowered. He could accept that his time had come, but he didn't deserve this torture. The soldiers turned away to continue their patrol, their raucous laughter echoing through the plaza. He huffed and wriggled, fighting the cords that stretched his arms back, while heads swam past, tilting and laughing. Legs were magnetized to the smutty ceiling of the world. A dog bristled and snapped its jaws as its surly owner allowed it just enough leash to torment him. Disrel stretched against his tethers, praying that the dog would not jump, that his fangs would fall short with every snap. The deadly growls blasted in his ears, and shoppers cast taunting remarks that faithfully reminded him that he was getting what every Pyron deserved. One salty old Kobalt lifted his cane and dealt several vicious blows to the back of his legs before staggering off, venting the injustices of his life. Disrel's arms burned as the shadows lengthened. Game over. The soldiers would come back and collect him in their wagon, take him to the Hold in chains. From there, it was either a beating and a release into the new Pyron sector, or a beating and the short one-way ride to Execution Square. The first course of fate was equally unappealing as the second, both leaving Solla to fend for herself.

The shining bald head of a bronze Kobalt paused in traffic. The man approached with ready hands, thick shoulders flexed. Disrel winced, preparing himself to become a human punching bag, waiting for the hands to wrap around his neck and throttle the life from him. One arm set tightly around Disrel's waist and cold steel hit the back of his arm.

"You look like you could use a little help."

Disrel's fingers tingled sharply as circulation returned. One by one the ropes tugged and released, then the stranger lowered him to the ground and gave him a hand up.

Disrel massaged his legs and stretched. "You're a good soul. Thank you."

"Think nothing of it. Can you run?" The benefactor stood with princely posture in his crimson garment, eyes glistening with kindness and his rueful lips framed by a beautiful beard and mustache.

"Yeah. Why?"

The sharp barks of soldiers rang out from the plaza above. Two patrolmen raised their weapons and took to the stairs.

"Get going!" The bald stranger struck out against the flow of pedestrian traffic.

Disrel stumbled after him, plowing into shoppers like a crazed ox chasing a red flag. He bounded under elbows and over baskets, pushing with his wide shoulders. The world gleamed with the brilliantly saturated hues of a sunset, and people funneled in droves toward the edges of the market. The crimson-clad man vanished, and Disrel spilled through a wide gate and into the street with the current of bodies.

A burst of red broke from the crowd and down a side street. Disrel bounded into the roadway. Corecycle wheels screeched and drivers cursed. Disrel's hands slapped down on the nose of a sliding vehicle and he danced onto the curb as the driver determined to run him over. He rounded into the alley and flew out into another street, finding the big Kobalt stopped in front of a shop window, hands akimbo, his chest rising and falling like bellows.

"Did they see you?"

Disrel shook his head and gasped. Millions of needle pricks stung his arms and legs as feeling returned.

"That was a pretty stupid stunt, throwing garbage at the soldiers." The bald man wiped his hand over his mouth.

"The lady got her bread, didn't she?"

"And you almost paid for it with your life."

Disrel glared at the ground. "They were running a two-for-one special. I thought it was a good deal."

The stranger chuckled.

Disrel offered his hand. "Thanks for looking out for me. I'm Disrel."

The man slap-grabbed it, gave it three quick pumps, and moved down the sidewalk.

"Tygo. It's what we do. I would have freed you sooner, but I had a little shopping to do first."

Disrel snorted. This man didn't have a single bag of groceries or goods on his person. "Who's 'we'?"

"Those of us who fight for Pyron."

Disrel bit his lip and studied Tygo cautiously as the distance between them widened. He carried himself like a soldier. "Why would you fight for my people?"

"Reasons. Same as I cut you free back there. Same as you had, maybe, for helping a stray lift some bread."

"Are you part of a resistance group?"

"You're free, aren't you? Get moving." Tygo turned down an alley.

Disrel followed. "Why did you do your shopping before helping me? Why would you leave whatever you bought for someone else to walk off with?"

"What if I bought food for the strays?"

"Look, man. I appreciate it. I was one of them once. But you know as well as I do that feeding strays won't turn things around. I want to fight for my people."

Tygo's teeth shone as he laughed. "Fight? You couldn't even get away with throwing garbage at the soldiers."

"That's not why I was there." Disrel raked a lock of black hair off his brow. "Sure, it was stupid. But nobody else was going to help her. I'm tired of seeing my people slaughtered like sheep. Just give me a chance. I can prove myself."

Tygo paused and looked him up and down.

Disrel straightened his shoulders. "Are you the leader?"

"No. But our leader is a highly selective man. He hasn't taken a new recruit in months."

"Why?"

"You can never be too careful when you're assembling an army to crush the regime. He keeps his men so compartmentalized that none have seen the extent of his forces. The left hand never knows what the right hand is doing. If any part of us is ratted out, it looks like the state has squashed a small rabble of dissenters. And the colony continues growing, like a tumor, unnoticed, slowly wrapping itself around the throat of the empire."

Determination simmered in Disrel's bones. "The state took everything from me. My father was just a walking skeleton at the Gelnitrak work camp three weeks ago. He died before I could speak to him. I've got nothing else, Tygo. I'll do anything. I just need this chance."

"Turns out we're all desperate men." Tygo scrubbed his chin and studied him. "Alright. I won't mention that I found you strung up in the market and I'll put in a good word for your heroic qualities. Come on."

Disrel's heart lightened with hope as he followed Tygo down the sloped street.

The sun perched on the western ridge like a gleaming phoenix, tracing everything its light touched with fire. The dark stone and metal structures of Tourmal penetrated the glowing evening sky and cast ominous shadows on the bustling cityscape. This capitol sector had always been Disrel's home, and it offered peace and prosperity to anyone and everyone who wasn't Pyron. Citizens whizzed along the dark, stone freeways straddling the sleek, open backs of corecycles, two and sometimes three-wheeled vehicles that made as little noise as a summer breeze. These were the stately horses a man could ride forever and a day, and they would never tire, nor overheat, nor consume food. Disrel's greatest pleasure was taking his boss's corecycle out on company errands, but he couldn't afford one of his own, even if he was one of those privileged and accursed Pyrons who had sold his soul in exchange for Kobalt citizenship. Like other Pyrons who held citizenship within the empire, he was still poor, but not as desperately poor as the strays—the orphans, the homeless, and others without ID cards.

Tygo led him across a walking bridge and down a wide street. He asked Disrel what he knew of weapons and martial arts and talked about the resistance group's plan to place the governing power in the hands of the people and localized governments. They soon arrived at an inconspicuous home on the south side of Tourmal.

The faces of the homes along the street glowed in the sunset. Lavender clouds rimmed in red gathered around rooftop spires, and a wet night air carried in the sickeningly sweet odors of fish and mollusks from the bay. Disrel brushed his cheek with his sleeve, thinking he had missed a spot. A shutter clapped back and forth in the wind, and a broken wind chime tolled its single forlorn bell like a grave watcher. Disrel rubbed the hair on his neck down as he passed a broken stained-glass window on the way up to the back porch. Homes this old had histories, and usually people who were not interested in moving out.

The stone porch step wobbled under his weight, displaced by the gnarled roots that contested for ground underneath it. Tygo leaned against the great door and rapped it rhythmically with his knuckles, then stepped back and thrust his hands in his pockets. Disrel shifted from foot to foot as a cricket chirped in a nearby bush. Tygo knocked a second time.

"We usually meet in an abandoned red brick building near the Grossings, over on Riverstone. But one of our officers, Teagen Faznog, has started a new recruitment there to guard a vast store of weapons and ammunition we've collected over the last five years. He keeps us well supplied."

The hair on Disrel's neck bristled. He shrugged his shoulders and glanced toward the street.

Blinding light slammed their liquid black shadows into the door. Disrel recoiled, hands splayed before his eyes, as three soldiers surrounded the porch, hedging the pair in with their polearms.

"On the ground! Get on the ground! Hands on your head! I said *get on the ground*!"

Disrel leaped over the railing corner, and a polearm caught him and threw him to the earth. He rolled in the grass, rising and wrestling the haft as two more soldiers rushed him like lions. The others had Tygo on his knees with a sack on his head, and more had come out through the door. A blunt stroke burned through

Disrel's shoulders and his knees buckled as a sack jerked over his head. Cold hard rings bit down into his wrists, and rough hands hauled him upright and marched him along. Sweat rolled down Disrel's neck, and he trembled, tripping up steps and into a wide room echoing with military voices. A heavy door clanked shut as they took Tygo into another room for questioning. Disrel was forced to kneel on the warped, unforgiving floor, and he drew each breath to the fullest, knowing that at any moment his chin would be jerked up and his neck bared to ruthless, biting qorzan steel. There were no trials for Pyrons.

Hands plunged through his pockets. The hard soles of boots ground a circle around him. A female voice, the voice of a sable, chilled Disrel's blood. "Conspiring to overthrow the government, along with all the others."

"Should we execute them here? Or save them for the arena?" A male voice said.

"Kill them all here."

Disrel's heart melted with dread. He kept his head down, counting each second, thinking of his sister, waiting for the sack to lift and a razor edge to kiss his throat. Bodies moved between the rooms. Doors opened and shut. Voices rose and fell. Minutes passed and his heart throbbed with ever-mounting anxiety, every ambient sound like a body hitting the floor, life gurgling from a slashed throat, one prisoner closer to his own last breath. A string of questions and guttural cries poured from a nearby room and were eventually silenced by a dull thumping. He strained against the cuffs and trembled. Sweat wicked through the fabric of his skyn and the air in the sack grew stagnant and stifling.

A door groaned on hinges and boots clomped as someone approached. The sack snapped away. Disrel's heart jolted at the crimson boots and armored legs planted right in front of him and the wicked execution knife that hovered just above.

"Who are you, Pyron?"

Disrel avoided the soldier's penetrating gaze, casting his eyes toward the presence he felt behind him. "You've seen my ID," he muttered. "It's pronounced, diz–REL."

"Did you honestly think you'd get away with your rebellion? That we wouldn't hunt you down, follow you to your leader?"

He followed the stout legs upward and stared brazenly into the enforcer's ruthless face.

The soldier sneered. "You're not afraid?"

Disrel's heart quivered. "No."

A hand seized his elbow from behind, wedging a bar between his cuffs and twisting. His scream choked short on his lips and he roared through his teeth.

"You should be. Where are the others?" The sable growled through clenched teeth.

Fire licked through each wrist and up Disrel's arms. "What others?"

The baton wrenched harder, and Disrel buckled over, gasping. The male officer grabbed a fistful of hair and jerked his face toward the light.

"The others in your little network. Give us the name of even one of their leaders or the location of their hideouts, and we'll let you go."

Disrel clamped his eyes shut and fought the pain. Teagen Faznog. He could give up the name. But if they let him go at all, it would be with broken wrists or a scarred face. His life wasn't worth more than all those men, all those weapons. They could do so much more for his people than he could. Tears spilled silently down his nose and onto the floor, each one crowned with agony and waves of fire.

"Crying won't get you any pity. Talk!" The soldier bellowed.

Disrel shook his head and the baton torqued harder, wringing a feral cry from his throat.

Suddenly, the sable released her pressure and stepped back. "What made you decide to throw your life away like this, Pyron? You had citizenship, a good job."

Disrel's eyes scorched on the floorboards like hot coals, and he sucked air through his teeth. He couldn't even plead with them for his sister's sake. They couldn't know she existed or they would use her to make him talk.

The enforcer brought a combat knife up against his throat. "You need to start thinking about how to survive tonight. Your actions have consequences."

So did inaction. Disrel pushed back, defying the sharp edge, staring into the soldier's electric blue eyes. "What good does it do me to survive one night as a coward to die the next as a traitor?"

The soldier kicked him over. "You're as stupid as they come. Get ready to meet your god, ashrat."

The other soldiers hauled Disrel up and thrust him against the wall, slamming his cheek into the old wallpaper, rusted and mildewed. Disrel's heart galloped and his throat knotted at the sound of a crossbow string clicking into place. He closed his eyes and swallowed, silent prayers pouring from his spirit. He projected all his love for Solla, hoping she would feel it long after he was gone. If only he had taken the time to hug her last night and tell her how much she meant to him. How long would it take for the world to fade once the bolt pierced his skull? Was it quick? Or would he writhe for minutes?

The nose of a crossbow pressed against his head, and burning energy jolted through his spine. The wall melted, and all feeling flushed away into a void.

Dead. Alone. Would Father come? Would Mother come? Anyone at all? Would he recognize them?

Breathe. Breathe.

Disrel's mind swam with panic. He was like a sleeper struggling up from a nightmare, aching, groping, straining, stretching to breach the veil into waking life. He slammed down on a hard surface and his eyes flashed open. A porch lamp hung high overhead, dull and dark. The great door towered on his right. His bearings returned, and he flexed his wrists. He was in a body. His body. His hands rested at his sides, free of the cuffs.

Was this death—existing in the same world but shut off from the living? Where were the soldiers? Disrel jerked to his feet and whirled on the porch, patting his head and clawing at the fabric clutching his throat. His hands slapped down his broad chest and straight stomach. Not a drop of blood. Not a scratch on his skin. He tore through his pockets and found his ID. *Thunder.* He raked his fingers through his short hair. Had it all been a prank? And who would play such a cruel joke? The stars twinkled brilliantly above. How long had he been out? Solla would be eating her knuckles with anxiety about now. But he was alive.

He leaped from the porch and raced toward home as hard as his shaking legs would carry him.

The moment Disrel opened his apartment door, his sister's arms snared his neck. Her tender eyes were rimmed in red and her curly black hair was frizzed from pulling.

"Rel! Thanks to God, you're alive. Where *were* you?"

Disrel pressed his face against her head and shushed her while he contemplated his gratitude. Solla was all he had in the world, and he meant as much to her. The night Father was arrested, Disrel had been forced to take on the roles of both parents: nurturing, providing, and protecting. But despite all his efforts, Solla was fragile, unable to cope with the changing, volatile world. Her anxieties crippled her in his absence, and there was no lying to her. If she suspected a lie, she grew worse.

He answered in his mother tongue, always encouraging her to preserve their language, even if they could only speak it among themselves. "The markets. Same places I've been going all month. I just had to hide a little longer this time."

Solla pulled back, her doe eyes searching his face, her soft mouth quivering. "Why do you throw yourself in front of the soldiers? You know they're going to get you one of these days."

"Have you forgotten when we were strays? We'd be dead right now if someone hadn't looked out for us."

She had that look again. "You know that's not why."

Disrel slumped down in his chair at their little table. Mother's beautiful face was a lucid vision in his empty hands; Father's was a haunting skeleton staring through the bars of a cage.

Solla clunked a bowl of warm food in front of him. "You can't bring them back. It's been years. We need to move on."

Disrel shot her a hard eye and pushed the bowl away. "Move on to where? To *what*? It's been three weeks since I saw Father, and I didn't even recognize him. I only learned who he was after they'd buried him. Should I think it was merciful that they *only* cut Mother's throat in the marketplace for trying to get home with medicine for you?"

Solla turned away, snubbing tears. She couldn't understand. She couldn't handle this pain. He was the one who had witnessed Mother's murder and ran home with the medicine. He was the one who had seen Father's corpse staggering around a labor camp and missed his chance to speak with him by three days.

Disrel ground his teeth. "I wasted years trying to make peace. I cut my hair like a Kobalt. I applied for citizenship. I adopted their customs. I learned their language—when all along I should have been fighting to preserve our ways."

"We need to stay safe, Rel. We both have good jobs, this apartment, food to eat. Stop giving everyone a reason to hate us."

"They hate without reason. And that night Father was arrested, what did he tell us?"

Solla wiped her eyes. "That he loved us and wanted us to be safe."

"He never said anything about safe. He said *free*, Solla! Free. And you watch. What happens in the other sectors will happen in Tourmal. They'll start moving all of us behind the walls of that new sector, and it'll look like we'll finally have a chance at peace. Then they'll shut the gates. Nobody gets out. They're making it easy to destroy every last one of us."

Solla's gentle face pinched at the horror. "I'm scared. Where can we go?"

Disrel pushed up from the table and moved toward his bedroom. "The other nations don't even want us. There was only ever one thing to do. Stand and fight."

"Listen to yourself, Rel. You sound crazy. Who are you going to fight? Do you really want to kill people? Get yourself killed? Get me killed?" The whites of her eyes glistened.

Disrel gripped the doorframe. "Maybe if we'd started fighting sooner, Mother and Father would still be alive. They've conditioned us to believe that if we push back we'll lose someone precious to us. We need to stop fearing death. Once we're all locked in the cage they want us in, we'll be facing it anyway." He released a deep sigh. "Goodnight, Solla. I'll see you tomorrow after work."

He closed his bedroom door, turned a slow circle, and wiped his face. Was he going crazy? Had he snapped? Or was he seeing what everyone else was afraid to acknowledge? Almost every day a new law went into effect—keeping Pyrons off the sidewalks after hours, limiting their purchases of various items, controlling the prices of their wares, limiting the numbers their families could reach with exorbitant fines and forced castrations upon those who could not pay. Where would it stop? When they had all of Pyron contained behind the walls of the new sector?

Or when all of Pyron was dead?

Kobalt people didn't simply despise Pyrons for their dark eyes, coal-black hair, and ivory complexion. They feared the strength Pyron spirit had to change the Kobalt culture like fire changes everything it touches. They feared power being invested in a myriad of elders instead of a single Kobalt tyrant. They feared Pyron beliefs and the strength of their warriors in old times, the knowledge of stone grids and wind harnessing being freely accessible to all so that they could not monopolize on wind and fire. With the people dependent on taxable energy, they could be controlled, made to work harder and sell their time in exchange for simple pleasures.

But Pyrons were nomadic, living off the land as they pleased. They were difficult to control. They were self-sufficient, holding to their traditional ways. The spirit of freedom sang in their hearts and its fire coursed through their veins. Pyrons were the last thing standing in the way of the Kobalt throne attaining absolute control of the people. That alone was reason enough to hate them.

Disrel bowed over his washbasin and scrubbed the filth from his face. He loosened the front of his white garment and pulled it down from his shoulders. A strained countenance glared from the mirror above the basin, looking beyond him, fixed on the reflection in the geometric window behind him. Seven pink stripes rippled through the musculature of his back, all crossed over the center and tattered from stretching as he had grown. They were still just as bright and livid as the day he had earned them, seventeen years ago. He hated every time a random reflection gave him a reminder of what the state had stolen from him and left him with instead. These were the marks of oppression and ownership. Kobalt power over his life on earth and the gate to the afterlife.

Disrel jerked the clothing from his body and pushed it into the sink. He scrubbed soap and water into the soiled fabric. It was his only garment, and he couldn't go to work the next day smelling like death. The multi-ply fabric of the skyn was soft and supple like fine leather and comfortable in most climates. It never bunched or clung, and it breathed. Most of its thread was spun from semi-precious stones that carried light and made it durable. A high-quality skyn resisted cuts, punctures, and snags. It shed water, wicked sweat, neutralized body odors, and to the hand it felt like the offspring of silk and eel skin. The adjustable collar covered halfway up his neck, and the legs were fitted all the way to his ankles. The sleeves had thumb loops for holding the fabric over the back of the hands, and when a shorter sleeve length was desired, the loops could be secured to buttons farther up the arms. A front closure ran from the throat to groin, magnetic and seamlessly interlocking. Disrel wrung the pearly fabric in his hands, firm and strong from taking on adult labors so young, then draped it on a body-form to dry.

The Tourmal cityscape twinkled peacefully beyond his window, but Disrel knew what the world out there was like in gutters and alleys, under tents and tables, under anything that could hide a body from wind, rain, rats, and Kobalt patrols. He remembered the day Solla had fallen ill, and he'd gone looking for work to buy medicine. A Kobalt woman had given him a job and paid him honestly. Miss Mazilyn—Heaven hold her. He could never forget her. It was only because of her kindness that he and Solla were in such a position of wealth and privilege. Their last apartment had been a mere closet, a single room like the one his father had afforded them, in a bad section of town. Disrel was so proud that their current apartment had three rooms.

A military corecycle, illuminated in crimson tracings, rolled down an avenue on patrol. Disrel took a reflexive step back from the window and clutched the curtain. Memory of the arrest chilled his blood. Why hadn't they killed him? And why had they left him on the porch? Everything about the soldiers had been authentic: their uniforms, their weapons, their actions. They were not a gang of civilians out to terrorize Pyrons for fun. Any gang capable of such a stunt would have actually killed him after making greater efforts to terrorize him.

Disrel rubbed his wrists and recalled details of his conversation with Tygo. It didn't add up. Nothing about that situation made sense. If only he had someone he could trust, someone he could talk to for guidance. Disrel turned his eyes to the stars. Father had often stood at their apartment window with his hands up, muttering, most often when he needed help. When Disrel had asked him about it once, he'd said he was speaking to his father in the sky.

Disrel raised his right hand to the stars. Father's prayers had gone unanswered, even after all these years. His hand fell back down. What if the stories were only stories? What if there was no life beyond death? What if the soul floated away and found no body to inhabit? But if the stories were true, and Father wasn't in a pit outside of a work camp but standing among the stars somewhere listening, could he even answer?

A haggard, sooty face approached in Disrel's memory.

Ravenous eyes bulged from deep sockets. Sunken cheeks clung to the teeth beneath, and lips were drawn, cracked, and downturned. It was a skeleton with skin on it, shouldering a burden from the mines. Rigid fence wires warped against Disrel's forehead. His heart yearned for it to be true and fainted at the very thought that it might be—but it probably wasn't. His hopes had been dashed twice at the last two work camps. Itzellen was a common name. And this camp had five.

"Ask if one of them has a son named Disrel, and a daughter called Solla."

The garbage boy snatched the candy from Disrel's palm and scampered back through the guarded gates.

Disrel's eyes swept the camp, scrutinizing the men going and coming from the mine. Each prisoner looked the same. Their skyns swung loosely around their bony frames, their hair was shaved close to their heads, and the light of individuality had faded from their eyes. One prisoner stretched out his skeletal hands and staggered over to the fence.

"Father!" Disrel strained against the wires, and stared into the dim, drained eyes.

Father's lips barely covered his front teeth—what was left of them. His gums were pale, cankered, and withdrawn. The protrusions of his skull and cheeks shone through his translucent skin. His beautiful black locks were now a gray stubble and his shoulders dipped where muscle had once been. He was a shadow of the man Disrel had known. Father's face contorted, but the tears could not come. There were no more tears left in that body. Disrel struggled to press himself through the fence and wrap him in his arms. No hardship of life on the streets could compare to the hardships of the labor camps. Death on the streets was for the careless and the frail. Death in the camps was for everyone.

"Don't just look at me. Please, Father. Say something. I need to hear your voice."

Father melted away with the blowing sand.

A soldier approached the fence from the other side. "What are you doing here, Pyron?"

Disrel shied back, stammering. "Looking for my father, sir. Please, I—"

"I know the one." The soldier averted his gaze, half-turned with his dark qorzan crossbow drooping in his arms. "You look remarkably like him when he first came here. We buried him three days ago. Pneumonia."

A whistle screeching from the street jerked Disrel back into the present. He wiped a tear from his eye. Disrel had lost and grieved Mother once, and Father twice, the second time so much more painful than the first. He'd never gotten that chance to speak to Father through the fence. It was all a fabrication, the dream that quieted his grieving heart. But no matter how many times he dreamed it, Father never answered. That ghastly face was seared into his memory, unforgettable, haunting. He struggled to piece together what Father had looked like the night he was arrested: the twinkling, hooded black eyes, the swarthy locks and thick eyebrows, the pleasant nose with wide nostrils that flared when he laughed, and his ever-smiling lips. He strained to hear Father's robust laughter and feel the muscles that rippled through his arms in his memories of being tickled and wrestled on the floor. What he would give to go back, or to have just one more moment.

What did Father look like now that death had freed him from the shell the Kobalt state had carved him into? What about Mother and his unborn sibling? Disrel closed his eyes and bowed his forehead against the window. Mirrors haunted him with Mother's eyes and Father's features. His fingers curled upon the glass, straining to stretch higher in prayerful reverence.

"I don't know if you can hear me, Father. A piece of me wants to believe you can. That night you took me to the elder in secret to receive the name I was to grow into, the soldiers caught us and striped our backs. They left me with scars in place of a name." Disrel's lips twisted. "Now there are no elders to bless me. Why do we let them steal our birthrights? Where are Pyron's warriors?" His free hand curled in his close-cut hair and another tear fell. "Death should have taken me twice today. Why am I still here? I have no place in Heaven, but I refuse to live in fear. If I must carry the scars of everything I've lost, I will set our people free or die trying."

Disrel opened his eyes and set them on a distant beacon to the north. The imperial flag swelled from its pole on the capitol grounds, and he lifted his chin, accepting its challenge.

2

Every rogue that Lieutenant Sable Commander Ambrosia had ever killed seemed to believe he was a born legend. She had proved them all wrong. And if they had been brazen enough to brand themselves by wearing some "heroic" emblem on their skyn, she'd braided a piece of their clothing over her duty belt. It was sable custom to sport a kill count on their belts, and Ambrosia's prowess in the Selenite sector had earned her a name given in contempt by the renegades she hunted and used reverently by her comrades and superiors. The Selenite Skynhound.

Ambrosia shouldered her crossbow and followed the humanoid dummy through her sights. The base's shooting range was rarely empty, but today she had it all to herself. In the last twenty minutes, she'd put eighteen bolts into the moving target's head and forty-something into its chest. She didn't consider herself any more skilled than the other women she shared a barracks with, and her duty belt was only more colorful than those of other sables because she'd been at all the right places at all the right times. At just twenty-three years of age and five years of service, she was only one step from taking command of the entire Selenite Sable Force, and two steps from becoming the Sable Queen. But Ambrosia had no such ambition. Commander would suit her just fine if she was ever granted the opportunity. And since sables served for life, opportunity only came through the death of another commander, either in combat, protecting the heads of state in their sector, or in contest for the position of Sable Queen. Ambrosia pulled the trigger and the faceless dummy staggered. Another lethal shot. She desperately needed a challenge, a running target.

Selen had been quiet the last couple of months, now that its Pyron population had been deported to the new walled sector at the Selen–Tourmal border. Sympathizers had either given up resisting or moved on to new battlegrounds. Ambrosia was sure it was the latter. There had been no attempt on Governor Tritium's life in several weeks, and the mobs of arsonists and brick throwers had vaporized after she'd captured her last renegade. She loved Selen for its richly historical inner city, mountainous skylines, and rural culture. It was home. And now it was safe.

The range door slid open, and a sable strode into the building with her weapon slung over her back. It was Ulyia, Ambrosia's friend and comrade from her first days at the Sable Academy. Ulyia dropped her gear at the nearest shooting window and pulled her cropped brown hair back into a ponytail.

"He didn't stop twitching after the first shot?"

Ambrosia smirked. "I didn't feel like walking all the way down there again when I had other areas to shoot."

Ulyia set a bolt on her crossbow and loaded two more in the reload chamber. She cycled the string back with a pump of the prod underneath the foregrip. "I'd love to get my hands on one of those triple-chamber bows they just came out with in Tourmal."

"Take your time. You don't need rapid fire to take down a running target." The Tourmaline military utilized the latest technology before selling it to any other sector. That edge kept the peace.

Ulyia huffed and peered down her sights. Her target swayed and paced like someone walking down the street before stopping, turning, and heading back the other way. The tracked movement made the target predictable. Ulyia fired and the qorzan bolt plunged into the dummy's stomach. She cursed.

"Don't be so hard on yourself." Ambrosia lifted her bow and studied her own target. "He's not going anywhere fast with that injury."

"I wanted a heart shot." Ulyia reset her string with a pump of the prod and glared through the sights.

Ambrosia studied her own faceless victim. There weren't many places left to aim for. Heart, lungs, and head were riddled with protruding fletchings and tips. But she didn't want to stop Ulyia just to go down range and retrieve her bolts.

The range door opened again and the bitter odor of black coffee told Ambrosia that the newcomer could only be her other friend Phaedra. Ambrosia pulled the trigger, and her bolt struck the dummy's groin.

Phaedra laughed and her amber eyes smirked over the rim of her cup. "Nice. You can't convince me that wasn't intentional."

Ambrosia set her bow down on a nearby table and ran her hand over its textured, lightweight metal frame. "You aren't going to shoot with us?"

"Doesn't look like there's much left to shoot at." Phaedra shrugged. "I was here yesterday, and I'm taking a bird up in a minute."

Phaedra should have been born with wings. When she straddled the pilot's seat of a xyraxaryx qorzanopteryx assault vehicle, or QAV-X, she became one with it. And though all QAV-X models handled well, they were not for the faint of heart. The pilot sat astride its open back the same way a rider rode a corecycle, with only a lap belt to prevent the riders from being thrown in downdrafts and sidewashes. Two corestone-powered turbines levitated within the QAV-X's gull-shaped wings, providing lift, thrust, and hovering capabilities.

Ulyia growled when her bow kicked, and the fired round struck her target's shoulder.

"You still hit him," Phaedra said.

"But not where I wanted to hit him." Ulyia reset her string and another round clicked into the flight groove. She set her eye to the sight.

Phaedra leaned against the shooting window and swirled her coffee. "Tourmal's Sable Commander died this morning."

"What?" Ulyia's bow fired, and the dummy staggered with a bolt in its forehead.

"Dead?" The word fell unbidden from Ambrosia's lips. "In combat?"

"Illness." Phaedra sipped her drink. "They're not giving details yet. But it sounds like she's been sick off and on for a while."

Ulyia pointed her hand at the distant target and made a sour face. "Slagging headshot. And I was going for the heart again."

"Maybe stop trying to be such a heartbreaker." Phaedra kicked Ulyia in the calf. "Aim for the groin and see what happens."

"Says the one with no love life," Ulyia kicked back, a smile creeping into her eyes as she resettled behind her sights.

Ambrosia wrestled with the shock of the news. She'd met Commander Riahn on several occasions. She was in her thirties, stood at five-foot, eleven-inches, and could bench press two hundred pounds with ease. It was difficult to imagine her succumbing to illness.

Phaedra downed the last of her coffee. "Anyway, there's a rumor that the Sable Queen is seeking fresh blood because of unrest in Tourmal. I wish they'd send me. I'd transfer just for a change of scenery."

"How do you hear all of these rumors?" Ulyia plucked three more bolts from her ammunition rack.

Phaedra smirked. "The same way I found out Tourmal's Sable Commander died. Commander Geiya received a letter from the Sable Queen wanting to know more about the Selenite Skynhound."

Ambrosia's blood ran cold, and she stared at her bolt-riddled mannequin on the other side of the range.

3

Disrel rose earlier than usual and shaved his face. He dried his smooth jaw, wet his fingers, and raked them through the loose coils of obsidian black hair that fell over his forehead, exposing his widow's peak. He brushed his thick eyebrows, tapped a fragrance oil on both sides of his neck, and held his own gaze. His irises were so dark he could not discern his own pupils. But there was nothing wrong with that. This was a face the world was going to hate simply because it was Pyron. Disrel gave himself an encouraging smile and recalled something Miss Mazilyn had told him years ago.

"There will always be people who have to look down on others to feel better about themselves, Disrel. They have to narrow their eyes because it hurts to look up. But a Pyron can look into the light without being blinded."

It was true. Kobalt people shielded their translucent eyes on sunny days, while a Pyron could comfortably follow a bird's flight across a clear sky. But society believed that Pyrons had a more stary look, and were therefore obstinate and less intelligent than their squinting neighbors.

Disrel returned to his bed and counted out a drawstring sack of coins to be sure he had a respectable amount. It equaled one month's rent. He checked an address scrawled on a scrap of paper and pushed it into his pocket. The wealthy district wasn't far, and it wasn't friendly, but one old friend might still live there.

He shouldered his backpack and eased out into the kitchen, a cramped aisle bordered by two counters and a cold box. He usually rose about the same time Solla did and walked a little of the way to work with her until their paths separated. But this morning he was going in a different direction.

He opened the cold box, pulled out a brown paper bag with his name on it, and peeked inside. Solla had made a crispy, savory potato flour pancake stuffed with bits of pork and served with a sweet vinegar dip. His mouth watered.

He pulled her lunch from the cold box and checked it. She'd packed herself the same thing, but with only half as much pork. Ridiculous. She worked just as hard as he did, if not harder, packing boxes at the packaging plant on a twelve-hour shift. So what if she only made half as much as he did? Disrel set the lunches out on the counter, raked meat filling from his pancake into hers, and rewrapped her lunch. He set it back in the cold box, precisely where he'd found it so she wouldn't suspect he'd tampered with it, then grabbed his own lunch, shouldered his backpack, and slipped out into the hall.

The tenant who lived four doors down squeezed out of his apartment at that same moment and shot an irritated glance at Disrel before racing to the elevator and summoning it. He punched the call button repeatedly as Disrel drew closer, and when the doors opened he rushed inside and hit the descent button.

Disrel walked past as the doors were closing. "Good morning, Turk."

The door shut over Turk's spiteful expression. Turk was strange. He'd moved rooms within the building three times in the last year trying to distance himself from Pyron neighbors, filed false accusations and complaints about odors, and left gossipy posted notes on doors, betraying his paranoia. Nobody liked Turk, but nobody ever complained: Kobalt neighbors saw no reason to and the Pyrons who dared were evicted. Turk thought of himself as the state's favorite vigilante, but he was a snitch who reeked of cheap cologne and ate only prawns, carrots, and cheese.

Disrel pushed into the stairwell and began the eleven-story descent. He trotted to the seventh floor, jumped the landings on the way past the sixth and fifth floors, performed a handstand walk past the fourth floor, jumped and rolled the landings through the third and second floors, and walked the rest of the way out of the building.

The elevator door opened and a dozen people streamed through the vehicle lot. Turk stopped in the flow of traffic, glaring so hard it seemed his eyes were filling with blood. The elevator must have made a stop at every floor along the way.

Fog hung between the skyscrapers, and the sky was brightening with gold and lavender, signaling another warm, cloudless day over Tourmal. Disrel whistled a tune as he took the sidewalk, and riders coasted silently down the streets on their corecycles. He turned a corner and drifted out of the path of an oncoming pedestrian. The woman's lips tightened, and she tossed her head, quickening her pace and stepping into the street without looking. Disrel reached for her, but there was no way he would get to her in time, and the oncoming cyclist blared his horn and swerved, missing her by inches. The woman raised her hands to her ears and straightened with a shriek while the rider struggled to save his balance and dropped his bike on the pavement. He clamored up and yelled at the woman, who only turned and cast the blame at Disrel.

But he'd given her all the sidewalk she needed. Disrel shrugged his backpack into place and marched on. He turned down a residential street lined with separated homes, set back from the street by a manicured lawn and surrounded by flower beds. The walks here were wider and shaded by ornamental trees. A man stepped out of his home and stood on the porch, noting Disrel with hard, cold eyes that glowed in contrast with his tanned skin. Disrel met his gaze and offered a faint, hopeful smile.

The man postured on his doorstep. "Stop staring, rat-eyes. This isn't your neighborhood."

Disrel averted his attention to the end of the street and sauntered on at a comfortable pace. He knew which homes were welcoming and which were not. Anyone who welcomed a Pyron's presence displayed something white. Usually, it was white flowers, planted outside or displayed in a vase; sometimes it was a painted porch step or paving stone.

Disrel pulled the address paper from his pocket and checked it with the house numbers he passed. He was close, if the address was even correct. He stopped in front of a dark little house with black stone corners, and his heart quickened. It was rude to be so early, but physicians were used to being called on at odd hours. Disrel strode up the walk and stepped carefully onto the porch, feeling like every eye in the neighborhood was on him. The man six doors down stood with his arms folded, glaring.

Disrel cleared his throat and drew a steadying breath, then knocked on the door. He stepped to the edge of the stone porch, squeezing his hands together and biting his lip, rehearsing his words in his head. *Doctor Kelsuq, you may not remember me, but I can never forget you.* Awkward. *Doctor Kelsuq, I owe you more than I could ever—* No. There was a limit. *Doctor Kelsuq, do you remember Miss Mazilyn?* If he didn't, that would be a dead end.

He knocked again, and another long minute passed. Maybe the old doctor wasn't home. Maybe he didn't live here anymore. Or maybe this was just the wrong house and its irritated resident was refusing to answer the door. Disrel forced himself to knock a third time.

The door cranked open and a bushy-browed man wrapped in a dark robe eyed him from head to toe.

"Doctor Kelsuq?" Disrel stammered.

One silvery brow twitched upward. "Yes?"

Disrel studied the aged physician's face. He looked nothing like he remembered, especially without his large medicine bag and medical apron. "I'm Disrel." He offered his hand and the doctor stared at it.

His wrinkled eyes wandered back up to Disrel's face. "I'm retired. And it's early."

"Yes, sir. I—I know." Disrel shed his backpack. "I'm sorry. I couldn't come later because I work. I know you don't remember me, but you treated me when I was young, and my sister, several times." He pulled the purse of credits from his bag and held it out. "I just wanted to put this toward our debt to you. And to thank you for helping us."

Doctor Kelsuq eyed the coin purse, and his expression softened. He pushed the door open and shuffled back. "Come in."

Disrel stepped into the foyer of a modestly furnished home, avoiding the rug that ran the length of the room. Savory aromas made his stomach rumble, and he noticed a table in the next room, with a place set and spread with food.

"I'm sorry for interrupting breakfast—"

"You're not interrupting anything. Come." The doctor walked into a sitting room and motioned to a cushioned armchair. "Sit. I want to know why you think you owe me money."

Disrel took the chair and set his backpack down at his feet. "You never charged the full cost of your services."

Doctor Kelsuq eased down into a chair opposite Disrel and gave him a meditative look. "But what I charged was paid, wasn't it?"

"I don't know."

The physician turned his palms up with a blissful shrug. "So, why are you here?"

Disrel rubbed the back of his neck and thought about his recent scrapes with death. "I saved up this money to give to the lady that took care of me and my sister. She would've paid you what you asked for, but I know you didn't charge her enough for what you did for us."

A light of recognition sparkled in the physician's eyes. "Are you Mazilyn's boy?"

"Yes, sir. But she's gone now. So my debt is to you."

"Gone?"

"She died."

"Oh." Doctor Kelsuq's brow knit as he rubbed his chin. "I'm sorry to hear that. She was still so young."

"She was murdered. Howlers." Disrel blinked tears back and clenched his jaw. It was too soon to think about this now, to wrestle with feelings of hatred toward his own people for blindly killing the woman who had become his second mother. Howlers were a nebulous group of Pyron supremacists originating from the tribe of the wolf after the tribe of the tiger had been purged. They believed themselves to be Pyron's elected warriors to bring freedom through fire and blood. And so they ran in packs, each led by an alpha, and usually struck during the night, slaughtering entire families and setting homes on fire.

The physician's face contorted with grief. "I'm so sorry."

Disrel fought his boiling emotions. He hadn't come to talk about another terrible loss in his life.

Doctor Kelsuq studied him. "Usually it's the dying who come to pay their debts. But all I see is a strong, healthy young man."

"I am dying, sir." He might as well speak for all of Pyron.

A light of understanding passed through the physician's eyes. "All of us are. And there's not a medicine in the world that can stop it from happening, ultimately. There's no miracle pill that can raise a dead man. I have written death notes for infants, children, newlyweds, and people far older than myself. So here's what I've learned: It's not when that counts, only how you died." A slow, knowing smile spread across his studious face. "Keep your money. What I did for you and your sister was my gift to your people. And as long as you live, that gift will keep on giving."

Disrel straightened, perplexed by the physician's words.

Doctor Kelsuq pushed himself out of the chair. "Now, you need to be on your way to work." He shuffled toward the table in the adjoining room. "Have you had breakfast today?"

"I'm not hungry." Disrel picked up his backpack and set the coin purse on the chair the doctor had vacated. His stomach growled, and the physician turned, brows arched.

"Well, then. Take something for when you do get hungry." Doctor Kelsuq opened a cloth napkin on the table and began to pile fruit in it.

"That's enough." His stomach roared, and he cleared his throat, choking back saliva.

The physician laid a variety of cheeses between two slices of heavy brown bread. "Do you like herring?"

Disrel's mouth watered. "Yes, sir."

The physician forked several of the little fish into the sandwich, wrapped it in paper, and set it in the napkin next to the fruit. He handed the bundle to Disrel with a smile.

"Doctor, I really can't—"

Doctor Kelsuq held up a finger and shushed him. "Do you see any lack in this house? Accept the gifts you are given, because if you pay it all back, my people will forever be indebted to you."

Disrel frowned at the physician's words. "Thank you, sir. From me and Solla."

The physician nodded with humble acceptance. "It was good to see you again, Disrel. Now, you left your sack of money on my chair in the next room. Don't forget it on your way out."

Disrel glanced at the clock on the factory wall. His heartbeat quickened with anticipation as the solar icon rolled closer to the dark hemisphere on the bottom half of the clock face. This wasn't just the end of any workday. He'd been preparing for this night all week. He raised the magnification on his loupe goggles and studied the supple fabric of a finished skyn under a light at his workbench. He brushed it with his thumbs and relished the rippling weight and suppleness against his hands. The cloth's finish was silky and flawless. He selected a smooth crystal chip from a test kit and inserted it into the port embedded in the side of the garment, then watched as the fabric gradually aligned itself to the information on the chip, cell by cell, until the entire piece had transitioned from a slate-gray to a complex patchwork of color and pattern. Iridescence rippled through the cloth, converting heat from his body into light where it lay over his arm and lap. This quality could only be found in fabrics with fibers spun from a stone called pyrelux. Amalite was a softer piezoelectric stone also used in fabrics, but it was usually preferred for flooring tiles. Some of the most elite fabrics the skyn factory carried became luminescent with every breath the wearer took.

The factory manager had allowed Disrel to create himself and Solla new skyns at a fraction of the cost, and even though sumptuary laws restricted the common person to a fitted one-piece, Disrel had still been able to use some of the finer fabrics to ensure that his skyn and Solla's were of a quality that would protect and endure. He'd fitted his own with layers of military-grade armor, hidden pockets, printed graphene circuits, and a port for a pattern chip, all skillfully concealed so it passed scrutiny. The mesh armor wouldn't stop projectiles as well as outerwear plate armor, but it would hold up against stabs and cuts. It added virtually nothing to his physical appearance, was too supple to notice when touching the outside of the skyn, and took nothing away from the fabric's breathability. The only areas without armor were his sleeves, because, when rolled, would have revealed the enhanced underside of the cloth, and concealing it with a lining layer would have made the sleeves too heavy and thick.

His skyn already drew enough attention, gleaming with warm rose gold tracings on the white fabric covering his arms, torso, and legs. Pyrons were special, different, they were told. They needed to stand out, to never hide their identity. Wear it with pride, with privilege. In Pyron culture, white was the most venerated color. It symbolized transcendence, the spiritual world, the change from one form to another. White was the color of the soul leaving the body and taking its flight to the heavenly plane, the color of a fresh cocoon, a dandelion head in full seed, a morphing cloud, a foaming wave, fresh snow, ashes after a fire. But here, it was just a gilded shackle, binding and hastening him toward the fate that awaited all Pyron blood under Kobalt rule.

Disrel dropped the chip back into the test kit and hung the garment on a rack. He was several orders ahead of schedule and running out of time to finish a personal project he had been sneaking time into all day. He pulled a chip from his pocket and set it upon prongs under a glass before adjusting the magnification on his goggles and scrolling the knobs and wheels on the bench, honing a beam of light onto the chip. He set his jaw and focused. Just one more edit and it would be perfect. The stench of burning stone wrung his nose, but it only smelled like fabric being cut. No one would know that a custom chip was being illegally designed on the fabric cutter. Disrel's stomach fluttered and his ears probed the hall for footsteps. His workstation was in the very back of the factory, away from coworkers, in a deep corner where visitors would never wander and find a Pyron working. But it was right next to the back door many employees used.

Disrel blew on the chip and pinched it reverently in his fingers. He pulled his loupe goggles from his face and cast them on the counter, then slid the chip into the port embedded in the seam to the right of his chest and watched an inky blackness devour his white garment. Subtle iridescent tracings accented his legs and bordered his torso armor. A pinkish, three-cornered prism gleamed on the breast of the garment. Its edges were tinged with green and yellow, and light rippled through it as he breathed, but the color was not as important as the details. Disrel picked up a crumpled paper and compared his crude sketch to the emblem on his chest. It was a good likeness. He had never designed a chip before. After several risky edits, he had something recognizable, something Pyron.

"Disrel!"

Disrel whipped the chip from the garment and plunged it into his pocket. His heart boxed his ears as Reem trundled along the counter, slapping it with a fat ring-studded hand.

"Everything going well today?"

"Yes, sir."

"Got any plans for the evening?"

If he said that he didn't, would he be rude to turn down what his boss suggested? Or if he said that he did, would Reem ask about his plans? Disrel turned through order sheets on his bench.

"Not really."

Reem hoisted a bolt of fabric onto the counter. "Come check out this sample we just got in. It's softer than anything I've ever seen, it's waterproof, and it could make you a walking ray of sunshine. Great stuff for working in dark, wet places."

Disrel ran his hands over the material. "I can't wait to work with this."

"Play with it as soon as you want." Reem pushed the bolt across the counter. "We already have a very wealthy customer wanting something unique and I wouldn't let anyone else in this factory touch the order."

Disrel moved the bolt to a fabric rack at the back of his workspace.

Reem leaned on the counter, twiddling his thumbs and going on about industry competition, rising textile prices, game night with friends, and a half dozen of his latest hobbies. The clock's heavenly bodies floated nearer the quitting hour positions. Disrel fussed with the garment on the rack and nodded, smiled, and affirmed his boss periodically, but his eyes wandered to the deep drawer below his workbench and his spirit groaned. If Reem stayed until the whistle blew, he'd have to wait until tomorrow to complete his project.

The gray caterpillars on Reem's forehead twitched. "Did you ever get one of the cinnamon rolls I left in the break room over lunch?"

"No, sir. I stayed here and had my lunch."

Reem's face furrowed. "I'm sorry. I should've sent someone down here."

The clock's solar orb dropped another tick. Fifteen minutes until closing.

A snub-nosed man with ears floating off the sides of his cropped head rounded the back hall corner with his knapsack on his back and his helmet in hand. His face was so heavily freckled it looked like it had been hit with a flying varnish brush, and his mouth was usually puckered like he was sucking sour candy.

"Hey, Ditzy! You missed out on pastries again. Too bad Reem keeps your ashy butt tucked away in the armpit of the factory." His voice cracked and broke like it was stuck in puberty.

Reem turned his head and looked Kommett square in the eye. "That's because I can trust him not to have overdue orders and camp out by the back door the last fifteen minutes of the workday."

Kommett pushed his helmet behind his butt and backpedaled around the corner.

Reem turned back to Disrel and shook his head. He slapped the counter and moved off down the hall. "Now we know who ate yours. Next time I'll bring you one. Alright, I'm done here. See you tomorrow, Disrel. Have a good evening."

As soon as Reem disappeared, Disrel jerked the drawer open and rummaged its depths. He pulled up a folded skyn, wide and heavy, and unfurled it on the cutting bench. Its clean white surface glowed under the bench light, and the bold black scrap letters sewn on both sides ran with iridescence under Disrel's hands. He set the cutter's light on the aligned corners of the skyn, punched two holes, and reinforced them with steel loops. A screeching whistle shot down the halls of the factory and doors groaned open under ready hands. Disrel wadded the skyn into his bulging backpack until the latter looked like a serpent struggling to swallow an egg. He set his knee into the top of the pack and drew it closed by inches, then swung it to his shoulder and strode out the back door of the factory.

Employees spurted from the building in droves and mounted their aerodynamic corecycles. Puddles filled every corner of the parking lot and the smell of rain was heavy in the air. Disrel kept his eyes on the pavement and marched steadily toward downtown Tourmal. A deep blue corecycle zoomed by, vaulting a wave of cold rainwater and drenching him from head to toe. The force of the spray gave the back of his head a new part. The cyclist whooped out a wild laugh and pumped his fist into the air as he turned out onto the main road. Kommett. Disrel gritted his teeth and shook water from his shoes. He'd just love seeing that kid's bike smashed in the road one day.

Many blocks later, Disrel reached the downtown area, a cramped, bustling maze of window shops with old homes nestled between. Inviting aromas poured into the streets as hungry customers opened the doors to restaurants along the walk, the windows of which showcased more customers dining in groups around massive platters of fine food. Disrel had taken Solla to a nice restaurant here for her sixteenth birthday. Now, a sign swung in the awning of that same restaurant: No

Pyrons Please. As if "please" made it any easier to read. The host standing in the alcove stepped in front of the door. Disrel straightened his posture and marched past. He only craved food that was warm and welcoming, like Pyron cuisine with all of its gloriously heaping plates of herb salad and delicious sauces for fresh bread and broiled meats.

Disrel slowed his step and paused before a toyshop window, brimming with every large and wonderful thing a child could want. Tucked in the far corner of the display, like an afterthought, stood an army of Kobalt soldiers, inches high and vividly painted, pinning their tiny polearms and crossbows upon a faceless character in glossy black. The solitary figure's hands were outstretched, his knees bent, opaque helmet fixed in rigid resistance upon the circle of steel. There was nothing notable about him, nothing to catch the passer's eye. But the smallest detail had drawn Disrel's attention and tugged at his heart: A distinctly pink three-sided emblem gleamed on the character's chest. It was the Pyron fifth element, spirit, the embodiment of freedom. Disrel slipped his hand into his hip pocket and rubbed the smooth chip. Was this unnameable character the spirit of Pyron? Was he trapped behind the walls of the new sector? He was breaking free tonight.

Disrel turned to face his onyx shadow, leaning down the sidewalk like a willowy giant, stoic and faceless, shrouded in burning orange. He shrugged his pack and trudged on, eyes fixed on the goal, the Capital Circle, that place where the senate convened and lashed Pyron with their pens upon paper. The Kobalt empire's capitol building was the crowning jewel of Tourmal. Rings of pavement and flowering gardens radiated outward from it, and rows of flagpoles carried the flags of every sector and territory in the empire—all except the new Pyron sector.

The tallest and most central flagpole bore the empirical flag, a mammoth swallowtail and tongue blazon of crimson and azure. The icon at the center embodied the elements of wind, water, earth, and fire, an amalgamation of Pyron symbolism under Kobalt ownership. But it lacked strength. It lacked a bonding agent. It lacked the fifth element—spirit—which cannot be taxed, regulated, or possessed.

The flag rolled and jerked over the seat of Kobalt authority like an overconfident dancer full of wine. Darkness engulfed Tourmal and beacons illuminated every flag in the Circle. Disrel paused by the rails while a train passed, then crouched down in an alley just opposite the capitol plaza. When the first star appeared, he slipped his handmade chip into his skyn and waited for the changing of the guard. His body melted right into the shadows, but he kept tight against the wall, feeling conspicuous. The rugged three-cornered emblem burned on his chest as Disrel pulled a helmet from his pack and placed it over his head. The visor darkened as it integrated with the energy running through his skyn, matching its colors and style. But he still had a perfect view of the world around him, an enhanced one almost as bright and clear as if it were day. He'd purchased the helmet in anticipation of one day affording a corecycle of his own, never imagining that he would use it to conceal his face.

At the edges of the plaza, guards approached to relieve the evening watch. Every second counted. There were twice as many guards, but they were too preoccupied with their comical routines to watch the world around them. Disrel went over his plan of approach and retreat, then stole out into the open, crouching and darting along walls and around bushes until he made it into the shadows of the Circle. He was just under the reach of the beacon, concealed behind the light that showered the top of the pole. At the base of the central flagpole he ripped the white skyn out of his pack and shook it open, hands trembling as they searched for the ringed edge. He looped the rings onto the flagpole's chain, dropped the flag, and pulled the chain from the cleats. The crimson standard fell a notch, and the edge of the white banner floated from the ground. He hauled on the chain again, pulling feverishly, hand over hand. The empirical flag dropped foot by foot until halfway down it met its Pyron conqueror. *Snap!* The white flag caught the breeze and unfurled over the city. Disrel's heart raced circles in his chest and he turned to mark his surroundings. The clanking of the chain and the snapping of the fabric were nothing unusual. Tourmal was always breezy, especially at night. But it wouldn't be long before someone noticed the disparity.

Pyron is Free. The flag flashed its Kobalt letters from one side and Pyron script from the other. Disrel caught the crimson banner by its tail and stripped it from its hooks. He punched it into his pack and sprinted across the square in the opposite direction. Shouts reverberated through the plaza, followed by the thundering of boots on pavement, and Disrel dove behind a wall near the outer ring.

"Stop! On your knees! Hands up!" A spotlight burned on him. Armor rattled.

Disrel pushed off the wall and tumbled. A javelin pelted the tile in his wake. He sprang up and dashed into the street, leaping high over a cyclist and causing another to swerve and crash into the soldiers. He rounded into a narrow alley and clamored up a lattice onto a second story ledge. The soldiers skidded after him and flashed their torches along the walls and ledges. A military canine towed his officer on the leash, foaming at the mouth and raging at the face of the building. Disrel skirted around the corner right before torchlight seared the outcropping where he had just been. His heartbeat roared in his ears, deafening him to what he was straining to hear. He inched his way up the side of the building to the roof and stood beneath an ornamental tree sprouting from a wide garden.

Nearby, a group of people lounged on furniture around a firepit and table, drinking and talking. Disrel toed the shadows, noting the other nearby rooftops and obstacles. Could he clear the distance to the next rooftop? A woman lowered her glass from her lips and peered into the darkness, raising a question about perceived movement. Her friends turned on their couches as Disrel clapped his hand over the emblem on his chest and ducked behind another tree.

The rooftop access door popped open, releasing a seething monster on a chain and an army of minions behind. The dog bolted, jerking its leash from the soldier's grip. Disrel scrambled across the roof, vaulting the couches and crashing over the table. Glasses smashed, spirits drained, and game pieces rolled. The dog exploded over the edge of the first couch and crashed down on the table with incisors flashing. Screams split the sky and the dog's chain wrapped the leg of the firepit, dragging it between the furniture and dumping it.

Disrel vaulted from the wall and tumbled onto the nearby rooftop. He scurried on, boots scraping on the stones. The soldiers hunkered against the wall and lowered their crossbows. Disrel caught a pole and slingshotted himself around a corner as steel bolts plunked across the rooftop. He plowed on from roof to roof, knowing that he would have to descend before the block was surrounded and aircraft began circling. He dropped down onto a balcony and caught a light pole, slid down into a street, and skulked down an alley toward home.

Once he'd gained several blocks and found a quiet street, Disrel removed the chip from his skyn, pulled his helmet from his head, and drew several slow, deep breaths. He glanced back toward the Capital Circle. The white flag was still hurling its treason over the city.

Pyron is free.

4

Two hours later, Disrel entered his apartment building and took the elevator up. He slipped into his room and eased the door latch. *Click.*

The room brightened and Solla glared from her chair at the table.

"Soldiers again?"

"Yeah. Why aren't you in bed?" Disrel made straight for his room with the bulging pack.

Solla got up and followed. "What are you up to?"

"It's none of your business."

"Why do you smell like alcohol?"

"Tripped into a drunk."

Her hand jerked on his elbow. "That's a lie. You're going to get us both arrested and you know it."

Disrel sighed. She was right. "Maybe it's time I find my own place."

"You can't do that. We can't afford it."

"I'll get a one-room and help pay for this one."

"That's ridiculous. Father would have wanted us to stick together."

"Our rotting corpses will be sticking together in a mass grave if we keep pretending things aren't heading that way! Is that what you want?"

Her lips quivered and she stepped back.

Disrel closed his eyes and released a slow breath, more angry with himself for taking out his frustrations on his sister. "Solla, sometimes I don't think you understand—"

"I understand completely." Her voice broke with emotion. "And I'm scared. Scared I'll lose you. Maybe I already have."

The drama. Disrel tossed his backpack into his room and blocked the door with his body. "I haven't killed anyone, and I wasn't drinking. Stop worrying about me. I'm fine."

"But you've changed. Since you found Father— The last month you've just— You're not you. And I need a guarantee that something in my life will stay the way it's supposed to forever."

Disrel clenched his jaw. She was right. When he found Father days too late, something inside of him snapped. A sigh burned through his nose. "The night Father was arrested, they were looking for someone, someone they called 'the renegade.' I don't know who he was or what he did, but just think, Solla. Someone risked everything for us."

"And they got Father killed and nothing changed."

Disrel balled his fists. "At least somebody was doing something. I'm not going to sit around and wait for my turn to die. Why can't you see I'm trying to protect you?"

She wrapped her arms around herself and looked away, eyes welling with tears.

"I'll pack up and find another place within the week, come check on you now and then. And I promise I'll stay in touch."

Solla's expression broke. "No. Please. You can't," she buried her head in her hands and sobbed fitfully. "I don't want to be alone."

Disrel closed his bedroom door softly in her face and ground his teeth. He didn't want to be alone either. He didn't want to leave her when she needed him most. But how else could he fight for their lives and keep her safe? He inwardly kicked himself for not securing another apartment sooner. He'd been too busy planning out all the other details. Fear ground through his chest like a hacksaw. What if there was a pounding at the door right then? The flag would betray them both.

He closed his window curtain and pulled the flag from his pack. How strange and out of place it was in his bedroom. Completely unfurled, it was large enough to cover the entire room. He couldn't risk taking it into the skyn shop to cut it into pieces, and the fabric was noncombustible. He would think of something. Maybe he could bury it in the bay. Disrel folded the flag into as tight a bundle as he could manage and stuffed it deep in a drawer under his bed.

Solla's heartbroken sobs wafted through the flimsy wall between their rooms. Disrel plopped down on his bed and removed his shoes. It killed him when Solla cried. Everything in him wanted to go to her and hug her and wipe away her pain. But eventually, she'd have to understand that he was doing what was best for her. If he told her he was staying just to stop her tears, he'd be lying. And lies weren't love.

Disrel touched the wall plate with his hand and the room's lights faded out. He pressed the chip back into the port on the side of his breast and gazed upon his creation. His heart quickened as light undulated through the crude emblem. It was both alien and kindred, heavenly and earthly, immortal and mortal, living yet stone. It spoke to him like a parent welcoming him home, like a song singing to the deepest desires of his heart. It resonated with him, kindled a flame in his spirit. Ever since his last return from Father's grave outside Gelnitrak, every time he'd passed that toyshop window and laid eyes on it, it had called to him, and the sorrows of his people consumed his heart. Every new anti-Pyron law stirred a fight in his bones, every unjust Pyron death a vengeance in his eye. He found no rest at night, and his appetite had withered. An invisible war raged out there. It was a war on Pyron's spirit and it was time to fight back.

Disrel slipped the chip back into his pocket. His skyn reverted to its default white, almost glowing in the darkness, and he fell back on the bed with a weary sigh. His mind swam with what-ifs and what-nexts. He needed to buy a knife, but he couldn't afford both a weapon and a separate apartment. His stupid stunt only endangered his life—and Solla's—for as long as he held that chip or the stolen flag. He felt like any other rebel painting the town and defacing statues in the night. What good was raising a flag going to do? He rubbed his face. How could any of his people fight back? They couldn't vote. They couldn't hold offices in government to undo the laws that had been on the books for generations. Fighting oppression was like fighting a sandstorm. There were no vitals, no heads to strike at. Most insurgent groups attacked public offices and clashed with the military, and over the years their numbers had declined.

Disrel pulled his old blanket over himself and stroked its worn areas. It was his only tangible memory of his parents, made from the remnants of the blanket they had all shared once. He and Solla had slept under it together while living on the streets. It made them feel like Mother and Father were still close by, watching, protecting. And while the years and elements had erased the scent of his parents, time had infused its cheap fibers with other memories he could not bear to replace. It had survived the streets with them, and so it always reminded him that they would survive tomorrow also.

A thunderous pounding shook Disrel from his turbulent slumber. Solla quivered at his bedside, clutching her blanket around her shoulders and pushing on his shoulder. Her panicked eyes gripped him.

"Disrel! Soldiers at the door!"

Disrel flew up from the bed and pulled her out into the living area. He wanted to shove her into a cabinet somewhere, just like his father had done to them, but now that they were grown, there was nowhere to hide. He pushed her into her room.

"Get back in bed!"

He shut Solla's bedroom door, determined to face the soldiers alone so that they might overlook Solla entirely. His crimes weren't hers.

"Open this door before we break it down!"

"I'm coming!" He bellowed in truculent Kobalt, squeezing his feet into his shoes.

He flung the apartment door open and recoiled as another barrage of fists and staves rained into the room. A dark gauntlet seized him by the shoulder and hurled him out into the hallway.

"Downstairs! All of you." The sergeant stepped into the room and glared. "Where's the other tenant?"

Disrel stared numbly at the officer, his jaw loose.

"I asked where your roommate is!"

His eyes darted from floor to wall. "I don't have a roommate."

The soldier got in Disrel's face. "Well your neighbor says you do."

Fear sent shocks through his stomach and he choked on his words. "My sister? I guess she's still in bed."

The sergeant motioned with his head and two of his soldiers made for Solla's bedroom. Two others pulled Disrel down the hallway and onto the elevator. A moment later, the others followed with Solla hyperventilating between them.

Disrel leaned his head against the wall and focused. This was about the flag. They had tracked him down and now Solla would suffer and die with him. The elevator descended, and Solla sucked little puffs of air through quivering lips. The young soldiers peered askance at her through their visors. When the doors opened to the dark outside world, the first thing to greet Disrel was the peeved face of a high-ranking sable. She snatched him from the elevator and pushed him to the ground in the courtyard.

"Finally. We've been waiting a long time for you."

Disrel kept low on his knees. "I sleep soundly."

The apartment's other tenants stood in rows, clutching blankets and yawning, shivering from shock. Solla shook like a leaf. A platoon of sables bristled along the walk and soldiers surrounded the assembly with arms ready.

The sable commander marched a circle around Disrel, her red boot heels ringing maliciously, her livid eyes scoring him. Her deep auburn hair was bunched on the back of her head like a sour cherry, and her strong nose plowed through space. Sables were as strong as men and twice as mean.

"An act of sedition was committed last night—Pyron, by the flavor of it. The empirical flag was stolen and a flag bearing the blasphemy 'Pyron is Free' was raised over the Circle. If any of you know who did this, it is your patriotic duty to turn them in immediately. Do not think that you can save your friend or family member with silence. If we discover the thief belongs to you, your entire family will be dishonored and die with him. Therefore, it is in your best interest to be the first one to report any tips or leads on his identity."

A soldier changed out the chip in the holoposter on the street corner, and its ethereal screen projected a three-second capture of a faceless black figure raising the white flag. The crude emblem on his chest was his only identifier.

The sable turned away from the group. "This is the skyn he was wearing when he committed the crime. As long as this impostor is free, you won't be. Do I make everything clear?"

Mutterings rippled through the group. The names "Selenite Skynhound" and "Tourmaline Renegade" were whispered several times.

The sable marched toward her troops, shoulders and hips swinging. "Now, back to bed."

A whiny male voice broke over the crowd.

"Why can't you ashrats learn to comply? I'm sick of you making life so hard for all of us!"

Disrel's neck tingled under the burning eyes of the other tenants. He pushed to his feet. "What do you know about a hard life, Turk? Pyrons don't even have choices anymore."

The sable about-faced, stomped back over, seized him by the neck, and forced him back down on his knees. Her curved blade glistened in her other hand. "Do you want to die now, or later?"

Disrel avoided her gaze. "Later is fine."

"Then shut up. We're also putting a curfew in place to keep things quiet until we've captured the renegade. So make sure you're home before sunset each night."

She lifted her hand and marched off with her sables toward the next apartment building.

A rock glanced off Disrel's back, sending pain through his ribs.

"Really? *Pyron is free*?" a neighbor from down the hall sneered.

Turk leaned over and glared. "We're in a new age. Old cultures and their old ideas just need to die off like old people."

Disrel's hands shook. "Maybe if you heard the stories of our elders, you'd see the cage you live in."

"Fairy tales." Another tenant paused at the apartment doors. "We only have curfews and safety taxes because of your kind."

The grumbling tenants funneled back into the complex to return to their beds. The few Pyrons hung back in silence, waiting for the halls to be clear of their Kobalt neighbors.

Solla's eyes burned at him, hot with tears. "You better not have had anything to do with this."

Disrel turned away. "Go back to bed. I'll be up in a minute."

Dark clouds shrouded Tourmal. He hung his head and kicked a rock across the courtyard. Every time Pyron kicked, the Kobalt noose tightened around his throat. And every time Pyron kept still, the Kobalt noose tightened again. The holoposter's light glared against the buildings, casting its images of the flag thief's skyn upon every mirror on the block. An overwhelming sense of inadequacy washed through Disrel. He was also alone.

"Would you like a little help?"

Disrel whirled upon the hedge behind him. "Who said that?"

"Over here."

Leaning up against the corner of the building, deep in the shadows, stood a man as stout as a tree, clad in aubergine, and wearing an opaque visored helmet.

Disrel clenched his fists. "Who are you? What do you want?"

"I saw you take the flag."

Disrel staggered backward, heart melting. "You're crazy. I didn't steal any flag."

The man didn't flinch. "I watched you take it. Then I followed you."

Disrel snorted. "*Porkskit.* Your evidence was too shaky to turn me in while there were soldiers about, but you think you can blackmail me? The state's reward is ten times higher than anything I could give you."

"You tried to join a resistance group last week." The stranger shifted closer but kept in the shadows. Disrel tracked his movements closely, watching for a weapon. "And what happened should've scared the fight out of you, for your sister's sake, at least. But you made another stupid move."

Disrel took another step backward, his heart punching up into his throat.

"How—how do you know that? You're not going to turn me in, are you?"

"No, son. I'm an ally. I fight for Pyron."

"Show yourself."

The helmet lifted, baring a bearded chin, two familiar eyes, and a shining bald head.

"What happened at the house on Bayfront was a test," Tygo said. "Most give up after tasting death. But you never sobbed, begged, or even flinched. I was impressed, so I followed you to see what you'd do next."

Disrel clenched his fists harder. Trust went both ways. It made sense that any good resistance group would test its recruits, but how could the recruits test the character of their leaders?

"I wouldn't give anyone the satisfaction of watching me cry for my life," he said. "Does this mean you're going to let me in?"

"I'll take you to the leader, if you're still interested. But only to talk about what you did tonight. And then it's up to him whether you can join us."

Disrel studied Tygo's face. "After that surprise test, I don't know that I trust you and your group."

Tygo nodded. "But you won't get very far on your own, throwing garbage and stealing flags. Trained soldiers can take out a lone warrior any day, and there are thousands of graffiti rebels and vandals who think they've got all the fight Pyron needs. I'm breaking rules tonight, taking personal risks, because there's something about you that sets you apart, and I don't want to see that wasted."

Disrel hesitated at the doors to the building. "There's nothing special about me. I'd just rather die fighting for my people than cowering with them."

Tygo's eyes narrowed, and he stroked his bearded chin. "How about this? No obligations, tests, or surprises, and your secret dies with me. I'll have you back here in time to get to work, and you can have a few days to think it over. Deal?"

Tygo offered his hand the Pyron way.

Disrel held Tygo's gaze, counting his other options. There were none. He accepted and shook hands.

Tygo held out a garment chip. "Camouflage. And make sure you have the Tourmaline chip on you."

"Tourmaline chip?"

"The one you were wearing when you took the flag. Mored won't see you without it."

Disrel pulled it from his pocket. Tygo glanced at it, then put his helmet back on and melted into the darkness. Disrel inserted the camouflage chip into his skyn, and the garment turned an incredible shade of black that drank the moonlight and made him feel like a shadow instead of a tangible thing. He followed Tygo's barely traceable outline behind the apartment and down a side street, listening to the sable's brassy voice echoing between the buildings as she briefed sleepy citizens on the new threat. Tygo opened a street drain cover and descended, shining a flashlight around the space, a pipe just large enough to stand in.

"I'm going to have to ask you to blindfold yourself." He pushed a sack into Disrel's hands.

Disrel clutched the sack with apprehension—but remembered that Tygo already knew his secret. The Kobalt had the power to coerce him into almost anything. He threw the sack over his head and let Tygo guide him for many steps.

The air grew dank. Squeaks and scurries echoed in the cavernous space, and water sloshed under Disrel's boots.

"You can take it off now."

Disrel removed the sack and Tygo's flashlight seared through the enveloping blackness, striking parts of an underground rail. The subways had been abandoned many years ago when deadly gasses permeated a fissure after an earthquake and silently killed hundreds. Murky water stagnated in the tunnel, deep in places but never covering the old rail. Mushrooms the size of corecycles bloomed from cracks in the walls, waves of bioluminescence tumbling through their translucent flesh. Stalactites and mineral columns added to the majesty. Pod invertebrates jerked their fluorescent heads and tentacles back into their bony carapaces as Tygo's light passed over them, and rodents the size of cats stared into the light with milky eyes.

"It's a world of its own down here," Tygo said, trudging up the incline at the center of the tunnel. "Don't worry about the gasses. The fungi and invertebrates thrive on it and keep the air clean."

Disrel stayed close to Tygo. Without the light, each step was a venture into nothingness, a plunge into the abyss. A strange vehicle, large enough to carry three people, hovered over the rail on four wings, looking like a manta ray in an aquatic kingdom. Its exterior glistened with vaporous luminescence, and lights shone from its front wings, illuminating the tunnel ahead. A glass windshield arced from its nose.

Tygo mounted the vehicle with a youthful hop and offered Disrel his arm.

"Hold tight. This one can scoot."

The vehicle lurched into motion like a bolt from a crossbow. The air hummed over its wings, holding it close to the magnetic rail, and Disrel's stomach whirled while his heart galloped. The wind caught his smiling lips and blasted his mouth with rank tunnel air as the vehicle banked around turns and its headlights split the channel for miles ahead. After some minutes, they slowed to a stop at the edge of a platform belonging to an old depot, long forgotten and unmarked by vagabonds and street artists. The signs and their lettering appeared ancient and included some destinations Disrel had never even heard of. Old subway cars sat at the end of the line, doors open, sitting exactly as they had been left the day people evacuated the station. Withered corpses slumped against the windows and in seats with browned skulls lolling grimly. They were dressed in fashions from a previous century, in fabrics that were mildewed and turning to dust.

Tygo turned a grim eye back at Disrel. "I'm so used to it I didn't even think to say something. So much death. It's tragic. People believe all these tunnels and stations are haunted. Even if they knew the air was safe, I doubt they'd come back for any remains, and that works well for us."

Tygo pulled the vehicle's keystone, and it sank closer to the rail, lights fading. He dismounted and hopped to the platform, then led Disrel upstairs and into the old depot. Tiles and concrete sealed every window and door from the outside. High stained-glass windows crowned the eaves and ceilings, and the massive corbels, arches, and crown molding spoke of a time forgotten. A ticket master's booth stood in the center of the room with its many windows facing the building's entrance. Tygo opened the door and motioned to a chair.

"Wait here. We have sentries around and they don't know you yet. But I'll need to walk off with your chip for a few minutes." Tygo's expression pleaded honesty. "The boss needs to see it before he will see you."

Disrel hesitated, calculating the risks of letting incriminating evidence out of his hand. But he was already in too deep.

"Actually, it's for me." Tygo mumbled with a hint of embarrassment. "I know you can't afford to let it go, but I put everything at stake bringing you here. And I'm sure I can make it your ticket to the real thing."

Was this another test? If Tygo had wanted to steal it he could have mugged him outside the apartment. Disrel turned it over in his hands and sighed. "Fine." He relinquished the chip and Tygo marched off through the station and disappeared through the double doors. While he waited, Disrel eased down on a padded stool and imagined himself as a ticket master from the past. He envisioned people flooding through the bricked entrances, lining up at the counter with their luggage. The tiles were faded and worn in distinct paths between the doors, the ticket counters, and the terminals. Hundreds of thousands of people had used just this one station. It must have seen all types and nationalities, as evidenced by the travelers who still remained aboard the trains.

A wailing echoed through the rafters, and Disrel jerked toward the sound, ears burning. Silence returned, and he counted his breaths through the passing minutes. A vehement growl roared through a pipe running overhead, turning his lungs to wax. Did the souls with no welcome in heaven linger on earth? He was trapped here, unable to find his way out of the station without Tygo. The growling faded, and Disrel eased back down in the chair, drumming his fingers underneath the counter. The threat of ghosts never felt more real than after having just seen the mildewed corpses of a hundred passengers in the seats of a last-century train car. But to Tygo they were common fixtures, apparent only because of the presence of someone new.

The minutes dragged on.

Slow steps knocked through the hall, and the doors opened under Tygo's hand. A well-groomed man followed, appearing to be in his late fifties, gripping a cane, his deep-set eyes peering trenchantly through the hall and straight into the ticket booth. He walked easily, except for a weakness in his right knee and a hump in his opposite shoulder. His garments were of a vintage color and cut, a stiff-collared gray military jacket over a forest-green skyn. His stern Kobalt features were both commanding and reverential, as if he had survived a war and come out of it much wiser than he had gone in.

A woman followed him with strides so graceful she seemed to float, dressed in layers of deep orange. Her thick, snowy hair was braided in a traditional Pyron style Disrel had not seen since the last festival Father had taken him to. The darkness of her eyes and her indigenous features told him she was Pyron, and her skin was radiant and smooth. She was either much younger than the man or defying her age; the few wrinkles she possessed reflected joy and hope.

All the way down the grand hall, the limping man grumbled and his hooded eyes bored right into Disrel. He rounded into the ticket booth and held the chip before Disrel's face.

"Where did you get this?"

"I made it."

"Why not some other design? What made you dress up as the Tourmaline Renegade to steal a flag from the capitol?"

Disrel met his gaze evenly. "It's a Pyron symbol, isn't it? The strays paint it on the walls of the alleys they sleep in for protection. I wanted to fight for my people with a piece of my culture as my identity."

The leader's gray eyes hardened and he withdrew the chip. "So you didn't know what you were doing."

Disrel folded his arms across his chest and spread his feet. He wasn't completely wrong.

Tygo shifted uncomfortably. The leader fell back into an armchair and turned the chip over in his fingers.

"It does belong to your people. More rightly belongs on your chest than any Kobalt traitor's. But the Tourmaline Renegade caused enough trouble to make that symbol his own before he failed in his fight for your people's freedom." He met Disrel's eyes. "You've resurrected a dead legend. Ignorantly. And made yourself the state's most wanted enemy."

Disrel straightened. "Assuming you're Mored, sir, I came here to see if you'll let me join your army."

Mored handed the chip back. "I don't want an impostor in my army. You want to run around in a mask and a fancy skyn? Take up any symbol but that one and the curse that follows it. It jeopardizes my resistance. Destroy that chip, and then we'll talk."

Tygo's mouth drew into a hard line. The woman kept still, her eyes trained upon Disrel's every reaction.

Disrel clutched the chip in his fist and studied Mored. It was a simple request. A small sacrifice in exchange for weapons, camaraderie, and potentially, a safer place to keep Solla through the conflict. He weighed the privilege of fighting with a larger resistance against fighting alone, without resources and direction. Why did this Kobalt leader expect him to give up a sacred piece of his culture for a chance to save his people? Disrel opened his hand and stared at the chip. The symbol glowed pink at its center. It whispered encouragement to his heart. It called to him like a distant dream, a memory, or a future self. He felt like he belonged to it, like it was holding him in its hand.

"I'm sorry. I can't do that. I want to reclaim it for my people."

Mored's aquiline gaze hardened. "What makes you think you can succeed?"

Disrel folded his arms across his breast. "What makes you think I'll fail?"

One of Mored's eyebrows ticked upward. "The Tourmaline Renegade had years of military experience and training. And what are you? A florist who thinks he's got what it takes to run around in a mask, steal flags, and take on the entire Kobalt military? When you become someone's hero, you're someone else's villain."

Then maybe the Tourmaline Renegade wasn't the failure Mored made him out to be. Disrel looked at Tygo, irritated. "I passed the test, didn't I? That mock execution you put me through?"

Mored scoffed. "So you proved you're brave, or maybe that you're stupid. I need men who respect and follow simple orders. If you want to fight in my group, destroy that chip and never wear anything like it again."

Disrel gazed down at the chip in his palm. He had so much to gain from joining a group: training, resources, protection, camaraderie. But he had so little to offer. Was Mored so desperate for men that he wouldn't consider him a risk as he was, the man who had stolen the flag and might be found out and arrested? And if this was another test, what answer did Mored want? The Tourmaline Renegade had brought hope to Pyron in the past. That hope was alive again, and this old man had no idea how much hope meant to dying people. A river of warmth coursed up Disrel's arm and he closed his hand around it.

Mored leaned back. "Don't be a fool. How long do you think you'll last running around like a lone wolf with absolutely no training? Two days? Maybe three?"

"Dying behind a piece of my culture is better than living to see Pyron freedom as a traitor."

"Traitor? I'm not asking you to renounce your culture," Mored laughed. "What is honor to a dead man? We all live with shame on our backs, regrets haunting us. Just choose another Pyron symbol to wear. Choose something from your family or tribe that has just as much meaning but won't have the military hunting you relentlessly."

Disrel hesitated. He didn't even know which tribe he had descended from. "This symbol speaks to me of everything I'm fighting for, sir. Even though it is Pyron, it excludes no one. It's not about revenge or retribution. It represents the gift of freedom for all people, and if you don't want that in your ranks, I'll go my own way." He pressed the chip into his pocket and set his hand on the door. "I must finish what I've started, even if it means I fight and die alone. Thank you for your time."

"You're a strong young man, Disrel. Don't waste yourself in this foolishness."

Disrel moved out of the ticket booth and looked to Tygo.

"It's a terrible shame for you to throw your life away like this. I see a great leader in you." Mored's eyes flashed and his large hands massaged the top of his cane. "Nothing I say will dissuade you?"

"Nothing."

Mored sucked air through his big nose. Tygo rooted in place, unwilling to take him back as promised. The woman's features bent with some strange admiration, and Disrel thought he saw tears glistening in her eyes.

"Before you go." Mored reached into his coat pocket. "If I can't stop you from wearing that pathetic copy, then I may as well give you the opportunity to wear the original." His demeanor humbled as he stretched forth a shining black chip, beckoning Disrel back into the ticket booth.

Disrel inched back in and accepted it with confusion. How else could this man have the original? "You're the Tourmaline Renegade?"

Mored rocked his cane. "*Was*. Until, in running with the hope of living to fight another day, I sustained an injury that nearly cost me my life. I thought I would recover in time and return to the fight, but time only showed me that, with this old knee, I would never perform as well as I had before. The extent of my injury left scars I couldn't push through. So I let the empire believe I was dead, lying somewhere at the bottom of the bay, and I continued my fight in secret. Since that time, I've built a network of contacts who are infiltrating the Kobalt military and government. I have other men like Tygo that I trust to be my eyes and ears in the world above."

Mored reached inside his coat and pulled out a photograph. His gray eyes misted as they poured over the image. "After accepting my death and defeat, I locked the chip away in a safe, never seeking someone else to fight in my place. But you've chosen it all on your own, and men are best known by their actions. I'm impressed by what you did. To see this."

He turned the photograph. Disrel's anonymous figure drew on the flag chain, the fiery element blazed on his chest, and his glossy, black helmet resisted the sky.

Mored motioned toward his hand. "Put it on. I want to see you in it."

Disrel inserted the chip into the port in the side of his skyn, and the fabric turned black, textured by scales on the sides and stomach, accentuating the layers of armor he had worked into his garment. Iridescent markings traced his arms, legs, and torso in warm pinks, cool greens, and yellow-orange. On his chest, a three-cornered symbol glowed pink, its multi-dimensional corners and interior accented by crimson. It was so much richer, clearer, and more beautiful than the design he had made.

Mored wiped his mouth. "Fifteen years." He sat forward on the edge of the chair, squeezing his cane with rapture. "A Pyron Tourmaline Renegade."

Tygo raked a hand over his mouth and grunted. "He wears it better."

Mored snorted. "Shut up, Tygo. This is your fault. You broke a cardinal rule just bringing him here, so as punishment, you will train him. And if he fails, I'll blame you." Mored turned to Disrel with a mirthful glint in his eyes. "You may be young and daring, but if you ever hope to have a chance at survival out there, you'll need to be fast and smart. Listen to Tygo and do everything he says. No hero rises alone. You will always need help, and as long as you're fighting for Pyron you will always have mine. But the Tourmaline Renegade still has no place in my army. You are not my soldier. You are a Pyron warrior and you will fight for Pyron as only a Pyron warrior ever could. I will not make any decisions for you, and you will not answer to me. It is as if we had never met and you continued stealing flags as you were. Understood?"

Disrel's chest swelled. "Yes, sir."

The woman moved forward, smiling sweetly, offering her hand, palm up. Pyron words dropped like honey from her lips. "Welcome to the family, Disrel. I'm Alta, and Mored is my husband. Please accept my apologies for using the baton on you the other night. I didn't injure you, did I?" Her hands smoothed over his wrist in search of bruises. "I was praying you wouldn't give up."

Disrel's heart skipped a beat. A Pyron woman playing a sable? He had seen the world's greatest paradox.

Alta's dark eyes were sincere and nurturing, and her presence was a quiet strength.

"Tell me about yourself. How old are you? Do you have any family?"

Disrel spoke softly to respect and give deference to the elder. It was one of a few Pyron customs he knew.

"I'm about twenty-four. I have a sister. She's eighteen. We've always lived in Tourmal."

"The blessing would have been outlawed by the time you were five. Were you ever?"

Disrel's chin shook, and he swallowed. "No, gracious one. I never received my birthright. I took a Kobalt haircut to gain citizenship and get a job, to get off the streets."

Alta's finger flew up to her mouth. "There is more strength in humility than there is in a warrior's braid. But I will see that you receive a new name the very next time you come here."

Joy curled Disrel's mouth and stole his breath. "Thank you. I regret that I'm so disconnected from my people, but I lost my parents when I was nine and a Kobalt woman took us off the streets and raised us. She taught me to speak Kobalt, but I try to speak Pyron with my sister as much as I can."

"So you better understand the good and evil on both sides of the struggle. That gives you a heart more worthy of Thelis."

"Thelis?" The word was like a cradle song dancing in a distant dream of his youth. Disrel couldn't remember the last time he had heard that word, nor did he understand what it meant.

Alta laid a finger against the liddicoatite on his chest. "Thelis may choose its warriors, but those warriors must completely surrender themselves if they hope to change the world."

Disrel looked down and reflected on her words. The trigonal pyramidal turned a deeper shade of pink. "I've already counted the cost of this fight. I'll do whatever it takes."

Mored scooted to the edge of his seat, interjecting with brassy Kobalt. "Do you have what it takes? Body armor? Weapons?"

Disrel brushed the front of his skyn. "I work at an apparel shop and the owner cut me a deal on materials for myself. I built military-grade armor into my skyn."

"Good! Weapons?"

"None yet."

"Corecycle?"

"Saving up for one. But I have a helmet."

Mored waved his hand dismissively. "One corecycle wouldn't last you more than a night anyway. Tygo will get you a standard-issue qorzan blade to start with. But here's what is most important: You must promise me one thing, Disrel. Above all else, promise that you will never reveal your identity to anyone."

"I promise."

Mored waved as if swatting an insect. "You think carrying secrets to the grave is an easy thing? I've been down here for fifteen years because of that skyn. Your sister must never know. No friend is ever, ever close enough to know. You will be living a double life. The moment your enemy suspects who you are, you and everyone you love are in grave danger. The second they see your face, the Tourmaline Renegade dies. The instant they can name you, they'll know how to bait and trap you. So swear to me that you'll die with your helmet on."

Disrel laid a hand over the symbol burning on his chest. "I swear. No one will ever know."

5

Less than twenty-four hours after the Tourmaline Renegade stole the imperial flag, his name was alive on every tongue in Tourmal. Ambrosia paused before the imposing double doors of the imperial palace dining room, tugged at the hem of her uniform, and tucked a stray auburn curl into her bun. She gazed down at the toes of her crimson boots, as glossy as candied apples. Stepping in front of the emperor would be like stepping in front of a camera, set to snap the moment she entered the frame and deliver a print of her intelligence, trustworthiness, competence, and usefulness to the empire. She had to look perfect, confident but not impetuous, groomed but not too done up, intelligent but not too shrewd to be trusted. And after spending her first twelve hours in Tourmal marching around blocks and shaking citizens from their beds, all she wanted was His Supremacy's approval.

What did he expect from the Selenite Skynhound? Was her new position as Tourmaline Sable Commander permanent? Or would they send her back to Selen once she had captured this flag thief? Those details hadn't been made clear in the correspondence. If her performance was impressive enough, the Sable Queen might insist that she remain in command. Ambrosia would miss the pastoral beauty of Selen, but the challenges offered by Tourmal's urban jungle and dense population excited her.

Ambrosia drew a deep breath and brushed flecks from her black sable skyn. At her nod, the guards pulled the towering doors open and stood aside. She strutted into the cavernous hall. An ornate rug ran down its length to the large picture windows bordered by beds of vegetation. A canopy of flowering plants climbed lattices, competing for light and framing the grand view of the palace grounds and gardens beyond. Serpentine figures of carved onyx glared down from their dark lofts in the highest corners of the ceiling, and the lucid teardrops of a crystal chandelier glimmered over an ostentatious glass table that sprawled down the center of the room. It was an aquarium, Ambrosia realized, filled with live coral, sunken treasures, and vibrant fish. Near the head of the table, a phlegmatic man sat in full military attire, his legs crossed, his elbow leaning on the table, his fingers pressed against his stubbled jaw. He appeared not over thirty-five years of age, but his face was hardened by experience. Still, he was gorgeously Kobalt, from the crown of his swarthy head to the soles of his boots.

Another man, broad-shouldered and elegantly dressed, turned at her entrance. His attire commanded respect, and his demeanor dripped with expectations of his due reverence. His eyebrows were dark cutlasses, and his almond eyes were deep pools of aquamarine, calculating, discerning, swallowing up her qualities and flaws and weighing them one against the other. His plump lips were framed by a perfectly etched beard of short, coarse stubble, and his wiry, brunette hair was cut close to his head. His nose was wide and strong, a token to his will and authority; and his complexion, like that of most Kobalt people, was a rich tan with warm undertones. As he extended his arm, his brocade suit and caped jacket moved lightly.

Ambrosia dropped to one knee and pressed her forehead to the back of his divine hand. Those beautiful blue shoes, ornamented by jeweled buttons on the tongues, were anchored into the carpet by his chiseled legs, sheathed in fitted black leggings that glistened as if encrusted with black diamonds. He was everything, and more than his pictures made him out to be.

"Supremacy." She pulled a breath, realizing that from the door to this point, she had forgotten to breathe.

"What a pleasure to have you in Tourmal, Commander Ambrosia. I hope you will feel right at home in our glorious capitol." He drew her to her feet. "Allow me to introduce you to General Gault."

The general rose and extended a hand. His lips drew into a grim line. "The Selenite Skynhound. Your photograph doesn't even do you justice, and your hair— Excuse me." He cleared his throat and swallowed hard. "I mean, in person, you're so much more . . . more . . . more . . ."

Ambrosia squared her shoulders and wished he would shut up. Sexier? Fatter? Boyish? More redheaded? More intelligent-looking?

Lord Cinnabar chuckled and took his seat at the head of the table. "Truer words have never been spoken as we stand in the presence of one of the empire's finest sables, one as deadly as she is beautiful. Please, take your seats."

Ambrosia's hands shook as she took her chair at the aquarium table. She let a falling lock of hair shield her burning face. The general wasn't a calloused, humped old piece of brass, and the emperor possessed remarkably good humor, but stiff-collared staff meetings still managed to be less awkward than private banquets.

General Gault adjusted his plateware until the utensils were perfectly aligned. His moody eyes sunk to the silty bottom of the aquarium to hide with the mud guppies.

Lord Cinnabar leaned back in his seat. "I was just telling General Gault how much I appreciate your coming on such short notice, and your willingness to jump in and take control of last night's situation. I rarely see such an initiative in transfers so soon."

Ambrosia brushed the lap of her uniform and folded her hands. "Thank you, sir. I will do everything in my power to keep Tourmal quiet for you."

Servants swept through the side doors bearing large trays of steaming food. The head chef paused at Cinnabar's shoulder and read him the menu in the order each dish was placed on the table and mouth-watering aromas filled the dining hall. Fish bolted down into the coral as the loaded trays landed on the glassy ceiling of their world. Lord Cinnabar extended his hand over the spread.

"Please. Fill your plates. I recommend the grott-pork and date pudding."

The servants left the room as quickly and as silently as they had come. Ambrosia contemplated the ingredients and the artistic arrangements on every platter. This was the finest food she had ever laid eyes on.

Lord Cinnabar folded his hands in his lap. "I understand that Tourmal is a very different landscape for you, Commander. Our population is eight times that of Selen and more concentrated."

"It does not intimidate me, sir. Selen's inner city is not much different, and that is where I made most of my catches."

"Excellent," the emperor said. "Then you'll feel right at home. The general's soldiers can handle the strays in the marketplaces and the occasional vandal. I requested your service here in Tourmal because there will be increasing resistance and unrest once we begin moving Pyrons into the new sector. That pathetic little white flag they decided to fly over Capital Circle last night is just the first clap of thunder in the oncoming storm. It was no benign joke. The insurrectionist dared to resurrect the Tourmaline Renegade's image from the grave and meant to stir all of Pyron into war with his flag. The faster we can make an example of this impostor, the faster we can crush the insolent spirit of Pyron."

Cinnabar's eyes gleamed. "My father wasted precious years trying to make slaves out of these people. All his work camps did was defile the beautiful landscapes and introduce rare diseases among our own. The reproduction taxes have done little to curb their exponential multiplication, and resentment festers in their children's blood from their conception. Just as last night's flag proclaimed, they think they are a free nation and reject the authority of the very empire they leech from."

Ambrosia stole a glance at Cinnabar while he filled his plate, meticulously spacing his portions. A pink web peeked subtly from behind the short hairs of the young emperor's beard, stretching from the corner of his mouth down around his jaw. A chalky foundation struggled to blend the scar with his olive complexion. Cinnabar was a champion fighter. He might have earned that wound by training in his youth or sparring with aristocrats.

Cinnabar laid three slices of grott-pork on his plate. "My father attended a Pyron festival once, hoping to ease the tensions between our modern ways and their feral traditions, and in full barbaric mockery, they sat him right among the lowliest of their people. The insult proved to me how incompatible the Pyron ways are with our culture. They will fill their children's heads with stories of their eternal Sky Father and teach them to respect their elders, and then dare to mock us at every opportunity. So I'm closing the work camps and relocating the prisoners to the new sector. In the upcoming weeks we'll clean the strays off our streets. Who could object to non-citizens being moved into a sector of their own? Or even criminals as we catch them? And the last will be the easiest, those Pyrons who hold citizenship. They're such a minority that there will be no good reason for them to remain in Kobalt society when Pyron has a sector of its very own. And when they're all securely tucked behind the walls of their own little nation, flying their little white flags of freedom, strays will no longer plague our beautiful marketplaces. Citizens won't have to compete with Pyrons for labor and wages. Housing quality will improve. Slums will disappear completely. It will be like night and day, the beauty and richness of the Kobalt Empire to the pasty, homogenous rabble that will eventually consume themselves to extinction."

General Gault lifted his glass in applause. "Well said, Supremacy. Your vision is so inexplicit that history will pen the tragedy upon Pyron ignorance and frailty. The universe is known both for mistakes and miracles, and the mistakes ought to be hastened into history by whatever means necessary, for the health of your glorious empire."

Lord Cinnabar carefully loaded his fork with an equal measure of food from each portion on his plate. "My father's negligence bred the Tourmaline Renegade right out of his own military. But I didn't let one hour pass before summoning the Selenite Skyhound to help us nip the buds of insurrection before they blossom into deadly fruit." His sculpted eyebrows arched in her direction. "How many renegades have you apprehended in your five years of service?"

Ambrosia's eyes flashed up to meet her emperor's. "Seven, sir."

General Gault's trenchant gaze lit on her. "Tourmal has more rogues in one night."

Cinnabar dismissed the general's remark with a wave of his utensil. "She has made far more than seven arrests. But of these seven, Governor Tritium assured me that every one of them were high-profile renegades, characters known for sabotage and assault against the Selen garrisons and offices, terrorists like that fox my father was chasing all over Tourmal some fifteen years ago. There was the Busq Market bomber, Howler Alpha Grynen . . ." Cinnabar trailed off, struggling to recall the others.

Ambrosia wiped her mouth with the napkin, her appetite suddenly shrunken and her stomach knotted into a little wad. What other swelling words had Governor Tritium included in his referral letter hoping to find favor in his emperor's eyes?

"Sego," Ambrosia said, "who led two hundred armed civilians against the governor's mansion, the South Station Slasher, the Grand Hall Ghost who cut the throats of five legislators and their families, and Cyruz, a joker who only wanted to see the world burn."

Cinnabar poked another bite between his smiling lips. "You heard it straight from the Skynhound's mouth, General. I'm excited to see her peacekeeping skills in action. Our little ghost of the long-dead Tourmaline Renegade won't last long with the Selenite Skynhound on his trail."

Ambrosia laid her loaded utensil down on her plate as her stomach flipped. "The sables you've placed under my command are very well trained and capable. And I'm confident that we can have your Tourmaline Renegade in chains before he incites insurrection."

"Yes, the Sable Queen ensures that we have only the best at our disposal. That's why she summoned you. She asked me to extend her apologies for her absence tonight and said she looks forward to meeting you."

Ambrosia had only met this Sable Queen once, at her graduation from the Sable Academy five years ago. That draconian face, with unfeeling eyes rimmed in dark purple and stern lips painted glossy black, was forever seared into her memory. Ambrosia shuddered. The Sable Queen was the reckoning drum every sable marched to. Her word was life and law. She enforced the sable code and every sable commander in the empire answered only to her. And any sable who fought for the position of Sable Queen—and won—relinquished her name for that title. It was the highest honor to be called Sable Queen. But Ambrosia could only remember sensing that this woman had lost more than her name.

Cinnabar took a slow draught from his crystal cup. "Commander Riahn's unexpected illness and death was almost fatefully timed. Mere days after the Sable Queen expressed interest in you taking command of our garrison, our little Tourmaline Renegade impostor made his appearance and necessitated your early arrival. I believe it to be fortune."

General Gault's astute gaze rested on Ambrosia, as though he had something to add, but his lips were drawn into a thin, hard line. Cinnabar pulled a small metal object from his breast pocket.

"Speaking of fortune." He turned the keepsake around for Ambrosia, showing a photograph of an exceptionally beautiful young woman with a sensual expression. Her lips were parted slightly, offering a glimpse of pearly white teeth, well set and of a good size. "You'll be the first to know that the governor of Euclase has accepted my daughter's proposal of marriage today."

Ambrosia smiled with genuine excitement for the royal family. "Congratulations, sir. Her Imperial Highness is a goddess."

General Gault scooted up in his seat. "And one who knows it."

Cinnabar smiled proudly. "Thank you. She takes after her mother so well, doesn't she? The wedding will be here in Tourmal in the spring of next year. I've recently created a variegated cross of the Zaelip and Zaelis perseus, and she plans on filling the wedding with them: bouquets, boats, baskets, and carriages."

Ambrosia and the general were obligated to turn and take notice of the flowering plants growing in the windows and vocalize their amazement at the mottled blossoms. The emperor's sanguine mood surprised Ambrosia. She had expected an austere personality, the face of deity and power expressed through his statues, photographs, paintings, and holograms. But Ambrosia's experience warned her that Cinnabar had other layers. His buoyancy masked his intelligence, his wit veiled his cunning, and his smile veneered a propensity for fury.

Cinnabar touched the photograph affectionately before tucking it back in his left breast pocket. "I'd like to have the land free of Pyrons in time for my daughter's wedding. And that freedom will double as her inheritance, since she will one day be empress in my stead."

The meal continued over a circular conversation of political unrest being the fault of Pyrons and how it weakened the strength and glory of the empire. Then Cinnabar dismissed himself and left Ambrosia and General Gault standing before the spread of cold food.

Ambrosia's uniform squeezed her full stomach, and her mind kept wandering beyond the dark windows and into the grounds beyond the mansion. The weather was perfect for walking, and she was unaccustomed to sitting. The moment the doors closed behind Cinnabar, Ambrosia turned to the general.

"I must also excuse myself, General."

General Gault reached out. "Please, Commander. Just a minute of your time." His eyes searched her face, and he fumbled. "I had no intention of insulting you with my comment about Tourmal's crime. I respect your record and I'm sure you'll add the Tourmaline Renegade's skyn to your belt before the month is out."

Ambrosia held his gaze, shocked that she was being offered an apology or a compliment, let alone both in the same breath. "Thank you, General. I understand how governors tend to bloat their officers' reputations to earn respect from their emperor. But the sables under my command are just as worthy of the honor and title they gave me."

A wide smile spread across his face, unveiling two rows of beautiful teeth, framed by wolfishly pointed canines. He bowed his head in an almost bashful manner. "Understandably. But no army goes to victory without a great officer leading the way. You have potential and you are fortunate the Sable Queen recognizes your talent. You've advanced so quickly that I believe you could one day become the empire's youngest Sable Queen."

Pricks and stings rolled over Ambrosia's cheeks. "I know so many others who would kill for the opportunity I have been given. So I don't take it lightly."

"Sometimes greatness is thrust upon us. But I know how transfers often snatch us away from friends, those we hate to lose more than anything else." His eyes glimmered with a burning intensity that kept arresting her gaze. He stood comfortably, arms hanging easily at his sides, a pleasant smile playing around the edges of his face.

"I was able to bring a few sables with me."

He tilted his head and his chest rumbled every time he spoke. "Forgive my candor, but I find it impossible to believe that a sable of your reputation and skill and"—his hands fumbled in an almost practiced manner—"beauty wouldn't have left a string of broken hearts in Selen."

Ambrosia clutched the hem of her jacket and stiffened, squinting over a standoffish, angry smile. What was he getting at? "Any heart that dances with a sable's is destined to be broken before it has a chance to do any crushing of its own," she said.

The corners of his eyes wrinkled as he caught the old military joke, normally played by soldiers, turned around and hurled at him like a dagger. "So you *are* all widows. Have you ever found a man you could respect?"

Ambrosia leveled her chin and stared off her nose. "Not yet. But I know of at least one with a sliver of potential. I would entertain a comrade sooner than anyone else, but I cannot afford any distractions until I have caught this Tourmaline Renegade."

The general's eyes were the most beautiful shade of hazel, smoky and vivid against his amber complexion. And for a moment, all Ambrosia felt was his gaze, intense and passionate, yet checked.

"Cleansing our land of Pyrons will be a straightforward campaign," he said. "And this new Tourmaline Renegade will be history in a matter of weeks with a sable of your caliber on his trail. Perhaps you'll allow me to take you down to the wharf sometime for seafood and drinks. Tourmal has much to offer, and I hope you'll feel at home here. The architecture is breathtaking, and the shipping offers us luxurious imports at half the price you might find in Selen. And once you've seen a Tourmal bay sunset, you'll want no other view."

His eyes twinkled. Ambrosia tugged at her jacket hem, hating the lack of self-possession she felt under his gaze.

"Thank you, General Gault. I'll consider the offer."

"Callon." He extended his hand. "If you ever need anything, this Kobalt will have your back."

Callon Gault. It fit him well. The wrinkles deepened at the corners of his smile and the grand dining hall fuzzed into a blurred fantasy. His hand enveloped hers firmly and her heart tumbled into those pools of hazel for one dizzying moment. Then his hand fell away.

Ambrosia turned and pulled a breath. She'd foregone her chances with many attractive ranking officers before, but this one was different. He was ruggedly handsome, mature, dangerously charming, and even a little humble. That combination was rare in men.

"Goodnight, Callon."

He nodded pleasantly, and Ambrosia marched off over the long rug and through the doors, her heart popping like a firecracker in time with her footfalls. She strode down the hall with wings on her heels, wanting at every turn to stop and catch her breath. But her legs were like horses pulling to run. What did the general want with her? He knew sables didn't marry. Nobody wanted them, not under oath and ceremony, not for more than a night. He knew sables with reputations for killing their lovers were called widows. And whether or not they chose to live the lie, a dark shadow followed the uniform. This was why people hid their little girls when the Sable Queen passed through the villages. Sablehood was no blessing of power or equality. It was a curse. Slavery of mind, body, and spirit. Soldiers enlisted and collected a salary, and once retired, received a pension. But sables were selected for a lifetime of service and held to a code outside of military and civilian law. A higher standard of fidelity. Because a sable's sole purpose was to protect her emperor's throne from traitors and renegades. They were the check and balance. The military police. The bodyguards of every government official from tax collectors to the imperial family.

Ambrosia hurled herself out into the gardens that surrounded the mansion to shake off the stress of the meal, her mind whirling with a confusing flurry of emotions. Lord Cinnabar had been more pleasant than she could have ever hoped, and his highest-ranking officer more attractive and cordial than any officer she had met. And the general's initial awkwardness paled under the warmth he'd extended in parting. It was impossible to deny the emotions boiling under his surface, and his bumbles were only those of a man with a smitten heart. How was such an attractive man not already in a committed relationship? Why was a man of such power interested in a sable at all?

Ambrosia walked the paved pathways through the topiary hedges and fountains, contemplating the fortunate evening. Dreamy lavender clouds striped with vermilion painted the evening sky. She paused by a lily pond with two white marble swans gleaming at its center. The black waters rippled around each lily pad, every crest cradling a ribbon of the neon sunset.

A young woman stared up at her from the pond's murky depths. Her shoulders were swept back and her frame resilient. Her chiseled face was weathered and framed by locks of deepest auburn. Her eyes were slits of cynicism and her lips forged into a sneer as rigid as the armor in her sable skyn. Her face seemed older, wiser than that of a girl of twenty-three, but in its depths a child was pressing to the front, beating against the bars in her eyes and screaming to be heard. There was hardly any room for the child in the staunch military mold, yet every time she moved tears pushed up into her eyes. What was this child doing in a sable's uniform? The girl belonged in the mountains of Selen, plaiting flower crowns and running with her herd of goats. Ambrosia's mind wandered back across the distance of time and space.

Great white ships in full sail clipped through a cerulean ocean over the peaks, and a warm summer breeze rattled berries from the vines. Ambrosia had been dawdling as usual, her lips, hands, and pockets stained with aubergine juices and her tangled red coils bouncing around her face in the wind as she splashed through a brook with the goats. She skipped into town with a crown of milk thistle and wildflowers on her head, a basket of herbs on her arm, a shepherd's song on her lips, and a trail of spotted kids bouncing behind her before tumbling straight into two black pillars with crimson boots at their bases. A hand jerked her up by her hair, and livid eyes bit into her face. Two glassy black lips parted, and a voice screeched—

"Perfect! Redheads make the finest sables."

A formation of stern women in black and crimson uniforms stood just behind, all holding giant ox goads with gleaming steel tips. Two of the women marched forward and dragged Ambrosia back into their line, cuffing her to them with their iron hands.

Mother gaped and clawed at the doorframe of their little home with its green door and oxen carved gables.

"Ambrosia! Ambrosia! No! No, you can't take my little girl! Please, she's not the one you want!" She tumbled out onto the lawn and fell on her face.

The woman with the inky black lips chucked a sack of money at Mother. "Ifayth's duty to the empire has been fulfilled. We will not seek another sable in this village for five more years."

Ambrosia pressed a fist to her pounding chest. She had passed the rigorous training, she had excelled in all of her studies, she had made friends she would not have traded for anything money could buy. But she had killed. She had cut and maimed and bludgeoned. She had passed the point of no return and made a name for herself, a name that had caught the attention of the Sable Queen and brought her to command in Tourmal. And yet, sometimes she still felt that child inside her, screaming and pulling against the amazonian women who held her. But there was nowhere to go. This was her life. This was her: the uniform, the belt, the boots. This was all she could ever be. Sables ended their lives in combat or in training the next generation for service. A sable died in her boots with honor or on her cross in shame.

Ambrosia's mind meandered back to that gabled cottage and through its lovely green door. She had visited it often in her dreams like a ghost, sailing through the familiar rooms and trying to catch the eyes of the people who dwelled there. How she missed hovering about the stove with Mother, helping to chop this and sprinkle that into a pot of bubbling joy that she could share with the family.

"Ambrosia made this," Mother sang as she set the pot on the table. Even though Ambrosia may have only helped a little, even by simply stirring the stew, Mother would give her all of the credit.

Ambrosia hunkered down behind her plate and relished the sight of Father and her elder brothers downing the hot food along with hunks of bread. The muscles in their shoulders rippled, and she felt a certain responsibility to help strengthen the arms that farmed the land to provide for them all. "Good food makes strong men," Mother would say. "And strong men can handle strong women."

"Hmmm! Hmmm!" Father patted his bulging stomach. "You could open your very own restaurant someday, Ambrosia. Once word spreads, everyone in the empire will come to taste your fine cooking!"

Seven-year-old Ambrosia grinned and hunched in her chair across from Father, secretly hoping to one day be married to a man as strong and handsome as he was and have children of her own.

Ambrosia wrenched away from the sad woman in the lily pond and continued her lonely walk through the gardens. What silly dreams children had. She had been granted a more fulfilling life than anything her parents or her lonely village could have offered her. She had traveled, trained, and received a higher education than the average civilian could afford. And the state had given it to her freely. It made sense to be grateful. But in gaining all of this, she had lost something far more precious. Her family. Love. Her own dreams. Her self.

The shadows deepened and the lamps in the garden flickered on. Ambrosia quickened her pace, knowing that she had things to take care of at the barracks before retiring. She stepped up into a wide, arched trellis that led to the garden doors of the palace. Tremulous voices crooned to each other in the breeze, just overhead.

"I'll be back soon, my darling flower!" The deep bass floated down from right above her.

Ambrosia pulled back into the climbing foliage as a giggle wafted over the lawn, chittering into words: "You're my only addiction, hummingbird. How can I ever say no?"

The sultry, silky smacks of lips caressing drifted down through the vining plants in the lattice. A window light cast off the side of the palace and onto the stone path, and within it the shadows of two people morphed into one undulating ball of passion. Ambrosia was not one to eavesdrop, but she also did not want to suffer the embarrassment of interrupting the intimate moment on her way to the door.

"Oh! If only my father would take another vacation, I would dare to let you stay an entire night. Here, don't forget your things."

A sack rustled, followed by another passionate kiss.

"My precious Zaelix. I will wait every evening for your white flowers to appear in the window. Until then!"

"Goodnight!"

An alluring face pressed its way into Ambrosia's mind—Cinnabar's daughter. Ambrosia held her breath and pressed deeper into the corner as a pair of bright shoes wedged themselves into the holes of the lattice. The white-clad stranger descended with a bulging sack slung across his shoulder. A Pyron. Ambrosia tensed, ready to spring. But the royal was watching from her window, and apparently she didn't see this man as an intruder. Ambrosia held herself to the lattice. The Pyron dropped to the ground and blew a kiss from his fingers to the window. He pulled a hood over his face and cast a furtive glance in all directions before diving into the garden foliage and scampering away into the night. The window latched, and the light faded with the drawing of curtains.

Ambrosia's stomach twisted with pain for the emperor. He was blissfully ignorant that his only child and heir, betrothed to a governor, had a Pyron lover. If he found out, all of Pyron would take the blame, and he still might disinherit his daughter. The Euclasian governor would have reason to demand a defamation settlement; worse, if the blame fell wholly on Pyron's lap, thousands of innocent people would die. No one would ever dare accuse Her Imperial Highness of an affair, not even a sable sworn to protect her from harm. There was no way to prove it other than to catch them in the act. Ambrosia considered reporting that she'd seen a Pyron sneaking around the grounds near the princess's chamber window. There was no harm in that. She could heighten security and prevent the man from coming back. She glared at the darkened window. And what if her sables caught Zaelix's lover? He would reveal his relationship, hoping the royal would have some power to spare his life. But even in this scenario, all parties lost.

Ambrosia looked out across the dark gardens at the illuminated fountain display where she had been standing earlier. The water danced and frothed. What did Cinnabar's daughter want with a common Pyron? Why had she bothered to propose herself in marriage to anyone if all she wanted was a secret affair, and with people her father found undesirable? Why not an aristocrat, someone with whom she had things in common? Ambrosia's stomach turned with unease. Time had a way of uncovering the truth. It was not worth being condemned to a sable's cross for slandering the imperial family. Her Imperial Highness could have her secrets.

Ambrosia turned and walked through the tunneling trellis. She had seen and heard nothing.

6

There was an hour yet until dawn, and the doves were already warbling in the rafters under the indigo skylights of the old Selenite subway. Shards and powder mingled with blood and sweat to form a rusty paste under Disrel's feet. Tygo squared himself, gripping a tile between his fists at chest level. Disrel plunged his hand into the brick, shattering it.

"Good! Again." Tygo whipped another target from a nearby stack.

Disrel punched, and the tile crumbled to the ground in pieces.

"Again." Tygo skipped a circle around Disrel, holding another overhead. Disrel leaped, kicked out, and missed.

"Keep your eye on it."

He jumped again and the tile hardly wobbled in Tygo's fist. Disrel licked sweat from his lip and growled. Tygo was moving the target at the last second.

"Your opponent isn't going to sit still and wait for you to hit him. You've got to be faster, less predictable."

Disrel's toe smacked the corner of the tile as he kicked again. As his feet returned to the station floor, Tygo swung the tile down and Disrel crunched it with an uppercut. Tygo's palm plunged into Disrel's chest, bowling him back onto the ground. Disrel rolled to his feet just as another tile whirled from Tygo's hand. He ducked, and the tile hissed over the top of his head. The bald ex-special forces soldier already had two more tiles in hand and hurled them one after the other. There was no dodging two, and the bruises on Disrel's body reminded him of Tygo's punishing accuracy. He leaped and spun, crushing one tile with his foot and narrowly missing the second. It smashed into his arm and shattered on the ground.

Tygo propped his hands on his hips and nodded. "Not bad for your first week of training."

Disrel rubbed his throbbing arm. "Why are we stopping?"

"Alta wants to give you your blessing before you go."

Disrel mopped his brow with a towel. A streak of blood tinged the fibers. "Can I come back tonight after work?"

Tygo offered a teasing smile. "I can't inject thirty years of combat experience into you like a drug. But if you can handle the abuse, I'll be here."

"I'm Pyron. I can handle whatever you throw at me."

A chalky scraping sound warned him that another tile had left the stack. He jerked aside and snapped the towel like a whip, cracking the missile into three pieces.

Tygo's eyes twinkled. "I'll make you prove it." He clamped his hand on Disrel's shoulder and gave him a shake and a hearty slap. "You've got potential. But I'm not going to be easy on you. I don't want to see you fail. I want you to have a fighting chance out there, so I'm going to push you all the way to your limit, and then push you right through it."

Disrel was counting on Tygo to teach him all he knew, and the mountain of muscle had a lot of skill to offer. His training was not restricted to one on one with Tygo at the station. Sometimes Tygo's friend Astros worked with him. Astros was closer to Disrel in weight and size, and he offered a completely different martial arts style. When the two of them weren't teaching Disrel how to fight, they gave him exercises for grip and core strength, coordination, and endurance that he could perform almost anywhere: at home, at work, while loitering on a street corner. Two of the most brutal exercises involved clinging to an edge by his fingertips and swinging, and crawling like a lizard over a mile of rail and back.

Disrel scraped the folded crimson flag off the ticket counter. He'd brought it with him on his second return to the Selenite subway to remove the evidence from his apartment and possession, and stashed it in a drawer behind the ticket counter. Today, though, he needed a gift for Alta, and the stolen Kobalt flag couldn't have been more appropriate.

He followed Tygo through the atrium. Just beyond the double doors lay an eatery filled with benches and tables. Glass awnings swept out over two long bars and crowned the doorways to the kitchens at the back of the hall. Empty glasses and bottles huddled on the buffet in sporadic clusters, and plates of withered, crusty food remnants and random personal belongings ornamented the tops of tables. Pans, cooling racks, and baking sheets lined the counters in the kitchen behind, many of them bearing ominous black lumps and husks. Dust covered every surface like hoarfrost, but the wood and stone trimmings on the walls and behind the bar were historic and pristine, and an artist's mural on one wall told a richly colored story of a station bustling with smiling patrons like the very ones who had suddenly disappeared and left everything in this room behind, undisturbed through the decades. It was similar in style to the mural that ran the length of one wall in the atrium.

Mored perched rigidly on a bench running alongside a row of tables, and all around him sat a score of faceless persons, armed but at ease, elbows leaning on the table. Cloth hoods shrouded their heads and some interior cloth concealed their faces except for their eyes. One could not be told from another, Kobalt or Pyron, without peering at the colors of their eyes or the complexion of their exposed hands. Perhaps they were all Pyrons, here to witness his blessing like brothers of his tribe. The far corner of the eatery was clear of tables and free of dust. Rugs and pillows were placed on the floor in a way that would make any Pyron feel at home. Alta rested on a large pillow, a cream robe spilling down from her shoulders and over the edges of her lap. A veil of intricately woven stone beads crowned her snowy head and coiffed around her neck and shoulders. Her face held a melancholy light, a meditative quality, and her hands tended a vial of incense and a cup of coals. The sight of her threw Disrel back into his childhood to the last time he had met with an elder, and he winced, throwing out a hand to block the lash. He rolled his shoulders as the scars on his back tingled, pretending that his awkward reaction had been voluntary as the masked men took note.

Alta beckoned him forward. "I'm sorry that we have no male elder among us to bless you. I hope you will not be offended."

"Not at all. I'm very thankful you can do this for me. Please accept this gift."

She took the flag and laid it aside with a pleased smile, and when she looked at him, her eyes twinkled. "Please sit and let me counsel you in the ways of our people."

Disrel eased down onto a pillow, mindful to keep his feet off the beautiful fabric like his mother had taught him.

Alta drew a meditative breath. "The ways of the Pyron, firebloods, tabernacles of light, temples of Thelis, star followers, seekers. Listen carefully to my counsel, young Disrel, that you may have joy and peace on your journey through this earth and may pass this wisdom to your children. We have no holy books or holy men. We have no temple to worship in, outside of the nature around us and the body we indwell. Your body is a gift from your Sky Father, a temple for Thelis. Keep it strong and healthy. Nourish it, but do not let it become your idol. Surrender it to your Sky Father and let Him use it in a life of love and service. This is the way of Thelis. This is a divine character that makes light in your temple for all the world to see. You must be a star shining on earth. As fire is light and power, so is Thelis in your veins. But great power only enhances the darkness or light that is already within our hearts. And what we choose to manifest, we become. We have no chosen ones, only given ones, those who give themselves in the purest love. And if you would overcome, master your tongue. It is wise to be reticent and soft-spoken and let only life come through your lips. Speak life. This is the way of our people. Will you follow it?"

"I will follow it."

"Which tribe did you descend from?"

Disrel's brow knit. He remembered the elder asking Father that question, but the soldiers had interrupted before Father could answer. "I'm not sure. My parents never spoke of our descent."

"Do you know which stars your ancestors followed?"

"No. Well... just once, Father told me that grandfather would chase the tiger from year to year, trying to catch him by his tail and force him to tell the secrets of the stars."

The men around Mored shifted and murmured.

Alta's eyes narrowed with some secret pleasure. "Could it be? A tiger survived the purge?" She scrutinized his face, as if looking for some trait that might confirm it.

Disrel sat back, his heart racing. He knew little about the purge, only that one of Pyron's tribes had been slaughtered to extinction during the reign of the previous emperor, and that it had happened right before he was born.

Alta opened her hand. "Answer me this question: What three things cause men to die?"

It was a familiar cradle riddle, one no Pyron could have grown up and forgotten. The answer was fear, hate, and pride.

"Love, Thelis, and sacrifice." Disrel cringed as words left his lips. Surely, she knew what he was trying to say.

Alta's eyes gleamed with approval, but she shook her head and repeated the words right back to him, stressing the unusual fricative that each required of a Pyron tongue. "Fear, hate, and pride." They were only one delicate sound apart.

He strained to replicate the sounds, and Alta demonstrated them again, moving more slowly so he could listen. Disrel stammered, a lump rising in his throat at the embarrassment of being unable to speak three simple words.

"Love, Thelis, and sacrifice. No. Worry, like cowering in the face of danger." There was no other word in the Pyron tongue for fear. Disrel scrambled for other ways to describe his intent. "Disliking someone so much you wish them dead."

Alta's eyes shimmered. "Your speech does not lie, Disrel. You are a tiger."

A tingling rushed through his spine as memories from the past fell into place like missing puzzle pieces.

Alta's face radiated hope, relief, joy. "You were always one of our smallest tribes, our most hated because you bred most of Pyron's warriors and protectors. Those who follow the tiger exhibit greater strength and willpower in the face of adversity, acting preemptively, sometimes without thinking because they trust their inherent strength and believe that good will always triumph. Your spirit is tenacious. But you must learn to trust in a power greater than your own strength, and learn that surrender is the first step on the long journey to victory and that the death of the flesh is the only way for the spirit to have a new life." Alta wiped a tear from the corner of her eye. "Are you ready to continue, Disrel Itzkyre?"

Disrel relished the sound of the name she had added. It meant "son of the tiger." He nodded. "I am."

Alta sprinkled a bundle of herbs with oil and laid them on the coals until they caught fire. Then she made him stand and wafted the smoldering bundle all around him. The smoke rose and fell in eddies, coiling around his head, shoulders, arms, torso, and legs. The pungent odor consumed Disrel's senses, and he closed his eyes. It was piney, musky, with a hint of spicy sweetness that made the air run cold through his nose and burn upon his skin. Alta laid the herbs down and took up a white feather, waving it to clear the air of the smoke. When the cleansing was done, they sat back down on the cushions. Disrel's heart skipped and every movement in the room turned his head. He clenched his fists, feeling that at any moment, soldiers would disrupt them and lay the whip to his back again, just as they had seventeen years ago.

"Quiet your spirit. Open your heart and ears to the Eternal One. Traditionally, this was done in the open air of the wild for an entire day, but we can only set aside a few minutes here. Always remember that your relationship with your Sky Father is your own private journey and you must draw close to Him on your own as often as you can."

Alta closed her eyes and lowered her head. Disrel sat there for a moment, feeling awkward. Would everyone else in the room participate? He dared not look back. He closed his eyes and waited. He had to be at work soon. How long would they sit like this? The bench groaned under shifting weight and someone coughed. The minutes rolled by and, little by little, his mind settled. His own breathing became more apparent, followed by the breathing of every other body in the room. The slightest sounds were sharp to his ears. And then they faded, and Disrel dropped deeper into himself and a strange feeling consumed the space around him. The air felt alive and quick with energy. Someone else was present. A hand touched him, shaking him to wakefulness.

Alta gave a comforting smile. "Rise to your knees."

Disrel obeyed, and Alta stood and placed both of her hands on his head. "This son of Pyron, descended from the tribe that follows the tiger, now carries the spirit of freedom and the light of Thelis in his temple. By receiving a sky name, he vows to let his life on this earth be the proof of divine love and adhere to the way of Thelis in all matters great and small. He vows to pass on our ways and our stories in their purest form to his children and all others who will listen, to preserve a free people upon a free earth. Who among us, no matter his tribe or nation, will bind his life with this child of heaven as a blood brother? Come, lay your hand upon him to bear witness to his pledge and yours."

The benches and tables groaned as the men rose and gathered around, stacking their hands on top of Alta's. Disrel peered at their boots on the mat around him and estimated more than a dozen, and yet more were gathering. Their heat grew, and the hands increased, resting on his shoulders and anywhere they could slip in and touch him.

"There is none chosen for greatness among the Pyron people." Alta's voice took on a hypnotic cadence. "There are only those who choose to give themselves for love and freedom. Therefore, I give you my maternal blessing, that you might be a leader who will soften the stony hearts of our people and all others, that you will be a powerful fighter, a protector of the weak and helpless, a true vessel of

Thelis. The Eternal Spirit reveals your new name, so that you will be able to walk this new path. Never boast of this gift or let pride consume your heart, or its power in your life will fly away. It is better to never speak this name at all, should you say it lightly and despise it as a small thing. This name is the secret of how you will overcome this life, so guard it well, hold it close to your heart. It is a token of your position in your sky family. May you live worthy of its tenor, Kyreasheluhn, white tiger of the people."

The men touching him repeated the name in unison, and Disrel's chest swelled as he meditated on it, replaying its sound in his memory so that he could always remember it. It was beautiful. It was his. It was *him*. Kyreasheluhn. It meant more than any tangible possession, than any sum of money, than any position in society he could have ever dreamed of attaining. He was different now, looking at the world through a new lens. The world would look back and never see him for what he was, but he would know. And he would carry himself differently, in the power of that knowledge. It changed everything, and he wondered how he had gone so long without it. Seventeen long years of waiting, without a tribe, without a family, without a name. The elder's words to Father echoed in Disrel's memory.

"Woe to those who have sharpened the tiger's stripes."

He thought the elder had been referring to Father, but now he knew. The elder had meant him.

The hands floated away, and the men dispersed. Disrel stood and turned. Now he was one of them, a fireblood by birth and blessing. Mored approached and clapped a firm hand on his shoulder.

"I'm sorry we cannot let you bring your sister here for her blessing."

"It's okay. In time. Maybe we can find another way for her to meet with an elder. I appreciate everything you and Alta are doing to help me." He patted his hip pocket where he kept the Tourmaline chip Mored had given him. "I need to get going or I'll be late for work."

"You know where the bikes are kept. Take your pick. Red drives faster." Mored gestured with his head and patted Disrel's back before moving off. "Just don't drive too fast or you'll have the aerial police on your tail."

Disrel thanked Mored, waved to Tygo and Astros, and headed out through the station with his helmet in hand. He took a tunnel out into one of the massive concrete and steel towers that bordered the subway station's surface complex. This was where Mored hid his stable of sleek, sturdy bikes, some vintage, some new, most ordinary models that would blend well on the roadways. One quarter of the silo floor was a dedicated workspace with benches, cables, and beams for hoisting the vehicles for service and customization. Some of these bikes had been birthed from scraps and parts right in this workshop.

Disrel swept a hand over a glossy black roadrunner and admired the wide, all-terrain druze tires. Druze offered excellent shock absorption and traction in the worst of riding conditions and freely allowed the repelling wind to flow between the netyardot rims, floating suspension arms, and drive wells. But this maglev technology was only possible because of two elements: the non-ferrous netyardot and the composite corestone that provided the pull to the netyardot's relentless push. It was a mysterious symbiosis of stone and metal, and the corestone's energy was only visible to the eye in darkness, an arcing, blueish-purplish ultraviolet light that rippled and washed over the surface of the corestone when a keystone's frequency contacted it. But Disrel was careful never to pull an engine apart for a look at a corestone. These energy cores were fixed behind shields to prevent them from causing swift and permanent vision damage when they were looked at directly.

Disrel threw his leg over a deep maroon-colored bike and slid into the seat, gripping the handlebars and rocking it with his weight. He put his helmet on, fastened the chinstrap, and pressed the keystone into the port on the bike's head joint. Energy hummed through the seat, and the rims and tracings on the vehicle illuminated, reflecting off nearby surfaces in the dim garage. The chassis raised several inches from the wheels as maglev wind flowed between them, then Disrel pushed off with his feet, setting the engine into motion and gliding toward the tunnel that wound underneath the streets of Selen for a half mile and came out on the other side of the business district. Soiled skylights barely illuminated the pathway to the elevator at the end. The bike's wheels skimmed into the giant box and the container sank under its burden. The room tilted, tipping the wall and floor outward, and they separated, delivering the bike gently into a quiet alley in the industrial section of Selen. The moment the bike's back wheel left the elevator, the container groaned back, closing itself off to the outside world and slowly reascending several feet. A counterweight returned fluidly through the caged center of the nearby water tower that loomed over the alley. It was a crafty one-way exit. Disrel cruised to the end of the alley, turned on his signal, and entered the busy trafficways of Selen.

He set his hand on the barrel of the bike and smiled as the gentle resonations of the engine pulsed up through his arm. Mored had designed these bikes to outrun military police. So how fast could it go? He pushed the throttle with his thumb, then pulled back a quarter when the bike bucked and almost left him hanging in the air. She was sensitive and responsive.

"Wow." A grin smeared his face. A bike with this much power was illegal, but Mored had managed to get his hands on some heavy corestones. The state inspected vehicles at bike shops on the regular, but even that didn't stop some from obtaining black-market corestones for loyal customers and upgrading the vehicles after purchase. Military police weren't doing random stops, either. A corestone's shields couldn't be dismantled without special tools, and no one was foolish enough to size up a corestone without protective eyewear.

Disrel turned onto the highway into Tourmal. The corecycle's front wheel devoured miles of pavement like a ravenous beast. Another rider moved up on Disrel's left quarter and glanced over his shoulder, lifting his visor and squinting in admiration at the maroon bike. Then he slapped his visor back down and motioned forward with his fingers. Disrel shook his head, and the other rider drew closer, taunting and weaving. He anticipated his movements and steered clear, but the other rider slowed in his path, begging to be passed. Disrel knew that the moment he did, the other rider would speed up and engage in a race. He studied the layout of the road ahead and smiled. The race was on.

He eased on the throttle and carved a path around his challenger. The other rider sped up, keeping pace next to him and throwing another taunting glance. Disrel hunkered down and burned ahead. The wind roared around his helmet. He glanced back to find the challenger riding right on his tail, moving alongside him again, pulling out in front. Disrel pressed conservatively against the throttle, unsure of the vehicle's true potential. He passed the Kobalt rider in a blur. If this bike even had gears, they'd shifted seamlessly. Disrel raced on ahead for miles, certain that his challenger had given up.

He rode the crest of a small hill, and the corecycle caught air. Disrel drew in his breath and clung to the handles, bracing himself for the drop, looking down, expecting to see the road rising to meet his wheels, waiting for the shock of landing. But the ground was dropping away and the bike was pushing him upward. Its front wheel had flipped on its side, horizontal to the earth, and four short balancing wings had sprouted from beneath the carriage. Panic stole Disrel's breath. The back wheel was oriented the same as the front and whirling like a fan.

Disrel drew back on the throttle and gripped the barrel of the bike with his legs as it dropped out from under him. The vehicle landed heavily on the road and bounced on its shocks. His seat slipped out from under him for a moment and the grinding road snatched his un-stirruped foot. Disrel wrestled with the tottering beast and narrowly avoided several collisions with other riders. People slowed and veered onto the highway shoulders in panic. Disrel anchored his feet back on the rests and hunkered down against the bike's barrel.

"Wow." His turbulent breaths thundered in his helmet.

Of course, Mored's bikes could fly.

Minutes later, Disrel rolled cautiously into the parking lot at the rear of the factory. An employee jerked about on the sidewalk, blinking stupidly at him. Another hung back in the doorway with curiosity. Disrel removed his helmet and raked his hair as the corecycle rocked back in the parking space, powering down and lowering on its kickstand. Let them gawk. He yanked the keystone from its port and dismounted without making eye contact. He didn't want questions. Not this early in the day. Let them assume for a while. Word would get around and they'd all drop by his workspace on their respective lunch breaks to get a straight scoop. He might even feed them all a different story to see what came back on the grapevine. Disrel pocketed the keystone and entered the building through the door closest to his area. He shifted to his workspace and busied himself with readying a finished order for pickup. Elbows hit the counter.

"Hey, Dizzy! What sort of raise should I ask Reem for? What does it cost to get a pair of wheels like that red bruiser you got?"

Disrel's face soured at the obtrusive voice. Kommett.

"It's not mine. Just borrowing from a friend."

"I was gonna say!" The freckled young man withdrew from the counter and swung his arms. "No Pyron should ever make more than me."

"You know how much I make?"

"Pff! It's more than you deserve."

"Maybe it is." He wanted to tell Kommett to go pound sand. His snaggle-toothed mouth was always flapping wide open and begging for a blow. "But I like to save my money instead of drinking it."

Kommett's bold laughter rang through the halls. "Save? The new homeland security tax is sucking seventy-five percent of my savings!"

"Not my fault the price of beer went up with it."

"That's a crime and a half," Kommett slapped the counter. "Hey, why don't you enjoy a drink with me after work sometime, come hang out with me and the boys?"

"I don't drink." Kommett knew this.

"Why not?"

Disrel turned his head and occupied his hands with folding his customer's skyns. Too often those hands had asked permission to choke Kommett. He only dropped by to rub salt in old Pyron wounds. "The same reason you don't come down here to enjoy an honest conversation. You don't like me. You even splashed me in the parking lot the other day."

"Come on, Dizzy! That was just a prank. You need to lighten up. You're too stiff. People would like you better if you cut loose once in a while. You know, I haven't ever seen a Pyron good and drunk before."

Of course he hadn't. They were smarter than that. No Pyron would make himself vulnerable in the presence of Kobalts.

"How about this evening at the wharf, and every glass you finish is on me?"

"How about this? You cut out all the pranks and I'll show you the bike right after work, here in the parking lot. And if you play nice for a full week, I might even let you sit in the seat and dream for a few minutes."

Kommett paced a circle before the counter, shaking his head and laughing. "Is that how you got Reem to give you a raise? You Pyrons drive hard bargains."

"We have to if we want to survive," Disrel grunted, scooping up his customer's order and stepping into the hall.

Kommett's arm shot into the wall, blocking his path. He flicked his chin upward and stared over his snub nose. His lip snarled, flashing a snaggled canine. "Who's the friend? Come on, Ditzy. Be honest for once. Where'd you get the new ride?"

Disrel met Kommett's hard gaze fearlessly. Laughter was soon to follow, wasn't it? It was another cruel joke. But Kommett had never looked so intense.

"Where'd you get the moneys? You a gambling man? Is it blood money? Huh? I can smell that Pyron sorcery on you. What are you smoking? Are you selling any of it?"

Disrel stepped right.

Kommett moved with him, back and forth like a cobra, his gray eyes digging like ice picks. "Are you selling Kobalt souls to the underworld? Huh? How many bikes is mine worth?"

Disrel held his ground. One blow to the nose and Kommett would be sobbing on the floor. But the Pyron would be the first one to lose his job. Kommett was willing to lose a battle to win a war. Disrel's hands crushed his customer's package. Just one punch. One well-placed blow.

Kommett pressed right up in his face, snarling. "You don't come hang out with me and the boys and let us spin on your bike whenever we want to, and I'm going to start taking that homeland security tax right out of your pocket every time I see you."

Disrel clenched his jaw and spat two Pyron words. "Try me."

Kommett launched a solid right hook into Disrel's cheekbone.

Disrel rolled with the momentum and wrapped the parcel around Kommett's head, smashing his face into the counter.

"Kommett!" Reem trundled toward them, clutching a roll of papers in his pudgy fist. His arms swung back and forth at twice the speed of his legs and his wiry red beard fuzzed from his jowls.

Kommett staggered to his feet, whirling in fear and anger, blood streaming from his lip. Disrel stood back and gazed evenly at the wilted coworker. His stomach flipped. Had Reem seen the whole thing? Or just enough to fire him for hitting Kommett?

"What is going on down here?" Reem slapped the papers on the counter next to Kommett.

Kommett cringed and pushed along the wall, holding his nose. "He called me a Kobalt pig and said he was going to beat the living skit out of me. These Pyrons are violent, Reem. He's flipped his skit. You have to fire him."

Lying coward. Disrel hung back, scowling at Kommett without remorse while his heartbeat thundered in his ears. He wanted to say that he hadn't touched Kommett. But did it matter that he'd used the parcel to snare his coworker's head?

Reem shook the roll of paper at Kommett. "I ought to fire you for even being down here. Don't let me *ever* catch you near Disrel's desk again, especially when you have more than three overdue orders to complete. Now get moving or I'll walk you to the door."

"I'm leaving the physician's bill on your desk," Kommett growled.

Reem looked to Disrel. "Do you need to see a physician?"

Disrel shrugged. "I'm alright."

Kommett muttered dark curses under his breath and slunk away.

Reem sighed and shook his head. "What brought him around so early in the day? He usually doesn't bother you until lunch."

Relief washed through his shoulders, and he rubbed his buzzing cheekbone. "The price of beer went up again and I think he actually got to bed on time last night."

Reem gave Disrel a swat to the stomach with the roll of papers. "That's what I thought. The man drinks like a sieve and expects me to raise his wages everytime the beer market hiccups. Now what about this new bike I'm hearing about?"

Disrel forced a half-smile. "It's on loan from a friend. Everyone knows I can't afford anything like that right now."

Reem nodded. "Tough times for all of us. And the world is only getting crazier." His bulbous cheeks pinked, and he twirled strands of red fuzz between two stubby fingers. He flicked the roll of papers. "I'm dishing out extra projects to keep people like Kommett too busy to socialize. I don't want to see anyone distracting my most skilled employee. Also, I need this place looking extra productive this week because we might be getting state visitors at any time. Apparently, Tourmal's new sable commander has been tasked with hunting down that prankster flag thief, and someone has the ridiculous notion that talented skynmakers waste their time making junk flags and flying them on state property."

Disrel's cheeks burned, and his breathing hitched. Sure, he'd thrown the flag together from scraps, but it had still required a good bit of skill.

Reem proffered a wary laugh. "Pretty serious business when they call in the sables. Rumor has it this new commander has a real reputation. They call her the 'Skynhound.' She's here to catch the new Tourmaline Renegade. Anyway, enough bad news. Carry on, and if Kommett dares to pay you a visit again this week, you make sure I hear about it."

Reem's eyes narrowed, and he waddled off to make his rounds and dish out a heavier workload.

Disrel sighed heavily and headed toward the lobby to deliver the customer's order to the front desk. He was grateful for Reem's trust and kindness, but if Reem knew the truth, how would he react? There were a few good Kobalt people who didn't buy the propaganda, who looked out for their Pyron neighbors. And sometimes they were rewarded evil for their kindness.

Disrel slid through the door to the lobby and braced himself for a brawling greeting, but Daimus wasn't lounging in her padded chair with her bare feet propped on the counter. Her glittering sandals weren't even under the desk where she always kicked them off, and her nail polish wasn't in its place, ready to touch up her nails throughout the day. The tattered, warped bucket seat was tucked under the desk.

It was still early. She was probably running late again. Disrel dropped his customer's pickup in the receptionist's box and took a piece of hard candy from Daimus's "good customer" jar.

The lobby doors pulled back in their grooves and a sharply dressed sable waltzed through, followed by an entourage of combat-ready women, each with her hair pulled back into a tight bun, undercut from nape to ear, some with designs etched against their scalps. It was such a trademark that it distinguished them even when they were not in uniform, and no woman who was not a sable ever dared style her hair this way.

"Sable Commander Ambrosia, Imperial Security." The lead sable pushed her flat chest out as if wanting him to notice the insignia emblazoned on her jacket. "I'm here to have a look around this factory and see if I can turn up any leads on the Tourmaline Renegade."

Disrel turned stiffly from the counter, his heart jackhammering into his stomach.

"I'm sorry. I just work in the back. Please have a seat and our receptionist will be here any minute."

The sable's eyes flickered like a spitting candle wick. "I've got a long list of businesses to visit today and I don't need a guided tour."

Disrel lowered his eyes and raised his hand in the direction of the door. "Then be our guests, ladies."

The commander narrowed her eyes and scanned him from head to toe. Was she upset he hadn't addressed her as commander? The other sables peered at him like cobras.

Disrel pressed himself against the drop box wall, his breath withering away and his eyes shifting on the floor. Their etched napes, sharp noses, and perfectly tailored uniforms made the bunch about as cuddly as a basket of baby ferrets. Ones with venomous bites.

"Aren't you that Pyron I almost arrested the night the flag was stolen?"

Disrel's jaw clenched, and he fought the rising lump in his throat as he wiped his hands down his legs. "Might be, Commander. But aren't we all a little grouchy in the wee hours of the morning?"

She whipped out a notepad and pen. "Name?"

Great. A writeup for what? Back talking?

"Disrel."

"Spelling?"

"You didn't get the other guy's name."

"Don't play with me, Pyron."

He wedged his hands in his front pockets and muttered out the letters.

The pen ground across the tablet and her eyes flashed over his face, looking for marks of distinction to describe him by.

"Residence?"

He pulled his ID card from his pocket and let her copy the information.

"I promise, my two-in-the-morning self and my eighth-hour self are two totally different people."

She wrinkled her nose and stuffed the tablet back into her jacket.

"Funny. Watch your step. I find you both extremely suspicious."

She strode past him into the factory with her sables trailing closely behind. Disrel slouched against the wall and sighed. He tipped his chin to the ceiling and let his shoulders droop. What sort of evidence would she look for? Should he leave now while he still had a chance? She'd looked at him like she suspected something. He didn't want to return to his workstation with any chance of passing that group in the halls again.

A minute later, the front doors pushed open again, and Daimus pranced through with her sparkling handbag swinging from the crook of her elbow. Her skyn shimmered with beige and silver scales.

"G'moining, Dis'el!" She sang like a tuba, whipping off her aubergine-tinted shades and flapping her bushy false eyelashes against her glittering cheekbones.

"Morning, Daimus. How are the children today?"

"On the mend." Daimus tossed her purse on the desktop and began unpacking everything she needed to survive the day. The items hit the counter in rapid succession: nail polish, lipstick, perfume, extra hair ties, makeup case, bag of application brushes, wrapped snacks, a heating pad, a pocket game, glass pens, and gel ink.

"The physician ce'tainly doesn't believe in offering a discount to come treat all three at once. I juggle multiple customers all day long and it's the same rate day in and day out. Wish I was paid by the problem."

Daimus dumped the handbag under the desk and plopped into her chair. She spun around, arching her eyebrows and batting the bushy black caterpillars that weighed down her eyelids and gave her a lukewarm expression.

"Now, what can I help you with?"

Disrel pushed off the wall. "I just wanted to let you know that some very important ladies from Imperial Security are giving themselves an invasive tour of the factory."

Daimus puckered her face and gawked in disbelief. "What? And you let them through without a hall pass?"

"They said the insignia on their uniforms was enough. And I wasn't going to stop them."

Daimus stacked invoice papers on her desk and smacked her lips. "You's smart not to stand in the shadow of those girls, Dis'el baby. Stay safe out there. And did you grab yourself some candy?"

"Yes, I did." He pulled the piece from his pocket.

"Have another. Thanks for holding down the fort."

Disrel caught the flying candy, thanked Daimus, and retreated to his workstation with caution. Were these sables looking to match something to evidence they already had? Would they check the equipment and try to pin the flag's manufacturing to this skyn factory? Were they scrutinizing employees? Were they on to him? The sables were five days too late to look for material scraps. Recycling had just picked up the container of remnants, so anything they found in that bin would not match up. The tension, settings, and specifications on the equipment changed from project to project. Was there any chance that an innocent coworker's loom, cutter, or seamer would reproduce the same details found on the Pyron flag?

Disrel pulled materials for his next project out of the drawers around his workstation and laid them out on his bench. That knot in his stomach was steadily tightening. The Skynhound's eyes had been too thorough on his body and had probed his face like fingers feeling for the edges of a mask, a lifting point from which to peel back the layers. Now he was on her suspect list. Disrel shuddered and considered using his first sick day for the year. In less than two hours on the clock, Kommett had assaulted him in the hallway and the Selenite Skynhound had considered arresting him in the lobby.

He brushed his hand over the pattern he had created for a new female customer. Ladies' clothing was always more complex and detailed. They loved a little extra sheen and shimmer in their skyns, even the everyday ones. This order called for a fabric containing extra fluorite. The customer wanted it to glow and was willing to pay the price. But that was why Disrel often served the wealthier customers. He was careful. He could work with expensive material and unrealistic expectations. He could design and create high-end skyns like few others could. And he loved raising the bar, surprising himself and Reem's customers. Of course, the customers never knew who touched their order. They had no way of finding out that their skyn's creator was a Pyron. Daimus was the face they saw. Their clothing fit. They shined. They felt good, and they minced like aristocrats past Pyron slums.

Disrel measured out the yards of fabric to the necessary minimum and made cuts on his cutting bench. Then he arranged the pieces and threw some of them over a form to nip and tuck them. After that, he would tailor them to the customer's measurements. It was routine, a pattern of movement he'd done too many times to count. But today, Disrel's heart raced with worry and dread. He fumbled and dropped pieces of fabric onto the floor. After several attempts and locking pieces together in the seamer, he threw them into a tub and stood there, raking his hands through his hair. He couldn't focus. He was too flustered to handle a project of this expense. One mistake and the company would lose hundreds of credits.

The hall rang with the clops of unforgiving boot heels. Here they came. Disrel moved behind the form and lowered his head, hoping they would miss him and march right on by. The squad slowed as they passed his window, their stiff shoulders swinging and staunch collars supporting their goose necks. Their poisonous eyes glared at the equipment. Disrel fussed with fabric on the form while the commander leaned on the counter, studying the area. Her eyes landed on the form and sharpened. She knew. She'd caught him. But if he could just squeak out into the hallway before they pulled out their handcuffs and made their move, he could bolt for the back door, leap on his corecycle, and fly for the hills.

Disrel stepped aside smoothly, acknowledging them with a brief nod and smile. One of the shorter women leaned in his open doorway, arms folded, staring over her snipped nose with copper-shaded eyes. Disrel scooped a tool off his workbench and ducked behind the form again, peeping over the mannequin's shoulder. The commander's gaze was intense.

"You're the only Pyron in this building."

Disrel cleared his throat, driving the lump back down. "I don't mind. Kind of makes me feel special."

"The bruise on your cheek says otherwise."

The tool clattered from his hand.

She tipped her round, perfect chin. "The coworker with the busted lip wants me to arrest you."

His breath turned to mud in his chest, and his heart skipped. He pressed back into his work, doing nothing much to the fabric, tucking and clamping, unclamping and retucking.

The sable's eyes circled the workspace like a hungry shark smelling blood. "Fortunately for you, I've got more important things to do than settle workplace quarrels between grown-ass men."

Disrel leaned against the garment form and drew a slow breath.

The commander laced her fingers together. "How long have you worked here?"

"Almost three years."

"What are you working on?"

"A woman's skyn."

"May I see it?"

"Well, it's not finished, but"—Disrel danced over to a large cabinet and pulled the door open—"when it is, it'll look something like this."

He snatched a glittering garment from the rack and waved its flowing edges around for the women to admire. He let them feel its waterfall hemlines and supportive bodice and showed off the unique features he had hidden in the garment's construction.

Their eyes twinkled with girlish visions of themselves in the garment, and one sable even pressed the gown to her breast and took opinions from her comrades. Disrel reached for a second garment and accidentally selected a skyn that had been designed for a tall, strong man. In a whirlwind of improvisation, he puppeteered the two garments into a complimentary dance before returning them both back to the wardrobe.

"Let's give those two their privacy." He leaned upon the doors and closed them.

The sables stifled amused giggles, a sound that surprised Disrel because of how sharply it contrasted with their severe demeanors, and the commander pulled rigidly back from the counter.

"Quickest way back to the lobby?"

"Take a left at the third intersection. Lobby doors are straight ahead."

The sables trickled down the hall, but the commander held back. Her hard lips softened and a civil light passed through her face.

"Thank you. The layout of this place is confusing." Her gaze dropped to the side and her tongue hesitated between her teeth. "And . . . you do beautiful work. It's not hard to see why your boss keeps you around."

Disrel nodded courteously and bent back over the pattern. Relief was the sound of sable bootsteps fading in the distance.

7

Ambrosia raised the lid of her foot locker and a wave of sweet vanilla and rustic autumn odors flowed out. She flipped through the layers of gear and personal belongings that she hadn't bothered to unpack, inwardly hoping that her stay in Tourmal would be too short to warrant it. She tossed a fresh uniform onto her bed and slapped the sides of the trunk. Had she forgotten to pack that dress? The only civilian garment she had ever purchased? The one she had instantly regretted buying but held on to with the hopes of one day having the chance to wear it, to be admired in it? She tore through the trunk again until a shimmer caught her eye and she pulled out a royal blue and cream skyn. She ran her fingers over the fabric and seams. It was nothing like the quality that Pyron was turning out on his bench at the first factory, but it was all she could afford and it would do. General Gault was only welcoming his comrade to the sector with a professional dinner date. Any suit dress was better than showing up in uniform. She pressed it to her body. It should still fit.

Ambrosia slipped into the skyn and turned herself in front of her mirror. Her naked shoulders glared back at her and she fussed with the bodice. Were her exposed arms too much skin? She wasn't used to going without sleeves, even if the rest of the garment covered from collarbone to ankle. Was it too tight at the waist and hips? A little risqué? Her breasts, like most sable's, were subtle and firm. They weren't a pair that turned men's heads, but her hips had done that before. She plucked at the fabric with her hands. Whatever. This outfit was no tighter than her uniform.

She dried her hair and wrapped it into the Sable Queen's high and tight style. Her eyes studied the stern, cynical face in the mirror with disapproval for a moment, and she ripped the bun apart. She tossed her hair around her shoulders, playing with the part, desperate to pull off something fresh, something playful. This was a new chapter in her life, a new setting. And since the general was an approachable man, she could experiment with something softer, welcoming, feminine. Her hair fell around her shoulders, and a young Selenite mountain woman stared back, looking uncomfortable, out of place, lost without her animals. That woman had dreams of leaving sablehood, of falling in love and finding emotional connection, of having a happy marriage and a quiet home and children to raise and to love.

Ambrosia shook herself, uncomfortable with the reflection of who she truly felt. That was the person she was in her dreams, wandering alone and lost in various wildernesses. No one was allowed to see that deepest part of her—that vulnerable, wounded inner child that had gone dormant the day she had entered the Sable Academy. Ambrosia raked her hair up tight around the edges of her head. Sables had teeth, backbone, grit. She hadn't been educated, trained, and built into a warrior just to walk around dolled up like prey, to need any man's love and affection, to want to go back to a peasant's life. Her skill had caught the attention of the Sable Queen. Now, she commanded the sable garrison in the capital sector. She had dined with the emperor in his palace. She had favor with the elite. She was a predator, an enforcer, a woman of power.

Ambrosia wrapped her hair back up into the Sable Queen's style and ruefully inspected the hard, chiseled appearance that she was so comfortable with. She pulled one curl onto her brow to soften the image. Balance. Perfection. She spritzed her neck with perfume and swept out of her quarters.

The general leaned against his military corecycle on the curb. His stiff-shouldered and open-collared black-and-gold suit flattered his athletic figure from every angle. The skyn's armor glistened with tracings of orange and bright blue. He raised his helmet visor and smiled.

"You look stunning, Commander."

Ambrosia wiped her hands down the front of the skyn. "It's just an old dress. We didn't have many social occasions in Selen."

The general slapped his visor back down and beckoned with his gloved hand. "You'll adjust to Tourmaline life before you know it. I'll have to show you the best place to have a skyn made."

Ambrosia swung a leg over the corecycle and took the back seat. In a moment, they were cruising down the wide streets toward the bay. The general's spicy cologne teased her mind toward scenarios of mutual attraction. Was this a dream, to be spending off-duty hours with Tourmal's highest-ranking military officer only days after being transferred to Tourmal? It could be nothing else.

On the wharf, a glass-covered building reflected its buoyant atmosphere into the lolling black waters, and two piers ran out into the bay. The dusky ombres of a matured sunset crowned the sky. Couples nestled in each other's arms on benches along the water's edge, and waves lapped against the concrete pylons. Salt and cypress teased Ambrosia's nose, along with the odors of grilling meats piped from the restaurant's kitchen. The general parked his corecycle in a reserved slot, stowed his helmet in the bike's barrel, and led the way.

He held the door, his hazel eyes tranquil and gentle in the twilight. "I think you'll come to love this place as much as I do. I rarely eat anywhere else."

Once they were seated at a quiet corner booth overlooking the water, he turned to the ready server. "The usual appetizer and drinks. Two extra for my guest. Everything on my tab."

He looked at her and his smile carved lines on either side of his eyes.

Ambrosia raked her hands on her lap. "I don't mean to seem stiff, General, but I don't drink."

"You're joking. We have the best drinks in Tourmal."

"I'm sure you do, but my command requires my highest vigilance and sobriety." A sable's life depended upon it. "I'm compelled to be boring while the Tourmaline Renegade is at large." She turned to the waiter. "Sparkling water, please."

The general relented. "Well, if you won't drink, do me the pleasure of calling me Callon."

Ambrosia offered a diplomatic smile. "I suppose that's not too much to ask."

She glanced at the menu and her heart dropped. Each dish was priced in the hundreds of credits. Appetizers cost twice as much as a common man's meal. This restaurant was no fisherman's quick stop. How often did the general eat here?

Callon's gaze wandered off through the restaurant and he twiddled his thumbs. When he excused himself abruptly, Ambrosia turned an eye back from the menu. He weaved to the back of the restaurant and stopped in the mouth of a hallway where a man leaned, his face concealed in the shadows. His skyn had a military cut to its edges, yet it was devoid of any insignia. He set his hand on his hip, pulling the edge of his cloak back. A weapon glinted on his belt. The two talked for a minute, then the general pulled a paper from his jacket and passed it underhand. The other nodded at some instruction, tucked the note in a breast pocket, and moved furtively down the hall. Suspicious. What government matters would the general be taking care of at a restaurant on the wharf at this hour? Maybe it was personal. Either way, with an impostor on the loose, everything was the Skynhound's business.

Ambrosia buried her eyes back in the menu the moment Callon turned back her way. He slid into the booth and recommended the day's fresh catch: butterflied Dunnego smothered in juri pearls and laid out on a bed of red rice. The waiter returned with the appetizer and drinks, took their orders, and left with the menus.

Ambrosia's mind turned constantly upon her open case, and her eyes scanned the restaurant for anything notable. Guilt consumed her for not being out there on the streets, working, watching. She was not accustomed to being at ease in public, wearing anything other than a uniform, sitting alone with a man. Diners looked up from their plates now and then. They were taking notice, watching the sable in civilian attire dining with an attractive military man. And they knew what sables were made of. And yet—a nearby diner caught Ambrosia's eye and then turned back to her food without reaction. The sight of a sable usually twisted faces and snarled lips. How freeing it was to sit in disguise, to be seen as a respectable woman. This was what life was like for others. This was what it was like to be seen as innocent until proven immoral. Ambrosia couldn't remember the last time she had worn anything civilian, or gone out on the town with anyone besides her sables. But she was in Tourmal now, a new place, a new position, a fresh start among new faces. And the general respected her. It was foolish to pass up a chance at a better life. Ambrosia sipped her water methodically, trying to look more at ease.

"We hit five skynshops, seven stonemasons, and a sail and flag maker today."

Callon sampled the appetizer. "Anything remarkable?"

"It was unsurprising."

"You don't have much to go on, do you? Not even a shoe tread."

"Unfortunately. The flag's construction is a standard all-weather skyn with lettering made from dark scraps. The maker had a solid understanding of both Kobalt and Pyron writing, or as is more likely, there was more than one person involved. Either way, the one behind the mask is of a typical build, so our footage of him offers no helpful clues."

Callon laced his fingers and leaned in. "He's probably a repeat offender. I would request a copy of everyone released from the Hold in the past month."

"Already have. Up to three months back. I'm waiting for confirmation that the names on the list are present in the new Pyron sector."

"It sounds like you have a good start on your suspect list."

Ambrosia crushed a knowing wince. Suspect lists. Ugh. The Pyron at that first skynshop was the only name she had taken down and only because he got under her skin.

Callon leaned back. "I must again express my amazement at your record. Seven high-profile renegades. Tourmal has been trembling since your first night here."

Ambrosia forced back a flattered smile. "Thank you, General."

"Callon, please. I know we're never truly off duty, but I rarely have the chance to let someone see me for who I am underneath the uniform."

Warmth flooded her heart. What a humble man. "It's so difficult, isn't it? I wish every one of my sables could have that opportunity."

"I thought a sable's uniform was a little tighter than a soldier's."

She narrowed her eyes. "What do you mean?"

"Haven't you all aborted a pregnancy or murdered a lover within the first year of service?"

Ambrosia's fist tightened in her lap. She squinted at Callon, trying to hide her disgust. "We're not all like that. I could vouch for half of the sables I've ever commanded."

"And the other half?"

"Casualties of the lies." Her heart throbbed with rising annoyance. What was Callon getting at?

"Lies?"

"The moment a girl is chosen for sablehood her family mourns like she has been sold into harlotry. We're all eventually disowned. We belong to the state. Every sable I have ever known, ever commanded, began her service with a determination to save herself for the man she would marry. But from the first day we step out onto the streets in uniform, the insults are cast in our faces. After so long, the words don't fall so harmlessly. We begin to believe them. They change us."

"But the statistics don't lie. The half you can't vouch for are responsible for ninety percent of the empire's prostitution."

Ambrosia shuffled her drink in circles. "Even if a sable remains a virgin for life, the uniform is a scarlet stain on her breast. The prophecy fulfills itself once she rationalizes she may as well reap the pleasures of the label she's forced to bear. And once she does that, why not make money? It's not like we're paid for our service the way your soldiers are." She wanted to add, *You know that*, but she bit her tongue and scrutinized his reaction. Why did he want her to spell it out?

"And where do you fall on the spectrum?"

Heat flushed up Ambrosia's neck. "I'd rather not comment on my personal history. Nor does it matter to me on which side of the fence any of my sables fall. We're family, sisters, and I'd fight and die for them all the same."

Callon chuckled. "The way my soldiers talk, there's no sable unturned."

"So you admit it's a two-way street. Their own mouths betray them and somehow they don't share our stigma. Or is the other ninety percent of the empire's prostitution committed by men who are not your soldiers?"

She handed him an icy glare. At home in Selen, she would have had no trouble leaving the restaurant. But she was on the general's turf now. She had to play along to get along.

Callon reined in a knowing smile. "You seem ashamed. Why? Doesn't your shame become your success? A freedom other women only dream of achieving? Monogamy isn't for everyone. You have an advantage. Equality. Even better, you're empowered."

"It's hardly equality. It's a double-edged sword to be feared and admired, respected and rejected. When your soldiers are ready to settle down, they marry socially upstanding women. But when is the last time any man has taken a sable's hand in marriage? Most men want a family, and what sable is allowed to bear a child? We belong to the state for life—mind, body, and spirit—and what we do at night is one thing they cannot control."

There was a tense pause, in which Callon simply handed her an understanding look. Then he said, "If I asked you to marry me, would you accept?"

Coldness splashed through Ambrosia's stomach. Was he mad? Why was he toying with her? "I don't answer rhetorical questions trussed with humor, General. I've had girls so crushed by repeated heartbreak and public shaming that they took their own lives. Those of us who are strong enough to bear a sable's reproach adopt a new code. If it's close enough to cuddle—"

"It's close enough to kill." Callon leaned back, smiling pensively. "It's always amazed me how sables can get away with murder."

"We live under the rules of war. Our battlefield is domestic. How could we keep the peace for our emperor if we hesitated to eliminate a threat?"

"So I take it you'd sooner kill a man than date him?"

Ambrosia shrugged. "Depends on the man."

"You're a very strong woman, Ambrosia. I'm honored to have you as a comrade-in-arms. If fortune smiles upon me, you'll allow me to get to know you better for who you are beyond the uniform."

Ambrosia rubbed her clenched jaw. "I'm sure there's always a possibility that could happen. But for now, empire before eros."

Callon lifted his drink in approval.

The waiter appeared and laid down plates of food. Tendrils of steam coiled up from the butterflied filets, heaped on mounds of rice and smothered in sauces. The savory aroma made Ambrosia salivate, and she inhaled deeply.

Callon picked up his utensils and cut into his fish with perfect etiquette. "Tell me: If sables never marry, why did you say that you had intentions to settle down one day?"

Ambrosia hesitated until she could swallow her morsel. "You're too interested in the personal lives of sables, General."

"Callon, please."

"General. And thank you." Her nostrils flared. "I think you're better off ignorant."

He laughed, drinking in her anger. "I see. Lie to me then."

Very well. Two could play this game. "Men come in all calibers. Is it a fantasy to hope that one day a man might have loved me for me?"

"No, Ambrosia. It's not." His gaze lingered on her face, steady and intense. "Not anymore."

Ambrosia's fork rattled against her plate, and she laid it down. The ambient lighting sculpted Callon's brow and cheekbone. He cleared his throat and turned his attention back on his food.

"You also said you'd entertain a comrade before any citizen, and that you know of at least one man with potential. Am I assuming too much by thinking you meant me?"

Ambrosia wiped her mouth with her napkin. "You aren't a man to mince words, are you?"

Callon proffered a sheepish smile. "I'm a military man. I've minced enemies, but never words. I realize that I hardly know you, that we only just met. And I know you think my intensity is a new level of insanity. But I'm beyond being offended by any sable's history or reputation. Perhaps, together, we can change the way the world sees you ladies, one marriage at a time."

"And what would that do to your reputation?"

"For the right woman, I'm prepared to sacrifice everything."

Ambrosia hesitated, taking time to temper her words. "You're a terrible sweet talker. I guess you're lucky I never had that on my checklist of an ideal man."

Callon wiped a hand over his mouth, and the corners of his eyes crinkled.

Ambrosia pushed food around on her plate and nibbled from the end of her fork. Her mind and stomach whirled dizzying circles, harder and faster every time those gorgeous hazel eyes embraced her. He offered a sample from his plate to try, and asked numerous questions about her adventures and upbringing, listening to every word with rapt attention. Until they had finished their plates, Ambrosia held back. But Callon was so down to earth, slow to interrupt, with a ready ear. And the more he drank, the more he loosened up and chattered and laughed until he was like an old friend Ambrosia had known from childhood. When he laughed hardest, he would throw back his head and flash those pointed canines. His short beard and thick eyebrows gave him the appearance of a grizzled alpha wolf. Callon polished the last drop from the bottom of his glass, chortling and wiping a tear from his eye.

"Justice served as cold revenge. No wonder they call you the Skynhound. It's a title that surpasses the glory of any rank and makes you a true legend."

"And now I must spend the rest of my life living up to it."

"The Sable Queen still fills her own boots well enough for her age. I'm sure you'll do just fine." He stretched his arms. "Well, the night is still young. Would you like to walk the pier and see the water?"

"Certainly."

They rose and left the restaurant through a side door. Callon turned his collar up and wedged his hands into his pockets. The stubble on his jaw sparkled in the moonlight. His muscular legs moved easily, unhindered by the many drinks he had downed, and his coattails swayed at his sides in the ocean breezes. The wharf was his other realm, the place he ruled in civilian attire. He cocked his head in her direction and proffered another charming half smile, one that said he was a winner. Gulls barked as they settled in on the nearby rooftops. Ships creaked and groaned in mournful song as their hulls made love to the piers. Couples strolled hand in hand along the water's edge, and the moon smiled down on them from her throne in the deep sky. Ambrosia leaned just a little closer to Callon as they walked.

Callon looked at the stars and pulled a deep breath, sighing. "What a perfect evening. Would you like to do it again sometime?"

"That would be nice."

"Maybe a few days from now. Early next week?"

"I can make time for that."

"And I will always make time for you, Ambrosia. I'm feeling something around you I've never felt around anyone else. I'm comfortable. At ease. Myself."

His large, warm hand slipped around her waist. Ambrosia stiffened, every muscle recalling its training to fling this attacker from the pier. But she fought it and chided herself. Her discomfort was her own issue. Callon was only expressing his fondness for her. He'd already expressed intentions for marriage, and this was only another step in that direction, as long as she didn't ruin her chances. What could that mean to all of her sables if she could lead by example, show them that love was possible? A sable's life wouldn't have to be an absolute curse. By demands of their duties they would still be forced to go childless, but a marriage without children was far better than men only looking their way with cheap intentions.

"I've always felt this way about the sea, though." Callon squeezed her waist and his fingers meandered up and down. "Loved the way it can go from tranquil to impetuous in minutes. It's unpredictable. Unconquerable. Kind of like a sable. But that challenge, that call for conquest, drives sailors to set their sails and risk their lives venturing upon it to glean its treasures." He turned his eyes down into the rippling waters. "Is the bay as beautiful as you expected it to be?"

Tourmal's lights twinkled through a fog along the opposite shore and the headlights of cyclists traversing the bay bridge made it a dreamy ribbon of black opal. "More. I'll have to come down here in the early morning to see the fishing boats letting out their nets."

"And maybe try fishing sometime?"

"Of course."

"With me, of course."

"Definitely."

Callon paused at the end of the pier and pointed out to sea.

"Some miles out that way sits a rocky, forlorn little crust of earth that was once a part of the peninsula. Fishermen won't go near it. They would rather drown with their ship than take their chances on it. They say it's haunted by hengebeast, humanoid creatures all burned out on pork and goat and salivating for human flesh."

His arm released her waist and wrapped around her shoulder. Ambrosia arched her neck and caught her breath, constricted by his armored breast near her cheek and his large hand fencing her in on the other side. Why could she not bring herself to melt against such an attractive man? Was it the odor of power that mulled caution in her core?

"Fishermen who claim to have spotted the creature say it's grotesque, all skin and bone, with sunken, lidless eyes like a fish. Gaping jaws and curved teeth that are hollow, like straws, and barbed. Ha! Fishermen's yarns. How would they know if they never drop anchor within a mile of the place? They say those teeth can get down between the strands of a military-grade skyn and the bite force alone can crush bone. If it were true, wouldn't dropping prisoners onto that island be a grand way to execute criminals?"

Ambrosia shuddered at the memory of a neighbor staggering back into her childhood village, his arm mangled and dangling like a tattered cloth, and his eyes livid with pain and terror. The inhuman timbers of his suffering still haunted her.

"What crime would warrant such a death?" She stole a look into Callon's face. "Treason, perhaps?"

"It's more merciful than a sable's condemnation for treason."

His fingers played in the hair at the base of her neck. Ambrosia pulled away, avoiding his gaze, trying not to encourage him. He was looking again, so much more closely than before.

"I was thinking that the firing squad was a touch too soft for preventing desertion among my troops." Callon's gaze remained, raising the hairs on her neck. "You never hear of such a thing among sables. It's been many, many years since we've had to hang a sable."

Ambrosia cleared her throat and spread her stance, consuming more space and keeping her elbows aimed at Callon. "Fortunately, yes. We're educated on the full extent of the law before we take our oath of loyalty." Not that a sable cadet had any choice in the matter. Taking the sable's oath and serving under sable law was far better than becoming a dorm slave for failing the academy and suffering that shame the rest of her life while class after class graduated and moved out into the world in uniform. Those poor girls were always badly abused, having no home to return to and nowhere else to go, sometimes suffering a fate as bad as if they had taken their oath and broken it.

Callon set his face to the sky. "You see? The sable code is the perfect example that severe punishments ensure the highest loyalty. That is how you prevent a society from breeding renegades. People are happier with heavy laws because they like to know where the boundaries are. It helps them feel safe."

Ambrosia stared off into the water, checking her rising temper. She was Tourmal's newest official. What if she was being watched? What if this was a test?

Callon glanced back toward the cityscape. "Except for Pyrons, who refuse to be happy unless they are chasing that illusion they call freedom. The freedom to chase the stars, to run themselves tirelessly in circles, never progressing as a society. Pyrons are as content to sit around their fires and tell stories of a sky spirit that gendered the universe solely for their pathetic existence, as apes are to sit in the trees and munch twigs."

At the word "fires," Ambrosia remembered the musky odor lingering around the Pyron whose name she'd written down. "I've come across some who smell of smoke. How do they hide their fires in a place as crowded as Tourmal?"

Callon tossed his head and laughed. "No. That's from the smoke bathing in some of their rituals. It's supposed to open up a channel for the fire spirit to flow through their veins or their god to come live in their bodies and give them increased strength and power. But once we started shaving their heads, they realized it was just a myth, that all that fight they thought their warriors had must have come from a little hard liquor and inhaling some herb they burned for incense."

The Pyron's comment about his two selves being different people resounded in her mind's ear. "They are strange people."

Callon turned his eyes back on her and raked her cheek with his thumb. "You know what's strange? The way you put fire in my veins."

He bent his head down against her hair, drinking in her perfume with greedily flaring nostrils and blasting hot air down her neck. Ambrosia glared out across the bay, transfixed with fear, her stomach jerking and knotting. It wouldn't be too difficult to throw him off the pier, but what were the consequences of resisting the empire's highest-ranking military officer?

"I can drink all day and never get drunk, yet your smell intoxicates me. You are like a garnet rose, Ambrosia. Sturdy of stem yet graceful."

Ambrosia peeled out of his arms. "With more thorns than petals."

"I think the reward of your sweet nectar is worth the pain of a few thorns. I've always been very passionate and sure of the things I want." He drew another deep breath against her skin.

Ambrosia's heart jarred her senses with every throb. "Callon, we only just met. And this is entirely unprofessional." She pushed back, sizing him up, giving him a warning look. What did he want? Why the sudden change?

"You should know I thirst for power, Ambrosia. It is my profession." His eyes drank her in as he leaned closer, falling upon her lips and half closing. "And you are a powerful woman."

Ambrosia planted a hand on his chest, checking him. Was he really going to ice an evening of insults with flattery?

Growling laughter rose from his chest and his eyes gleamed with hunger for a challenge. Callon pressed in and clamped his mouth over her lips, his slimy tongue slicking as she clenched her jaw, wrestling for an appropriate response. What made him think she craved power? She hadn't transferred to Tourmal of her own will. None of her military training had ever covered a graceful escape from undesired passion. Could she be charged for assaulting Tourmal's top military general? Or did she even want to resist? What if she ruined her only chance at marriage? There were far more frightening consequences than this undesired interlude, which would pass in a moment. A group of fishermen whistled and cheered from a nearby boat, and Ambrosia relented. She couldn't embarrass the general before all these people. The only way to protect herself and her sables was to let him have his moment. If only she'd worn a uniform, this would never have happened. She'd made a mistake by seeming eager to go out. She'd led him to believe she returned his affections. Ambrosia dug her nails into a pressure point on his wrist, forcing his release.

"Callon. I'm not ready to be this close. Let's slow things down."

Callon's eyes were dark with desire, and his hand threatened her throat. "You're too strong for me, Ambrosia. I can't."

His hand wrenched into her hair and he came down again, pinching her mouth between his lips, his tongue rasping over her teeth, spearing into her mouth. His other hand battled past her arms and down to her hips, searching, groping. Ambrosia locked down like a stapler.

"Argh! Scrag it!" Callon staggered back, pinching his bleeding mouth.

"General Gault!" She trembled, boiling inside. "It's getting late."

He wiped blood on his thumb and laughed. "You warned me you had a few thorns. My dear Ambrosia, what made me believe you wanted to end the night with something sweet back at my place?"

Ambrosia backed, hands wadded into fists, her jaw rigid with the desire to spit.

"I really can't imagine. Some things can't be bought at the price of a meal, even a two-hundred-credit meal. And you should know better than anyone, General, that the Selenite Skynhound's heart isn't one of those things."

"You could have been more upfront with your intentions, Commander."

"'Empire before eros' wasn't clear enough?" She wanted to scream in his face.

"You led me to believe that you were willing to test the waters before committing."

"Your mistake, General."

Callon raised his head and stared down his nose. "I think an apology is in order, Commander."

His tone had a dark edge to it, and his eyes gave a warning. Ambrosia's chest heaved and her focus flitted around the pier. And what if she didn't? Would she and her sables suffer? Would she end up dead like Commander Riahn? She clenched her jaw and tempered her words.

"I—I'm sorry, General. I don't know what I was thinking."

A look of approval returned. "That's better." A little smile returned to his face, but it was cold and victorious. "We shouldn't let little things come between us. We're a team," He sighed. "I just want you to know that I'm more than happy to drive you back to the barracks and we'll just forget this little incident ever happened."

She would never forget. Ambrosia collected herself and raised her head, even though she was too disgusted to look at him. "I'd rather walk. Goodnight, General Gault. I'll keep you posted on anything I turn up on the renegade."

The pier thundered under her boots as she marched toward the restaurant. The entire walk back to her barracks might not even dissipate her embarrassment. She spat, trying to cleanse her palette of his alcoholic breath. She had been in close scrapes before, but never felt so robbed of her dignity. She chided herself for not trusting her gut, for not sticking to a fresh uniform, for thinking that at long last, one man respected a sable as something more than a whore in armor and combat boots. The general had not acted differently than any other soldier might have, but his power demanded that others respond differently to his actions. And Ambrosia had failed.

Her hands shook. She could cripple any man that dared touch her like that. But not the general. Not a man who leaned on Lord Cinnabar's right arm. Not a man who commanded the Imperial Army. Few men were strong or even brave enough to rape any sable, but that man had the power to rape a sable using fear alone.

Rage boiled up in her chest. Blue light flashed over the spires of Tourmal, and the sky vented her anger with repartees of thunder as large, cold drops splashed down on the pavement and splattered on Ambrosia's bent head. She trudged on, cursing her life. Her childhood friend Lyka was, no doubt, happily married to the butcher's son by now, and dancing on the sunny slopes with her blue-speckled swine and a fat baby strapped to her back. But fate had chosen little Ambrosia the day the Sable Queen had passed through. Fate had chosen very different dreams for little Ambrosia, dreams that were nightmarish realities some days. If she could catch this renegade soon, she might be sent back to Selen. If fate was kind, it would give the renegade's life in place of her own.

The rain soaked through Ambrosia's skyn and her boots squeaked on the wet stone. Crimson curls plastered to her face. She was going to throw this outfit in the dumpster the moment she could peel it and its seductive curse from her body. She brushed past two men huddled under an awning outside of an empty building. One of them whistled.

"Hey, hot sauce. Gimme a smile and make my night sweeter."

Ambrosia leveled the speaker with three swift blows, jerked a knife from her boot, and faced the other. "Go home to your wife, deadbeat, before I cut your chicken neck."

The man shuffled into the alcove like a dog with its tail tucked between its legs.

Ambrosia stepped over the groaning man and marched on, fists pumping, cheeks burning. Their loss for not knowing she was an Imperial Sable in civilian skyn. How easy it was to put rogues in their places when they didn't wield imperial power.

At the base, Ambrosia collapsed against the door to her barracks and pushed in. The roar of the pouring rain and crashing thunder echoed through the rooms, rousing her sables.

Phaedra tottered around the corner, an open book in her hand and a robe wrapped loosely around her goddess figure. Her rueful eyes studied her commander's dripping face.

"He didn't have the manners to drop you off at the door?"

Ambrosia had been granted permission for two of her sables to transfer with her, and now she regretted pulling her friends into this hell.

Ulyia's inquisitive face popped over Phaedra's shoulder. "So, how was the general?"

Ambrosia suppressed a shudder and clenched her fists. She wanted to break something. "It was a platonic dinner date. And the general is fine."

"Uh oh." Phaedra gave her a knowing look.

Ambrosia felt seen and turned away. "We talked about the Tourmaline Renegade and political affairs. That's all it was supposed to be."

Ulyia looked her up and down as if she was seeing the same thing Phaedra was. "And so what if it was something more? You're the Selenite Skynhound. General Gault is a powerful man. He's bound to be attracted to you."

Ambrosia shot Ulyia a warning glance. "There's more to it than attraction. I'm not ready to talk about it."

Phaedra fell back against the hall corner. "Ugh. Sounds like it was a disappointment."

That was putting it mildly. Ambrosia dragged her soggy feet up the stairs and into her private quarters. She collapsed against the wall, her lips withered and her brow contorted. Why was fighting terrorists and Pyron rebels easier than having dinner with a colleague? She squeezed out of her boots and peeled the dripping garment off, casting it onto the shower floor to drain out—or rot. How kind the general was to offer to forget about the incident. He should be the one begging her to forgive, let alone ever try to forget. She pulled a robe around her shivering body and hugged herself. If it was only the smell of a rose that turned a man into a beast, she could easily help him control himself. She jerked the top off her perfume bottle, poured it down the sink drain, and slammed it in the trash. Then she rinsed her mouth with salt water, over and over again. But his breath was haunting, permeating her mind. Even if he truly forgot, she would never. She slammed her bathroom door and slumped on the bed, cocooning in the blanket and remembering how her mother would tuck her in tightly when she was ill or hurting.

Her own misfortune at Callon's hand would go unavenged. Phaedra and Ulyia might sympathize, but they had no more power than she did. Men like Callon were why sables never fought over men, never let jealousy come between them. The rumors of sables killing their lovers were true, but it was rarely ever unjust. There was no revenge that could be wrought upon the head of a man as powerful as the Imperial General. Ambrosia thought of Commander Riahn and wished she had mentioned her over dinner and watched Callon's reaction. He wanted something more than her body. He wanted power—power over her.

Ambrosia gritted her teeth. What had it gained her to resist and be forced to apologize? She'd lost that battle. She'd shown him that he could flex and she would acquiesce. But what if she was attracted to him? How would life be different if she'd loved his hands and his kisses and willingly gone home with him? Had Commander Riahn? Or was Ambrosia to believe that she had something Callon couldn't find anywhere else? What was the point in resisting the lie? There was no accolade for virgin sables, no medal for their breasts, no salute or ceremonial weapon. She could have been lying in the general's silk bed right now, against all his naked flesh, and no one in the world would have thought any differently of her. They expected it.

Ambrosia shivered, and her teeth rattled. She would never give Callon—or any other man—her heart or her body. It was easier to kill than to love. Love demanded weakness, vulnerability, trust. It was a shackle ready to bind her will, a remorseless thief. Love was a monster that demanded submission, surrender, and sacrifice.

8

Ambrosia pumped up the imperial palace's central staircase, taking two and three carpeted stairs at a bound. Six sables trailed her and the courier kept just ahead, spewing as much as he knew into her ear.

"The servant girl's shrieks rocked the halls, and when the guards reached Her Imperial Highness's room, they found only the man's skyn left on her bed. Her Highness is terribly distressed. She claims a Pyron man attacked her while she slept."

Ambrosia hit the landing and turned down the hall toward the royal bedchamber.

"I'll take it from here. Thank you."

The courier stopped behind a guard's polearm, and Ambrosia marched into the glittering apartment with her sables. She took everything in with a sweeping glance: the furniture, the carpet, the mangled bedsheets, the items on the royal's vanity. The perpetrator's dark skyn lay across the end of the bed. Ambrosia picked up a corner of the garment and rolled it between her fingers. A strong, spicy cologne infused a terrible memory upon her mind, and she dropped her jaw, wishing for a can to spit into. Into the room swept two guards, prodding a blubbering girl along between them.

"This is the one who came upon the scene, Commander."

The girl's sky-blue eyes wheeled like swallows around the room and her light, silky hair trembled around her shoulders. She shook her finger at the window where Phaedra leaned out and surveyed the outer sill.

"He jumped out through that window, right there, as naked as a newborn."

"Was he Pyron or Kobalt?"

"Pyron. He had the blackest hair."

"Are you sure it wasn't dark brown?"

"I know a Pyron when I see one, miss!" The girl wrung her hands at a speed that rivaled that of her tongue. "He glared at me with those ratty, black eyes, bared his teeth, and hissed." She demonstrated by arcing her fingers into fangs and squinting her eyes. "And his body was as bright as milk. I swear it was."

Ambrosia rolled the fabric between her fingers again, hunting for an emboss-ment, a designer's mark. But it was material commonly worn by men of all classes. She stuffed her hand into the pockets. Empty. On the floor below the sill, a blue vase lay shattered, its white flowers crushed and smeared into the rug. Did the princess have more than one lover? More than one Pyron admirer? How could she be sure this skyn belonged to the same man she'd witnessed descending from the window two-and-a-half weeks earlier?

"Oh, please don't let Her Imperial Highness hurt me. I was just coming in to get her bath ready. I don't want to die for what my eyes didn't intend to see, miss! Please."

Ambrosia turned to the soldiers. "Leave her here with us in case we have more questions."

The soldiers retreated from the room, and the teenage girl quivered in place, scrutinizing everything they touched. Ambrosia moved to the window and con-ferred with Phaedra. Knowing what she did, it was hard to believe that the girl was lying, but there were still reasons she might. Other than the skyn, the disheveled bed, and the broken vase, there was nothing to go on.

"Commander, look at this." Phaedra ran her hand along the outer windowsill.

Ambrosia touched the strip of wood that formed a groove for the window to nestle between. It was several inches tall, and on the outdoor side, a difference in paint color revealed where the vase had sat.

"The vase should've fallen outside the window." Phaedra demonstrated with empty hands. "But it's well inside, like it was picked up and thrown onto the floor."

Ambrosia admired Phaedra's astute observation.

Phaedra turned and gave the servant a hard eye. "Are you sure he was absolutely naked?"

"Yes! Nothing at all."

"Then where are his shoes?"

The girl bit her whitening lips. "He grabbed his shoes and flew out the window with the strength of an ape. It was animal!"

Time would tell. The servant girl did seem full of exaggerations. Had she really seen what she was describing, or was she working hard to convince herself? Ambrosia laid the skyn back on the bed. "Where is Her Imperial Highness now?"

"Confined to her summer chambers, Commander. Her father's orders."

"Stay here with my sables. No one is allowed to touch you until we're done with our investigation."

Ambrosia marched out of the chamber and into the long hall as Cinnabar descended from the opposite wing with an angry, brooding look in his eyes. She paused and saluted him.

Cinnabar looked at her with a glimmer of hope. "I trust you will have a lead in this madness soon, Commander."

"We're doing our best, Supremacy. I was just going to speak with Her Imperial Highness now."

Cinnabar nodded and wiped his hand over his mouth. "I'm fortunate to have you here in Tourmal for such a time as this."

"Have you spoken with your daughter yet?"

"I have. And she swears to me that the ashrat put a knife to her throat and forced her into silence. They mock me, breaching my palace windows and disgracing my daughter. It's as if they're trying to seed a half-blood for my throne."

Ambrosia swallowed back an urge to tell Cinnabar about the Pyron she had seen. Maybe this recent visitor had assaulted the princess. Maybe she had not consented. "I'm sorry the heightened security around your palace was not enough to deter this attack, Supremacy. But please allow me, for the time being, the suspicion that the man did not enter or exit through the window until I find clearer evidence."

Cinnabar gave her a look of displeasure, then seemed willing to tolerate it. "Hmm." Was all he said.

Ambrosia collected herself. "I've always worked by thinking like the criminal I am hunting, sir, and so I have to wonder why any Pyron who manages to breach your palace walls and windows into your daughter's bedroom wouldn't have taken her life while he had the opportunity."

"Are you insinuating that my daughter is a liar? Or worse, that she's in love with a Pyron and let one in through her window?"

Ambrosia stammered and shook her head. "I dare not, sir. I simply meant that we have no evidence the man was Pyron. The skyn is tailored for a very large man, with an athletic stature, and few Pyrons are even six feet tall."

"I see. Well, don't let thinking like these terrorists water down your brilliant mind." Cinnabar looked her up and down. "Anyway, what Kobalt would stoop so low?"

Ambrosia clamped her lips as Callon's behavior came back to mind. "I am rarely surprised by the faces people wear underneath their masks anymore, sir. Let me look for bruises on your daughter and try to gain her trust. Time has a way of uncovering the truth." She could only hope Cinnabar was ready to face it.

The emperor nodded. "I trust you, Commander. The security of my throne rests on your shoulders."

Ambrosia saluted, backed from the emperor's presence, and ducked through a draped doorway. There were two sides to this coin. What she had witnessed outside the royal's window had been completely consensual, and the man most definitely Pyron. Which face would the royal heir apparent use to her advantage?

Ambrosia acknowledged the guards at the door and turned into Zaelix's summer chamber, now her prison through the storm. She closed the chamber doors softly behind her. The royal hunched on the side of the bed like a gargoyle, turning her dark-rimmed eyes upon her visitor.

Ambrosia eased over and settled down on the side of the bed.

"You can trust me, Highness. My sables and I will do everything in our power to protect you and bring the creature that attacked you to justice. But we need your help."

Zaelix's eyes pined for Ambrosia like a hurting child to its mother, like she might fling herself into her breast for a hug.

"Could you identify the man? His face or anything about him?"

She pinched her lips and shook her head. She picked at the folds of her garment and tears welled up in her eyes.

"Was he Pyron?"

Zaelix bit her lip.

"Was he Kobalt?"

Her breath halted.

"Was he a palace servant?"

Zaelix kept still.

"Was he a soldier?"

She cast Ambrosia a bitter glance, but that pain was still there, that look Ambrosia saw in sables' faces when they regretted a relationship. It was a look she still felt whenever she thought of Callon and their dinner on the wharf. It was like a ring with empty settings, a flower head devoid of petals, a bird hopping along without wings. It was like anything that had been utterly robbed of its value and purpose. She laid her hand on Zaelix's knee.

"You can trust me, Highness. Please trust me. No matter who it is, he's not powerful enough to hurt you."

Zaelix sniffed and turned her face to the window. "Even an empress could not overpower this man."

"Do you have any marks or bruises?"

The royal eyes gouged at her with suspicion. There were no bruises on her neck or shoulders, nothing visible even on her chest or wrists. Perhaps the knife he held to her throat was invisible, a metaphor for the control he wielded.

Zaelix slouched back against the bedpost, two words squeaking from her lips. "I'm afraid."

"Of who?"

Her jaw tightened, and her eyes wandered.

"Describe his face. What did he look like?"

Zaelix swallowed, and her gaze shifted on the floor. It seemed like the words were moving behind her eyes but stopping short behind her lips.

Ambrosia leaned closer. "I believe you. I can see that you're afraid. But I don't think you're afraid of the Pyron man who comes to your window when you set the blue vase with white flowers there."

The royal's eyes grew three sizes, and her lips quivered.

"There's someone else, isn't there?" Ambrosia pressed. "Someone you under-estimated. Your safety is my highest priority, Highness. I'm sworn to give my life for your protection. Please trust me."

"You haven't told anyone about that. Tell me you haven't! You can't!"

"It's between me and you, Highness. But if this other man forced you, I need to avenge your dignity."

Zaelix clenched her jaw, and a tear coursed down her cheek.

"I'm a lost cause, Sable. You need to watch your own back now. Pyrons should be the least of your worries here in Tourmal."

Ambrosia's neck prickled. She wanted to choke everything Zaelix knew right out of her. "Speak plainly."

"Commander Riahn tried to protect me. Do yourself a favor: Trust no one and stop investigating. The less you pry, the longer you'll live."

Ambrosia lifted her chin. Callon was looking more and more suspicious. It would be easier to pull the truth out of the servant girl, but Ambrosia thought she might try the royal once more.

"Let's pretend for a moment that I found something of General Gault's in the pocket of that black skyn we found on your bed. Would your father hesitate to have him executed for assaulting you?"

Zaelix dug her fingernails into her palms and forced a laugh. "Do you really believe my attacker fled through the palace naked?" She stopped herself, realizing she had betrayed valuable information. "Or even out of the window and through the garden. If there had been anyone at all, someone would have seen him. Killa's lying. She doesn't know what she saw."

Useful. Maybe the servant girl had been instructed what to say. There was still a way to run the equation of lies backward to find the truth. It would be easier, now that she knew the attacker had left through the palace, most likely fully clothed.

"Is that all you wish to tell me at this time?"

"I'm trying to protect the person I love, Commander." She gave her a warning stare.

Ambrosia rose from the bed. The broken vase flashed in her mind, connecting somehow with Callon. But that made no sense. The vase and its white flowers had been a signal for Zaelix's Pyron lover. She either hadn't been attacked at all, or there were two men involved—her lover and the attacker.

"Fair enough. But please understand that my priority is your protection. My sables will be close by until we figure this out. Do not hesitate to call for me anytime you're ready to talk, Highness."

Ambrosia retreated into the hall. Servants congregated in the corners and alcoves, dusting and polishing and hissing about the palace affair. How many maids did it take to dust one tapestry, and so fervently, in the late hours of the night? Below the balcony, waters gurgled down the rock wall and into the emerald pool with its golden koi swimming dreamy circles, each fish so vibrant and shimmering like polished metal. On the right, two walnut doors swung open, and two military figures stepped in. Ambrosia pulled back from the railing at the first glimpse of Callon's curly head.

"Get it done tonight, before she runs her mouth. And don't let me see you again until you're finished." He said to the man on his right.

The aide raised a hand to his dark helmet visor and peeled away from the general's side like a hawk on the hunt. No insignia marked any corner of his skyn. Callon ascended the stairs, fastening the front of his military jacket. He noticed Ambrosia and a subtle smirk moved behind his features.

"So you have yet another renegade to catch, Commander. Have you any leads on the Pyron rapist?"

"What evidence do you have to call him Pyron, General?"

A sardonic smile moved through Callon's lips. "You think one of our own people dared to assault Her Imperial Highness in her own bedroom?"

Ambrosia's jaw tightened. "In my experience, anyone is capable of animalistic behavior."

Callon lowered his chin and knit his brow. "Ooh, that felt personal. I thought we had agreed to forget about our . . . accident on the pier."

"You agreed to forget, General."

His eyes wandered across the room and he moved off, dragging his fingers across the lavish banister. "And I have. But you and I both know Her Imperial Highness was letting Pyrons in and out through her window, so let's look out for each other, shall we? Let Cinnabar discover on his own that his daughter is a little minx."

Ambrosia held back, pressing her lips and letting Callon slink down the hall. The pit of her stomach was burning, thrumming, warning her that the general was not a man to trifle with. She bounded down the stairs and whisked out into the gardens to check on her sables.

Two hours into the search and the women had turned up no sign that anyone had climbed down the lattice or dropped to the ground below the window and fled. It was as if he had sprouted wings on the sill and flown away. Zaelix had told the truth. Only a Kobalt could have fled through the palace, and maybe he hadn't fled at all. Maybe he was still walking among them.

The servant girl, Killa, shadowed Phaedra on the stone walk like a glum little troll, stooped and ambling. Ambrosia pulled her over to a bench and sat her down.

"I already know he was Kobalt and I know he didn't leave through the window. So give me the truth. Who was the man in Zaelix's room?"

Killa trembled and buried her face in her hands. "I don't know, miss! He could've been anybody. I didn't see his face."

"Why did the blue vase and the flowers fall inside the room instead of outside?"

Killa started and scootched back on the bench. "What about them?"

"You tell me, child. The secret Zaelix forced you to keep for her. Were there two men?"

"Oh! I wish I had never been here tonight! I can't tell you or Her Imperial Highness will kill me."

"You know what you saw. And Zaelix knows what you saw. And you're both afraid for your lives. Now, be a brave girl. I cannot protect her life or yours if I don't know the truth."

Killa blubbered and snotted into her hands. "Who can tell Lord Cinnabar that Her Imperial Highness has a Pyron lover? She will prove me a liar to keep her lover safe and I'll be executed for defaming her! Please, miss! I don't want to die!"

"Enough with the tears! Stick with my sables and no one can touch you. Now tell me the truth. Was the man that was here tonight a Pyron?"

Killa bowed forward, hands pressed to her face, staring down at the path. "No."

"Was he a palace guard or servant?"

"No."

"Was he a civilian?"

Killa's chest heaved as she moaned. "Please, miss. You don't understand—"

"Was he a civilian?"

"No. No!"

"A palace guard then?"

Killa groaned and rocked, rubbing her eyes and blubbering.

"Look at me." Ambrosia shook her. "Was it General Gault?"

Tears rolled from Killa's red eyes and her face continued spasming.

A sable skidded onto the terrace overlooking the gardens. Her hands slammed down on the stonework as she leaned over the edge.

"Commander! Quick! The lawn below Her Imperial Highness's chamber windows."

Ambrosia's heart leaped and her legs catapulted her from the bench and across the lawn. Her sables bolted like darts from a bowstring toward the eastern side of the palace. The urgency in the sable's voice was a call to war. Ambrosia vaulted over the low stone wall, dropping into the courtyard below the royal chamber. A crumpled form lay on the stonework, auburn hair splayed out on bricks, the silky garment entwined around the contorted limbs.

"Highness!" Ambrosia descended on the body and gave it a push. "No. No. She didn't! She wouldn't have!"

Limp. Cooling. Lifeless. The slitted eyes were crossed. Blood oozed from a cut on her scalp. Ambrosia slid her hand under Zaelix's neck and palpated it for fractures. The window was only three stories high, hardly a guaranteed fatality for anyone attempting suicide. Ambrosia pulled the robe's excess over the royal's pained face. The sables moved lightly around the body, hands on hips, pacing, distraught that there was nothing they could do.

How was it possible? Why would Zaelix take her own life? Had she feared public shame and divorce from her royal titles more than death itself? Was this how she chose to protect the identity of her Pyron lover?

Ambrosia commanded her sables to remain around the body and to not let anyone near. She marched into the palace and flew up the stairs, knocking servants aside as she darted through the antechambers, bolting past the door guards and into the royal's summer chamber. The sheets were peeled back from the bed, twisted on the end in a tangled mass. The tabletop items had been rearranged, not quite where she remembered them sitting. The drapes were unbalanced on the rod. The princess's slippers were at odds with one another, one by the bed, the other by the window. A notebook and pen lay on the floor below the sill. She picked it up and flipped through the pages. The royal's musings were scrawled on the first ten, a poem or two. Then a blank page. Another blank. The next one, scrawled in a brawling, offhand manner.

Pyron is free.

Ambrosia tucked the notebook into her jacket and hovered in the window. Her sables paced solemnly around the body on the stones below, rubbing their faces and shaking their heads. The death of any royal, especially an heir to the throne, was distressing, but a sable's most important duty was to protect the throne, and now, only a couple of weeks into her service in Tourmal, she had to bring this failure to Cinnabar's ears. Would he think her incompetent, incapable of keeping himself and his own house safe, let alone the rest of Tourmal? Was he a man to have his officials executed at the slightest dissatisfaction?

Her stomach twisted and she scuffed off to deliver the tragic news.

Ambrosia slipped through the doors of Cinnabar's private library and waited for him to acknowledge her presence. The emperor glanced up from a document on the table before him with expectant surprise.

"I take it you've caught the animal? Or perhaps Zaelix was able to identify him?"

She clenched her fists at her sides and straightened her shoulders. "I want nothing more than for that to be true, Supremacy. Less than fifteen minutes ago, while we were conducting a sweep of the gardens, my sables discovered Her Imperial Highness lying dead outside her window."

"No!" Cinnabar bolted to his feet, agony shooting through his face, a terrible gasp wicking through his open mouth. Just as quickly, he fell back into the chair, hands limp and mouth drawn. "Dead? My little flower, crushed while she bloomed."

The air in the library was suddenly thick as tar, and the perpetual motion figure on the reading table rolled tepid circuits. Cinnabar's eyes dropped numb and cold in his bereaved hands. Ambrosia was at a loss for comforting words as her mind whirled with much speculation but scant evidence. She reached into her jacket and pulled forth the notebook, opening it to the page last written upon and laying it before him.

"This is the first thing I noticed when I inspected the room. It lay just under the sill as though she had written it while sitting in the window."

Cinnabar's brow darkened ten shades as he smashed a fist into the page. "This is the Tourmaline Renegade's doing. The flag was a warning, the start of Pyron's regicidal campaign. What more evidence do we need? Pyron has written its own death warrant upon my daughter's body, signed it with her divine blood."

"Sir, when I spoke to your daughter, she seemed fearful for her life. And I'm convinced her chambermaid, Killa, knows that the threat lies within your own palace walls."

One sharp brow unshielded an intense aquamarine eye. "Who? Who would dare do this to my flesh and blood?"

"Well, the skyn we found was made for a big man and—"

A walnut door gave way to Callon's imposing figure. He read the room at a glance and bowed.

"My heart cries for your loss, Supremacy. Please forgive my intrusion, but some new evidence was just brought to my attention. The servants were turning through Her Imperial Highness's bed and collected these hairs, all black as charcoal. What other people in our empire grow hair of such a lackluster color as Pyrons?"

He set a glass vial down on the open notebook and Cinnabar glared at it, deepening shades of red smearing across his face. Callon rested his fingers on the notebook, read the writing, and shook his head as anger licked through his eyes.

"My soldiers are ready to avenge your daughter upon Pyron's head, sir. They are not free. They are all dead where they stand."

Ambrosia pulled back from the table a half-step. How could she accuse the general now, or even suggest that some of the evidence was contradictory? And who could prove the hairs had been planted or even found in the bed at all?

Cinnabar turned away stiffly, his fist clenched, his jaw working as he fought back tears.

"You were right, Commander. What Pyron would assault my daughter and not kill her? Her own notebook wants me to believe it was the Tourmaline Renegade's doing, and it will not be enough justice to tear every bone from his body when we have caught him. Both of you, prepare your troops. I will drain every Pyron throat and feed the flowers around my daughter's shrine with their blood before her wedding day. I swear it. Fate help me."

9

Disrel shook the contents of his backpack onto his bed and sorted through the items, replacing some, leaving others: Pain reducers. Helmet. Second pair of shoes. Gloves. Towel. Through his bedroom window, a deep orange sun falling between two neighboring towers illuminated clouds of dust milling in a sea of golden light. Billboards mounted on the structures' angular faces broadcasted a cyclical choreography of wanted posters and anti-Pyron propaganda, intensified by the heir apparent's recent murder. Of course, all of Pyron would suffer for the actions of one. No other malefactor would dare enter the imperial palace through a window to rape and murder the princess but the Tourmaline Renegade.

Disrel yanked the window curtain closed and turned back to his pack. Pyron was out of time. He was out of time. He could only train so hard and so fast. When the killing started, he wouldn't be ready. He needed to talk to Mored about finding a safe place for Solla to stay, because it wouldn't be long until Reem would be forced to lay him off, and Solla would lose her job at the packagers, and the apartments would begin evicting their Pyrons. Both of them would be required to register in the Pyron sector to begin a new life behind tall concrete and razor wire walls—*prison*. He had called it months ago. The Pyron sector was a death-row prison. They had to resist. Everyone had to resist. But so many Pyrons had families, large families, young children, elderly relatives.

The apartment door groaned. Disrel scraped up his pack and stepped into the living area. Solla frisked him with a glance. She knew he was leaving and that he wouldn't tell her where he was going, just like the last several weeks. She yanked open the cold box lid, her eyes rifling for something to eat, and ended up rummaging through a brown paper sack. She jerked it out.

"What's this?"

"Harutk." Solla was too young to remember how good Mother's harutk tasted, but this wasn't the first traditional Pyron meal he had brought home and left in the cold box for her.

"Where are you getting this stuff? We can't afford restaurant food."

"I got it from a friend at work."

"You aren't dating a Kobalt girl, are you? Is that why you smelled like beer?"

Disrel shrugged the pack onto his shoulder. "Relax, Solla. I'm not seeing any-one."

"How am I supposed to know that? We don't even talk anymore. You're only home long enough to sneak stuff into that backpack and leave again, and if I'm going to be alone here every evening, I need to know what is going on."

"I told you I took up a night job. I have to get there before curfew and come back when curfew is over."

"Why do you need a second job? Do you even sleep anymore?"

"I get a few hours."

"How much are they paying you?"

"Enough."

"I haven't seen any extra salary."

"It's coming." He pulled on the apartment door.

Solla dropped the container on the table, her eyes reduced to peevish slits. "I don't believe you. You're limping around, rubbing your back, and popping pills."

He let the door fall closed and approached the table.

"Solla, I told you, I've been working really hard lately. It's a lot more physical than what I do at the skynshop. And the company feeds me on the job and sometimes I get to bring the leftovers home for you. You've got to trust me."

"Then stop lying to me." Tears bubbled up in her eyes and her lips twisted. "I'm scared, Rel. I don't want you to be arrested and tortured and die like Father did. I can't survive without you. I have no one but you. No one."

He stared hard at the floor and pulled in a stiff breath. She wasn't alone. He was just as afraid as she was. And if soldiers ever came for them, there was little he could do to protect her. But she had always leaned on him for strength, trusted him to be everything she needed as the world went dark.

Solla wiped her eyes. "Why are we all being blamed for Zaelix's murder? And why can't we just be treated like everyone else? Why do we have to be different?"

"I don't know." Words of comfort were so hard to find. They were harder to believe.

"Why can't they see that some of us aren't like other Pyrons?"

Disrel clenched his fists. "What other Pyrons? Now is not the time to be a pacifist."

"Well, I don't think fighting back is going to solve anything! It just hurts good people out there, like Miss Mazilyn, and it's going to start a stupid civil war."

Disrel ground his teeth. He hated the Howlers for murdering the kind old woman for no other reason than their own blind hatred. But extremes didn't prove her point.

"You know that was Howlers. And so what? The state wants a war. You want to make peace by going to the prison sector? Go see how you like it."

Solla's lips bunched as she huffed through her nose. "You're not listening. We should pray for the people that hate us."

"You're naïve, Solla. It's ugly out there and it's not going to miraculously get better. Pyron's freedom wasn't taken in a day, and it won't be restored in a day. We might spend our whole lives fighting just so our children can have freedom. Just so we can even have children at all."

Solla scoffed. "If you are running in a gang at night, I hope you get beat up so badly that it knocks some sense into you and you learn to stay home."

Heat blew through Disrel's head and he jerked the apartment door back open. "I'm done here."

He slammed the door and trudged down the hall. Prayer hadn't fixed people like Kommett, and decades of Pyron prayers had only left them standing on the brink of genocide. It was time for action, for living like a true fireblood before the world.

By the time Disrel reached the Selenite subway station, a hopeless feeling had started creeping through his bones. He hadn't figured Solla into all of this, or how she would crumble inside if he was caught. Or what the state was capable of doing to her if his identity was ever discovered. He would take any sort of pain for her, but he could never forgive himself if he had to watch her suffer. His mind wandered through a museum of nefarious Kobalt tortures while he performed a dead hang after an hour of climbing. How could one man fight an army? There was only strength in numbers, and all of the numbers were on the Kobalt side. Going up against Tygo and Astros in the ring was a reality check. The muscular ex-special forces warriors could break bricks with their knuckles and chew through skyns with their teeth. If Tygo could snap his neck before he ever saw him coming, how long would it be before some other Kobalt soldier succeeded?

He dropped to the ground and wiped his face with a towel.

Tygo coiled a rope and laid it aside. "Your form is improving."

"Thanks. When do you think I'll be ready?"

"When do *you* think you'll be ready?"

"Maybe when I can whip you ten out of ten in the ring."

Tygo laughed. "You gave me my money's worth in six out of ten rounds last time. Listen. Even if you could whip me ten out of ten, you must never stop learning. Always continue to hone your abilities and improve yourself. No matter how hard we train, every soldier on the battlefield wishes he had one more day to prepare. Nothing can stop death from choosing the strongest among us and writing his name on the smallest arrow."

Disrel turned away, clawing at the back of his neck.

Tygo eyed him. "What's that look about?"

"I wasn't thinking long term. I was angry the state killed my father and I didn't have a plan beyond stealing that flag. So what if it was just a lucky stunt?"

Tygo searched his face steadily. "You're doubting yourself now?"

"It's worse than that," Disrel scrunched his fist in his forelock and wrestled internally. "I'm lying to my sister's face and she knows it."

Tygo grunted.

"We've never fought like this. We were always close. Soon after we moved into our apartment, we lost contact with the few friends we had—actually lost the one friend we owe everything to. If we can't turn things around soon, we'll lose the apartment, our jobs. I'll be fighting from the streets again, back to square one, needing another rich Kobalt to come lift me out of the gutter and give me a bath so I can amount to something."

Tygo sat down on the pile of rope. "So what's your next move?"

"Find somewhere safe for Solla."

"You'd have to leave Tourmal, and yet Tourmal is still the safest sector for Pyrons."

Disrel rubbed a hand over his mouth and met Tygo's gaze.

Tygo rested his elbows on his knees. "We got word from the palace. Cinnabar has sworn to fertilize his daughter's memorial garden with your ashes and blood. War is like chess: If you mess around, play defensive, your opponent will force you to make a move. And your best move will still cost you. Don't wait for that to happen." Tygo stood up. "Ready to keep going?"

Disrel sighed. "Yeah. What's next?"

"Escaping impossible restraints."

When the night's training had ended, Disrel showered and sprawled out on a bench in the atrium for a few hours of rest. Alta roused him at daybreak and handed him the usual heavy paper sack and a maternal smile.

"Was it enough to hold you last time?"

"Yes. It was delicious, thank you." Alta's cooking had a mother's touch, and every bite carried Disrel home to his childhood, to a safe, comforting place.

"I cut back on breakfast a little today to pack you extra for lunch."

Disrel worked the sack into his backpack. He'd gone without a morning meal for so long, but Alta and Tygo insisted he ate more to supplement what he burned in training. "I'm sorry I didn't bring your other containers back. I didn't have time to wash them before I left."

"Don't worry about it." The corners of Alta's eyes wrinkled. "I've been packing you extra because I know you're sharing with your sister."

Disrel's cheeks flushed with fire. "I'm sorry."

"Don't be. Just let her know the cook sends her love with the meal."

Disrel hauled himself off the bench. That wouldn't go over well, and the day he found any of Alta's cooking dumped in the garbage would be the last he shared any of it with Solla.

The drive back into Tourmal was pleasant, despite the numerous holoposters along the roadway blazing anti-Pyron propaganda. Disrel entered the back door of the skyn factory closest to his workstation. He turned the corner to his secluded area and halted.

Kommett slouched against Disrel's workbench, rolling an adjustment wheel back and forth under his butt like an animal marking its territory. He whipped his head back and forth to some offkey tune and snapped out a beat with his fingers. Disrel dropped his backpack on the counter, shaking the young Kobalt out of his jam. Kommett stumbled off the edge of the cutter and moved back, reptilian eyes popping, jaw flapping noiselessly.

Disrel gave his coworker a quizzical look. Did Kommett wipe his butt around his workstation every morning? Maybe he didn't want to know. "What are you doing?"

Kommett's expression shifted to anger. "What are *you* doing? You're not supposed to be here!"

Disrel spread his hands and looked around. "Where am I supposed to be, Kommett?"

"Prison!"

Disrel rolled his eyes and tightened the wheel on the cutter. "Sorry to crash your party and break your heart."

Kommett's eyes fluttered along the floor in disbelief and muddled reckoning.

"But the military police raided your apartment building late last night and took everyone to the Hold. It's all over Tourmal. They caught the flag thief." Kommett usually mocked like a cat with canary feathers fresh upon his lips, but today he was grimly serious.

Disrel's heart dropped into his stomach, and he choked back a wave of bile.

"Don't believe me? Ask anyone in this building the name of the Tourmaline Renegade."

Disrel's fists tightened. It would take only a minute to turn on the machines and sew Kommett right into a body bag. He whirled at his coworker. "Is this how you settle a personal score, Kommett? You think it's funny to condemn a building full of innocent people?"

Kommett staggered behind a garment form and slipped around the cutting table, keeping two sides always between them. "I didn't rat! A police dog smelled him out and they matched a print to his shoe tread."

"What else do you know, Kommett?" Disrel followed him doggedly.

"His execution is in an hour, along with everyone else they arrested!"

Cold sweat wicked onto his forehead and he turned about, sucking quick breaths. Solla. They had Solla. He vaulted over the table, snatched his backpack from the counter, and plowed back down the hall and out the door, mounting the corecycle without bothering to secure his helmet strap and pushing out through the lot. Without checking for traffic, he lurched out onto the roadway and rocketed toward his apartment building.

The evidence was clear long before he skidded to a stop at the apartment's main entrance. The doors to the building were wide open and passersby loitered at the curb, wagging their heads. Heaven have mercy. The insanity of condemning dozens for the actions of one. He couldn't lose Solla like this. He couldn't forgive himself for letting her go in anger. Disrel drove like a demon, splitting lanes and cutting off other riders, eating up mile after mile at deadly speeds. It was impossible to get into that arena to free the prisoners, not with it brimming with soldiers and mounted bows. But someone had to do something. Could Mored's army move in less than an hour?

From the westbound lanes, a corecycle left the pavement and dove across the grassy median. The driver came straight at him, then turned with the intent to cut him off. At the sight of a familiar orange skyn, he pulled onto the shoulder and slowed, cruising beside the other rider until they came to a stop.

"Alta! I need your help, please! They have Solla. Does Mored know?"

Alta raised her visor and unbuckled a bulging backpack from her body. "We heard right after you left." She tossed it over. "But this is your fight, Kyreasheluhn. Showing yourself and the flag is the only way to prove their innocence."

"You have to help me get Solla out of there. What if they continue with the execution?"

"They think they have the real Tourmaline Renegade. But, son, you are the real Tourmaline Renegade now. My husband had that chip embedded in a crystal vault for fifteen years. The only reason he brought it out was because of what you did. And I believe you can finish what you started. Do you have your chip?"

"Yes."

"Then get going. You don't have much time."

She kicked at his bike and peeled off into traffic, knocking her helmet visor back down.

Disrel turned back toward inner-sector Tourmal. Drivers shook their hands and threw fingers, cursing him for his reckless abandon. But now was not the time for courtesy. He would be too late to stop the first few executions and could only pray that Solla was near the back of the line.

The arena's burnished stones gleamed like gold in the morning light. Her many flags snapped in the wind like drum corp snares. She was a specter of death, a reaper of souls, a mosaic of bloody stones. Her walls offered shade, seats, and comfort to the public. But all she offered the condemned was a certain place to die. Execution Square had provided these services to hundreds of thousands in Disrel's lifetime, and hundreds of thousands before that, when she was nothing more than an open plaza. Her morbid shadow streaked across the cityscape, prophesying death to multitudes more.

The chilling tones of the gongs and trumpets carried on the wind to Disrel's ears. The feverish thrumming of hands and feet roared through the arena arches, accompanied by pitched screams of patriotic fervor. This was the execution of the decade. The Tourmaline Renegade would fall under Kobalt justice and take many others with him.

Disrel turned off the main road and paused on a quiet backstreet bordering a row of small shops. He opened the pack Alta had given him and found a standard seven-inch qorzan blade and scabbard rolled up in the flag's fabric. He cinched the weapon around his thigh and pressed the Tourmaline chip into the receptacle on the side of his left breast. His helmet visor darkened and an inky blackness swept down his arms and legs. The pink liddicoatite shimmered lucidly in the lower middle of his chest, and he swallowed down his fear. He couldn't do this. But he had no other choice. Solla was all he had left. His fight was for her, and the state had brought the fight home. He rolled the flag under his arm and cruised slowly around the block, every joint and limb aching, his heart galloping faster with every revolution. A line of food wagons trimmed both sides of the street, and a sea of pedestrian traffic ebbed and flowed between them and the colossal structure.

Disrel jumped the curb and plowed down a walk, coursing up to the wide ramp of the arena's central gate and its yawning tunnel. The sea of people parted, screaming and dropping crates of food and drinks. A burly man lunged, and Disrel mashed the throttle, streaking past him. Two guards moved into the walkway and lowered their crossbows. Three more stood with polearms along the tunnel's darkly gaping throat. Disrel hunched under his windshield, leaned hard to one side, and drifted down underneath a traffic gate. He caught the spiral at the tunnel's mouth and ramped the wall with a fresh burst of speed, skimming the ceiling and sailing over the soldiers' heads before arcing down the opposite wall and catapulting straight into the heart of the arena. From the pinching tunnel to the breath-snatching expanse, the turning bike floated out over the crowds and over the heads of soldiers goading a long line of prisoners toward a grizzly machine bearing a polished blade grinning for a naked neck. Disrel looked down for Solla and cast out his arm. The crimson banner unfurled from his side and snatched from his grip. Its dark shadow swallowed the neck-slashing machine and the executioner as the flag cloaked them both in silent objection. Ten thousand spectators burst from their seats and roared.

Disrel gripped the bike between his legs and braced for the descent. The corecycle touched down and skimmed over the sprawling mosaic floor, smoke coiling and gravel flying from the squealing back wheel. He raced a wide circle around the line of prisoners. Solla hunched like a wilting flower near the back of the line, her hands and feet bound in supple skyn cable ties. Disrel sailed up to her and pulled his blade, nipping through her ties and jerking her onto the seat behind him.

"Hold on to me!"

She squeezed his middle with a death grip, and the corecycle lurched forward. Disrel turned parallel to the wall of oncoming soldiers and headed back around the arena floor. Cinnabar shot out of his seat and glared at the chaos, and blame and anger rushed down the chain of command around him. Disrel continued his wide circle around the edges of the arena, as if making a victory lap instead of bolting for the exit. All the floor-level gates led to holding cells deep within the sloped walls. There was no escape.

Arrows pounded down from the four guns mounted in turrets around the top of the arena. The line of prisoners dissolved into a mad rabble, fighting the soldiers for weapons and freedom. A steel-shafted arrow plunged into the tiles in Disrel's path, blasting shards into the air, and Solla's scream numbed his ears as her fingers gouged into his diaphragm. Debris pelted his helmet and body. In the next second, a thunderbolt could skewer them both. They would never hear or see it coming.

Disrel pulled the corecycle closer to the arena wall and opened the throttle. There was a slant in one of the buttresses ahead. He threw his head back toward Solla.

"We're going up! Don't fall off!"

Solla shrieked when the corecycle began climbing the sloped support. They mounted the wall and jumped rows of spectators, ramping another curved buttress and dropping into a clearing in the stands. Solla tumbled, dragging him off his seat a little as the back end swerved. Disrel planted his foot and reclaimed his balance, tugging her back on behind him as soldiers waded through the stands. He pushed the throttle and the bike lurched forward, carrying them into a dark exit tunnel where lights blurred and refracted around them. People flung themselves into the walls all throughout the spiraling passage, casting aside food and drinks and pulling children to safety. Solla's screams cut high above the chaos.

They burst out into the streets and weaved through lanes of traffic, taking the shoulders and medians. Disrel glanced back every few seconds, anticipating a military pursuit. He cut onto the highway. The wind roared around his helmet and whipped his skyn against his body. Solla continued squeezing his ribs with all she had.

Disrel's heart rattled, and fear arced through him in bursts. Flying into a packed arena and overturning an execution at the last second may have looked like the most brazen rescue ever, but he didn't feel like a hero. He felt lucky. A million and one things could have gone wrong, resulting in his capture and death. He glanced into the rearview mirrors every couple of seconds, watching for police bikes. Solla twittered with amazement and gratitude, but the wind snatched every word. After many miles, the traffic cleared and Disrel slowed.

Solla was still jabbering. "You're the one they're looking for! You took the flag from the capital!"

Disrel kept his face trained forward and prayed that his visor was perfectly opaque. Roadway signs welcomed them to the Selenite sector. He turned off the highway and onto quieter back roads. There was no going back to the apartment, even if the group's innocence was declared. It was too risky. He would have to leave her somewhere for now and hope she could stay hidden until he came back for her. Selen was much more forested, more secluded with its rolling farmland and unpaved lanes. The homes on this road were well-spaced, with fenced acreage, ponds, and rows of trees bowing over the dirt lanes. A patch of woods bordered the closest manor. It was the perfect place to hide. Disrel noted one wealthy home, and its single white marble porch step. Only the bottom step of the three that led to the porch was white, as if it had been replaced, added on recently. It had to be a sign that the resident was sympathetic toward Pyrons.

Solla continued bubbling as she hugged from behind. "No one will ever believe that I was saved by the real Tourmaline Renegade! Who are you? Oops, that's a stupid question. I know you're the Tourmaline Renegade, of course. But I wish I could know who you really are, your name or your face so I could always remember you. I know you don't owe me any of that, but still. That was so heroic, I'll remember it every day of my life, how you came flying in and raced up to me and—" Her face numbed. "All those other people. What's going to happen to them? Why did you save me?"

Disrel turned and gazed into her beautiful eyes. He wanted to wrap her up in a crushing hug and never let go. He wanted to ask Mored and Alta to give her a place in their home, but he couldn't impose her on them like that. He roughened his voice so Solla wouldn't recognize it.

"I'm going to have to drop you off here."

"Drop me off? I don't know where we are. Please don't leave me."

"We're right across the border in Selen. It's safer than Tourmal." He pulled the blade from his leg and cut the remains of the restraints from her wrists and ankles. "They're probably watching your building and would arrest you if you went back there."

"But I have family in Tourmal. My brother will look for me. . . or maybe not." Her voice cracked and she paused. "The last time I saw him we fought and—" The tears came.

The blade shook in his hand as he resheathed it. "Younger brother?"

"Older." She sniffled. "His name is Disrel."

"Hmm. I'm going back into Tourmal. If I happen to see your brother, I'll let him know where to find you."

Solla dismounted, wiping her wet eyes. She was probably processing what had almost happened to her. "How do you know this area is safe? I don't know my way around Selen."

Disrel pointed. "See that home with the white porch step?"

She looked at the grand house.

"People who are friendly to Pyrons usually leave something white in their windows or outside their homes."

Solla wrung her hands and stared anxiously between him and the unfamiliar house.

"I feel safer with you. I know I don't know you any better than the people who live in that house, but—"

"It's too dangerous to be with me." He glanced at the sky, almost expecting to see military aircraft.

Solla's eyes flitted up and down the road. "I feel like a stray again. No home. No job. Why did you steal that flag and start all of this?"

Disrel turned his head toward the sprawling home. "I'm finishing what started before you were born. No Pyron is ever a stray. That's a Kobalt label for a spirit they cannot control, cannot enslave. You were born to be free. And I'm fighting so you can have that birthright."

Solla stood there quivering and nodding. "Well, thank you. I don't know why you chose me out of all those others. But whoever you are, my brother and I are indebted to you. And I wish I could help you somehow."

"Maybe someday you'll have that chance." Disrel kicked the corecycle into motion and looked through his mirror at Solla standing in the middle of the dirt lane. It was all he could do to keep from squeezing her to his chest. He had almost lost her, the one person he had to live for, and now he was leaving her again, in an unfamiliar neighborhood, in the hands of strangers.

10

Execution Square was a stomped anthill. Every inch of pavement within ten miles crawled with frenetic vehicle and pedestrian traffic. Disrel worked his way back toward the apartment on a slate-gray corecycle he had taken from Mored's garage before leaving Selen. He couldn't have felt any safer in his skyn, now restored to its usual white. The military police patrolled the street corners in packs, interested only in red bikes and dark-skynned characters. Less than four hours after the Tourmaline Renegade had dropped the flag in the arena, the prisoners had been justified and released, except for the Pyrons, who had been taken back to the Hold to be transported to the walled Pyron sector.

Disrel cruised a wide path around his apartment building, watching for police in case they had a warrant for his arrest. After several laps around the block, he pulled into the parking lot. Trash and leaves danced passionate, dizzying circles around the broken entrance. The geometric windows were glazed, dead eyes from which shadowy human forms winked. Looters. No matter how low-income the housing, Tourmal always had someone who thought there might be something worth taking. There was no going in for anything now, not even for that old blanket. It was time to move on.

He was homeless again, and after this experience the landlord would probably never rent to Pyrons again. Few places rented to Pyrons anymore, and none of them were anywhere as decent as this building, with its narrow halls and threadbare walls and unheated water. Now that he didn't have to walk to work, he could look someplace farther, perhaps on the outskirts of the sector. Disrel rode out and parked several streets over on a hill that gave him a clear view of the building. Relocating was always a mess. It seemed that as soon as he and Solla got comfortable in one place, they were forced to move soon after, as if heaven were gently reminding them of their nomadic ancestry.

A nearby hologlass flashed its life-sized sequences of the Tourmaline Renegade riding through the arena. Disrel leaned over the handlebars and studied the motion pictures of his ride. As numb as he had been through it all, he couldn't have ever imagined he would look like such a champion standing in the saddle and unfurling the flag. The arena cameras had even captured the finer details of his helmet and skyn. Every twenty seconds, a monotone recording played:

If you see this person, report him to the authorities immediately. It is your patriotic duty. Keep your sector safe.

Safe? The regime was apathetic, at its best, toward Pyron safety and human rights. The billboard's message was clearly not for people like him.

"What are you doing here, Pyron?"

Disrel pushed upright in his seat and turned, his heart jumping around in his chest. A deep sable uniform glared on his right. Two intense eyes narrowed upon him from behind the tinted helmet visor.

"Existing, just like everyone else."

"Pyron's don't just exist. They live for anarchy."

"I think freedom is a better word choice."

She snatched the keystone from the bike, and the engine died.

"Freedom outside of Kobalt rule *is* anarchy. Show me your ID."

Burning auburn wisps leaked down inside her helmet. It was an unmistakable shade. This was the sable commander who had been cordial enough to ask if he wanted to die later, the one who had barged into the skyn shop with her weaselly entourage and asked for directions to the exit. Disrel sighed and leaned back, fishing through his pockets.

"If you want to keep in touch, you could just ask for my contact information."

Her sloped nose wrinkled. "You're not my type, and you don't have what it takes to impress me."

"Are you sure?"

The hologlass fired off its motion picture series of the Tourmaline Renegade soaring into the arena with the flag flaming behind him.

"Unless you can do that, you'll never impress me," she said. "And even then, it's a slim chance. I hunt renegades for sport and eat them for breakfast."

He shrugged. "The way you keep hanging around, you must find me a little attractive."

"I find you suspicious and annoying." She cuffed him across the helmet. "Helmet off, Pyron. I can't even see your face."

Disrel sighed and fidgeted with the chinstrap. He pulled the helmet off and set it on the barrel of the bike. A light of recognition passed through her face.

"Not bad, is it?"

Her eyes sharpened. "I've seen worse. ID. Now."

He pulled his card out of his breast pocket, praying she would send him on his way in a moment.

She snatched it from his hand and scanned it with her eyes. "DIZ-ral?"

"Diz-REL. And your name is?"

"You live in that apartment we raided last night. Why aren't you with the others waiting for a train to Pyron?"

"Did I give you my old card? Sorry. I have a Pyron sector pass now."

She flicked her fingers, throwing the ID card up under his nose. "Then let me see it."

He fished in his pocket once more, replacing his ID with the false Pyron pass Alta had made for him.

The sable waved her hand at the white card. "That's all I need to see. At least you're obeying some of our laws. Starting tomorrow, Tourmaline Pyrons will have three weeks to relocate to their new sector, by direction of General Gault. Move along and don't let me catch you loitering again."

She handed him his keystone and marched off toward her military corecycle.

Disrel set his helmet back on his head and pushed his vehicle away from the curb. "It was nice meeting you, too!"

A sable's presence always put an ache in his stomach, this one more than others. She looked at him like she was smelling something sour—someone guilty.

Disrel merged into traffic and headed for Selen. As long as he had breath in his body, he wouldn't let anyone force him and Solla into the prison sector. If he was to continue his fight, he had to be close to Tourmal, preferably in the city. He could handle the streets again, but Solla couldn't. Really, Solla couldn't manage being away from him anywhere. It wasn't like people in the farthest corners of the empire or its bordering nations were opening their doors to fleeing Pyrons anyway. It was the same everywhere. Apathy.

Disrel cruised down the back roads along the Selenite border. The rolling farmland and thickets all looked the same, bend after bend. He'd been too shaken to take careful notice of just where he had left her, too nervous she would recognize him, but eventually, he came across a familiar fenced estate with a winding lane that led his eyes to the home nestled back in a grove of trees: a sprawling dark stone mansion with a white porch step. There were footprints up and down the edge of the road. If these were Solla's—and they had to be—she hadn't gone to the house. The tracks followed the road some distance away from the home and disappeared into the grass. Disrel paused next to the black stone fence that bordered the property. The acreage allowed the residences along this road to breathe and blend with the environment. What a contrast to the megalithic jungle of inner Tourmal. The wide blue door on the face of the home slid open, and a man leaned out and waved his arms.

Disrel nudged the corecycle forward.

"Hold up!" The golden-haired Kobalt trotted across the lawn, smiling and waving every couple of paces. Gold bands traced through his simple, navy-blue skyn, and his tousled pompadour flopped to one side. "Are you looking for your sister?"

Disrel hesitated, giving the man a closer look. "Yeah."

"She's inside."

Disrel braked and set his feet down.

The young man slowed at the fence, breathless. "She's only been standing at the window watching for you since she came in. She told me all about what happened in Tourmal, so if you need a place to stay, I live by myself and have room for you both."

Disrel glanced at the grand house with conflicted eyes. How did one man afford so much roof? And why was he so eager to share it with strangers? The offer was too good to be true. It was closer to Mored's hideout and still within decent range of the skynshop. "Your home is beautiful."

"Thank you. There's a stable in the back where you can keep your vehicle hidden. And I have a safe room in the basement. I know Pyrons never arrive with much, so I have supplies of anything you might need. Why don't you come on in, rest a while, and eat something? Or if you have somewhere to be, you can take some necessities and be on your way. But you probably already know that Selen has almost finished deporting Pyrons to that prison sector."

Disrel locked eyes with the man. "Thank you. I really don't know what to—"

"Koti. My full name would choke a hippo, so don't ask. It's just Koti." He offered a tawny hand, smiling as he gave a solid shake. "Disrel, right? Come inside before the neighbors see you."

Disrel followed Koti down the driveway and parked the bike in the shade. As he ascended the steps to the door, Solla burst out onto the porch.

"Disrel! You'll never believe this. While you were gone, they found the Tourmaline Renegade in our apartment building. Only he wasn't the *real* renegade because when they took us all to Execution Square—"

Disrel advanced, wrapping his arms around her and squeezing her to his chest. He rocked back and forth as he pushed her back inside. Safe. He couldn't believe it. Heaven had smiled upon them, given them a place to stay. Another Miss Mazilyn. Another friendly Kobalt soul. The moment he released her head, she resumed her babbling.

"—the *actual* Tourmaline Renegade came flying in on a red corecycle and threw a giant flag over the beheader. And then he zoomed around the arena and cut me out of the line and told me to get on and to hang on tight and then *whoosh!* We zipped around the arena again and the turrets started firing the thunderbolts at us and it was like *bang bang bang*—and broken tiles were pelting us and there was no way out because the floor-level gates only lead to holding cells and it's a maze down there!" Her eyes grew three sizes as she came up for air.

Disrel clasped her cheeks in his hands and shook his head. "The same renegade who stole the flag?"

"Yes. But his skyn was much prettier than the wanted posters show." She gripped his wrists and jumped up and down with childish excitement. "And then we ramped the wall and jumped into the stands and people fell out of their seats and we flew through a tunnel and when I opened my eyes we were blistering the highway. I've never gone so fast in my entire life. And he brought me here and said he would let you know where to find me! Did you talk to him? How did he find you?"

Disrel scrambled for a lie. "I found a message at the apartment telling me to come here."

Solla's cheeks flushed as a dreamy sigh escaped her. "Oh. He is so nice to help us like this! I wish you could've met him. His voice was *so* beautiful and kind. I'll never forget it."

Disrel turned, wiping a finger down his nose. Ick. He'd tried to sound tough.

A man stood up from the couch in the adjoining room. His face was obscure, serene, princely, smoothly shaven and black as obsidian. Disrel had never seen anyone with such a dark complexion. The stranger flashed a bright smile and extended a hand.

"Hello, Disrel." He rumbled like a double bass. "I'm Voss. I've been a close friend of Koti's since medical school."

Disrel halted. He'd never heard such fluent Pyron off the tongue of an outlander. He slapped his hand into Voss's large palm and gave it a vigorous shake.

"Nice to meet you, Voss. Where did you sprout from, and how did you learn to speak Pyron so well?"

"I'm from the blue sands of Jadkwe, across the sea. I came to Selen eight years ago to study medicine and treated many Pyrons in exchange for anything they could give me. Most of them could neither speak Kobalt nor Jadkwean, so I had to learn their language to better treat them."

Disrel's respect for the outlander swelled. "Why haven't you taken your knowledge of medicine back to your own people? Why would you treat people who have nothing to give you?"

The lines around Voss's wide mouth deepened. "Because I have no people to return to. Soon after I completed my internship, I received word that my nation had been taken over by our neighbors and many of my people killed and enslaved."

Disrel's brow knit. "I'm sorry. Man, I—I don't know what to say."

"The world is always changing, both in good ways and in bad. So I have sworn myself to Pyron's cause. Your people are my people, and my home is your home."

Disrel pushed his hands into his pockets, inadequate phrases of thanks pressing on his lips.

A slender and petite woman swept her golden auburn hair from her eyes as she moved into the room and extended a hand. "I'm Doni, Koti's half sister." Her tone was breathless and bright. Her cheeks plumped and dimpled when she smiled, and her eyebrows were thick and sculpted.

"Half sister?" Disrel stammered, lost in her magnetic smile. He kicked himself for repeating that part like an idiot.

Doni's brow twisted, but she continued smiling at him like he'd done something adorable. "Yeah. We have the same mother."

Disrel forced out another string of disjointed syllables. "I'm sorry. Doni. I mean—not about your mother. I meant to say nice to meet you."

She laughed. "That's okay. I can imagine today has been stressful. I work as a part-time nurse under Voss, and the rest of the week I'm shuffling paperwork for Koti. Solla's been telling us all about you over the last few hours."

Fire flashed through Disrel's cheeks. Her Pyron was almost as good as Voss's. "No lies, I hope."

Doni's glittering blue eyes skipped around the room. "All good things." She shrugged her petite shoulders, wedged her hands into her hip pockets, and crossed her short legs. "I hear you're talented. Your skynmaking skills are incredible. Solla showed me how you hid armor in her garment and said you can do special features like hidden pockets and convertibility for different occasions and activities. I've been wanting something custom for a long time. Nothing illegal, obviously. I'm just built kind of curvy and longer in the waist, and I've never had a skyn that stretched in all the right places and was still versatile, you know?"

Disrel raked his neck and gave Doni's gorgeous hourglass figure a once-over. She embodied the word *cute* from the tip of her button nose to her dainty feet.

"I know how to do it. But it's expensive and I'm backed up several months." He turned to Koti. "Do you speak Pyron too?"

Koti's eyes darted back and forth. "A few beetles kissed?"

Solla giggled.

An instant change came over Koti's face, and he resigned to Kobalt speech. "No. I clearly do not speak Pyron. The few words I know, I butcher." He pulled two shining copper cups from a cabinet. "Can I get any of you something to drink? Disrel? Solla?"

Disrel turned in the center of the room, gazing up at the vaulted ceiling spaces, skylights, and high windows. "Yes. Thank you."

Koti filled the cups and passed them out. "I'll show you around the house and the supply closet, and after dinner, if you're up to it, we can play a game. Or if you just need time to settle in, we'll leave you alone to rest."

Solla exploded. "Yes! I haven't played a game in years!"

Disrel wrapped his arm around her shoulder and gave her a squeeze. He'd have to goad her into bed as early as possible to get ahead of her stress-induced vomiting episodes.

"We'll probably take a nap before supper."

Koti moved toward the stairs. "Then I'll show you your rooms."

Koti's wide home had all the amenities a refugee could have wanted. There was a natural hot spring pool in the basement, an exercise room, and a private patio facing the wood in the back. A bubbling creek coursed along the edge of the forest. On the upstairs level, Koti showed them two small bedrooms, connected by a washroom. Each room was minimally furnished with a floor mattress, a lamp, floor cushions, and a case of reading materials. A few traditional woven hangings graced the walls.

"Purchased those from some homeless Pyrons here in Selen before they were moved out." Koti squeezed a hand over his cleft chin. "I thought they'd make my future guests feel more at home."

Disrel nodded and wondered if Koti had paid more than what the poor Pyron had asked for them. The macramé and beadwork brought back memories of Mother sitting cross-legged by the window and poking beads on the strands. Sometimes, she'd let him stack beads on the spools in the orders she needed for the pattern. Seeing the woven pieces resurfaced a longing he'd spent years suppressing, and he ached to see Mother's warm smile and hear her deep, pleasant laughter one more time. A misty feeling crept up in his face, and he turned away from Koti, sniffling.

"It's not a Pyron home without these," Disrel grunted, fighting to hold his composure and believe the goodness around him.

"If there's anything else that will make it feel more like home, let me know." Koti moved back toward the door. "Or change things however you want them. These are your rooms for as long as you decide to stay."

"It's good. You've done enough. Thank you, Koti. I'd like to rest now."

Koti, Doni, and Voss went back downstairs, and Disrel sprawled out on the mattress in Solla's room. Solla paced before the bedroom door, itching to follow her new friends for more excitement, until Disrel slapped the mattress and reminded her how embarrassing it would be if she threw up on Koti's nice furniture. Solla came and sat down beside him. She hugged herself and shivered as her attention darted from one thing to the next. All of the day's adrenaline was draining, clearly leaving her weak and anxious. Disrel rubbed her back and tried to distract her with small talk.

And then she heaved, clasping her hands to her mouth and staggering toward the bathroom. Disrel jumped up and rushed her along. She shuddered under his hands and he pulled her braid back from the basin. It was hard not to scold. She was old enough to know when she had reached her limit, but given the day's twists and turns, he bit his tongue.

There was no way she could return to work at the packager's. She would have to stay hidden here until it was safe again, and she might be a prisoner to the refuge of this house for much longer than she could imagine.

Disrel raked his fingers down her spine. The little comforting things always seemed to stop the dry heaving. He led her back to the bed and let her curl up under his arm like she had when they were children. She was too grown up for it now, but after almost losing her to a beheading blade, he wanted her no farther away. Her lips quivered and her eyes darted all around the room as she twittered the day's perils afresh in his ear. Disrel listened, interjecting with yawns and groggy "hmm-hmms" until her voice faded away.

Laughter rang through the ducts in the walls from the floor below. Solla was gone. Disrel pushed himself up, straining through heavy eyelids. The sun hand was sinking down the face of the clock. He had overslept by an hour. He struggled off the mattress and to the washroom, freshened up, and slipped quietly down the stairs, where the inviting aromas of fried food saturated the air. A fan vented the oily clouds out of the house through a pipe. Koti leaned against the marble counter, clutching a bowl to his black apron all splattered with flour, whisking and laughing as Voss juggled limes and balanced a shot glass on his nose. Doni and Solla sat at the table, turning game pieces over in their fingers and reading a pamphlet of rules. A tiny silver hammer punished a tinkling bell above the fryer, and Koti wrestled his eyes from Voss's impressive act to pull meat from the grease.

"Hey! The chief is awake!" Voss leaned forward and caught the shot glass.

Disrel ambled into the chaos, rubbing his eyes.

"I moved your corecycle around back in the stable." Koti salted the fried morsels. "Your keystone is in the vestibule."

"Thanks. I'm leaving for work tomorrow, but Solla won't be. I hope she won't be a burden if she hangs around here."

"She's fine. Just be discreet. I don't want the neighbors on the hill to see you. We don't know their political positions yet."

Disrel leaned on the kitchen island. "Also, my hours are a little strange. Got an odd night job that I can't talk about."

"That's okay. Solla was telling us you do garment work down in Tourmal, right?"

Voss slid onto a stool at the island. "Since you're so knowledgeable about skyns, help me figure this one out. You've seen the Tourmaline Renegade's skyn, haven't you?"

"On posters, yeah."

"As far as I can tell, it's identical to the one the original Tourmaline Renegade wore over fifteen years ago. It really shows off that armor and has a lot of texture. Tourmaline security says none of the factories in the area have any record of making a garment like that. Do you think he could've made it himself?"

"That's unlikely. Maybe he had it made in another sector."

Voss scratched his chin. "Probably under the table. Or he had help. That corecycle must've cost a heavy credit."

"He'd have to have some expensive equipment and a place to store and run it all. It's more likely he's wearing an integrated skyn. He can change the chip out and walk through a crowd unnoticed."

Doni made her way over to the island, eyes glistening with interest, and spoke Pyron. "How did you sleep, Disrel?"

He cast a furtive glance, responding in Kobalt. "Pleasantly."

"Mind if I ask you a few more questions about the skyn I want made?"

"How about over supper?" Koti pulled a stack of plateware from the shelves and set out drinks on the counter. "Disrel, Solla, you first."

The group filled their plates and gathered at the table, chatting about the food, the fine company they shared, and the game to follow. Disrel plowed through his meal. The fried food crackled and crunched between his teeth, and the sweet, tangy sauces wrung saliva with every bite. Doni glanced over every twenty seconds or so, but Disrel's gaze never left his plate until he'd finished a second helping. Less than seven minutes into the meal, the conversation drifted back to the Tourmaline Renegade.

Doni bumped Disrel's arm with her elbow. "Stealing that flag and flying a Pyron one was brazen."

Disrel tried to shake the feeling that the comment had exposed him. "Yeah. Crazy."

Koti pulled a face. "That doesn't even compare to the steel guts it takes to go cruising down into Execution Square on a corecycle. And from what did they say?

The fifth level? That's a mad drop. And those thunderbolts weigh five pounds apiece and they're moving eight hundred feet per second. He drove into a hornet's nest and got out unscathed."

Voss pointed his fork at Koti. "How did he manage to get the bike up out of that death pit with a passenger on the back? That's some wizardry."

Disrel chewed a fried strip steadily, moving his attention from speaker to speaker. Rapture smeared Solla's face as she listened to her new friends' accolades for her hero.

Doni folded her napkin. "His skill makes me think he might be an ex-special forces soldier. It's frightening, but somehow it's all so exciting. I can't wait to see what he'll do next."

As if this were a show. Disrel swelled a little at Doni's assumption. So he was on par with the Kobalt special forces already? Tygo was a fine instructor.

Voss shook his head. "The stakes will get higher every time he shows himself. If he's that good, he could have picked his way to the top, assassin-style, and taken out Cinnabar and his cabinet before the world even knew he existed. He's messing around, flapping flags in front of the bull. 'Hey, Cinnabar. I'm here. I'm ready to cause some trouble. Come get me.' No. He's either a young kid who's going to get himself killed soon enough, or a state puppet they're using for an excuse to tighten Pyron's noose."

Doni slid a newsposter onto the table and laid a hand on the central photograph of the renegade hoisting the flag. "And why couldn't he be a brave Pyron warrior? He chose Solla out of all those other prisoners."

Disrel forcibly swallowed an unchewed morsel. Doni had looked straight into him as she said, "brave Pyron warrior."

"There were other Pyrons in the line," he said. "Weren't there, Solla? Our neighbors?"

"I can see Cinnabar using a stuntman," Voss countered easily. "Why invent a new fake enemy when you can use an old dead one to funnel Pyrons into that sector? People still remember the Tourmaline Renegade. They're just too afraid to admit it."

Solla straightened. "He spoke fluent Pyron to me the whole time I was with him."

"As fluent or more fluently than I can?" Voss slumped back in his seat with an apologetic expression.

Solla sniffed and dropped her gaze.

Doni's eyes drank in the photograph. "What does it matter? He might be biracial for all we know. But I'd bet my blue corecycle there's a ruggedly handsome face behind that visor. What do you think?" She turned to Disrel.

Disrel raised his glass. "Do I think he's handsome?"

"Is he on our side?" Voss countered.

Disrel took a calculated sip.

"I know he's gorgeous." Solla gushed with stars in her eyes. "No guy with a voice like that could ever have a face that isn't perfect."

Disrel struggled to swallow as a burning heat rose through his collar. Her ignorance was his pain and her bliss. He set his cup down on the table with a hard knock and made a face. "Ew, Solla. You don't even know the guy. What if he has warts between his toes?"

She gave him a deadpan stare. "He does not."

"You don't know. What if he doesn't brush his teeth?"

She huffed. "Someone as nice as the renegade brushes at least three times a day. You should take notes."

"Solla got to hug him," Doni wiggled her eyebrows. "So lucky."

Solla blushed. "He had very nice arms and wide, strong shoulders. I'm sure he has a face to match."

"But there's a possibility he doesn't." Disrel pressed.

"None of you can prove a word you're saying." Koti stood up and gathered plates. "Anyone care to speculate on what's for dessert?"

Everyone rose from the table and helped to clear it while Koti procured a gorgeous fruit trifle and served it into smaller glasses. Voss wandered into the living area and picked up a carved wooden box.

"This is that old mountaineer's game you Selenites love so much." He looked at Disrel. "Do you know how to play?"

"Never heard of it."

Voss chuckled. "It's kind of like Pyrons, Kobalts, and the Tourmaline Renegade. Each player gets a role—some rabbits, some foxes. But there is only one white rabbit. He's the most fun, but also the most vulnerable role. His job is to single-handedly pick off the foxes before they kill off the other rabbits, all without revealing his identity to any of the foxes or rabbits. The foxes not only have the advantage of numbers, but can win by either killing all of the rabbits or discovering the white rabbit. Once the white rabbit's identity is revealed, the foxes win, even if the white rabbit has taken down more foxes than they have rabbits. It requires a lot of strategy, secret keeping, and teamwork."

Doni plopped eagerly onto the couch with her trifle. "This game always gets my blood pumping!"

Everyone gathered in the living room with their dessert, and the role cards, tokens, and NPC decks were dealt out. Disrel shielded his card with his hand and peeked at it. A strong-shouldered white rabbit stared back.

11

Ambrosia's ongoing investigation depended upon her attending Callon's private party—as reluctantly as possible. She didn't want to appear too eager and betray that she suspected Callon of murdering Cinnabar's daughter. Whether it'd been carried out by the general's own hands or through the hiring of another's didn't matter. Ambrosia needed answers, motives. Zaelix's death couldn't be the result of one or even two jealous lovers. The timing of everything was suspicious: Commander Riahn's illness and death, the Tourmaline Renegade's resurrection, and Callon's immediate interest in her and coldness after his assault. If Commander Riahn had discovered something that cost her her life, Ambrosia needed to discover the same thing without anyone knowing. She would not be intimidated. Rogues were the same everywhere: desperate, greedy. Some just dressed in ostentatious skyns and drank finer beverages.

General Callon Gault's mansion was almost as spacious and sumptuously furnished as the emperor's palace. Ambrosia narrowly dodged the services of a protrusive usher at the entrance and wandered through the east wing for half an hour before locating the ballroom. Arriving unannounced was the only way to get a self-guided tour of as much of Callon's home as she could see at her own pace. The halls and rooms were somber and moody. Dark blues predominated in the walls, floors, and furniture. The spaces lacked art with any meaning and instead abounded with old military artifacts and foreign pieces. What few paintings, sculptures, and decorative accents Ambrosia found were abstract and whimsical and exuded melancholy.

After making her observations and finding no clues, Ambrosia followed the festive sounds of the four hundred and something aristocrats and other military guests. If Callon was stirring fractiousness under Cinnabar's nose, it would betray itself in the constrained interactions between the wealthy families.

Ambrosia squeezed through a throng of aristocrats and military brass conversing in one of the ballroom's doorways. She trampled the hem of a holographic party gown, leaving tread marks on the damaged fabric that would no longer shift from emerald green to vibrant pink as the wearer moved. Another woman struggled along in a restrictive metallic costume that hobbled her knees. The stiffened fabric radiated from her body like sheets of polished metal depicting rays of light. Her headpiece was a chaotic display of prismatic fractals turning circles on coiled wires, and it seemed her whole purpose in existing was to garner compliments for herself.

That woman laughed in the face of another woman wearing a dress that looked like a broken mirror. "That was so brilliant of me, don't you think?"

The other woman smirked. "Yes, Andolith, you certainly are . . . hm, overbearingly radiant." She touched one of the reflective shards on her scant outfit and surveyed the room as if to remind everyone of a symbolism she intended her outfit to portray.

The men strutted about in ruffled, shoulder-exaggerating styles and pants so fitted around the hips and crotch as to flaunt the size and lay of their genitals. The entire ballroom was the finest display of power dressing Ambrosia had ever seen.

The ballroom itself rivaled one Ambrosia had glimpsed within the imperial palace. It was bright marble and scarlet, drenched in gold and accented with Kobalt blue. Crystalline figurines sparkled from ledges between the balconied upper floor, and the ceiling was all stained glass.

Ambrosia meandered along the outer edges of the room, her ears screening the myriad conversations. Laughter rang from pillar to pillar and glasses tinkled upon trays held aloft by servants. Candlelight cast rosy hues upon the tables set in an open adjoining room. Guests mingled around trays of hors d'oeuvres and strutted about like peacocks with fluted glasses dangling between their fingers.

Another set of doors led to a tulle-draped pergola that crowned a spacious rooftop garden. Tiny candle-laden ships bobbed around a pool edged in green tile. On the opposite side of the pool sat a covered bar, with bartenders hastening to fix drinks to order. Callon leaned against the bar, laughing and chatting with a dozen of his fawning subordinates. The moment he laid eyes on Ambrosia, his smile dissipated. He lowered his drink and excused himself. Ambrosia brushed the hem of her uniform and pushed through the sea of people, back into the ballroom.

Callon caught her elbow, and she whirled to face him.

"Commander. You came dressed to kill." He smiled, but it was hardly charming.

Was he really going to open with sarcasm? Ambrosia squinted and jerked from his grip. "I'm always on duty, General."

His smile widened. "I've noticed. Are you ever able to relax and have fun?"

She squared up with him. "Never had a good experience. I'm tough to please."

"I'm sorry to hear that. Your sables have been having a good time." He motioned toward a corner of the ballroom where several women were interacting with a group of modestly dressed men with military haircuts. The women were dressed in party skyns, but not as ridiculously as the aristocrats. The only way anyone could have known they were sables was by the style of their hair: worn up, undercut from nape to temple, with patterns etched against their scalp.

Ambrosia's annoyance toward Callon simmered. Only sables who engaged in prostitution could afford the cost of ballroom attire. Was he insinuating that her sexual restraint was unattractive to her office? That her coming in uniform was somehow distasteful while he and his officers sported decorated military outfits? Had Commander Riahn put up with this same pressure? Had her resistance to manipulation led to her death?

"I don't live for good times, General. Especially not for anyone else's pleasure."

He lowered his head. "Well, thank you for taking time out of your busy schedule to attend. Have you tried the hors d'oeuvres? The loaded oysters are my chef's best."

He was pretending to play nice now, trying to make himself less suspect of having murdered the royal heir.

"I'm sure I will before I leave." Ambrosia tempered her tone and forced a little smile.

"Already thinking of leaving?" Callon sobered and cleared his throat. "I see. Well, Ambrosia, I think we got off on the wrong foot. About what happened on the pier . . . I'm sorry we had a misunderstanding and that it upset you. And I want you to know that I meant what I said about having your back."

Ambrosia peered at him. A misunderstanding? Only that it upset her?

He stammered as his hazel eyes flashed up and down between her and his hands.

"Since we met, you've stirred something inside of me that I've never felt toward anyone else. I can tell you're not like other sables, and I respect that. You'll just have to remember that I'm a high-strung, passionate man, and you—for a moment or two—seemed receptive."

Not like other sables? Ambrosia blinked in disbelief. Was this his apology? Was he insinuating that she was more virtuous and worthy of respect than the women under her command, and yet blaming her for his own lack of self-control?

"And as much as I wish we could go back in time and do everything differently, we can't. So I'm sorry, Ambrosia, for assuming you were anything like them." He nodded in the direction of the partying sables. "And to show you how much I respect you and try to put any awkwardness behind us, I have a gift for you. I hope you won't hate me too much to accept it. Even if you can't accept my apology, the gift is custom-made for you."

Ambrosia couldn't stop herself from shaking her head in amazement. What an utterly feckless, blame-shedding apology. Assumed she was like what? A prostitute who should've felt privileged to have his favor? As if any sable had chosen to be kidnapped by state authorities and pressed into a lifetime of service with only a meager allowance to spend on things the state didn't supply them. As if a sable who took money to sleep around was any more disgusting than these aristocrats who were doing the same without any want of money—who were practically advertising themselves openly in ballrooms across the empire.

Callon bowed his head. "I know you don't want it, but please, at least have a look at it. It's just a gift, intended only to mend things back to a professional, platonic level."

Alright then, General. I'll play along. Ambrosia reasoned as her curiosity rose. At the very least, he'd made an attempt. "I'll take a look."

A smile spread through Callon's face and he backed up, beckoning with youthful enthusiasm for her to follow. They pressed their way out of the ballroom and Callon stopped a servant in the hall, asking him to bring the gift for his comrade. Then he directed Ambrosia into a smaller side room and stood by an empty fireplace, making small talk about hosting the party and the history of his home.

The servant returned, handed a soft, wrapped parcel to Callon, and left. Callon passed it to her with hope in his eyes.

"No more attending social events in uniform unless you truly want to."

Ambrosia plucked at the paper and string until a skyn of liquid silver tumbled open on the floor and shimmered. Her breathing hitched. A formal gown, as luxurious as anything the aristocrats were wearing. And not just any gown: This was the same garment the Pyron skynmaker had danced before her and her sables.

Callon raised his brow with anticipation. "Do you like it?"

Ambrosia grimaced inside and fussed with re-bundling the garment. Did Callon want her to look like she was the most expensive sable prostitute in Tourmal? Or had he bought this for her to honor her apparent respectability? Was she supposed to feel flattered and stare down her nose at all of her comrades? She was just like them. No matter their individual choices, they all suffered the same in uniform.

"It's gorgeous." She smiled up at him, feigning gratitude, determined to support her sables with a show of solidarity. She was just like all of them—the virgins, asexuals, jaded hearts, seducers, the willing and reluctant prostitutes. They were all innocent girls who had been pressed into an infamous establishment, where the only way to find healing from their shame was by owning their labels with pride.

Callon leaned on the fireplace mantel. "I hope it's not too forward. Please consider it a token of my respect for your professional record."

Respect? No. This man had none and deserved none. The supple, holographic skyn reflected rainbows of light as it moved in Ambrosia's hands. "I appreciate the gesture. Is there somewhere I can go to try it on?"

"Even if you don't wear it tonight, I'm sure you'll have another opportunity. Allow me to show you to the ladies' room."

Ambrosia pressed the garment to her chest and gauged Callon's reaction. It would be easier to blend with other guests now. If she played her part well, she'd find what she'd come for.

In the ladies' room, Ambrosia removed her duty belt and sable skyn and slipped into the formal gown. She looked into a floor-length mirror and felt transformed, like a butterfly fresh from its cocoon, like a goddess rising to take her place. She ran her hand along her waist and hips. There was not a seam to be seen or felt. It was perfect. She tugged at her bun and her hair tumbled down around her shoulders. All she needed was one shred of evidence tonight and she might have her eighth renegade. Two for one, if the Tourmaline Renegade was one of Callon's henchmen.

Ambrosia swept back into the ballroom just as the doleful timbres of the stringed table harps and golden flutes raised above the cacophony. Women drew their men toward the middle of the room, but a black-skynned character with a sallow complexion remained stationary in the shadow of a pillar with a drink in hand, watching Ambrosia. The moment Ambrosia met his gaze, he deflected and pulled back so she couldn't make out his face. His skyn had a military look about it but bore no insignia or pattern. No aristocrat would dress so simply. Ambrosia moved around the perimeter of the room, sampling hors d'oeuvres and weaving between guests who preferred not to dance. The ominous man studied her new position and shifted, raising the glass to his lips and pretending to watch the dance.

Ambrosia noted his face, rigid and so bland and generic that it could mask him in a crowd. But he almost didn't need a face. He was Callon's shadow, lop-shouldered, hunched a little to one side, and up to no good. Ambrosia circled another pillar, biting into a cracker laden with smoked fish and cheese. The stranger's pillar stood empty. The hairs on the back of Ambrosia's neck tingled as she scanned the dance floor. He couldn't have gone far. There were no doors for several yards in either direction, but there were so many guests in dark colors. Had her Tourmaline Renegade just slipped off in the crowd? She worked her way toward his last position in search of clues: a scent, a dropped item.

Callon intercepted from the sidelines. "I'm pleased you like it. It compliments you."

Ambrosia tossed hair out of her eyes. If only he knew a Pyron had made it.

She brushed her hands down her waist. "I can't get over how comfortable it is."

"Is it comfortable enough to dance with me?" he offered an imploring smile.

"Just barely." Ambrosia forced a half-smile and took his hand. For clues, she could bear the pain of dancing with him. She would dance all night if it kept him talking.

Rosy, golden baubles of light orbited tepid ellipses around Ambrosia. Garment hems swished and hissed over the floor. Her own skyn reflected every color like a mirror and shimmered like bursts of fireworks. Maroon teardrops and gold ribbing ornamented Callon's skyn, and his coat fell to the middle of his thighs. She rested her hand on his broad chest and his chiseled beard wrinkled at the corners of his smile.

"Everyone is looking," he muttered in her ear.

"Everyone?" She pulled back a little.

He furrowed his brow and shook his head, emphasizing, "*Everyone.*"

"Why?"

"I think the aristocrats envy the empress in you."

Lies. Most of the room was still dancing, and those who were staring could only be thinking the worst of her. Why would Callon want to show off his comrade? But now was not the time to throw the flattery back in his face.

Ambrosia sighed. "What a shame fate chose sablehood for me."

"But it was not fate that made you the Selenite Skynhound, and now Sable Commander of Tourmal. Fate is malleable at times, like iron in the fire. You just have to know when to strike, and where to strike it."

She massaged Callon's shoulder. "Maybe it's better to leave fate untouched. We might meddle and ruin an otherwise perfect future."

Callon squinted one eye at her and half smiled. "What do you mean?"

"You spoke of fate before the Tourmaline Renegade murdered Zaelix. Now it seems that fate found you more worthy, and moved you in line for the throne."

His gaze swept the ballroom before returning. "And I don't esteem that lightly. But Cinnabar is still young. He might choose to remarry and produce another heir."

"You've disproved your own point, Callon. You admit that fate is untouchable, unbendable, unbreakable."

"That is what fire is for. It changes everything it touches."

But who will handle the fire without getting burned? Ambrosia let a knowing smile creep into her face. Callon could have easily hired Pyrons to murder Zaelix, making promises for their freedom only to allow Cinnabar to consume himself with plans to annihilate them.

"Like Pyrons?"

Callon tossed his head and laughed with a toothy, wolfish grin. "Pyrons. That sector is a burning candle in a sealed jar. I'm hoping to begin the deportation a few days earlier as payment for the Tourmaline Renegade's little stunt in Execution Square."

"Hmm." Ambrosia reconsidered and decided to follow the flow of conversation to avoid suspicion. "It was impressive, wasn't it? You thought you had him first in line for beheading and then there he was, doing laps while your bowmen destroyed the mosaic."

Callon looked beyond her with a tolerant expression. "Our dogs' noses are rarely wrong."

"They're probably never wrong. But if you give them a wrong scent, it's a false lead, and your entire case is doomed. Sometimes it takes more than a matching scent to catch a renegade." Ambrosia studied his face for signs that the soldiers in the arena had been ordered to miss the renegade, that the Tourmaline Renegade was a puppet enemy.

Callon offered a compliment on her reputation, and the crowd dissipated back toward the sides of the room for food and drink when the dance ended. Then he politely excused himself and mingled with a few of his other guests.

Ambrosia moved from one end of the room to the other, ears tuned, eyes turning. Would Cinnabar believe a dog's nose if it pinned Callon as Zaelix's killer? If only it were that simple. There had to be something more. The hole went deeper. Someone else had pushed the imperial princess from her window. She may not find all the pieces she needed tonight, but if Callon was plotting to dethrone Cinnabar, she needed only to continue watching.

Ambrosia leaned on a pillar by the pool. The little ships bobbed and jostled against one another, casting their candle flames into the eddies all around. A well-figured young woman in a deep cherry skyn moved up on the other side of the pillar and slumped against it, tapping her wineglass with her tinted nails and grinning.

"Aww, look who's finally cut loose."

"He's not opening up," Ambrosia hissed, more to herself than Ulyia.

"Who?"

"Callon." Ambrosia spat the name.

Ulyia wrinkled her nose. "Doesn't sound like you want him to."

"I'm on duty, Ulyia. I didn't come to party."

Ulyia made a sarcastic face. "Oh! I assumed you came to clean the toilets. Where'd you get the gown?"

Ambrosia pulled a stiff breath and shot her comrade a serious look. "It's Callon's *apology* gift."

Ulyia pursed her lips and bugged her eyes.

"Don't get any ideas." Ambrosia gave the room another scan. "It was pathetic and insulting."

"Insulting?" Ulyia splayed her hands toward the dress. "That is one of the nicest designer pieces I've ever seen."

Ambrosia swished the hem and turned her shoulder to her cheek, winking. "It's Pyron-made."

"No!" Ulyia's jaw hung as she rolled the fabric between her fingers. "Is that the garment that Pyron at the first skyn factory showed us?"

"I believe so." Ambrosia shifted closer to Ulyia. "How many sables did Callon invite?"

"No idea. Neris and Serilda are here. Dian and Vyti. I came as Lieutenant Brody's guest. We're going on two weeks and he is so hot I might keep him a little longer." She pointed out a handsome young man standing around Callon and his other peers.

The men possessed the somber camaraderie of gravestones, surveying the room with forbidding reverence. The ominous stranger who had been watching Ambrosia earlier moved among them, working his way toward Callon.

Ulyia moved closer and pointed past her nose. "He's the tall, hot one, there, with the cleft chin and the bigger shoulders. See?"

All of the officers were tall, athletic, eye candy in uniform, but the tip-shouldered stranger without insignia moved through their midst and leaned on Callon's ear. His gait was distinct, like that of the man who had been shadowing Callon just before Zaelix's murder.

"Not that one. Look three over to the left." Ulyia pointed.

"I see him." Ambrosia remained fixated on the suspicious man, straining to read his and Callon's lips while Ulyia spoke of the lieutenant.

Suddenly, Ulyia's tone shifted. "You didn't tell me why the gift is insulting."

Ambrosia jerked toward her comrade, frowning. "Later."

"It's obvious the general fancies you."

"He fancies something he wants from me."

Ulyia lifted an hors d'oeuvre from a passing servant's platter. "You two have great chemistry. I watched you dance."

"It was an act on both ends."

"Hah. It wouldn't be an act for me. A dance with General Gault? Ooh–ooh–ooh." She pumped her shoulders and licked her upper lip flirtatiously.

"I can't stand a man who is used to getting everything he wants." Ambrosia pushed back around the pillar and watched Callon pat the man on the shoulder, dismissing him.

She caught Ulyia by the arm. "See that man with the short shoulder? I need you to keep your eye on him."

"I'm off duty tonight. And I'm with Brody."

"Last-minute schedule change. I want to know everything about him. Follow him. Vamp him. Get him talking."

"He's one of Callon's aides. And you match his rank better than I do. Why can't you?"

"Because he's on to me. And I've a hunch the Tourmaline Renegade is here. Quick, he's leaving. Go."

Ulyia scooted straight out across the room. The musicians struck up another song and guests eased back out onto the dance floor. Callon approached Ambrosia and asked for her hand once more. She accepted and swept along in his arms, an admiring smile plastered to her face and one eye on Ulyia. The room turned circles until Ulyia and the officer disappeared in the sea of people.

Callon leaned in, blasting warm breath on Ambrosia's neck.

"Looking for someone?"

"Just taking it all in. The fashion. The architecture."

Callon's gaze swaggered out through the floor. "You actually seem to be enjoying yourself for once."

Ambrosia rolled back a tense smile. "It's a nice party, and so far, a pleasant evening."

"Because you found what you came for?"

Her eyes dropped off his shoulder. Did he mean himself?

His eyes radiated passion as he tucked a strand of hair back from her face. "Mind if I tell you why you came tonight?" He leaned in close to her ear, dropping every half-whispered, ruthless word with hacked cadence. "You think you're going to find evidence that I murdered Cinnabar's royal little tart. But I'll advise you to watch your step. You're one move from checkmate."

Ambrosia's gaze cemented to the ballroom floor. The spaces in the tiles glared underfoot. Icy shocks rocked through her spine and into her toes. She forced her head up and locked eyes with Callon.

"You're mad."

A marauding smile creeped behind cold eyes. "But I'm not wrong."

They stumbled together as the hem of her skyn caught under his foot, and Callon drew her tight against his muscular chest.

"You'll never be able to bring me down without hanging yourself. I will not only prove you wrong on every charge you bring against me, but I will prove you guilty. And you know what sables get for treason."

"Do not underestimate me, General." She wrestled from his grasp and marched out of the ballroom, quivering from head to toe.

His threats were far from idle. He knew. She glanced down at her dress and a sick feeling swept over her. The apology, the gift, his every word to her since she'd arrived—he'd known. And every second more she spent in this dress, she continued to play his game, dance to his will like a marionette.

Ambrosia rushed to the ladies' room and reached inside the wardrobe where she'd left her uniform, pushing aside skyns on hangers. Gone. Her breath turned to a sponge in her throat. She turned circles, scanning shelves and vanity tops. She tore back through the wardrobe, going over each garment carefully. Her dread mounted and her heart raced, knowing it was gone—knowing, to a degree, why it was gone. Only her duty belt remained where she'd left it. She growled and scrunched her fists in her hair, heat flushing through her, wanting to rip Callon's throat out, feeling cornered, afraid. What if she'd already taken the bait, eaten the poison? She'd be dead soon, just like Commander Riahn. She crossed an arm over her stomach, put the back of her hand to her forehead and did a quick assessment of how she was feeling. More irate than faint. She coached herself to breathe until she felt a little more composed.

After a while, Ambrosia stepped out of the ladies' room clutching her duty belt. Callon leaned inches from the door, hands folded.

"Looking for something, Commander?"

Her upper lip curled. "You know what I'm looking for. Where is it?"

He smirked. "Wouldn't it be right where you left it? In my bedroom?"

A hundred filthy names for Callon boiled through Ambrosia's mind.

"What is this dirty game you're playing, General? What is your obsession with proving I'm promiscuous? And who should care? My uniform proves nothing."

He smiled and shrugged.

"What do you want?" She could not check her biting tone.

He pushed off the wall. "Your compliance. The pieces of evidence I have against you are my little tokens of . . . security, assurance that you will behave yourself while I wield my own fate."

Anger made her vision pop and crackle with strands of darkness.

"Evidence of *what* exactly?"

His smile turned cold and predatory. "Any crime I need you to be guilty of. Treason would look good on you."

She looked away, heart hammering, jaw clenching, fists pumping around her duty belt. Was she one move from being put in checkmate, or checkmating him? Either way, she still had one move to make. He might not have her cornered. There might be a way out of his trap, a way to spring it on him instead.

"Go on," he said with a sardonic smile. "Tell the Sable Queen. Tell Cinnabar."

Her gaze snapped back to Callon, and she wanted to spit. He was going to seize the Kobalt throne, and she could do nothing. He had muzzled the Skynhound with a diamond-studded cloth.

She pushed past him and stormed down the hall, the silvery hems of the dress popping like lightning in her wake. There was no defense for a sable accused of treason, no lawyer who might intercede for her. The martial court was loaded with Callon's minions, and if Cinnabar even knew his danger, he could only turn to his sables. Did the Sable Queen support Callon instead of Cinnabar? And if so, why had she summoned Ambrosia to Tourmal at all?

Ambrosia passed a group of sables standing in one of the ballroom's doorways. They gazed at her in collective silence, as if they knew. How many of them were compromised, either by fear or by choice? Could she even trust Ulyia, or Phaedra? Or was she alone?

Was the push to have Pyron contained in that sector intended to create a smoother usurpation of power? Was the Tourmaline Renegade a red herring, a cog in Callon's coup? A thousand more questions haunted Ambrosia.

She stumbled out into the visitor's lot and fell upon her corecycle. The gown glittered like a silver waterfall around her. What an irony that her shackles had been spun by the hands of a condemned man, a Pyron. Once Callon held the throne, he would never trust her to protect his life as she was supposed to protect Cinnabar's. She was nothing more than a pawn in his hand. Disposable, like Sable Commander Riahn.

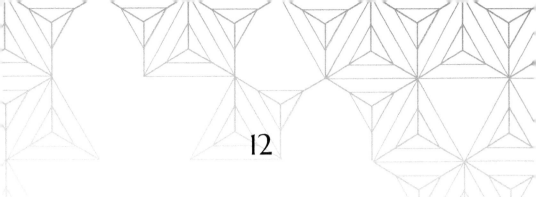

12

Reem trundled into Disrel's work area, puffing, face like a tomato. He'd never looked so angry.

"Up! You need to leave right now. They're searching the factory."

Disrel stumbled from his chair under Reem's hands. "What? Who?"

"General Gault mandated that Tourmal be Pyron-free by the end of the week. They're rounding you all up and taking you by train to that slaughter yard."

"What about Kommett?"

"I can manage that boy." Reem stuffed a chip into Disrel's palm. "Put this on, get your helmet, and go straight out the back door." He clutched Disrel's hand and shook it, a mist hanging in his usually lucid eyes. "I'm sorry. I had to destroy your paycheck and records. But I hope this makes up for it, your key to freedom. I'll miss you terribly. And good luck, young man."

The sinister, damnatory rhythm of combat boots droned through the halls. Disrel pressed the chip into his skyn and bolted for the back door. His white garment morphed into deep blue with creamy blades accenting his torso and legs. He had never imagined Reem was capable of something so illegal. Kommett's accusations could send Reem to prison for life.

Disrel pushed his helmet onto his head and plowed from the building. The air flushed with early morning rays, and flower petals showered from budding trees. Military corecycles rolled through the business park, the heavier tricorecycles towing enclosed metal wagons. Soldiers stood about hugging compact crossbows to their breastplates, ready for an organized sweep, street by street, building by building. Disrel threw his leg over his corecycle and pushed out. His chest constricted with the mounting tension. If he was caught wearing anything other than the white Pyron skyn the law required, he could be executed where he stood, without trial, without plea. He pulled out onto the access road and cruised by the convoy, giving the soldiers a nod. It was unusual for an employee to be leaving at the start of the day, but all he needed was a head start. He paused at a junction for an opportunity to move out into traffic. Corecycle after corecycle blew by, too narrowly spaced to risk it. Lights flashed in Disrel's mirrors, and his heart beat a ragtime. Two military corecycles pulled up behind him.

"Not today." Disrel squeezed the bike with his legs and propelled into traffic.

Horns blared, wheels screeched, and three riders skidded off the road and tumbled from their bikes. The chaos in his wake was perfect. He weaved furiously and took to the shoulder when a lane became impassable, cobalt light strobing in his mirrors. But the chase was still young. He trained his eyes on the road and carved his way around the long merchant wagons, using them for cover and forcing the drivers to hit their brakes and jam traffic. The military corecycles zoomed up on his left and the closest soldier aimed his crossbow. Disrel whipped right, cutting off four traffic lanes and catching the offramp to the intersector highway while the military corecycles continued helplessly along the overpass. He pulled a deep breath and pressed on. He had to get to Mored. Tourmal was Pyron's last stand. If every Pyron was forced behind walls, there would be no resistance, no hope.

Once across the Selenite line, he merged onto the coarse road to the abandoned subway station and slowed. It was a constant struggle not to drive at the speed of his thumping heart, but he couldn't afford to draw the attention of the military police again.

A corecycle rushed up on his right and the rider grabbed for his keystone. Disrel kicked and swerved left, smashing into another military bike. The vehicles slid into the curb as one grinding pile of metal, and he tumbled down the sidewalk.

"Thunder!" he exclaimed. Why hadn't he seen them overtaking him?

As the two soldiers pushed out from under their bikes, Disrel scrambled to his feet and tore down a side street. Their footsteps pounded behind him, their shouts and curses echoing between the buildings. One set of boots halted and gear clanked, signaling the retrieval of a semi-automatic crossbow from its sling. Disrel caught a corner and swung into an alley. A metal construction fence bottlenecked the corridor and he collided with several workers. A paving machine squatted directly in the way, feeding a grooved slab from its mouth into the street. Disrel seized a handlebar on the side of the paver and vaulted onto the rolling slab, but the slab slammed down from the gaping mouth, sending him stumbling headlong over another construction fence and down into a black pit. He slapped down into a bed of mud and standing water, which rushed back from the walls of the street drain and washed over him, trickling into his helmet. He spat and clambered up on loose knees, hugging the concrete walls of his prison and watching the square of light high above. Murky water sloshed around his legs. Voices reverberated like stricken gongs. *Thunder.* He'd not only wrecked Mored's corecycle, but he'd trapped himself in a storm drain.

Two military helmets glistened in the sunlight above. Disrel wedged deeper into the corner and clutched a hand to his chest to silence his heartbeat. A breeze passed over his wet body. He inched farther into the darkness and the wall opened up. His fingers groped the smooth lip of a round pipe and he scraped himself along its curved edge while the voices of the men above continued in debate over ladders and lights. He had to keep moving, find another way out. He scootched along the pipe for some distance. It was impossible to tell how far. The stifling darkness was a serpentine universe. He crouched down on all fours and raised his helmet visor. His breaths hummed in the dark around him, and a moaning returned to his ears in the sifting air. Perhaps it was the sound of vehicles on the road above. There had to be another opening nearby.

A hissing, scurrying sound echoed. Rats. Disrel shuddered and pulled his hands back to himself. There was no way to pinpoint the direction of any sound or the number of sources. One sound became a hundred, and the hundred became a thousand. The space opened into a square with pipes branching off each side. He chose one and shuffled on, crouching, groping up and out with each step. A faint light glowed in the distance. He pressed toward it, and it disappeared, leaving him disoriented and uneasy. His neck crawled. Steps echoed parallel to his own. He paused. Something large scraped by on his right and water rippled around his shoes. Disrel pressed his spine into the curve of the pipe. It was foolish to ask if anyone was there. *Something* was there, and it knew where he was. He clenched a fist.

A leathery arm lassoed his neck and dragged him to his back, choking his cry in his throat. He bucked and writhed, twisting under the iron noose and sucking a breath.

"Oh, gohel!"

Water sloshed in the pipe's trough as he struggled. His attacker's legs wrapped his stomach and the vise around his throat clamped his airway shut. Disrel's lungs burned and the air around his head boiled with colors. He had only seconds before he would pass out, and everything Tygo had taught him was failing him now. Was this one of the military police who had descended through a nearby drain and caught him? Disrel resorted to clawing desperately at the chokehold as his hands turned to putty. His fingernails scraped the familiar textures of fabric, and then his arms tumbled down into the chilling water, and the clenching noose faded away.

In the next instant, a grinding scuffling raged through the air. Disrel gathered his senses and immediately remembered the events leading up to this dark moment. He tugged his aching wrists, but they were pinned together behind him by a flexible band. His helmet was gone. The air was rusty, pungent. It was still black, mostly. A shocking whiteness speared his eyes, shattering his night vision, and his own angry cry snarled back from the concrete surfaces. He lowered his head against the light until it moved away from his face. Pyron words tumbled from behind it.

"What are you doing down here, son of Pyron?" The voice was grim and smoky.

Disrel hesitated, waiting for his eyes to readjust so he could make out who had spoken. "I fell into an open storm drain back there. Just trying to find my way back up."

"How could you just fall in? The Kobs are working on it."

"I was being chased by soldiers. They're rounding us up in Tourmal and shipping us out by train. I've got somewhere to be and I'm no threat to you, so you can take these cuffs off and show me the way out."

"You're lucky you spoke out when you did." The light raised and flicked down the pipe. "By your skyn, I thought you were one of them."

Disrel glared at the figure towering behind the light. "And what if I was?"

"You'd be dead." The pipe echoed with the force of that last word.

Disrel weighed his next words. This Pyron had no reservations about murdering Kobalt people. He might have no trouble killing any Pyron who disagreed with his actions.

"Well, it's a relief to run into a brother in such desperate times. Will you please uncuff me and show me out?"

"The only way out is through our leader."

"I'm already part of a resistance group."

"Kobalt leader?"

Disrel squinted. "The group lets me work independently." And they're not so coercive, he wanted to add.

"Who leads the group?"

"I don't know. It's very compartmentalized."

"Pyrons must lead Pyrons. Any Kobalt who says he fights for Pyron has something in it for himself. He'll use you as his pawn, use your pain to gain power. You will come with me."

Disrel clamped down on his tongue and strained against the cuffs, putting Tygo's lessons into practice, but his wrists chafed with little success. "Alright, then. Let's not waste any more time, shall we? You first? Or me? Whichever."

The light moved forward and a hand picked him up and led him along.

Disrel eyed the shadowy Pyron that held him. "What's your name?"

"You don't need to know that."

"Oh? Why haven't you asked my name?"

"Because I already know it. Now shut up."

Disrel bit his tongue and wondered. They passed a street access and turned at an intersection, which Disrel marked. He stumbled here and there, until the man's reactions became less heightened, and with each stumble, he rotated his wrists, working a thumb free and finally slipping one hand free of the ropes. He thanked Tygo inwardly and held his hands together. At the next junction, he erupted, seizing the man's light-wielding arm, swinging at his head, and striking into the back of his knees. The pipe thundered with a roar and the man tumbled to the ground. Disrel knelt on him, jerked the cloth mask off the stranger's lower face, and turned the light down onto him.

"Normally, I'd apologize for having to go back on my word. But anyone who would take me anywhere in cuffs doesn't get that courtesy." He smashed his elbows across the man's face, sprang up, and rushed through the pipe with the light flashing before him.

A blade rang from its scabbard, and Disrel sprinted harder. He turned off through an angled pipe that went on forever, but it was dry, and the light scorched a fissure in the bottom, filled with knurled roots and just wide enough to step right over. His shoes ground to the edge and he turned the light down. It struck rails. A subway tunnel. He had a fifty-fifty chance of following that rail straight to Mored. He clamped the light between his teeth and lowered himself down, clutching roots and broken stone. His feet dangled, and he kicked in the darkness, seeking a toehold. It seemed he might drop into an endless abyss. All of his being wanted to climb up, not down into hell. But down was the only way to escape his tormentors above.

Disrel tucked his chin hard to his chest and aimed the light down. Solid ground seemed just within reach. He took the light from his mouth, braced himself, and dropped.

Shocks blistered his ankles and shins. His lungs seized and the smell of blood filled his nose as the light tumbled from his hand and clattered over the tile. His own groan startled him to rise and fight. He scrambled on hands and knees for the light and searched for the fissure above. It was a farther drop than he had realized, one he would have never attempted if he had known. It had been impossible to anticipate the roll in a blind jump. He shined the light along the rail and all around the tunnel. He was so close to help, too close to come across a split in the tunnel. He would walk a mile or two, counting grooves in the rail, and if he had not yet reached the old Selenite station, he would turn back. Disrel climbed up the incline, set his hand upon the stone conduit, and began his trek.

A ghostly ambience of dripping water, moaning reverberations, and phantom breezes filled the tunnel. The rising hum seemed only a haunting imagination until the rail itself buzzed with energy and emitted a soft glow. Disrel released it and tripped his way down to the outer wall, tucking the light under his arm so he could not be seen. A light appeared in the distance and rushed along the rail. He recognized the rail runner and its orange-skynned rider and signaled with his flashlight.

"Alta! It's Disrel."

The vehicle slowed to a stop. "Disrel? What are you doing all the way out here?"

"I'm trying to get to Mored. We need help. They're loading the trains in Tourmal and if we don't stop them—"

"Get up here. I'm heading there now."

He clamored up the rail and onto the back of the vehicle. They rushed onward and pulled into the station less than a minute later. He had been heading the wrong direction.

Disrel grabbed the sacks of groceries and followed Alta through the station's halls and down into the auxiliary rooms she and Mored called home.

"You've got some strange guys lurking around out there."

"Our sentries?"

"I don't know. Would they bring me in cuffs to Mored just for wandering down in a storm drain?"

Alta frowned. "How many did you see?"

"Just one. And whoever he was almost killed me without question."

She paused and looked upset. "I'll have a talk with Tygo."

Disrel set the sacks on the kitchen table and marched straight into Mored's study, where he pleaded his case.

Mored scribbled in a notebook, never once glancing up. "So, what are you going to do about it?"

"I came to you for help."

"Aren't you the Tourmaline Renegade?"

"Well, yes. But... weren't you? Surely you had help from time to time."

"What would you do if Tygo had never found you? I can't see you boarding the train with the rest of them."

Disrel's face burned as he turned away, scratching the back of his head. "I can't stop a train by myself. And you seem to have enough henchmen haunting these tunnels. Why can't you send them to stop the deportation, blow up the rail or something?"

Mored shrugged and scribbled on. "We've fought for years to stop this war on your people, to stop it from coming to this. And it's clear we're failing. Damaging the rail is a brilliant idea. Maybe the Tourmaline Renegade should get the credit for that one."

Disrel turned circles before Mored's armchair, rubbing his jaw. "Well, if you and your army are failing, how am I supposed to succeed?"

"What makes you think you'll fail?" Mored's gray eyes lit on him and twinkled.

Disrel avoided eye contact, remembering when he'd cast that sentiment at Mored on their first meeting. He'd been willing to fight and risk his life without training then. Why was he doubting himself now?

"I'm not your mentor." Mored returned to his scribbling. "I'm a dead legend. Remember that: dead. Your people are counting on you now. And so am I."

Disrel sighed. "Well, I need a new helmet."

"You know where we keep them."

"And a new corecycle."

Mored's gaze seized him once more.

"I'm sorry, I—" Disrel wiped a finger down his nose. "I wrecked it evading soldiers."

"Hmm." Mored laid his pen down and his brow furrowed. "Have you given much thought to the certainty that, sooner or later, you will have to take lives to save lives?"

"I can't not think about it. Tygo is training me for it, but I hope I never have to."

"And if you only wound them, won't they see you as weak and ineffective? Will you hold one soldier at knifepoint and expect the others to drop their weapons? Isn't wounding just as immoral as killing if the injury is permanently crippling? The gruesome reality of struggles like this one is that you will find yourself in situations where it's your life or another's. And then, like a god, you will snuff out a life and live every day after having to tell yourself that you did the right thing."

He wrestled with imaginations of what it might be like to kill a man. Even one death would class him as a terrorist of the state.

"What about killing a woman?"

Disrel raked his neck. "Why would I ever have to do that?"

"You've never heard of sables?" Mored laced his fingers. "Too many men like to pretend they could never be defeated by a woman. But sables aren't just women. They're engineered in mind and body for a lifetime of killing. They don't fall back for hostages. And the Selenite Skynhound has one job: to bring your head to her emperor, attached or unattached."

Disrel met Mored's gaze evenly. "I'd have no problem killing a sable."

Mored laughed and reached for an old news pamphlet. "How do you think she earned the name Skynhound?" He flipped through the pages, then stopped and turned it around, tapping a photograph. "Here she is. One of Cinnabar's renegade-catching machines. Isn't she just beautiful? Hm! Just look at those eyes and that hair."

Disrel bunched his lips and frowned. "I'm not afraid of her."

"You ought to be. Pity her one second too long, and she'll castrate you before you hit the ground and braid your skyn into her belt. She won't hesitate to cut your throat because she thinks you're cute."

"I get it. Don't worry. I won't get sidetracked." Disrel moved to a large map framed on the wall and folded his arms.

Mored closed the pamphlet. "If you destroy the rail in a remote area, it could take more than a month to repair."

Disrel traced the railway with his index finger. "If I hijack the train halfway out, I can release the people into the suburbs. You said you have a network of civilians who can house them?"

"Some of them. And not permanently. But we can give them chips, cards, and disguises to help them hide in plain sight."

"Can you have your men leave me a few getaway vehicles along the railway?"

Mored nodded.

"I'll create a diversion at the station, board the train just as it's leaving, and stop it halfway to Pyron." Disrel's hand fell from the map. "And then pray that I make it out alive."

The train spanned the Tourmal station platform like a bloated python. Disrel squatted in the crook of a roofing brace and gazed through his darkened helmet visor upon the chaos below. Pyrons funneled like sheep toward the cars under the goading polearms of soldiers. Mothers pressed their wailing children to their bodies. Every dark eye watched with dread and heads bent with sorrow. A group of men railed as one against the soldiers and were promptly shot for their efforts. A young woman ran forward and fainted upon one of the executed and had to be dragged bodily to the train. Her limp hands streaked the platform with his blood.

Disrel glanced at the station's clock tower. The soldiers were behind schedule and had another train to load after this one. A toddler tottered circles in an open area, hands outstretched, mouth twisted, tears washing paths down its soiled cheeks. A soldier grabbed the child's braid, lifted him from the ground, and hauled him toward the car as though he were a suitcase. The child's screams echoed off the glass ceilings and mingled with the pandemonium. A lithe sable whirled from her line of passengers and intercepted the soldier, twisting his free arm into an awkward position. The soldier submitted, fear and pain glazing his eyes, and the sable bowed over him and screamed into his face.

"Unnecessary use of force, soldier! Can you not handle a child?"

"He should have stayed with his mother!"

"You should have been watching your line!" She carved the toddler from his grasp.

The soldier backed away, flexing his arm and scowling. Another time, his face sneered.

The sable set the child on her hip and brushed its hair from its eyes. She pressed it to her breastplate and smudged the tears while her lips moved with consolation, then carried it over to the open car where the arms of many women gladly received him. She set her empty hands on her hips and surveyed the bustling platform with strained, weary eyes. After a moment, she hustled straight for the adjacent line and paused it for a tottering elder, giving the people time to lift him and his bags into the car.

Disrel leaned back on his perch and studied her. A sable showing compassion, to Pyrons, no less? This was a strange thing. Who was this anomaly?

Two more trains waited in the station yard, destined to leave in the hours following. The soldiers halted the lines and closed the doors, sealing them one by one with padlocks. Four soldiers mounted the engine car, clinging to its sides like schoolboys, with bolt-clips and crossbows strapped across their backs. Divided families screamed to each other from the platform and car windows, determined to reconnect at their destination.

Disrel pulled three grenades from a pouch on his belt, plucked the pins, and hurled them through the terminal. Flashes of light blistered the interior of the station and thunderings pounded the glass ceiling. Smoke fountained where each grenade had landed, drawing the soldiers in multiple directions while people screamed and pushed and broke the lines. Disrel slid down the pole and sprinted across the platform with the moving train. He darted around people and shoved others aside, unnoticed in the madness as he caught the side of a car, leaped into the gangway, and crouched, catching his breath while the station faded into the past.

The rail hissed under the car connector. Twenty cars. Two hundred miles. Less than one hour to take control. He clung to a handlebar, watching the ground rush beneath the gangway like a hissing, raging river of death. He tightened the cuffs on his gloves and patted his gear. Sunlight strobed through the flying treetops, and the liddicoatite on his chest flashed. Thelis. That mysterious force that wanted to express itself by pressing into every human fiber. It had called him to this. Disrel plucked a hatchet and crowbar from his thigh and battered the lock on the carriage door. The jostling of the cars rattled the crowbar's teeth off the pressure point. Seven strokes and the bolt loosened. Five more and the seal exploded with a shower of sparks. Disrel hooked the ax head into the door and forced it open. A hundred terrified faces gawked from the dingy interior. Children screamed and clutched their parents. Those nearest the door pressed back.

One of the men shouted: "Who are you? What are you doing?"

Disrel strode down the aisle. "When I stop the train, run as far and as fast as you can. There are people in the communities who will help you hide."

"And when we're caught, we'll be butchered on the spot." A thick-browed man pointed his finger vindictively at Disrel's chest. "You're the reason we're even on this train!"

"Then stay aboard and let them give you a red ribbon for your loyalty to the state. I'm here for the ones who are being taken against their will." He pushed to the other end of the car. "You are Pyron's last stand. Don't go like sheep to slaughter."

Children hugged their parents' necks and gawked at him. Mothers whispered encouraging words into their babes' ears, and fathers postured like a fighting spirit was stirring within them.

Disrel worked the door open several inches and struck at the padlock on the outside until it flew apart. He proceeded into the gangway and destroyed the lock on the next car. The reaction from each car of passengers was the same: shock, awe, and a few angry men.

"Are you Pyron?" some asked. "Or are you Kobalt?"

"Why are you hiding? Show us your face."

"He's probably deformed or scarred."

"You're a traitor Kobalt, aren't you?"

"No. He's biracial. He's got to protect his identity."

"A few good deeds won't save his soul."

Disrel moved swiftly, breaking through the doors that barred him from the engine car where his greatest challenge waited. These hundreds of desperate, homeless people were counting on him to stop the train, but the soldiers would hear him smashing through the last lock. He turned to the people.

"Alright, first class! Are you ready to help me stop this train and run to freedom? I want children under the tables and seats. Women in the back. Able-bodied men and boys at the front. Let's go!"

The people shuffled through the car like the pieces of a chaotic slider puzzler. Disrel stood to the side of the door, hatchet in hand, knife at the ready. His heartbeat drummed in his ears. This could be the moment where he would have to take a life, even four lives, to save hundreds. He scanned the car, watching the people squeezing up and down the aisle. Children hunkered under the seats, their gleaming eyes turned up with hope upon him, the Tourmaline Renegade. This was Pyron's future. They alone were worth any cost.

"I want you all to shake this car until they open the door. Let's make some noise, Pyron." Disrel stepped away from the door and shook himself.

The car erupted with frenzied shouts and pitched shrieks. Some threw themselves against the walls, rocking the carriage on the rail. In less than a minute, the car door rolled open.

Disrel thrust the ax head out, bludgeoning a soldier's jaw. He seized the man by the vest and jerked him down the aisle, laying him across the feet of the men. The second soldier raised his crossbow. Disrel smashed the ax across it and the bolt ricocheted off the outside of the car. He hooked the bow with the ax head and slung it from the train. The soldiers fell back into the engine car, but Disrel raged through the gangway, driving blows and dealing kicks. The moment the second soldier fell, Disrel tossed a flash grenade and pulled the engine car's door shut. Two bolts thundered against the steel, followed by panicked cries and a deafening explosion. The train lurched and Disrel slammed into the door and fell to his knees, inches from the edge of the gangway. He rolled the door and plunged into the smoke, remembering his training for tight spaces.

He moved like an animal, slamming the soldiers into the walls, crossbows clattering to the floor. Disrel snared a neck and shoulder with his legs and cranked another's head forward in a brutal headlock. The third soldier stumbled and heaved in the dark cloud. The driver crawled under the smoke canopy, a short blade in hand. The moment Disrel's triangle-choke victim went lax, he released and twisted, kicking the blade from the driver's hand and dealing a terrible kick to his face. The driver collapsed. Disrel dropped the other soldier from his choke and punched his exposed throat for good measure. He rose, moved to the control panel, pushed the drive lever into neutral, and mashed the emergency brake. The train's deceleration threw him across the control panel and sent him sliding to his knees. The men rolled down the aisle and collected in a groaning heap. Disrel whipped the keystone from the panel and stuffed it into his pocket before rifling weapons from the soldiers and punishing them for resistance.

The driver's eyes liquefied as Disrel advanced. "Please! I have a family."

"So does everyone else on this train." His voice was disembodied, savage, foreign to his own ears. He shook with rage, a little from fear. "Turn around and put your hands behind your heads. Quickly."

The four officers obeyed, but a weight wrapped around Disrel's throat, pulling him back and cranking his chin up. Disrel squatted and twisted, dropping the soldier over his shoulder into the gangway. Already the other three were up, scrambling down the length of the engine car for the pile of weapons. Disrel torqued the fallen soldier's arm and smashed his ax down into the helmet visor.

"Back! All of you!"

They immediately reversed.

"Up!" Disrel forced the soldier into the car. "If even one of you moves from this car, you're all dead men." He tossed the weapons out into the gangway, pulled the door shut, and wedged several crossbolts into the jam. Engine car doors were not made to lock from the outside, but it would hold for a little while. Fear might hold them there longer. Prisoners poured from the first four cars into the grassy acres on either side of the rail. There were still seventeen cars to open. Disrel marched down through the empty cars and wailed on the locks of the unsealed carriages. The people trembled as the doors rolled back.

"Run! Go, go, go!" Disrel rushed them from the cars, counting on the young and strong to carry the feeble and elderly with them.

None dared to question him, and he moved on, swinging the dented hatchet. The second train would be whistling down the track all too soon. Worse, if the stationmaster realized the line was blocked, forces would be dispatched. Car after car fell open, and Pyrons streamed for the woods. As soon as he opened the last car, Disrel raced like an arrow back through the line to the engine.

He glanced up at the sky. Five black crosses dotted the horizon in formation. QAV-Xs. Craft that could hover and maneuver tight spaces with ease. Their bodies and wings doubled as landing gear, and each wing held a circular turbine that tilted by degrees. The stabilizing tail wings gave them a signature, threatening silhouette—one that assured renegades they would soon be crossed off the wanted list. Disrel noted that these were the heavier QAV-X5s, built for carrying a pilot and four military units, unlike the QAV-X3s which held a pilot and two snipers. He leaped to the ground, sprinted to the front of the engine, pulled a compact explosive from his belt, and planted it on the rail. He wound the key tight, delaying detonation, and jerked the pin. The QAV-Xs soared a wide circle around the train, their mounted riders leaning over the sides to survey the situation.

Disrel sprinted for the woods. It wasn't enough to make it into the tree line; he needed to locate his getaway vehicle. The tall grass hissed and zipped around his pounding legs, his arms pumped and his breathing rasped his ears. Thunder shook the ground, throwing him forward. He tumbled down and rolled. A thick shadow fell across him and the grass swirled in a cyclone under the QAV-X's energy. The machine settled low overhead, preparing to drop its passengers. A dozen yards remained. Disrel crawled through the grasses, sprang up, and plunged onward, glancing back to see the damage to the rail.

A lithe figure sailed down toward him on a rope, crimson boots poised for a crushing blow. He hurled off course, tumbling back down into the grass and shooting up again a few yards later. The sable's boots struck the earth and never missed a beat. She pursued fast and hard, like a leopard locked on to a stag, devouring the distance with ease. Strands of fire licked from the edges of her helmet.

Disrel threw himself headlong into the wood and drew his blade. He leaped over a fallen tree and turned to face her, bouncing lightly on his feet, weapon held high, but her boot connected with his head, throwing him into the base of a tree. A chilling numbness engulfed his chest on impact. His lungs seemed to crystallize and shatter. Two sables swung back and forth like pendulums, colliding and passing repeatedly until they condensed into one bristling tower of black and crimson.

"Huh." Her blade rang from its scabbard. "I thought you'd be a little taller, more muscular."

Disrel gasped a lungful of air. Her ruthless eyes bit into him, searching the visor for a face. It was the commander. The Selenite Skynhound. She pounced and slashed. He smacked his heel into her visor and rolled away from the tree, scrambling up and darting off through the brush.

"Cowards are always easy prey." Her brassy tone rasped a little. The laugh before the kill. The lust for renegade blood. Her footfalls menaced, dissonant like an executioner's drum.

Disrel tore left and right through the brush. He couldn't find the corecycle with her nipping at his heels, and sooner or later she would draw a ranged weapon and take a shot. He planted his feet, skidding in the leaves and pointing his knife at her throat.

"Don't judge me too quickly, Sable."

She gazed right through the webs in her visor, right past his steel, and her lips pulled back over gleaming teeth. She knocked his arm aside and delivered a solid kick to his ribs. He doubled back, and she slashed at his chest. He took another backward step as she closed in, sweeping his leg out from under him and dropping him to the ground. She flew down on top of him, knees pinning his waist, blade diving for his neck. He diverted the blow into the soft earth and caught her wrist.

Her snarl twisted into a bitter smile, and her feral eyes probed his visor. "Your kind usually aren't this difficult to kill. But I like a challenge."

They grappled for a moment, neither one able to overpower the other.

She huffed, "Who are you?"

Disrel struggled for control of her blade. "Wouldn't you like to know?"

She gave the base of his helmet a fierce tug. "I'd love to see what you've got—"

Disrel knocked into her elbows and rolled her, pinning her underneath him. "Let's slow down, get to know each other better."

He wrestled the blade from her grip, delivered a blunt stroke to the side of her neck, and sprang free. Soldiers hacked their way through the brush in search of prisoners as the dark QAV-Xs hummed over the canopy. Disrel sprinted on, scanning the terrain for the vehicle, whispering prayers of desperate need. He was close, but so were his enemies. In a small clearing, three troopers descended on ropes, blocking his escape. He turned toward a rocky impasse where boulders sloughed from a broken hillside. There, partially concealed in a bush between the boulders, sat a black corecycle. The troopers closed in from the right, raising their crossbows, and the sable was up again and running. A bolt hissed over his shoulder. Disrel bounded up the rocks and bolts pelted the stones at his heels, spraying shards and sparks. He lunged and landed astride the seat. The bike bounced and jerked on its shocks as he thrust the keystone in, pushed off with his feet, and opened the throttle. The bike's back wheel ate the soil and slid sideways before gaining traction.

The sable towered on the rocks and took aim with her bow. Disrel weaved left and right among the trees. *Thwack.* Her bolt glanced off his helmet.

13

Cinnabar turned from Ambrosia and glared into the aquarium that served as a partitioning wall in the study. A piebald shark moseyed along the glass, then darted away from the emperor's gaze.

Ambrosia clenched her jaw and squeezed her fists against her legs. He seemed to be handling the news better than she'd expected. Or was his reticence her worst nightmare? Leaders who railed on incompetence were predictable, readable. The ones who listened and brooded in silence were to be feared. Part of her expected him to hurl his glass of alcohol into the side of the aquarium.

But he scratched at his sideburns and sighed. "How is my Skynhound bested by a combative Pyron in a costume?"

"He's tough. But he's no legend. My mistake was trying to remove his helmet, hoping to learn his identity and bring him to you alive. I am positive I will have him next time."

Cinnabar raised his drink to his lips and stared over the rim. The fish in the tank were mesmerizing to watch, but he seemed to be looking beyond them. He lowered the drink and swirled it, gazing down at the deep red liquid.

"What he did today delayed the deportation of Pyrons by a month or more, so I'll be hosting games at Execution Square to free up room in our prisons and to instill fear into treacherous minds. It's times like these that bring renegades out of the royal woodwork." His eyes darkened, and he ran his finger around the rim of his drink until it sang. "We're long overdue for a court execution. Rooting out just one renegade from within my palace would dispel all other treacherous fantasies."

"My honor as a sable is to keep you safe, Supremacy. But Tourmal's affairs have proved more intricate than anything I've ever dealt with before."

"Are you confessing incompetence, Commander?" He turned and gave her an analytical stare.

"No, sir. But men who wield power don't move as carelessly as street insurgents. Another traitor may be lurking in your court, and until I can present more certain evidence, may I and my sables guard you more closely?"

"Who do you suspect?"

Ambrosia hesitated, remembering Callon's warning. It was best to let Cinnabar be the one to make the accusation.

"It is my duty to suspect anyone in line for the throne."

Cinnabar sat down in an armchair and rubbed his face. "I've had little time to consider this since my daughter's death. But General Gault is a very scrupulous and upstanding man. He is my right arm and I've never sensed any resentment in his presence."

"With respect to Your Supremacy, things are not always as they seem on the surface."

Cinnabar leaned back and watched her. "And what way do they seem underneath the surface, Commander?"

Ambrosia's heart drummed as she wiped her slick palms against her legs. "They seem to have preceded my service in Tourmal, sir. Both Commander Riahn's death and the Tourmaline Renegade's appearance may be connected. I only began to suspect it when I marked a familiar cologne lingering in Her Imperial Highness's chamber prior to her murder."

Cinnabar looked as though a rotting stench had passed under his nose.

Ambrosia squeezed her hands to keep herself from shaking. "I didn't mention it sooner because the odor dissipated, and contrary physical evidence was presented."

Cinnabar downed his drink and set it aside. His fingers drummed the armrest of his chair and he wiped his chin. "Do you realize how serious such an accusation is, Commander? Dare you defame my daughter's honor with such flaccid evidence? Would you prove she had a consensual affair with a Pyron right under my nose while simultaneously lending herself to my general?"

Her gaze fluttered over the floor as she wrapped her hands together, bowing slightly. "I apologize, Supremacy. I realize that until we find the traitor, all deductions will appear to cast a shadow on Her Imperial Highness's name. But if time is any tool in the hand of fate, the truth will honor and vindicate your daughter, while preserving your own life. Until then, please allow my sables to stand by you more closely."

Cinnabar pondered her words. "I'll allow it. Just be careful, Commander. I won't tolerate false accusations or slander against my dead child. You cannot understand the pain of such loss."

An unaccepted truth had the potential to hurt worse than any lie. If Cinnabar could only understand what his daughter had done, his eyes would be opened to who his general truly was. Ambrosia bowed from his presence, stomach quivering, joints aching, flesh burning with phantom tortures of a sable's cross.

Her anxiety mounted with each passing day. Each moment in Callon's presence was a stalemate. Any evidence she could hope to uncover would be an intentionally dropped crumb, and if taken to Cinnabar would only condemn her instead of Callon. Both sides of the coin were a loss. Even if she submitted to silence, he would find another way to puppeteer her to a shadowy fate.

That same week, Cinnabar hosted a series of deathmatches at Execution Square, and Ambrosia set twice as many sables about the imperial box for his protection. The stadium shook each time a prisoner fell and the other leaped upon him for the kill.

Ambrosia perched in the shadow of the outer wall arches, her eyes narrow with disgust. She could witness a just execution and never cringe. She could watch an honorable duel to the death and never cry for the deceased. But these Pyron men, hacking each other to pieces on the floor below, would learn the truth much too late. After slaying his cellmate, the victor would be granted life by his emperor, only to be taken back to the Hold and kept for a future game. Day after day, all these men took away from the carnage was the revelation that they had killed their brother for a ruse.

From the cells on the sidelines, a prisoner broke from the soldiers' hands and rushed toward the imperial dais. He shook his fists, screaming unintelligible Pyron curses. He had fought for his freedom before, and now he wanted to tell the world about the lie, but his voice was drowned by the pleasured roars from the stands. The soldiers dragged him back to the shaded pens on the sidelines and chose another.

Ambrosia turned her face to the sunset-drenched cityscape beyond the arena and longed for a place to be alone with her thoughts. Tourmal bustled all hours of the day and night. There was no hope of transferring back to Selen, or to any other sector. Even after she brought the Tourmaline Renegade to justice, she would remain and serve until death. The glossy black facade of a skyscraper peered at her with all the likeness of that renegade helmet, a faceless entity, a dark mirror of reckoning, warning her not to judge him too quickly. Who was this man she had chased through the woods?

"Wouldn't you like to know?"

No Pyron accent laced his words. No Kobalt cruelty ground the edges of his tone. The voice was rich, silvery, the kind of voice that painted the most handsome face into her mind and set upon it the eyes of God. But he was no god. And no rogue could be attractive. Who had dared to put on a defeated traitor's skyn and bear the emblem of Pyron rebellion on his chest? She'd been one second away from unmasking him. The helmet had slipped just an inch, revealing the stubbled skin of his throat. And the next instant he was staring down at her, serving humor like it was just a game, an awkward moment between lovers. Why had he stunned her with the handle of her knife instead of dealing a lethal blow? She had so many questions, and if she killed him, she would get no answers. Yet killing him would be a mercy compared to delivering him alive for interrogation—and torture.

Syncopated movement within the emperor's box drew her eyes. A sable sprawled on the floor near Cinnabar's feet. Another knelt by her, and Cinnabar leaned over the arm of his throne with concern. Soldiers and sables converged on the box from all corners of the arena. Ambrosia leaped from her perch and ran down the terraces and stairs. She planted her polearm and vaulted onto the platform. Officials drained from the exits without objection from the soldiers rushing the stairs. A tense standoff ensued, crossbows and polearms pointing both ways, and Cinnabar castling behind his sables. The deathmatch below went ignored as the crowds fixed their attention on the imperial balcony.

"Neris! Phaedra! Help His Imperial Supremacy to a private room." Ambrosia motioned to several other sables to attend them.

The game master turned his commentary to the tension on the balcony, leading the crowd into speculation that an assassination attempt had been made. Ambrosia pointed at the soldiers frozen in confusion with their weapons drawn. "Will one of you shut him up before we have a riot? And you, call a physician from below."

The soldiers obeyed reluctantly, and Ambrosia moved over to the group of sables gathered around their collapsed comrade. They prodded and called her name, but she remained unresponsive, her skin pallid and glistening with sweat. Ambrosia knelt and looked at her face. It was Dian, another impressive and robust woman, like Commander Riahn.

"Commander, I can't find a pulse." Cygnus's normally powerful tone wavered.

Ambrosia set her fingers on Dian's neck and focused. There was nothing. "Was she feeling ill? I would've given her the day off."

"She was her usual self. Laughing. Talking. Had the same breakfast we all did."

"What about right before she collapsed?"

"She was tottering a little, breathing hard for the last hour. Then she started seizing and fell."

Ambrosia grimaced as she accepted the truth. Dian was dead.

"That was a bit of a scare." The loudspeakers cast the game master's voice across the arena. "But not to worry, citizens. His Supremacy is safe. It's clear that a sable simply collapsed and died at her post. We should be able to resume today's games in just a few minutes."

Ambrosia snorted and cast Dian's stoic face another glance. That's right. No salute or solemn moment for a sable. She only collapsed and died at her post next to the emperor. There was nothing suspicious about that.

One of the arena physicians arrived and confirmed Dian dead before taking the body for an autopsy. The games continued with a tense collection of soldiers and sables surrounding the dais, and Cinnabar left unannounced.

Ambrosia caught the apprehension in her sables' eyes. Many of them had admired Dian and looked to her for strength. Now, they were checking in on themselves every few minutes, each assuring herself that she hadn't contacted any lethal dose of poison. What else could it have been? Did Cinnabar see now that Callon had made his move, and the blow had luckily been absorbed by someone else? Or would the autopsy show that Dian had succumbed to some rare, non-transmittable disease? Ambrosia could not make a fool of herself by throwing sloppy evidence in her emperor's lap again. The Skynhound was better than this.

She left the arena early and tracked down the location of Dian's body. Two burly soldiers checked her at the door to the lab, and the physician emerged when a ruckus ensued.

Ambrosia gripped the crossed polearms.

"I would like to take my own samples."

The physician's heavy brow pinched. "Why?"

"I want to have them analyzed at another lab."

"I'll send samples to whichever other lab you want them sent to."

"I'd rather take them and get the results myself."

The physician bristled. "You perceive me as untrustworthy?"

"With the emperor's life on the line, I can trust no one. Who called you to collect the body?"

"You're not authorized to access that information."

"I'm Tourmal's Sable Commander. Anything that threatens my emperor's life is my business."

"One sable dropping dead on a hot day does not constitute a threat on His Supremacy's life. Now I'll give you some vials I've already drawn, but I can't let you anywhere near the body."

"She's my sable."

"And now she's my cadaver." He motioned to the soldiers and withdrew from the lab door.

Ambrosia backed away, grinding her teeth as the soldiers moved to grab her.

"Don't touch me."

A moment later, the physician returned with a sealed bag.

"Your samples, Commander."

She whipped the bag from his hand and marched from the building. Another dead end. Still, she would have it tested and see what the results offered.

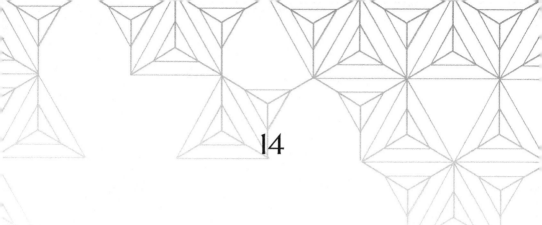

14

Astros dropped the last combat knife on the corner of the track and stepped back. "Try it again. Elbows down. Don't accelerate into the corner. Keep your eyes on the track in the direction you're going. Go."

Disrel clenched his teeth with determination and pushed his bike forward. Tygo sank down in the seat of his corecycle and prepared to give chase. Disrel opened the throttle and made one lap around the empty warehouse to gain speed, then chose an apex off the corner and let off his accelerator, leaning in and reaching his right hand down to the pavement, attempting to spot the knife in his limited peripheral and grab it.

"Chin up!" Astros coached. "Eyes on the track."

Disrel's fingers skimmed the knife handle as he passed, spinning the weapon where it lay. His bike wobbled, and he fought for balance as he clipped the corner. A miss.

Tygo rode up on his left, pinning him to the inside of the track. Disrel straightened his bike and launched out of the corner, fixating on the next bend where another knife waited. Tygo bore down, forcing him toward a much too early apex. This type of training was nothing short of madness, but Disrel couldn't expect anything different from two ex-special forces soldiers.

He shifted his weight over the seat and swept his hand out, snatching up the weapon before knocking into Tygo. Both of them were heading for the dangerous edge of the track. Disrel hit the brakes, the rear of his bike hopped and skidded, and he instinctively dropped his foot, only to have it punished by his own speed. He recentered himself and rocketed down the straightway toward a ringed target with the knife in hand. Focus. Tygo was only a distraction. Aim. He eased off the throttle, steadying his speed through the apex of the next corner, and cast. The knife struck the bottom edge of the ring below the bullseye. Disrel shook his head with irritation and skimmed out into the next straight. Astros was yelling again, but he knew exactly what he'd done wrong. Tygo was on his right now, hogging space, threatening to wreck him.

"Dominate with momentum!" Astros thundered.

Disrel gripped the corecycle's barrel with his legs and plotted his path toward the ax lying in the next curve. Tygo kicked out in an attempt to throw him, but Disrel held his center of gravity, pushed ahead of his opponent, and scraped the ax off the pavement.

"Eat that corner." Astros gestured emphatically from the median where he stood.

Disrel hurled the ax at the next target, and it stuck. He opened the throttle and rocketed through the straightaway, hoping to distance himself from Tygo and have more space in the next corner, a tricky double-blind curve. He kept his eyes trained on his chosen apex, shifted down in his seat, and reached for the pavement. The weight of the ax hit his hand, and he maintained an even speed, gauging his trajectory through the next bend. A wall of old tires shielded him from the target. He envisioned the approximate height and distance of the bullseye and readied himself just as Tygo emerged on his inner corner, forcing him over. The tire wall ended, exposing the target. Disrel made a hasty cast and looked back, thinking he'd completely missed the board.

His bike lurched, and he felt himself lift from the seat helplessly. He struck the pavement, and before he could process another thought, he collided with the line of old tires. His breath was tinged with a metallic odor, and he groaned involuntarily, hobbling to his feet. He gritted his teeth as his face burned, cursing himself for wrecking another one of Mored's bikes. It happened so quickly he wasn't sure what he'd done wrong other than looking back. But it was on the straightaway. What had he struck?

Astros trotted over.

"This game is too dangerous," Disrel grunted, testing the strength of his shaking legs.

Tygo's corecycle was lying on its side down the track, wheels spinning freely. Tygo climbed to his feet, grimacing and dusting off his gloved hands.

"Out there"—Astros gripped Disrel by the shoulder and pointed to the warehouse wall—"it's not a game." His bright aquamarine eyes shifted over Disrel's helmeted face, harsh and scolding. "Soldier One just kicked you off your bike. I'm here to put you in cuffs. Now fight." He threw a fist and Disrel blocked it, buckled down, and cast his weight into Astros.

They scuffled together on the track, Disrel attempting to pull his opponent's legs out from under him while his head whirled and his chest ached. Astros shoved a solid fist into his stomach, and Disrel ate it and pushed back. Astros clapped his hands against Disrel's chest and roughed his shoulders, a faint smile creeping through his eyes as he relented.

"Alright, that's enough. Not bad."

Disrel hunched, resting his hands on his knees and breathing hard. He unlatched his helmet and removed it as Tygo walked up, a guilty twist in the set of his lips.

"You alright?"

Disrel sneered, unable to hide his irritation that Tygo would gamble with his life.

"I'd like to take my deadly risks out there, if that's alright with you."

"I want you to make every mistake you can possibly make right here." Astros got between them and faced Disrel. "That way, you won't have any mistakes left to make when your life depends on perfection."

"My life depends on him not kicking my bike over." Electric energy surged through Disrel's muscles as he struggled not to engage with Tygo.

"He didn't kick you." Astros smiled broadly, like the accident couldn't possibly have broken any bones.

Disrel gave both men a hard, questioning look.

Tygo scratched at his jaw and glanced sheepishly across the track at his damaged corecycle. "I lost control. Happens to the best of us." He grunted and flashed a proud smile. "Anyway, that's what I get for pushing you. You were driving so well I had to stretch my own limits to push you harder. Lesson learned. Good job."

Astros nodded in agreement, then looked Disrel up and down. "Don't let it get to your head. You still need to work on being faster than the Skynhound's bolts."

"Feed the kid a compliment every now and then. It won't hurt his ego." Tygo chuckled and tossed his dented helmet aside.

"He got a bone from you."

"He needs to hear one from you. You're the riding instructor."

Astros set a toothpick between his jaws and turned his narrowed eyes toward the wrecked bikes. "Good job giving the bike a few new scratches. It'll live. Go pick it up and we'll work on shooting the crossbow from it. The next time you're riding away from the Skynhound, and her bolts are singing off your helmet, you can return fire."

15

Dian's test results arrived by mail in only three days. Ambrosia slumped against the mail dock wall at the command center, clutching the papers in her hands, shaking from anger. Poison. Not recreational drugs, but a powerful neurotoxin.

Her heart popped like a firecracker. Cinnabar must know before it was too late. She parted the command center doors, and a line of soldiers raised their crossbows. Fear knifed through her veins but her eyes snapped with rage. A barrage of fierce demands flooded her ears, and she had no choice but to drop her weapon as four soldiers rushed forward and wrestled her arms behind her. The lab report and its envelope were plucked from her hand. She bucked and raged as the cuffs clattered around each wrist.

"What have I done? Why are you arresting me?"

Callon leaned around the pillar on the porch of the command center, a condescending smile smearing his face as he accepted the lab report from the soldier's hand. "All we are here to do, my dear sable, is to catch a renegade. Who would have ever imagined Tourmal's new Sable Commander was plotting to poison her emperor?"

"What? I never—Only cowards use poison. I swear I will haunt you every night of your miserable life. I hate you!"

"What a shame I don't believe in ghosts. Lock her up."

Ambrosia danced under the soldiers' pushing and pulling, her heart leaping like a hare at every forced step. "I want a hearing with His Supremacy and the Sable Queen. And I will tell them you took my lab report!"

Callon turned away, rubbing a wicked smile on his lips. "Tell them whatever you like."

A sandy blond man with an unremarkable face approached Callon and whispered something about a transaction and Lieutenant General Tharik. Ambrosia missed a moment of lipreading each time the soldiers pushed her forward, and she struggled to look back once more.

Callon nodded and clapped the man on the shoulder before handing him the lab report. "Thank you, Crossfire. Bring me all the evidence for the trial before you leave."

"Right away, General."

Ambrosia's jaw loosened as she recognized the slightly tilted stature, the unmarked uniform, and the mediocre expression of Callon's aide. Crossfire locked eyes with her for a moment, the corner of his mouth twisting sardonically before he shuffled off.

The gates of the Hold thundered shut, and the soldiers forced Ambrosia into a high-security cell. They removed her cuffs, and the thick glass door of the cell hissed into its seal. Ambrosia panted, every breath caught in a vise. She slammed her fists against the glass and glared down the hallway, screeching her demands for a hearing.

And then she realized she wasn't alone. Ulyia slouched on a bench in the nearest cell, her lips quivering, her face numb. Three more sables leaned in the other corners: Serilda, fighting tears. Lolez, cursing and pacing her perimeter. Cemryn, glassy-eyed and still. Ambrosia sank against the corner of the cell, fists balled against her stomach, stifling the profanities that clawed up her throat. What good would a trial do any of them? Callon would not have arrested her without having the support of every judge and lawyer in the imperial court.

A few hours later, a score of soldiers transported Ambrosia to a narrow courtroom located in one of the upper levels of the Hold. A retired officer sat in the judicial seat, cloaked in deep orange. Cinnabar glared from his throne on the judge's right and the Sable Queen loomed like a specter in the opposite corner of the room. A panel of nine officers sat behind a long table just below the judicial platform, and other military persons sat at the back of the room to witness. Callon entered the room late and assumed the tenth seat on the panel. The charges were read and the evidence presented: her uniform, Dian's autopsy report, forged correspondence, and a receipt for a vial of poison.

The judge stared down his bulbous nose at Ambrosia.

"How do you plead?"

She spat through clenched teeth. "Not guilty."

A smugness glimmered throughout the room, followed by twittering laughter and snorts. The judge wiped a hand across his mouth.

"Have you anyone to speak on your behalf?"

Ambrosia stood, cuffs and shackles tinkling.

"Your Honor, please overlook my mistrust for your office, but I realize this circus is full of persons who support General Gault's plan to seize Lord Cinnabar's throne. I will not place any of my sables in harm's way by asking them to testify on my behalf. Every fiber of my being is sworn to protect my emperor's life and throne from any and all who would try to damage or steal it. I have no ambition apart from cleaning the capitol of its renegades, as I was transferred here to do."

The judge laced his fingers. "The panel may proceed with the interrogation."

One of the ten consulted his papers a moment before looking down at her.

"Sable Commander Ambrosia, the night of General Gault's party, did you or did you not attempt to seduce him in an effort to undermine his moral character and have his position of heir presumptive revoked?"

Ambrosia looked straight to Cinnabar. "Supremacy, I object to this line of questioning."

The judge straightened and jerked on his orange cloak. "Commander, you are not to appeal to the royal chair."

She stared hard at the panel. "I have never attempted to seduce anyone."

Laughter rippled through the room.

"Did you or did you not deliver a passionate bite to the general's lip on a pier after dining with him some weeks ago?"

Blood boiled in her ears. "He assaulted me and it was out of self-defense that I—"

The judge raised his hand. "The floor is not open for you to bring charges against General Gault. Either say that you did or that you did not."

"I am aware, Your Honor. But these questions are designed to make me appear guilty of all the things that General Gault has done."

"It is you who are on trial here, and further accusations against the Imperial General will result in the panel making an early decision. Do you understand?"

She simmered behind her desk. "Yes, sir."

"Did you bite General Gault's lip?"

Her teeth ground like chalk and her eyes stabbed Callon's unprotected throat. "I wish I had bitten harder."

Callon smirked, and the judge warned her that her words could be considered contempt of court.

"Did you not leave the party early, wearing the formal skyn once the general resisted your advances?"

She glared at the officer. "Please rephrase the question to omit the presumption that I attempted to seduce the general."

The judge intervened once more, and Ambrosia slammed her chains down on the desk before her.

"Your Honor, at the beginning of this trial, you demanded the truth from my lips, yet you allow these mud guppies to spin the truth into lies with asinine questions. If you'll only allow me to elaborate—"

The judge shouted over her, slamming the gavel repeatedly. "Speak over me again, Commander, and I'll allow the panel to try you without the privilege of questioning."

The next panel member glanced up from his papers. "Commander, the day that sable Dian fell dead at the emperor's side, did you not appear at the lab where her autopsy was being conducted and demand access to the cadaver?"

"I came to take my own samples to another lab, and I had the report at the time of my arrest but—"

"Your Honor, the accused has just admitted to intent to tamper with the evidence. I have no further questions."

The jaundiced interrogation continued and the corrupt judge cut her every attempt at defense short. After a brief deliberation of the panel, the gavel thundered down one last time.

"Sable Commander Ambrosia, the court finds you guilty of high treason against our supreme emperor and his throne. You will be stripped of your titles and hung on a sable's cross within Execution Square from morning until sunset three days from now. If you are found alive at sunset, you will have your throat cut where you hang. Do you have any last words for the court?"

Oh, did she have words.

"Specifically, any apology for your victims?" the judge added.

Ambrosia stood on shaking legs and collected herself, looking straight to Cinnabar, who seemed at ease with the verdict.

"To my emperor, I offer this apology: that I failed to defend you from every renegade in this court. To the Sable Queen: my sincere appreciation for the opportunity I was given to serve here in Tourmal. And to General Gault: a reminder that fate will avenge me and reward you well."

Callon laughed and whispered something in the ear of the officer next to him. Victorious conversations bubbled throughout the room, and another knock from the gavel dismissed them all. Rough hands plucked Ambrosia from her desk and whisked her back to her cell. The sentencing for the other four sables would transpire in similar fashion, swiftly and unjustly.

Ambrosia paced, tugging at her hair and fighting tears—so unbecoming to a sable. She could not let Callon have this victory, though she could not imagine how she could deny him any pleasure while she dangled from her cross. The darkness wrapped around her like a comforting blanket. Red hair poured like blood around her face. She was so lost, so young, damned from the moment she had been selected for sablehood. That moment had forged her into a shape of evil that no amount of goodness could recast. There was no bank where she might withdraw credits for her good deeds or positive influences and buy herself more time. Whether she had lived a life of evil or good, the outcome was all the same: She would fade into nothingness just as Callon would at the end of his road. They would be equal someday, despite their different choices. How was that fair? What could exist beyond the veil of death? Was death just an empty blackness like the womb that birthed the universe, or was it a place where a freed consciousness could manifest anything into unlimited reality? What if the Pyron stories held some truth? Did people from the sky come and gather their loved ones to another place? Or maybe only Pyron families cared enough about each other to come collect their dead.

Ambrosia melted down the cell wall. Even her own family had rejected her. There would be no one to come gather her to an afterlife. No one wanted a sable.

"Commander?" The familiar voice dripped with remorse and grief.

"Phaedra." Ambrosia pulled herself to her feet and hugged the glass door, nose to nose with her closest friend.

Phaedra's golden eyes leaked tears, and her lips quivered. "They're going to give me your position tomorrow, even though I told them I wasn't going to—didn't want to—"

"Shave my head?" It was a custom for any sable who took the office of a sable condemned for a crime. It erased the etchings on the nape and shamed the guilty as one who belonged to no one, who fit in nowhere, who was less than the lowest of society.

Phaedra nodded. "Because I declined, General Gault suggested I help put you on your cross. And Cinnabar agreed." She bowed her head and shook with repressed sobbing. "I'm so sorry, Ambrosia."

"Scrag, Callon!" Ambrosia boiled with curses inside. But she couldn't bring herself to speak against Cinnabar, even if her fate was already sealed.

"Why can't we do anything to stop this? How does one man hold such power?"

"Phaedra, listen to me. I predict Callon will make a second attempt on Cinnabar's life at the execution. He wants an audience, or he wouldn't have let so many easy strikes slip by. Keep a score of sables around Cinnabar at all times and watch out for a man with a drooping shoulder. He goes by Crossfire."

16

Disrel buckled a bathing towel about his naked hips and stepped down into the hot spring pool, which bubbled and frothed with jets of water. The swaths of green and yellow bruising on his back and chest melted below the foaming surface, and he sighed. After tangling with the Selenite Skynhound in that wood, he dreaded his next endeavor. She was every bit as ruthless as Mored had said, and he was still thanking Heaven that her bolt had glanced from his helmet instead of plunging into his back.

He clenched his jaw at the thought of the many slow and elderly being shot down like pigs and left to scavengers in that forest. What had seeded such a hateful tumor in the human heart? Why did some find pleasure in killing? He'd held the Skynhound's own knife in his hand and could not bring himself to cut her throat. The Pyron warriors of the past must have frowned upon him then, maybe laughed a little when the bolt had clacked off the side of his helmet and shattered him with fear. The Skynhound's hypnotic eyes bored back at him from the churning water.

"Who are you?"

He remembered her weight pinning his hips and her athletic shoulders darkening the sky. It had felt like his helmet was actually going to slide off, like somehow she had managed to unbuckle the chinstrap. One split second. Instead of wedging in her blade and finishing him there, she had tried to unmask him. And that moment had cost her the battle.

Voices whispered from the bubbling surface.

"You're a traitor Kobalt, aren't you?"

"A few good deeds won't save his soul."

"You're the reason we're even on this train."

"Who are you?"

He was what they saw: the Tourmaline Renegade with the spirit of Pyron blazing on his chest. They could love him or hate him for his actions, but never for his ethnicity. He was Thelis wrapped in skyn.

The basement door rolled back, and Koti descended with a tray.

"Hey, Disrel. I thought I might find you down here. Mind if I join you?"

"Not at all." He lowered himself until the water lapped at his neck. His scars were an intimate piece of himself, and he wasn't ready to lie about the bruises.

Koti set the tray down on the edge of the pool, and a sweet, buttery comfort teased Disrel's nose.

"Solla and I were baking. They're fresh out of the oven."

"Awesome. Thank you." The plate of cookies and glass of nut milk beckoned him to rise from the water. A newsposter lay under the plate like a placemat.

Koti moved toward a room divider, tugging the front of his garment open.

"Thank you for straightening the shelves in the washroom and fixing that leaking faucet. I've been so wrapped up in my studies and reports that I never got around to it."

"It's nothing." Disrel pushed up on the stone seat, dried his hand on a nearby towel, and pulled the pamphlet free. A stern sable visage glared from the cover of the newsposter, bordered by a severe crimson headline: *"Selenite Skyhound's Fall From Grace: Attempt to Seize the Throne."*

"I hope you're not going stir-crazy around here without a job."

"It's not too bad. I've still got that night job."

Training with Tygo often left Disrel exhausted and seeking sleep during the day. And that left Solla alone while Koti was at work.

"Well, if Solla keeps baking, we'll have enough cookies to get us through a cataclysm. She keeps itching to dig around in the flowerbeds, but we just can't risk either of you being seen by the neighbors."

Disrel flipped from page to page, scanning for the article advertised on the cover while his other hand groped up two cookies and pressed them to his lips. This was the same sable who had almost killed him in the woods. He would not have to tangle with her again. Pyron's freedom would be so much easier to secure without her nipping at his heels the entire way.

"Doni asked if she could come over this evening. Are you going to be here?"

I'm not sure. Disrel responded internally and refocused on the Skynhound's visage.

There was a pause before Koti spoke again. "Are you?"

"Hm?" Disrel shook himself from the newsposter. "Sorry. Maybe. I don't know. This newsposter. Is it today's news?"

"Yeah. Unbelievable, isn't it? It would seem everyone has forgotten the Tour-maline Renegade. I have to wonder who wanted her out of their way." Koti moved back around the divider, buckling a towel around his narrow hips.

Disrel jerked the pamphlet in front of his chest, snatched another cookie, and dropped back down into the water.

"Looks like four of her sables are going to hang with her." Koti stepped down into the pool. "I know they're psychopathic killers, but I couldn't wish a death like that on anyone. Death alone is enough punishment and a fair crime deterrent. It's a shame we feel the need to make a show of it."

Disrel consumed the article with mixed emotions. He could stare at her and not be stricken for brazenness. Ambrosia. It hardly matched her hoydenish appear-ance, even if it implied strength. The only names that fit sables appropriately were names like Shank, Measles, Malice, Whiplash, Arsenic. Shank was the one who had arrested Father. Arsenic had killed Mother. Naming them had given Disrel a shard of power over two moments in his life where he had been completely powerless.

But there was something about Ambrosia that set her apart from her comrades. She had protected a child on the platform at the train station. She had paid him a compliment about his work at the skynshop, and it seemed genuine.

Koti's voice broke through. "It must feel like a small victory for Pyron, anyway."

Disrel shrugged and laid the pamphlet on the side of the pool. "It's not like she signed up for the job." He leaned his head back and closed his eyes. Poison was too risky, and a coward's weapon. Someone was framing these women for their own unfortunate miscalculations against Cinnabar's life. If anyone was going to take down Cinnabar, dozens of sables would die. It was part of the price of bringing down a tyrant.

But as much as Disrel detested sables, he couldn't find pleasure in an unmerited punishment. They were not like the soldiers who enlisted. They were slaves, forced to obey or hang in shame, a shame so great that "sable" was an oath used by soldiers and sailors alike, and the sign of their cross was used to profane things. It was possible that there were some as capable of being as good and kind as Miss Mazilyn, if only they could escape.

Koti stirred the water around himself.

"This set them back so hard they published last week's article on the hijacked train late. They could not put more than three words together without admitting just how soundly the Tourmaline Renegade whipped them. The soldiers on board said his fighting style was amateurish and that they would capture him the next time he showed himself, but no one admitted the skill it would take to single-handedly stop a train and let every single one of your enemies live to tell about it. And then this condemned sable said she almost had him in the woods."

Disrel folded his arms across his chest. "She probably did. How do you think she earned the name Skynhound?"

"There cannot possibly be any more room in the Pyron sector. I don't even know how they planned on introducing Tourmal's Pyrons should those trains have arrived."

Disrel's eyes scored the stone floor of the pool. "They planned on making room."

Koti sat like a statue, processing horrors in his mind's eye.

"Maybe they already did." All the feelings of victory felt swept away in the churning water. He'd saved one trainload—several hundred people—and delayed the deportation of thousands more. What could he have done to stop the slaughter of thousands behind those walls? What could he do now? Disrel took a reassuring breath and spread his hands against the currents.

"I wish I could go see it for myself. See what they're not telling us."

Koti's lips pulled into a ribbon. "Are you prepared to see more than you want to?"

"I'm not afraid of the dark. I lived on Tourmal's streets for years. Kobalt gangs would knife us to death for fun and tally us with the sewer rats."

Koti's eyes slanted with pity.

Disrel clenched his fists under the water. "I hate not knowing where they're at with their death camp project. I just want to see where Solla and I will be if—if we're caught."

"We could go today. It's a good hour-and-forty-minute drive one way, and we'll have maybe an hour to look around."

"Let's do that." Disrel jumped up a few inches and then dropped back into the water. "Wait. I can't go. They'll let me in, but how do I make sure I get out?"

"I'll go as myself, a psychologist interested in studying Pyron–Kobalt relationships at the wall for a paper I'm writing. And we'll fix you up to look like a Kobalt student. A little hair color, foundation, and bronzer."

"And these eyes?"

"I have everything you'll need, right down to colored contact lenses. Let me show you."

Koti pulled himself from the pool and rinsed the minerals from his body under a showerhead in the corner of the room. The moment he moved behind the divider, Disrel climbed from the pool and raced through the shower. He snatched a towel around his shoulders just as Koti reemerged, fully clothed.

"Meet me in the upstairs washroom. I'll have everything laid out."

Disrel dried off, dressed, and met Koti upstairs. Tubes and jars and applicators littered the counter.

"This is washable hair wax." Koti slapped a jar into his hand. "We'll shoot for a medium brown color."

Disrel lifted out a glob with his fingers and combed it through his hair, while Koti sorted through a box of paper envelopes and rattled off words like, "ocean mist," "stormy skies," "amber," "sapphire," and "honey-hazel."

"Any of the blues are good." Disrel struggled with the lenses a while, having never placed anything on his eye before. The first one he tried leaped from his eye four times before Koti offered to help. Disrel leaned his head back and pried his eyelids open.

Solla entered the washroom just as the second lens slid into place. "Koti? Where can I find the—"

Disrel turned toward her, blinking away tears and solution.

She stumbled back, peering at him with confusion.

"I'm sorry, Koti. I didn't know you had a friend over."

Disrel laughed. "Solla?"

She stared hard. "Uhm. I don't think I've met—"

"Solla. It's me."

"What?" She shook her head and pressed her fingers to her temples. "I feel like I should know you—and your voice—but . . . Rel?"

"Solla? Are you feeling alright?" Laughter bubbled from his chest and he spread his arms open for a hug.

Solla turned away with a pained expression, like she had been violated by a devious prank. "I'm so confused."

Koti grinned and dusted a brush through a cake of medium tan foundation. "That should be comforting. If your own sister can't recognize you, nobody else will."

Solla turned back and squared up with hands on hips. "Where are you going?"

The brush batted his cheek and nose. Disrel contorted his face, fighting a sneeze. Koti worked quickly. "If you want, I could take some clay and give you a nose job or a prosthetic chin."

Disrel glanced at the mirror. "Don't fix what isn't broken."

"Can I come?"

"Eh, well. Kobalt power dressing, you know? The larger the nose—"

"There are exceptions."

"Can I come?"

"But if we built it up in the middle and made your brow look heavier, you'd be more intimidating, and nobody will mess with you."

"And when we're in a scuffle and my opponent takes a grab at my face and comes away with my most prominent feature sogging in his hand, then what? Or if I get punched and my nose pops off and goes flying?"

Koti made a face. "Ugh. That would make an unpleasant surprise. And I doubt the soldiers will just be playing 'I've got your nose.'"

"It's too risky. I could go to wipe it and smudge it off center. Or sneeze and it just drops off."

"Can I come?"

Koti's brush caught Disrel in the eye as he turned to Solla. "Bro, hold still."

"Ugh, Solla, I promise you don't want to come. It's not—"

"Safe?" She scowled and left the room.

Disrel rolled a brush back and forth on the counter while Koti finished the disguise. It seemed Solla was realizing that she was just as much a prisoner to Koti's home as others were to the Pyron sector. The only difference was, this prison offered a luxury stay.

"There." Koti stepped back. "How do you like it?"

Disrel stared at the stranger in the mirror and wrestled with guilt. He liked it too much. It offered a taste of freedom and a glimpse of power. And yet, he was equally disgusted that he looked too much like all the people who had hurt him through his life. He felt dirty, and then ashamed for feeling that way, lost and like he didn't belong anywhere. There was nothing wrong with clear Kobalt eyes and light Kobalt hair, no more than there was anything inferior about Pyron genetics. And if he could choose to be reborn, he'd choose to be Pyron again. It was who he was. His fight was not just for his people, but for a love that could erase all boundaries. For now, he would accept being reincarnated to experience the struggle from the side of Kobalt privilege, just for a glimpse of his people behind those concrete walls.

Koti shrugged. "You won't offend me if you don't like it. I can honestly say I'd have an identity crisis if I suddenly looked like a Pyron. The human mind links physical appearance to our sense of personal identity, and any substantial transformation will be distressing."

"Something's off."

"I agree." Koti folded one arm across his chest and tapped his chin. "I cannot put my finger on it. But you look choleric."

Disrel raised his eyebrows, trying to soften his expression.

"There it is. We forgot your eyebrows." Koti dipped a finger into the wax and applied it. "Doni is coming over this evening. She'll keep Solla company."

Disrel stared into his reflection's strangely deep blue eyes, searching for any recognizable piece of himself. He felt no more Kobalt than he did female. He was a Pyron man, and any other disguise, no matter how thick and how convincing, was a lie. But how it made him feel wasn't the point. The ruse was for everyone else to believe.

He sighed, recalling his sister's displeasure at being left out. How long until a girl like Solla could sit outside and enjoy the sun and wind on her face? Even if the regime crumbled tomorrow, civil war might rend the empire for years and spill just as much Pyron blood. How could one renegade from Tourmal possibly do enough?

Two hours later, Disrel and Koti slowed their corecycles at the Selen–Pyron border. Soldiers meandered about the checkpoint, weapons dangling from their elbows. A grim stone wall snaked for miles, crowned with coils of razor wire and segmented by watchtowers clinging to the outer face. Dark and light blotches brindled the lower half, censoring graffiti. A few odd-angled structures stood proudly above the wall from the inside, their windows offering tenants a view of the world outside. Koti spoke with the guards about the nature of his visit.

"You don't want to go through this gate." The guard's lips twisted as he pointed to the number four crowning the entrance. "It's riddled with disease here. Go to gate nine on the south side."

"We want to see as much as we can for research. If we come out through another gate, could someone give us a ride back to where we parked?"

"I don't see why not." The guard shrugged. "But I've warned you. It's rank on this side and you'll enter at your own risk."

Disrel and Koti parked their corecycles next to the guardhouse and stowed their helmets in the barrels of the bikes. A terrible stench blasted through the open gateway, feces and decay mixed with smoke. Disrel hesitated and Koti looked back with a hint of concern.

"Having second thoughts about this, chief?" He said.

Disrel shook himself into motion. "No. Let's go."

The moment they crossed the threshold, it was just as terrible as he had expected, worse even. Dark eyes peered up from under stretched canvases and the shadows of wooden crates. Some pulled deeper into their tents, but others never stirred. One old man was undeniably three days into decomposition. Carrion flies droned over puddles of sludge and clouds of gnats dithered in the pathways while dogs seethed and strained at their chains, their mangy skin stretched over racks of ribs. Disrel's shoes sank and squelched in dung-sodden earth—both human and animal. A bent woman squatted beside a fire and stabbed a steaming kettle with a narrow spoon, chopping a brown slurry and muttering. Her headscarf, worn thin in places, barely shielded her balding head from the sun. She glared up at them and slung a spoonful of slurry at their legs, spitting a vicious string of incoherent words through her pocked mouth. Pot-bellied children staggered about in the nude, chewing on strips of leather and pieces of wood, black hair matted over their sooty foreheads. Girls gawked with feral expressions from darkened doorways and clutched veils over their sunken cheeks. Even in their suffering, they were beautiful—preciously beautiful. Disrel glimpsed two cankered, bleeding feet just before a young woman minced back from her doorway in shame. His face burned as he blinked away tears. He had been here once before: hungry, impoverished, trapped, and alone.

Koti moved closer. "Do you want to turn around now?"

Disrel moved up to the drifting doorway and spoke gentle Pyron words to the young woman with the cankered feet, just trying to give her a little hope, reaching out with his hands to let her know it would be okay. She jerked back screaming and hurled a dry corn cob. Disrel bowed, and it ricocheted off his head. He backed from the doorway, avoiding Koti's analytical gaze. Was he a traitor for walking in as a Kobalt? They would spit on him if they knew.

A mile in, the landscape changed dramatically. Wood and wire fences separated the homeless from a neighborhood of modest cement boxes and stucco-sided cabins. Steel shipping containers served as homes for some and barns for animals. Some lived right among their animals in lean-tos. A cat streaked across their path, dancing around Disrel's shadow and stopping to hiss at him once on the other side. Spangled gamefowl pecked around the doorsteps and went in and out of the drab dwellings freely. A young woman spilled in front of Koti, scooping up a small hen and rushing back into her shack with it. Disrel turned and spoke to her in calm, even tones, but she shirked back into the darkness, eyes darting back and forth between them both.

Koti leaned on Disrel's shoulder. "What did you say?"

"That we won't hurt her or her animals. They're all so afraid of us." His brow pinched as he realized he couldn't blame them. How could they know which Kobalts to fear and which ones to trust?

Men hunched around fires, whittling small pieces of stone and wood. They lowered their tones and leered as Koti and Disrel passed. Another mile, and the streets became drier and cleaner. The spicy aromas of authentic Pyron cuisine carried on the breeze, the buildings took on colorful faces, women sat in circles plaiting ropes and knotting beads along them, children followed with curious faces. They tugged on Koti's skyn, and he jumped.

"Hey! Wow. What do they want?"

"Anything." Disrel crouched and pulled a handful of hard candies from his pocket. Their faces lit up as they tore through the candies until his hand was bare. They smiled with gaping jaws as Pyron words dropped smoothly from his lips.

Another mile, and tents and tables filled with wares swallowed the streets. Vendors moved in and pressed their goods into the hands of other Kobalt visitors, desperate to make a sale at almost any price. The main street led straight to another gate, crowned with the number ten, and all around it was multi-level housing and paved streets and restaurants with outdoor seating. Disrel leaned up against the corner of a building, picking apart a grass blade, his mind troubled by the factions it seemed his own people had built. Or was this prosperous section a state-funded theater for tourists to see that Pyron was happy behind their walls?

Koti hung close, hands in his pockets, and beyond him a shifty-eyed Kobalt man skulked along a line of tables with an entourage of infantrymen shadowing him like subordinates. His black boots and coat had a military look but lacked insignia of any kind. The man paused in front of a blacksmith's shop, leaning heavily on the service table, one shoulder more sharply sloped and a little shorter than the other. The smith raised from his crouch over the anvil, gave his customer a gesture of recognition, and pulled a wrapped parcel from underneath the table. The eyes of the two men cleared the area before the smith unwrapped the item.

Disrel pushed off the building and ambled down the street with Koti in tow. Bright steel glistened in the folds of the cloth, and the smith turned a beautiful knife before the eyes of his customers. The soldiers looked upon the weapon without emotion.

Koti brushed shoulders with Disrel. "That looks shady."

"Yeah." There was no way bladesmithing was legal here. Disrel inched closer and plucked a reed flute from a table. The slant-shouldered man said something about "the general," but the rest of the conversation was diluted in the market cacophony. If only he could read lips.

"I'll go around the other side." Koti moved off, scanning tables like he had never seen finer things.

"Five credit? Four? How much? You want flute?"

Disrel started at a touch on his elbow. A young man, maybe fifteen years old, looked between him and the flute with an open hand.

"All perfect pitch. Many keys. Hear?" He piped out a folk song with impeccable rhythm and tone.

"Yeah, uh—" Disrel glanced back at the short-shouldered man, who was wrestling a wad of money from inside his coat. A small black object dropped, unnoticed, between his boots. The smith ferried the money under the table and his customer wrapped the knife back up in the cloth.

"Three credits for three flutes?"

Disrel fished in his pocket and pushed a ten-credit piece into the young man's hand.

The vendor gawked at the coin before reaching to make change.

"No. Keep the change."

"Take ten flutes!" The vendor scraped up a fistful of the little instruments and pushed them at Disrel.

"No. Just one flute. Please." Disrel backed away and looked toward the smith. The craftsman hammered a rudimentary tool on the anvil, but his strange customer and the soldiers were gone. Disrel whirled circles in the street. Koti was gone too. He ambled by the smith's table, his eyes scouring the ground between rounds of feigned interest in tools and metal art. The smith lifted his head.

"Help you?"

"How much for the cauldron?" The soil was packed hard around his feet. Had they picked up the item while he was distracted? Might it just have been a coin or a card? Had it rolled farther under the table?

The smith's brow bounced. "You speak Pyron like it's your mother tongue."

Disrel clenched his jaw, and intentionally stumbled through a response with as heavy of a Kobalt accent as he could manage without sounding ridiculous. "Funny. I thought the same when you spoke up."

The smith glared. "That's because I am Pyron. You understand?"

"Well enough." Disrel shrugged. "How much do you want for the cauldron?"

"Three hundred credits."

"Would you take—?"

"Firm."

Disrel handed the craftsman a shrewd look and sighed while he fished in his pocket, working his purse out backward and spilling coins on the ground. He feigned awkwardness and embarrassment about having to bow and kneel to retrieve them all. He pushed under the tablecloth and groped through the grass. The underside of the table was lined with boxes, and the smith lifted the cloth from the other side and glared. Disrel's hand came down on a shining card and he scooted back, lumping it with his retrieved credits. He stood and raked his fingers through his hair.

"I'm sorry. I didn't bring enough."

The smith dismissed him with a wave of his hand and returned to pounding on his anvil.

Disrel shoved his hand back in his pocket but clung to the data chip as he retreated down a side street, following the tantalizing odor of frying food and spicy stews. His stomach gurgled and his mouth watered, and he ambled up to an open-air restaurant where a cook lowered a string of lamb shanks into a fryer. If only this food could be carried back to the starving. A wrapped figure stumbled behind him, poking the earth with a cane and tilting its hooded head this way and that like a bird. It probed around his left and a ghostly hand snagged his arm with terrifying force. Disrel jerked back, and the hood fell away from a bulbous puff of white hair and two milky pools banded by immersive wrinkles.

"I have found him! I have found him!"

Disrel shrugged her from his arm while others looked on.

"I don't know you, woman. Leave me be."

A watery smile cracked her chalky lips and her bony hand patted up his chest to his shoulder and to his neck and jaw. "I know you by your stripes, Kyreasheluhn."

His tongue numbed. How could she know? She was as sightless as a worm. He stepped from her reach.

"You won't shirk your blessing, will you?" The milky orbs darted back and forth, searching, and her fingers groped the air. "I must have the right one. I feel it. Yes. Thelis is strong within you." She seized him again and her fingers palpated his face without shame.

Mocking laughter rippled through the dining crowd as people wagged their heads.

Disrel stared down into her sightless orbs and mumbled in Pyron, "Elder, I'm sorry. I came to see behind the walls."

"Ah, the walls. There are so many, so high around human hearts. Today your strand begins to weave with another's. So many have failed because they could not hold true to Thelis. Please, do not fail us, Kyreasheluhn."

Her hand drifted from the center of his chest, and she puttered away. Disrel watched her go, feeling ashamed, rebuked, and angry with himself. She knew his skyname. All these people had laughed at her for approaching a man so obviously Kobalt as though he were Pyron's chosen savior. But in her blindness, what did she really see? Disrel gripped his arm where the elder had first touched him and pondered her words. He pushed his hand down into his pocket, pulled the chip out, and studied both sides. It was too large for a skyn chip. It was either a key or a holoposter card.

Suddenly, Koti was at his side again.

"Sorry, I lost you. I kept looking for your other face. What did you buy?"

Disrel pushed the chip deep in his pocket and flicked the flute between his fingers. "It's a gift for Solla. Which way did they go?"

"I don't know." Koti smirked and held up a woven hair accessory.

Disrel moved down the street, noting the apparent age of the buildings and the reaction of each person he made eye contact with. The quality of living varied from street to street in an eclectic conglomerate of agrarian and urban living. Sometimes shipping container shanties were butted right up alongside multi-level apartments or grocers. He walked a slow mile toward gate number three, until a cry rocked through a narrow alley and cemented his feet to the road. Two soldiers jerked a garment from a young woman's upper body, laughing and taunting her while groping at her exposed breasts and suckling them. She wrestled helplessly, flinging her head back and forth, her wrists pinned together in a third soldier's fist.

"Please, don't. Please, stop. Please."

Each "please" moved Disrel's feet toward her, turning him toward the alley. The tip-shouldered man in black unfurled a short lash and cracked it at his side as he approached the girl, speaking to her with a lusty smile. Disrel's stomach torqued, his hands bunched, and his breath staunched. The edges of his vision swirled and narrowed. Someone tugged at his shoulder, and he whirled with hands taut, ready to strangle. Koti flinched.

"Hey. Let's go. There's nothing we can do."

Disrel ground his teeth as the lash hissed across the woman's chest. His eyes pinched shut and his back stiffened. *A stinging sensation shot raw and acidic from shoulder to shoulder, snatching him back to that alley where he and Father stood, facing each other with their arms tethered above their heads. The elder's wretched moans echoed each growl of the soldier's whip. A shock ripped through Disrel's lungs, followed by a wash of yellow and livid fire that twisted his insides like brown paper sacks, warping his screams into animal sounds.*

Koti jerked his arm. "Come on. We've seen enough."

The lash cracked, and the woman's wail was a nail through his heart. Every fiber of his being strained to move toward her. His blood boiled toward those men, those cowards, those animals. He would rip them apart with his bare hands and strangle the one with his own whip.

"Disrel, they will kill you. There's nothing you can do. Let's go."

He noted the faces of the soldiers and wrenched his feet into motion after Koti. If he ever saw these men again, he would gut them alive and rip their throats out.

The drive back to Koti's was twice as long, yet it failed to erode the pain. Disrel scrubbed the filth from his shoes behind the house a while longer, while Koti went in ahead to unlock the basement door from inside. Disrel stepped in and pushed the flute against his friend's chest.

"Give this to Solla for me. Please. I can't—"

Koti pushed it back. "Take your time. I'll make sure no one comes down here."

"I'm going to need more than time."

The pain must have been glaring from his face, because Koti actually took the flute. Disrel didn't regret going, but he regretted underestimating how it would affect him. He shook his head and turned a circle, raking his fingers through his hair.

"I'll probably sit here until Doni leaves."

Koti headed up the stairs. Muffled voices discussed his absence for a moment, then dropped away on a note of sadness.

Disrel tottered around the edge of the pool, rubbing his face, feeling like the world's greatest coward, and trying to wash Pyron suffering from his mind. The faces of starving children burned in his mind's eye like afterimages, grotesque and neon. The young woman's cries haunted him. He wanted to jump on his corecycle and drive all the way back to search for her, to fight for her, but was she even alive now? The men would be gone. He didn't blame Koti, either. There was nothing either of them could have done that wouldn't have resulted in their deaths. He scratched his chest and sighed, feeling like the blind elder's touch was still there, comforting somehow.

He pulled the chip from his pocket and stared at its grooved edge. It seemed made for glass and light, like a holoposter chip. Then he remembered that Koti had a screen in the reading room.

Disrel went into the next room, pushed the chip into the port at the base of a glass mounted on the wall, and dialed up the light. A vibrant portrait filled the entire glass surface, bordered by streams of text. Five words seemed out of place from all the rest, glaring, contradictory one to another: *"His Supremacy, Lord Callon Gault."*

Disrel's face pinched. This wasn't Cinnabar's visage. Wasn't this the name and face of the empire's highest-ranking military officer? General Gault? His jaw loosened as he stepped back, understanding the poster with fresh eyes. Of course. The reason five sables were condemned to hang. Cinnabar's general was preparing to announce his ascent to the throne via billboards and holoposters. The dip-shouldered man must have been one of Gault's henchmen, picking up a Pyron-made assassination weapon. Disrel rubbed his coarse jaw. So Pyron was to be blamed for Cinnabar's assassination.

But what if this news was released earlier than scheduled? What if Cinnabar kept his throne and remained unable to trust anyone?

Mored needed to know. Disrel plucked the chip from the screen and plunged out the basement door to the open garage. He donned his helmet, mounted his corecycle, and pushed off down the long drive.

"I should have seen it coming. Gault was posturing for this over a decade ago," Mored chuckled darkly. "No. He doesn't serve our cause. But even if he's no supporter of Pyron, it might be nice to let someone else take out Cinnabar for us."

Disrel folded his arms across his breast. "I've seen his men at work. We don't want them in power."

"You'd choose Cinnabar as the lesser of two evils?"

Disrel's eyes flew to the corner of the study, as if confronting one of his demons there. "For now. Can this be duplicated?"

"Sure. You could probably make five copies in an hour."

"I need forty before tomorrow morning."

A roguish light twinkled Mored's eyes. "Why?"

Disrel rubbed the card under his thumb and considered the torture the lop-shouldered man in black would face. "I want to slip them into screens and billboards around Tourmal just before the sables' execution. It might be fun to let the cat out of the bag a little early and see what happens."

Mored leaned back in his seat. "Cinnabar has more renegades on his hands than he could have ever dreamed of. But he'll never thank you for exposing them. If we're careful, we can use this turmoil to our advantage, move more men into position." Mored frowned and stared at his fingers, speaking softly. "I'll have to hold off on the shipment until things settle. Have Tygo train the new meetpoint operator instead. But we can't afford to lose our contact in Euclase. And time is running out. Or—" His gray eyes lit with inspiration. "We'll kill two birds with one stone. How would you like to see another corner of the empire for just a day or two?"

Until recently, he'd never been outside of Tourmal. He'd only read about and seen photos of other sectors. "Sure."

"Alright. I'll help you make as many copies of that holoposter card as you need if you'll do something for me in return."

17

Morning light wept through the trapezoidal gateway under the stands of Execution Square. Ambrosia quivered in a narrow holding cell, looking up every other minute at the construction on the arena floor. A tractor dropped a metal pole into a well shaft and a crew of soldiers bent around the base, their impact drivers ringing and rattling against bolts. They laid a smaller rod and a pile of rope at the base of each pole they erected.

Ambrosia hugged her legs to her aching chest to keep from shaking apart. Her heart quivered and skipped. She had brought so many others to this end, and now she faced death's door, waiting her turn to cross the river and fade into the soil and take her place among time's forgotten.

Vinegar, salt, and cooking grease, mingled with the sweetness of beer, carried on the breeze. Ambrosia suppressed a gag. She and her sables had been given a last meal, but only Cemryn had touched her food, hoping to find it poisoned. The ambient noise rose as the stands filled with spectators. Then the soldiers came and dragged the condemned out of the cells and into the light.

Ulyia's face blanched as they forced her toward the poles. Ambrosia clenched her jaw to keep her teeth from chattering. She shook her shoulders, finding the touch of the men painful and humiliating. She and her sables would fight to be killed where they stood if they were not bound so tightly. Desperation led Ambrosia to believe that she possessed enough power to snap her bonds, if she willed it. But if she tested her strength and found it inadequate, she would buckle with despair. Her only hope was to die with as much grace as she was allowed and leave Callon in fate's merciless hands.

The soldier turned her to face the imperial dais, ablaze with banners and carpets and self-important people in glittering skyns. Lieutenant Brody stood among the entourage at Callon's side, his uniform sparkling and his pompadour holding up the sky. He conversed and moved with ease, and Ulyia's face turned cold when she noticed him.

Phaedra and twelve sables stood around the Sable Queen and the governors and officials in attendance. Her eyes followed Callon's every move, and the eyes of her sables wheeled about the royal box.

Callon sat slantwise, leaning a little over his armrest, sipping a beer and chatting with Cinnabar like a bachelor at a sporting event. An officer ascended the stairs to the dais, bent over the back of Callon's seat, and whispered in his ear. Color drained from Callon's face and his hand dropped to his lap. He shifted and scooted in his chair, then fired something back into the officer's ear. He tugged at his stiff collar and settled, rubbing his hand down his thigh and forcing calmness into his face before resuming conversation with Cinnabar.

A moment later, a sable climbed the stairs to Phaedra's position and whispered in her ear. Fire lit Phaedra's eyes, and she cast an order to her sables. Word reached the Sable Queen's ears, and she seized in her chair before twisting and delivering Cinnabar a scornful glare. Callon took one look at Phaedra, whipped from his seat, and disappeared through the draped doorways at the back of the imperial box. Cinnabar cast a questioning glance at his general's empty chair, said something to the officers standing there scratching themselves like a bunch of addled monkeys, then resumed watching the condemned.

A rod was pushed through Ambrosia's elbows, and ropes laced about her arms. The soldiers left her hands cuffed and her ankles bound and backed her up to her pole. The beam clicked into the mount that would carry her from the ground. She breathed deeply, savoring her last moments of unhindered breathing, searching for peace. She wanted to scream at Callon, but a show of rage would only make her end sweeter to him. Suffering was a choice. She would go silently, denying him that satisfaction.

Serilda shuttered and sobbed as she backed up to her pole, choking out claims of innocence in the face of her executioners' curses. The stands rippled with dissonance. Sables and soldiers scuffled around the throne. One officer turned and fled, and then another, and another, until all at once, the last eight broke as one for the back door. Cinnabar climbed up from the floor of the box, clutching a limp sable to his chest. He dropped her on his throne and lifted a trumpet to his lips.

"Release the Skynhound."

18

Disrel smashed the lock on a billboard maintenance box and clawed it open, his hands shaking with adrenaline. The data card clattered against the receptacle before sliding in, and fresh light filled the glass, proclaiming General Callon Gault as divinely-appointed emperor to all eyes on the block just north of Execution Square. A dissonant roar wept through the arches of the stadium, and a sharp voice rang through loudspeakers.

"Release the Skynhound."

A chill swept his heart. Release? He slammed the box closed and threw a dark leg over his corecycle. Word had finally reached Cinnabar's ears. The coup had crumbled. The traitors must have fled. And the cruel, short-shouldered man would have no more time to molest Pyron girls.

Disrel pulled the chip from his skyn in the cover of an alley, and his garment converted to its default white with gold details. He thought of the Skynhound being set free from her cross, and a strange peace washed through him. How could he feel that way, though? Once she finished tracking down the traitors, she would return to hunting him. Perhaps this relief came from knowing she wasn't suffering unjustly. Sables were what they were, but not of their own choice. It was time in service that warped them, one evil stacking upon another and convincing them they were irredeemable—that they might as well be as cruel and evil as they could be.

Disrel rode the miles to the train station and paid for parking. Travelers cast him sideways glances in the ticket line and clutched their luggage more tightly. When Disrel approached the counter and handed the ticket master his fake Pyron-sector

ID card, the man's expression scrunched and he held the card under his nose as if sniffing it. After a barrage of questions about his reasons for traveling, the ticket master slid his ID and a ticket under the glass and let him through the gate. Disrel meandered down the wide platform, watching the glass screens flickering out destinations and departure and transit times in bright greens and blues. Behemoth double-decker cars stretched through the station like a pod of geometric whales.

Life-sized images of Tourmal's most wanted banded the pillars along the platform. On the nearest, a fur-caped figure hunched in a half turn, his qorzan hatchet clamped in a gray paw. A voluminous tail dangled between its human legs, and two wide ears sprouted from the grizzly head, made ghoulish by its hollow, canine eyes. War paint stained Howler muzzles. Human blood. Disrel spit on the image. They were no liberators nor avengers. They were hateful misfits, terrorists, supremacists who kept their ax heads wet with Kobalt blood and seized credit for every nasty thing that happened. Too many hurting Pyrons caved to their influence, abandoning the wisdom of the elders and the teachings of Thelis for this new way of blood and retribution—life for life, pound for pound, drop for drop.

Disrel hated their blindness. They'd snuffed another maternal light from his life—Miss Mazilyn. And for what? Because she wasn't Pyron. Because she looked like people they believed needed to die to settle an incalculable score of injustices. All that precious woman had ever done for him and Solla meant nothing to them. Any good anyone could do for his people they tossed into the bottomless pit of debts owed to Pyron. They accepted Kobalt benevolence without gratitude and repaid it with fire and carnage. They were insatiable, creating their own injustices and giving the world more than enough reasons to hate and fear Pyrons.

Disrel followed the cords that stretched the Howler's bounty poster to the opposite side, where an artist's rendition of the Tourmaline Renegade postured like a rabid monster. Blocks of text explained the unique details of his skyn and offered what little they knew of him. They had drawn his shoulders wide enough, but surely he wasn't that skinny. Had they failed to notice that Alta's supplemental meals and Tygo's training had helped him bulk up since his first appearance? They'd missed some of the ribbing in the stomach armor, but altogether the rendition was half-flattering. A monotone female voice called through an overhead speaker.

"Train to Euclase, boarding now."

Disrel jerked his ticket up and studied the screens above the trains. He glanced from the glass to his ticket, counting out the characters. He closed one eye and held his thumb up, blocking out parts of the word on the screen and then dragging his other thumb across his ticket and comparing the glyphs there, like Miss Mazilyn had taught him. It kept the difficult lettering of the Kobalt language from scrambling. Euclase. Two large men tumbled around him, knocking him into the pillar and its poster in their dash for the train.

"Hey, there's room for all of us," Disrel growled.

The shorter of the two half turned, hurling a middle finger from under his dark cloak and mouthing a curse. Disrel scraped his ticket from the ground and cleaned it on his leg. Ratscat. Nothing short of toe-kissing and lavish apologies was acceptable from a Pyron. If a Kobalt ran into a Pyron, it was the Pyron who was expected to say "excuse me." Whatever. The universe had a way of serving equilibrium to people like them.

The two hooded men pushed through a line of people funneling into a car. If they were as important as they believed they were, why didn't they have their own private car?

"Last call for Euclase."

Disrel joined the line for one of the end cars, hoping for a quiet seat, a corner where he could avoid rude comments and leering glances. Would people even notice a Pyron if he dressed like everyone else? A soldier pulled Disrel aside at the door and let the line continue while he asked a half dozen questions in the usual order: What was he doing? Where was he going? How long would he be abroad?

Who had signed his pass? At last, he was allowed on the train and the windowless door sealed behind him.

The interior was spacious, bright, and modern, with trapezoidal doors partitioning the cars. A line of single seats hugged the left and two wider seats spread on the opposite side of the aisle. Passengers stowed their bags in overhead storage bins and shuffled for the stairs and upper deck seating. It was a full train. Disrel took a window seat and reclined it slightly, hoping for a little peace and shut-eye, but something punched the lumbar of his seat twice, then a third time, with obvious intention. A red face scowled overhead.

"Put your seat up!"

Disrel straightened his chair and stared forward. Just one swat and the guy would sleep the entire trip, or else have something real to complain about. But any argument would only end in the Pyron being thrown off the train and denied passage, or worse, arrested and hauled off to the Pyron sector. Disrel leaned his head against the window and let his eyes relax. After etching copies of posters all night, he just needed twenty minutes.

Train employees directed those still standing to take seats, and the train shuddered into motion. A heaviness pressed Disrel into the seat until the train's velocity leveled out; when that happened, musical tones and lights signaled permission to move about, and seatbelts unlatched throughout the car. Daylight strobed into his eyes, and he turned a dial to darken the glass. In his periphery, a burst of color caught his attention as a head of hair the color of dark red wine bobbed at the front of the car, and the angular door rolled aside under an arm sheathed in a sable skyn. Several passengers moved down the aisle after her, obstructing Disrel's view with tall shoulders and wide hips. He laid his head against the window and shut his eyes, his feet fussing around the leg of the seat in front, itching for a little more room.

A sharp voice echoed in his memory, releasing the Skynhound again and again, stirring him farther and farther from sleep until his eyes shot open. It had to be her. He'd never seen auburn hair so deeply cherry and chocolate anywhere else.

He rose and walked the cars, keeping his hands off the backs of the seats after a woman smacked him in the crotch with a rolled-up magazine. His leg scraped a knee that had spread into the aisle.

"Sorry. Excuse me." Disrel backed up, expecting retaliation.

The man pulled his hood farther over his face and coiled into the window, grumbling. Disrel noted the design of the hooded jacket. This was one of the men who had pushed him on the platform, but he wasn't such a tough guy now. Disrel gave him a warning eye and moved on.

Passengers glanced up from their reading material just to scowl at the limber Pyron who had dared to move from his seat. Two cars up the line, a familiar voice tumbled down from the upper deck, causing Disrel to pause behind the stair wall.

"I watched them both board. I know they're here. Start on the second level and keep checking the lavatories. I'll run the bottom again."

His heart twinged. It *was* her. The Skynhound. She marched down the stairs and turned the corner, sweeping right into him. Her chest pressed against his before she pushed back and gave him a thorny glare.

Disrel spread his hands and forced a grin, cringing as he realized it probably looked more like he was gritting his teeth. "Hey, Ambrosia! Crazy running into you here. What's taking you to Euclase?"

Her eyes sharpened. "Do I know you?"

"Come on, it's me. Disrel? We met on Overlook, remember?"

Suspicion smeared her face. "I talk to a lot of Pyrons. It's part of the job."

"But we had something. You asked for my information. I smiled. You hit me over the head. There was some chemistry."

Her eyes scored him and she smashed a delicate finger into his sternum, moving him back a step. "Is that supposed to be funny? I've never been attracted to a Pyron."

His breastbone tingled, and he tugged on his sleeves. "Love is a choice. Maybe if you tried dating one, you'd find—"

Her open hand cracked over his jaw and he skidded down the aisle on his shoulder. The shape of her hand rode his cheekbone like a wrathful hornet.

"I wouldn't date a Pyron if he saved my life." She tramped down the aisle. "Now put your butt in a seat and keep it there."

Passengers snickered and shared cruel sable–Pyron jokes. Disrel stretched his neck and wiggled his jaw. He hadn't intended to flirt, but her presence was so unexpected that his nerves had spurred his tongue. She was rabidly pursuing the men who had condemned her, and he'd been foolish enough to stand in her way and toy with her. He dragged his feet up the stairs to the second level, chastising himself. He didn't like her. He couldn't. She might've shown concern for one Pyron child, but she'd helped put all the others in that prison sector. She was helping murder his people. He'd only hoped to know what his headhunter was made of and find a vulnerability in her armor. It was comforting that she couldn't remember him, but when he thought about her kinder moments, he almost wished she did.

A salty, metallic flavor tingled in his mouth. He wiped his throbbing lip and brought away a blood-smeared hand. The lavatory sign beckoned from the middle of the car, and Disrel moved toward it as an athletic man lumbered from the opposite aisle with a hood pulled down over the upper half of his face. He rushed the door, pushing Disrel back as they met. Not today, Kobalt. Disrel forced himself through the door.

"Hey, man, I'm bleeding. Just let me have some towels."

They wrestled in the doorway until an attendant noticed, and the man relented, allowing Disrel in with him and shutting the door.

"Fine. Just mind your own business." The hooded stranger turned away in the cramped lavatory, shrugging a backpack from under his cloak.

Disrel turned the tap, rinsed his lip, and wetted a towel as the man pulled out two magnetic gloves. He stood on the toilet and turned the emergency escape latch.

"She's after you, isn't she? The Skynhound and her sables."

The man turned an electric eye on him. "Do you fancy drowning in a train toilet, ashrat?" He jerked out the emergency latch and air screeched through the seal. The window dropped away and wind blasted the cramped lavatory, tearing tissues from the dispenser and cycloning them. The hood snapped back from a choleric, blood-stained face.

Disrel scowled. "Who are you calling ashrat, *Callon*? Pyrons don't treat their women like playing cards."

Callon swung the backpack at his head and Disrel ducked, twisting to strike Callon in the neck and wrestle with the straps. They slammed back and forth in the narrow space. Callon clawed the toilet seat up and dragged Disrel toward it, but Disrel wrapped the pack strap around Callon's neck. Callon recoiled, and the pack tumbled out the window and into the rushing vacuum, clunking down the side of the train.

The train lurched, and Disrel caught the sides of the toilet seat. A deafening explosion rocked the lavatory, and they slammed into the wall and stuck there while the rail screeched like a siren. Human screams pierced through the thunder. Stars of light burst in Disrel's vision and a tangy metallic odor filled his nose. For what seemed like an hour, breath would not come. He slid down the wall as Callon emitted a low groan, then lay still, slumped next to the toilet like a dead man.

Slowly, air trickled back into Disrel's lungs and he groped his way out of the pitch-black lavatory. Outside, only the aisle lighting remained on. The floor vibrated, as if the train had lost its magnetic lift, and passengers picked themselves up with groans and sighs, collecting handheld belongings and children. The train stuttered and jerked, and they grasped tables and seats. Disrel staggered down the stairs. Had Callon's pack contained explosives? And if so, had they detonated when they struck the side of the train or the magnetic rail? Or was it something entirely unrelated? An attendant clutched an open doorway with ashy lips and frenzied eyes.

"We need everyone to stay calm and remain seated. Do not panic."

Disrel pushed toward the end car.

Another attendant stopped him with her hand. "Sir, I need you to take the nearest seat."

He slipped from her grasp. "I'm looking for the red-haired sable. It's important."

The farther he went, the more tense and agitated the people were. At the gangway to the last car, passengers took turns running down the aisle and heaving their bodies against the door. Between their attempts, a bullish man standing to the side swung a hefty crowbar at the glass, each blow insurmountable and perfectly futile. The partition boomed and flexed and rattled, unimpressed with heroic efforts. On the other side of the door, passengers were smothering each other and clawing the glass. Smoke coiled, blanketing them in darkness, wringing beads of sweat and hoarse coughs from wilting bodies as eyes rolled white with dread. Disrel spied Ambrosia, deep within the car, fighting her way toward the door, stooping under the canopy of smoke and clutching her baton. She was unflinching, collected, trying to keep order while keeping her own head.

The screaming, wailing, grinding of the chassis dragging on the rail corroded Disrel's senses. Stress fractures crinkled through the groaning floor as the gangway warped and twisted like a carnival funhouse. The bullish man dropped his crowbar and retreated, ordering the runners back from the condemned car. Disrel wriggled up to him, his forehead barely lining up with the man's knotty chin.

"Excuse me. I'd like to try."

The group gave him that look all Pyrons received for intervening. Disgust.

"Try what? We've tried everything." The ripped Kobalt spread his sinewy arms in exasperation. "The upper-level door is jammed and this one is emergency locked."

"What about the override switch?"

"Hit it all you want. It does nothing. It would take an engineer with a proper toolkit at least thirty minutes to get that door open, and the car will be gone in less than two."

"Then I've got two minutes."

Disrel approached the door with caution and opened the maintenance box on the lower left side. Cables and wires webbed the interface. He was no mechanic, but the door's resilience had already been proven by the largest, toughest men on board. He grabbed a wire and yanked. Sparks spat from the interface as air hissed through a new fracture between his feet. He sucked his buzzing fingers and studied the door while the passengers behind him made derisive comments, as if he should be ashamed to even try where they had failed. Meanwhile, Ambrosia glared at him from within her broiling prison and jammed her baton into the seal on her side. Disrel ran his fingers along the magnetic bar lock. He needed a shield, something thin and insulating to interrupt the flow of energy. He snatched a newsposter from a seat pocket, folded it once, wedged it up between the bars, and motioned to Ambrosia.

"We need to pull together."

The cries of the suffering rose over the grinding friction on the chassis. The gangway popped and shook, rattling Disrel's knees until he couldn't feel the floor through his feet. Another portal hissed in the floorboard as he picked up the titan's dropped crowbar and wedged the teeth into the door handle. Ambrosia stabbed the seal with her baton, and together they pushed. The door screeched open an inch, releasing streams of caustic smoke. Disrel gritted his teeth and focused his strength through his core. His knuckles whitened around the bar and his palms burned against the metal; his arms shuddered as the door gave another inch. The sable leaned over her iron, hurling her weight in rhythm with his effort. Finally, the magnetic lock lost its hold and the door ground back into the warped door frame under eager hands.

Disrel ordered his audience of mockers to move up and make room. Ambrosia stepped back and ushered passengers through the opening, just wide enough for one to squeeze through at a time. They flooded into the next car like water under pressure, carrying the stench of burning metal with them. Some stumbled and fell, and Disrel snatched a boy from under trampling feet. Ambrosia dragged an unconscious woman to the door and passed her through.

As the last passenger crossed over, the couplings creaked and the gangway serrated. The car tilted, rear sinking, front rising. Ambrosia caught hold of the door frame and her boots raked the carpet as a bright blue sky opened up overhead and debris showered down from the upper gangway. Disrel jumped the exposed coupling and gripped a handle, reaching down to Ambrosia with every inch he had. His vision condensed to a dark tunnel, everything shrouded but her, dangling there, auburn coils whipping around her frightened face.

"Grab my hand!"

She clamped her hand around his wrist, and he pushed up. She set her feet on the edge, and he caught her duty belt and lifted again. Their momentum sent him staggering backward and sprawling into the aisle. She thudded down on his chest, velvety hair bathing his face while he sputtered and clawed strands out of his mouth. With a feral screech, the trailing carriage flew free. It rolled and bounced along the track, spraying debris as it disintegrated completely.

Disrel's head dropped back to the floor. He quivered like a pile of jelly, very aware that Ambrosia's eyes were fixed on him. They were like peridot, bright and glistening with amazement, gratitude, a little indignation, and something else he couldn't name. Then her lips drew together and she pushed herself to her feet, stepped over him, and marched up the train, ordering passengers to make as much room as possible for each other and stay put while people blubbered into spread hands, processing their scrape with death. Raucous coughing raked the car from end to end, and the air was rank with smoke and human odors. The back door to the car was finally drawn closed and locked.

Disrel leaned against a seat and drew deep, calming breaths. From the start of this trip, all he had wanted was twenty minutes of peace and shut-eye.

He could still feel Ambrosia's weight on his chest. What was that look in her eye? Respect? Admiration? Regret? Worse: Why was his enemy so alluring? How had he just saved her life again—twice in one day? None of this would have happened if Callon hadn't—

Callon. Disrel jumped up and pushed down the aisles, knocking standing passengers into the laps of others. Five cars up, Ambrosia wheeled around a blind corner, jaw clenched, fists balled.

"I told you to take a seat."

He balked and stared over her shoulder. Two sables knelt over a man stretched in a dark corner. A rusty color spotted his railway uniform from neck to waist and crusted his hands. A blood trail smeared the carpet from the door to the corner where he had crawled, or been dragged.

"What happened?"

"The captain's injured. Now move. I'm looking for someone."

"I know. I saw him in the lavatory. He's tall, dark, and—"

Whump. The side of his face collided with the stair wall, then his arm was searing from wrist to shoulder as she contorted it behind his back. A pointy elbow squeezed into his jaw, pressing his face against the unforgiving metal.

"Are you trying to get hurt?"

"No, I'm trying to help! One has a bad shoulder. The other slithers around like a snake."

Her eyes branded his cheek. "You're too late. That snake has already killed the captain and destroyed the engine. The E-brakes are melted and the switch is jammed, and unless I can find a way to stop this train, we're all on the fast track to oblivion."

A jagged rope of brunette hung across her eyes, diluting their poison. Now he couldn't read her.

"Please. I still want to help."

"Huh! Unless you're an engineer or a soldier, you can help by finding a seat and staying put."

"And if I'd listened, you and two hundred other people would be having out-of-body experiences in a field ten miles back."

Her arm pressed him all the more tightly, and her lip curled. "You think hacking a door lock is impressive? You'll have to do better than that, skynmaker."

"I want to live as much as you do. Just let me try."

Evacuation lights flared, paired with a nerve-shredding *whoooop*.

She flung him down the aisle. "Fine. You want to impress me? Stop this train."

Disrel careened off a seat and marched toward the control room, raking his bristling neck. Ambrosia stomped three paces behind him the whole way. If he failed, they would all die in a firestorm of glory. If he succeeded, he might get thrown around a little more by the temperamental beauty. Disrel rubbed his nose and thought that he might not mind.

The control room door looked as if a beast had fisted it open, and the panel strobed like a psychotic circus. A screen showed the train's location on a map of railways alongside a countdown to the end of the line. Seventeen minutes, forty-three seconds. The throttle flopped loosely in its slot. He toyed with several other switches and knobs, and the panel responded with puffs of smoke and the smell of hot wires. Even if he could cut the power now, they'd need more than seventeen minutes to coast off this speed.

"It's not as easy as hacking a door lock, is it, skynmaker?"

He turned and offered his right hand, open and up. "Disrel. Nice to meet you."

She tossed her head and mashed a button repeatedly. "I'm not about to let all these people die while you make small talk."

"Since when do sables care about saving lives?"

She cast him a sideways glance. "You don't know me, Pyron. Don't act like you do."

"Fair enough." He pulled a receiver from its slot and handed it to her. "Get on the intercom and tell everyone to strap in. I'll try uncoupling the engine car. Hopefully we can catch enough air resistance before we derail."

Ambrosia covered the receiver with her hand.

"And if we don't?"

"Then it won't matter if you're impressed with me or not." He tore up a portion of the gangway flooring and examined the magnetic coupling. They couldn't override it with the engine stuck wide open, and this was nothing he could hack with a wad of paper. He turned and jerked the captain's toolbox open. His fingers stuck to something tacky on the handle. Blood. Where were Callon and his slope-shouldered imp now? Why had they bothered to sabotage the train when they could have simply jumped to their deaths? Or were they evil enough to sacrifice a thousand innocent lives just to bring down the Skynhound? He dragged out a cutting torch and connected the lines to a portable canister of fuel.

"Do you know how to use that?" Ambrosia towered over him, hands on hips.

He struck the torch and adjusted the flame, then set it against the coupling, warming the metal. The rushing wind worked against him, cooling it. The track whistled below. He glanced at the screen—fourteen minutes. Conversation always helped with tension.

"So, who's the man with the bad shoulder?"

"What's he to you?"

He shrugged. "I've seen him around the Pyron sector. Seems like a terrible guy to work with."

"He just does all the dirty work for the other one."

"Callon?"

Those green eyes ate his face like acid. Maybe conversation didn't always help tension.

Sparks gored the rail.

A dark figure dropped onto the control room floor and hurtled down the aisle toward them. Disrel pulled the gas line, snagging the toe of the runner's boot and sending him tumbling into the empty car. Ambrosia sailed after him in one airborne leap and straddled his back, slamming his face into the floor with furious blows from her hard-knuckle gloves.

"Where's your smirk now, renegade? You should have kept your mask on."

Disrel cringed as Ambrosia pounded the man's face.

The hood flopped back, and Callon smiled coldly through the globs of blood. His breath rattled through his mashed nose. "Do your worst, Skynhound. Drag my head back to Cinnabar and see if that redeems you." He laughed. "It wasn't your fault the Sable Queen threw you in my way. Otherwise, I might have loved you. But fate will have you crucified. I swear it."

Another cloaked man thudded in the aisle and rushed the gangway.

Ambrosia, struggling to hold Callon, twisted Disrel's direction. "Grab Crossfire!"

Disrel dropped the torch and recoiled, sweeping an elbow into Crossfire's face as he passed. Crossfire staggered. Disrel caught his neck and hammered him between the legs with his knee. Crossfire buckled and his face turned purple. Disrel wrenched his arms behind his back and leaned down to put his lips near his ear.

"That's for the Pyron girl you raped in that alley."

Crossfire's piggish eyes watered and he sank to the floor, gasping for air.

Ambrosia mashed Callon until his eyes went dull and he quit struggling. "Filthy cad." She rolled him and snapped a pair of cuffs around his wrists. "Royal plate of meat."

Then she came over and cuffed Crossfire while Disrel held his wrists. Disrel reclaimed the torch and fixed its flame back on the metal, hands shaking. Some dark part of him wanted to run the torch over Crossfire's back. *No.* Cruelty was an unnecessary retribution. He would suffer enough at the hands of the state.

Two sables emerged and dragged the prisoners into the empty car. Eleven minutes.

"Come on, come on," Disrel hissed through his teeth at the steel connector. If this was his time, he had peace that he would see his loved ones. But he wasn't ready to leave Solla behind. He wasn't willing to leave the fight for his people's freedom in another's hands. The Tourmaline Renegade couldn't die like *this.*

Disrel's palms slipped around the torch handles and he wiped them on his legs. He glanced back up at the panel in the engine car. Nine minutes. The torch hissed as the flame devoured the last inch of steel. The coupling parted and the engine car plowed on freely.

Disrel's shoulders dropped and he extinguished the flame. Saved. He took a series of deep breaths, letting the tightness out of his chest as he watched the space between the broken coupling and the runaway engine car widen. He murmured a prayer of thanks. The bald side of a mountain towered on the horizon, with panels of colored lights flashing along its sculptured face. A contrary wind made Disrel take a step back from the edge, and hope splashed through his chest. It would help to slow the line of passenger cars.

Ambrosia stepped to his side. Sprays of hair whipped her face and the hem of her jacket swung around her hips.

"We did it." She sounded breathless and looked straight into him, eyes warmer than he'd ever seen them. "I can't believe—I mean, you—you actually—" She laughed and her eyes fluttered away for a moment as she collected herself. "You should be proud of yourself. You saved many lives today."

"Thanks." His heart jittered up into his throat. She'd actually complimented him. He replayed her words over in his mind, questioning if she'd really spoken at all.

"Disrel, right?"

"Yeah." He wedged his hands into his pockets.

"It's different. I've never heard a name like it before."

"It's Pyron."

"Strange. I mean, it's pretty. Kind of has a soft sound to it."

"Thanks. So does yours."

"I don't find many men with softer names. But sometimes, I think they wear better than the strong-sounding ones."

"Oh?" He wiped his chin. A little blood smeared from his lip.

Her gaze snapped toward the floor. "Sorry about what happened earlier. I hope you don't think I'm always such a piece of work."

"Don't worry about it. You had those two on your hands."

"If you only knew what I've—" She clutched the hem of her uniform and seemed uninterested in finishing her thought.

He rubbed the back of his neck and thought about how she must have felt when he suggested—in front of so many passengers—that she stoop from her already infamous rank to date an undesirable Pyron. And after standing in the shadow of her cross that morning, falsely condemned.

"Actually, I'm the one who should apologize for offending you in front of everyone. I didn't mean to be ridiculous."

Her lips hung apart and her eyes fluttered back and forth. A smile creeped into her face and she bit her lip. "So, what's taking you to Euclase?"

He looked at the miles of open rail before them. "This train was. Now I'm not sure."

Her lips tightened, but her eyes glimmered with amusement. "Are you always like this?"

He cleared his throat. "Only when I'm hungry and tired."

When she couldn't hide her smile, she looked away and rolled her eyes. "Then tell me why you boarded this train for Euclase."

"I wanted to see someplace new. I've never been out of Tourmal before."

She hummed and studied him comfortably. "There are so many beautiful sectors out there. I've been privileged to see quite a few. Next time you get the chance, visit Morion's painted canyon and hot springs, during the migration season. You'll never forget the sounds of the wildlife."

She drew back as if chiding herself for being too friendly and saying too much. "Anyway, it looks like we'll be stopping within three miles of a station. I need to send a message back to base and secure a new route to return with my prisoners. Would you be interested in coming with me?"

Disrel clasped a hand to his growling stomach, hoping to find something to eat. "Sure."

A ball of blue and orange fire billowed from the side of the mountain as the engine car finally struck it. They stood firm, counting the seconds until the shock wave washed over them.

19

Disrel sat on the edge of the car connector and let his feet dangle. The explosion of the engine's corestones must have been heard for miles. In the distance, workmen left a construction site and approached the smoldering wreckage, probably in search of survivors, and the previously empty station platform bustled with curious townspeople watching the line of cars sitting dead on the rail. Several dozen yards up the line, Ambrosia spoke with a group of soldiers.

Disrel caught only pieces of their conversation as she explained that they had been hijacked en route from Tourmal to Euclase, that they had a cadaver on board, many passengers in need of medical attention, and two traitors in custody. One of the men pointed at the wrecked engine car several miles in the distance and the conversation grew tense. Another pointed at Disrel and said something about Pyrons. Ambrosia's reply made them angry but, after a minute, they seemed to relent. She turned back to the train and motioned.

"Come with me."

Disrel hopped down and walked toward her. The soldiers gave him irritable looks as he passed. He caught up to Ambrosia, marching alongside the rail toward the station.

His boots crunched on pine needles and he took deep breaths of cool, boreal air. Even though he was tired, the walk was refreshing. He shivered a little as adrenaline drained from his system and noted the sable commander's sullen expression.

"Is everything okay?"

"We're in Zois."

"Never heard of it."

"Exactly. It's a gridlocked third-world sector hundreds of miles from Euclase." Ambrosia's steps pounded with irritation. "The only other rail out of here is miles to the north, and that line is a long roundabout way back to Tourmal. We'll have to get transportation up there, and then it could take days to get a train out of here."

He would miss his contact in Euclase. Mored would be disappointed. Even if the incident was out of his control, Disrel felt like he'd let him down.

"Don't you have the authority to make them—"

"Yes, and no." She huffed and gripped the hem of her jacket. "I have to choose my battles wisely." She slowed her pace and glanced at him. "They wanted to hold you and the other Pyron passengers in their prison until we secure a train out of here."

Disrel's lips parted, but he didn't know what to say. His heart simply warmed toward her. She cared.

"When Crossfire murdered the captain, every passenger on that train—Pyron or not—became my responsibility. Including the captain's body." Her eyes flashed. "I suspect Callon steered the train off the Euclasian line to avoid military police at the original destination and any junctions along the way."

Disrel proffered a half smile. "I'll do whatever I can to help. Even if I have to put my butt in a seat and keep it there."

Her lips twitched with amusement, but she kept her gaze trained hard on the path ahead. They climbed a steep bank of earth and pushed onto the crowded platform. Zoisite citizens stared at Disrel like they had never seen a Pyron before. It was more likely that they'd never seen a Pyron walking unbound next to a sable—especially the Selenite Skynhound. Disrel noted the unfashionable cut of their skyns and outdated colors. The fabrics were those of the working classes, lacking the luster and sparkle of amalite, fluorite, and quartz. By comparison, his white skyn looked like something the gentry would wear. The people parted from Ambrosia's path, whispering and chittering in a truncated western dialect.

Ambrosia stopped at the foot of a flight of stairs and pointed to a row of shops built along the platform.

"I doubt you'll find anything better than the onboard snacks, but see if they'll serve you and then wait for me here. I don't know how long I'll be."

Before he could reply, she marched up the steps and disappeared through a door.

Disrel moved along the station's bricked wall, looking for eatery signs and shivering with exhaustion. The people watched him with mistrust, keeping their distance. Nestled in the corner of the building was a gift shop showcasing local craftsmanship and a literature store full of outdated magazines. On the other end of the platform sat a quaint little confectionery. Disrel moseyed over and gazed through the glass at the displays of chocolates and soft candies. When a young woman approached the counter, he stepped back instinctively. But instead of chasing him away, she served him pleasantly, asking questions about the explosion, happenings across the empire, and where he was from.

"There are still Pyrons living in Tourmal?" She placed a dozen filled chocolates on a scale. "My great-great-grandmother was Pyron."

Disrel marked her clear eyes and blonde hair again. But she wasn't lying. There were indigenous strains in her face, and likely only from that one ancestor. Pyron traits swallowed Kobalt genes: Every child born to a Kobalt–Pyron couple inherited the black hair and eyes from their Pyron parent, and it took at least three generations of breeding Kobalt genes back in to produce a clear-eyed child. If a biethnic person committed to marrying Kobalt people, and their offspring the same, the great-grandchildren still had only a twenty-five percent chance of passing as Kobalt without a blood test.

"Most of my relatives were exiled from Zois because their Pyron features were too strong." The candymaker scooped his chosen soft candies into a brown paper bag. "They're probably in the Pyron sector now."

"I'm sorry."

"I'm hopeful, as long as the Tourmaline Renegade lives." She looked up and smiled. "Anything else?"

Word of the Tourmaline Renegade had reached even secluded Zois? Disrel scanned the displays. "Some pistachio fudge and buttercream chocolates, please."

She wrapped the fudge squares in paper, weighed them, and placed them in the bag.

"Your total is eighteen credits." She watched him carefully. "I'm surprised you had no reaction to that name."

Disrel counted out coins. "I didn't? How should I have reacted?"

She shrugged and drummed her splayed hands on the counter. "As a Pyron, shouldn't it mean a great deal to you?"

Disrel extended his money. "May I ask what it means to you?"

She took the credits and handed him his candy. "A freedom born of love rather than legislation. I know that a world without Pyrons is a world without light."

The words stirred his heart. They were the truth, and it was good to hear from a stranger in a faraway place. Disrel bowed his head toward her, a smile twitching the corners of his lips. "Thank you, Eylin. I will never forget that."

She gave him a quizzical stare. "How do you know my name?"

He gave her a big, warm smile. "Well, it happens to be embroidered on your apron."

She fussed with her attire and laughed. "Wait. That's not fair. We're not even until you tell me your name and what the Tourmaline Renegade means to you."

He paused and turned back toward the counter, taking another look at her face so he could remember her. "Disrel."

She seemed entranced and repeated it softly.

"And the renegade . . . he's just a man. So I put my faith in the mark of Thelis on his skyn. I'm sure he puts just as much hope in it as I do."

"Then what does Thelis mean to you?" Eylin was sincere in her question. Having only one Pyron ancestor, she probably knew little of it.

He bit his lip and looked at the ground. He'd never had to put it into words before. But he needed to give it to her honestly. "Everything. Life—whether or not one renegade can free us."

"You have a skyname, then."

Disrel nodded humbly. "And you?"

"No." Eylin smiled sadly. "But the Tourmaline Renegade is fighting for my birthright."

His heart moved for the young woman. "Keep on hoping."

After bidding the shopkeeper farewell, Disrel wandered over to a bench and sat down. The crowd of curious Zoisites had left the platform and ventured closer to the line of cars. A group of soldiers stopped them. Disrel opened his paper sack and ate some candy. It was fresh and soft and he sank against the backrest, closing his eyes and sighing, relishing the sweetness. He wanted to make it last however many hours it would take to get back to Tourmal. Or would Ambrosia put him on a train to the Pyron sector? He almost choked on a piece of candy as his heart jumped. Even though he'd stopped Tourmal's deportation of Pyrons, the law was still in effect. He didn't belong outside of the Pyron sector anymore. But she seemed fond of him. She'd asked him to walk with her—not a comrade, not a train employee or another passenger. Him. A Pyron.

Disrel opened the sack again and pulled out a filled chocolate. He ate it carefully, savoring its velvety richness and wishing for a glass of cold nut milk. Candy was always a rare treat. He would have to save some pieces for Solla, especially the fudge. The closest he'd ever come to sweets on tap was his coworker Daimus's candy jar. Memories of the skyn factory, Reem, and coworkers flooded his mind, followed by a sense of longing for the better days that had been. He didn't miss Kommett, but he missed the sense of normalcy the job and salary had provided.

The only thing normal about Kommett's presence in his life had been the bully's consistency.

Footsteps echoed through the terminal and Ambrosia appeared at his side, her cheeks burning, her eyes narrowed.

"That toad-sucking idiot. Pretend I'm not second-in-command to the Sable Queen and see if I don't put a bolt up your—"

Disrel raised an eyebrow and held the bag of candy out toward her.

She stifled her swearing, shook her head, and motioned for him to get up. "Let's go. We got the train."

Disrel retrieved his backpack and helped transfer passengers' luggage onto transport wagons. Then he sat on the ground with a dozen other Pyrons, apart from the Kobalt passengers, to wait. Medics gave aid to the injured, applying salves to burns and bandages to abrasions, offering ice wraps, medicines, and slings for those with limbs that were possibly broken. The people paid for the services with what they had. An hour later, more wagons arrived to carry them all some miles southwest to another station.

Ambrosia remained in a state of high tension and no tolerance. She deputized the train employees and divided her sables among the groups of passengers, and they all endured a jarring two-hour ride over broken roads.

Once at the western station, the passengers boarded in groups of fifty; Callon and Crossfire were transferred last. Disrel passed them on his way to the back of the last car, and Callon lifted his stubbly, blood-crusted face and cursed him, flexing against the cuffs that chained him to his seat. Those who swore the loudest were often the most powerless.

Disrel put his backpack in the overhead bin and slid into his seat with his bag of candy. It was strange that Ambrosia had assigned him to the same car as the prisoners. The seats all around him were empty, with the nearest passenger four rows up, but only because the captain's wrapped corpse deserved a respectful distance. Even though the train was older and less comfortable than the one they'd taken from Tourmal, it offered a little more space.

Disrel glared through the window on his right at the sun setting over a forested mountain peak and darkened his window to keep the car cool. His eyelids drooped as he sank into his seat and rubbed his face. It had been over twenty-four hours since he'd slept last. His stomach growled as he reached into his bag and ate a candy.

Ambrosia came down the aisle, taking names and marking a paper. When she reached his seat, her eyes warmed.

"Last but not least, Disrel." She made a check mark, motioned to a sable standing in the gangway, and dropped into the seat next to him, sighing. "It's been a long day."

"It's not over yet." He held a piece of filled chocolate out to her.

She stared at him as though she was seeing him for the very first time and wanted to memorize his face. Then her confusion melted away. "Thank you. But I really shouldn't. It's yours. You paid for it."

"And I'm giving it to you. Please. Take it."

She glanced guiltily at the confection in his hand and slowly accepted it. "Thank you." She popped it into her mouth and chewed instead of savoring. "Sorry there wasn't an eatery at the station. Everyone's famished and cranky right now."

The train rode silently forward on the rail.

"The sooner I return with those two scumbags, the sooner they'll release Ulyia," she muttered.

"Who's Ulyia?"

"A comrade. A close friend. Cinnabar kept four of my sables in the Hold as insurance that I would return."

"I see." He extended another piece of chocolate, which she ate much like the first.

"This Zoisite captain expects each of us to reimburse him double fare for inconveniencing him into leaving his pissbucket sector to see a more civilized part of the world. I think we got clearance to run through most of the junctions without stopping. It will be late when we get back, and then I'll have reports to write."

He selected a darker piece of chocolate and dropped it into her fidgeting hands.

Her brow knit and she searched his eyes. "What are you doing?"

"You're still worrying."

She suppressed a guilty smile and fingered the candy. "I have a lot on my mind and more on my shoulders than anyone should carry."

He hummed and watched her, trying to decipher the pain in her averted eyes.

"I need a shower. A quiet room. Solitude."

He had plans for all the same things when he got back to Koti's. "I know what you mean."

Her eyes jumped into his with a quizzical expression.

"Wait— I meant I want all those things too." He stammered quickly. "I didn't mean what it sounded like I meant."

She laughed and looked out the opposite window, shaking her head and kneading the chocolate square between her fingers forgetfully. "Let's just—we're both tired. It's okay."

Disrel cleared his throat in the pause between them, gauging his own level of embarrassment against what he perceived in her. Then he stole several glances, working up the nerve to speak again. She continued pinching the chocolate absentmindedly, and he nodded toward it. "You should try eating that one slowly."

She pushed it into her mouth and sat back, savoring it, apparently deep in thought.

Disrel set his bag of sweets in a holder and stretched his legs out under the seat in front of him. Was she going to sit next to him the entire ride back? He didn't mind, even if it was a little strange to be so close to the person whose greatest duty was to capture or kill him. If she knew he was the Tourmaline Renegade, she'd chain him to a seat right across from Callon and Crossfire, and they would all die together.

Ambrosia angled toward him, her mouth parted and her gaze shifting. "To be honest, I just sat down here to ask if . . . well, about what I said earlier today—maybe it wouldn't be so ridiculous to, you know—" Her eyes lifted to his. "Meet up again sometime, if you're still interested."

"Meet up?" Disrel wiped his hand over his mouth to reset his face. His heart thumped erratically.

"Nothing committed. It's just a chance to talk more about what happened today. And see how the other person is doing. I've never gotten to know a Pyron before, and—" She dropped her eyes and a loose strand of hair fell forward.

He dipped his head a little, seeking her gaze. "And?"

"And I owe it to you."

"You don't owe me anything."

"Respect."

He gazed into her eyes and felt welcome in her presence. "I appreciate that."

She stared shamelessly at him. "If I write you a pass, can you make it to Tourmal? Or would you rather I came to you?"

Disrel propped his elbow on the armrest, doing his best to appear calm. "I can come to Tourmal."

Was this actually happening? A date with the Skynhound? A chance to learn his enemy? How could he turn her down?

The corners of her eyes wrinkled a little. "I'm off most evenings. How about a week from now, when things have settled down?"

"Sure. Where should we meet?"

"There's a waterfront park by the base. It's private and empty most evenings."

Disrel tugged at his collar and rubbed his nose. "I'll be there."

20

Callon's arms quivered in the white restraints of the Sable Queen's chair, a hoary throne of reckoning where every tainted thought and word and deed was paid for with sweat and blood. His haggard eyes reached for Ambrosia like a beggar's blistered hands.

"Look what you've done to me." His chest pumped, and he leaned forward. The scooped back of the chair was webbed and smeared with crimson. Raw flesh bulged from a swollen cut on his side, another on his shoulder. Bruises covered his chest, arms, and legs.

Ambrosia set her lips together and barred pity from her face. She didn't care that he'd been begging to see her every hour for the last two days. It was only the Sable Queen's request that had brought her to this infamous room she had desired to never see. It was more clinical than she expected, with bright bars of light in a white ceiling and a well-drained floor of green slate, but the air was turbid and heavy and each wall a numb face, haunted by the excruciation it was forced to witness.

"I see only what you brought upon yourself," she said at length, keeping her gaze trained and indifferent.

"I cannot breathe without suffering. Her poison feels like razors flaying the flesh from my bones."

"Her Imperial Highness Zaelix," she replied. "Sable Commander Riahn. Sable Dian. The train captain. . . . They and many others no longer breathe at all because you loved no one better than you love yourself."

"Death comes for everyone sooner or later," he rasped, a smile twisting through his pained expression. "But the Sable Queen won't let it come soon enough for me. I would rather be beaten to death than face her again. She knows just how far to take you, and then she brings you up again for a little rest. I have felt death's sting a thousand times at her hand, and now I desire it just as much as I fear it. It claims a hundred souls a day, but refuses to take me."

Rolling tables sat around the chair, laden with vials, syringes, and other ordinary medical utensils. A statuesque blade rested like a serpent upon a spread of crude cloth, its shining edges whispering deadly intentions.

Callon's expression darkened when he looked at it. "That was intended for Cinnabar. It's Pyron-made." He almost grinned when she picked it up. "After all that I did to you, wouldn't you relish the irony of cutting my throat with it?"

"That pleasure belongs to Cinnabar, for what you did to his daughter."

His gaze liquefied. "He denied me that mercy."

Ambrosia's brow twisted. She'd expected Cinnabar to execute Callon in military fashion, with a bolt to the head, or as an aristocrat, by beheading. "Then how will you die?"

He almost snarled, but a running tear marred it, and he choked on the words.

"On your cross." His breathing hitched as he lifted his eyes to her face. "Don't you love the irony, Sable?" He quivered, watching her with ferocious intensity through the silence. "Say something. Why don't you laugh in my face? When was the last time any man hung on a sable's cross?"

She laid the knife back on its cloth and turned away. How fitting that Callon should die a sable's death. "There is a rumor on the streets that the Tourmaline Renegade published your treason. Whether it's true, or not, I have one question for you: Is he one of yours?"

"No."

Callon's eyes were so dead, it had to be the truth. His hand shivered under its band, pining for the knife. Without his uniform or his riches, he could have been any sinner from Tourmal's streets.

She turned for the door.

The restraints creaked. "And when I tell the Sable Queen that you've befriend-ed a Pyron? Disrel?"

Ambrosia cast him an unfeeling smile. "I thought you knew sables better, Callon. I went on a date with you and soon after caught my eighth renegade. Every tryst is just another intricate facet of rooting out a terrorist."

Disrel was no terrorist. But she would leave Callon believing that she had dutiful reasons for meeting up with the heroic Pyron. It stripped Callon down to the helpless, naked wretch that he was.

The bright door slid back into the wall, and a robust woman stepped through, glossy black lips carved into an omniscient smirk, silver hair polished against her angular head and tiered into a serpentine coil at the back.

"Ah, Commander Ambrosia. I was hoping I'd find you here." Her eyes, rimmed in draconian midnight and purple, burned over Callon like flaming icicles. "I've had splendid success with this one. The most sincere apology is the humility of suffering, to which he responds very well. You're welcome to stay and watch."

Callon's groan made her step back. Even if his suffering was the only sincere apology he could give, she didn't want it.

"Thank you, my Queen. But I've already gleaned all the information I came for."

"Ah. Well, you're still welcome to try your hand at it. After all, it was you he falsely condemned." She pulled her stool out from behind a table. "Have a seat."

Her sinking stomach ached. "I really have somewhere to be this evening. A prior obligation that might present a lead on the Tourmaline Renegade."

The Sable Queen's whip-like eyebrows twisted. "You're too dutiful, Comman-der." She picked up a syringe and twirled the cap. "I summoned you to lead my sables in Tourmal because you have potential. And this experience would serve you well when the empire requires its next Sable Queen."

Ambrosia met her superior's gaze breathlessly. "I'm honored by your faith in me. Perhaps another time."

"Yes. Perhaps we can work together on the Tourmaline Renegade when you've caught him, if all goes well tonight."

Ambrosia bowed, squirming with regrets. "Thank you for the opportunity, my Queen."

She stepped from the room and melted against the wall. Her heart urged her to leave, but her feet rooted to the stones with the fear that her mask had come loose, that her superior had seen the Selenite mountain girl, that piece of her that had survived the academy. Torture her next renegade? Cutting his throat would be her kiss of love for him. A piece of her died every time she killed someone in a fight, when her training took over and left her riding like a passenger in her own body. It had happened more than once. A fury-driven strike. A simple pull of the trigger. A blow to the head from which they never regained consciousness.

But justice was different here in Tourmal. The Sable Queen was a monster worse than death, and anyone unlucky enough to find themselves in her chair longed for death to take them. The Sable Queen didn't want help torturing any renegade. It was well known she hated audiences while she worked. She expected Ambrosia to succeed her. She expected to test that potential for cruelty, to condition her, to numb her so that when it was time for a new queen, Ambrosia would either be so feared that she had no contenders, or be so ruthless that she could cut down her closest friend and take the throne with a smile. For this, she wished the Sable Queen a very long life. But sometimes, she wondered if taking a few more lives in the contest for the title would be a justifiable sacrifice if it meant she could lead with kindness. Others would kill for power. But she could begin a new era, where all that was wrong with sablehood was reinvented for good. She was so close now, one step away from changing life for thousands of girls just like herself, and thousands more yet to be selected—enslaved. Ambrosia shook her head. Salvation was not so simple. She would have to become evil to defeat darkness, and she feared, more than anything, losing her soul in the fight.

Ambrosia flung herself from the wall and marched down that terrible, endless corridor, crossing puddles of light and oceans of darkness, each step ringing like a cymbal. Death lurked here, slithering and whispering along the stones, making love to the condemned only to seed the floor and laugh in their faces. They loved death's nearness for the hope that it might soon ferry them away from their pain, and hated it for its elusiveness, its neglect, its apathy. When death did not want to take a man, he was a most miserable wretch.

A feral wail leaped upon her neck like a thrashing beast. Her veins stagnated, her spine rushed, every hair on her body tingled. There was a raucous drawing of breath, a choked pause, and a savage, unbridled release.

Ambrosia charged up the stairs, stopping her ears. If only she had killed him on the train. But she'd chosen to bring him back alive. She'd wanted to make him stand where she stood, live her nightmare, feel her pain. Around her, Pyron prisoners shook from their cell bunks and paced, wringing their hands and clawing at their heads. They did not recognize these as the cries of their enemy. How could they? Pain was no judge. It did not discriminate between the kind and the cruel. It served the newborns and innocents just as freely as those who deserved it. To these condemned Pyrons, Callon's screams were the cries of a brother, another mortal heart like their own weeping for a merciful savior. Ambrosia dropped her hands and steadied her march through the hall of glass cells so that Tourmal's Sable Commander would not be seen possessing a human heart. How she hated this mask she was forced to wear just to survive another day.

Outside the Hold's street-side gate, she dusted her uniform, smoothed her hair, and collected her mind. She crossed the street and walked along the main road to the base to settle her rattling stomach. She could not fault herself for following orders. It was nothing short of a miracle that someone had publicly broadcast evidence of Callon's coup hours too early, and that Cinnabar had released her, trusting her to bring the traitor back alive to vindicate her and her comrades. Upon her return, Cinnabar released the other four sables and granted her a fair percentage of Callon's wealth; Ambrosia divided it equally between herself, the four falsely accused, and the eight who had boarded the train with her. The rest of Callon's estate Cinnabar took for reparations, leaving Callon's relatives and heirs destitute.

Ambrosia watched oncoming freeway traffic, scanning for riders clad in white. She wiped her hands on her legs and chided herself for feeling nervous about a Pyron man. It had only been a week since she'd seen him last—since he'd pulled her from the burning car, since he'd saved the train. She owed him a little kindness for his courage, because she could never thank him for saving her life. And the news would never publish Pyron heroism.

Each time she'd paid him even a crumb of respect, his eyes warmed and he accepted it gracefully. Some of the worst names she had ever been called had spewed off Pyron lips, but this man had only mocked her by suggesting she date him, by pretending she liked him. She did a little. And not because of his muscular figure, or because he was a little taller than her, who stood sixty-eight inches without her boots on. It wasn't even because he had a just, unassuming nose, defined jaw, prominent cheekbones, and pleasant lips. There was something about him that was as unique and attractive as his name, like soothing rays of sun, not strong enough to scorch, just warm and invigorating. She needed a friendship like that, even if it was fated to end under her emperor's vendetta. She might be able to better understand these people and their strange beliefs after a platonic date or two. Perhaps associating with a Pyron might lead her to discover something invaluable about the Tourmaline Renegade, and once he was brought to justice Cinnabar might leave Pyrons alone to thrive in their sector. And maybe after the renegade was dead, all the unrest and problems would fade away.

Wishful thinking.

Disrel had slept most of the roundabout ride back to Tourmal station, curled up in the last two seats with his hands tucked under his head and his bag of candy protected under his elbow—existing, peaceful. How confused he had been when she had roused him to give him a snack and a pillow from the first-class menu, and a little ice for his swollen lip. She'd never forget how he'd scratched at his stubbled jaw, squinted up at her in a groggy stupor, and then apologized for sleeping. Apologized. Like such a necessary behavior was somehow offensive or criminal. It hadn't taken more than a little assurance to get him to take the pillow and go back to sleep. As they'd stepped off the train and parted ways, he'd given an honest and level nod and a smile, eyes gleaming with a sincerity that promised he would show tonight.

A slate-gray corecycle glided through the open gate and along the curb, its white-skynned rider bowing over the handles. A gloved hand raised the tinted helmet visor in salute, and two warm onyx eyes twinkled at her.

"Commander. Help has arrived."

Ambrosia reigned in her amusement and allowed herself a glance at his strong shoulders and posture on the bike's seat. "I suppose you'll do. Leave your bike by the curb and we'll walk across the base to the water."

He set his kickstand down and pulled off his helmet, raking back a chunk of wavy black hair as it tumbled over his forehead. "How are you recovering from everything?"

She shrugged. "I'm still catching up on sleep. How's your lip?" His lip looked fine now, apart from a scab where it had bled; and she was glad she had withheld the full strength of that strike, knowing that years of slapping marble made most sables capable of fracturing skulls.

"Much better. The ice helped." He dismounted and walked alongside her, pushing his key deep into a hip pocket. "When is the execution?"

"Twenty-seven co-conspirators were beheaded yesterday. Callon and Crossfire die tomorrow."

"Any word on the condition of the rail?"

"They located the derailed car, but there wasn't much left to salvage. The rail was declared sound today, and they ran the first train since the accident. I suspect if Callon had explosives in his pack, they were meant for breaking a coupling and running the first car far beyond Euclase."

"Did you finish your reports?"

She gave him a relieved glance. "Finally."

His obsidian eyes climbed the dark stone walls of a barracks as they passed. "Which one is yours?"

She pointed to a balcony facing the bay. "Up there. Some nights when I can't sleep, I sit outside and read."

"Is that what you'd be doing now if we weren't hanging out?"

Her lips kneaded together and dragged in the corners. The wind whipped past her ears and she shuddered, thinking she'd caught a piece of Callon's agonized screaming. She glanced back at the Hold, fearing the Sable Queen's gaze. "No. But this is much better."

They crossed a storm surge gate and followed the steps down. The walk snaked to the water's edge, where the heavy boughs of trees dipped close to the waves. Ducks and geese hunkered down in their beds among the roots and rocks, bills buried deep in their down, eyes peeping at the intruders. A hefty gander raised his head and rattled his tail with a warning honk. Ambrosia pressed her hands into her jacket pockets.

"So, what were you really asking for when you suggested I date you?" she asked.

He shrugged. "A friend."

"Why do you mock me so boldly?"

His almond eyes plead honesty. "I meant that."

"Then tell me what you want out of this friendship."

"Maybe a look at the world through your eyes."

She kicked a stone in the path. "There are far nicer perspectives to explore."

A few steps on, he picked up the stone and skipped it across the water. "Have you ever seen the world through a Pyron's eyes?"

She stopped. "That's one reason I agreed to hang out."

"Looks like we both share a healthy curiosity." He cast a crooked smile and skipped another stone.

"And bad reputations."

His white skyn glowed in the moonlight, casting its supernal halo upon her dark uniform. The shocking colorlessness proclaimed his supposedly inferior genetics and dangerous beliefs, much like her scarlet collar chained her to a reputation of promiscuity and a life of murder.

He picked up another smooth stone, rubbing it in his hands while those midnight orbs searched her. "That's probably why we don't have many friendships outside of our own."

"Do you have any family?"

He cast the stone over the water. "A younger sister. Parents are dead."

"Illness?"

"Justice." He stared shamelessly into her. "Mother was butchered in the market street for resisting arrest, trying to get home with medicine for Solla. Father died in a work camp for no good reason. What about yours?"

She shrugged lightly. "They're alive and well, I think. They have a farm in the mountains of Selen."

"Do you ever get to visit?"

"I don't anymore. The academy issued us two days each year to see family. My graduation year was the last I went. Over five years ago."

"They must miss you."

She rubbed a pained smile from her face. "No. I grew into a stranger. Each visit, their welcomes became colder. They didn't know me, and I didn't really know them."

He stole sideways glances, reading the pain that must have been showing on her face.

"I'd walk into the village in uniform and the people would disappear. I wasn't the child they once loved. No one pitied me once I was grown. My parents would just look at me and cry, my brother went into the fields, not wanting to see me. They wouldn't speak to me, even when I told them I was still a virgin. And on my last visit, my eldest brother told me I was dead to them, and by returning I continued to shame my family—that I was a whore. So I left with a determination to fulfill their prophecy."

His gaze rested on her, unjudging, and his lips remained still.

Her heart pounded, and her neck burned. But she continued anyway.

"It's still my deepest regret. I found an attractive soldier and gave it all away. Used protection. Left him thinking he was horrible, and never did it again." *Scrag it.* He didn't need her personal history. Ambrosia balled her fists. "I know it's impossible for people to believe that we're not all rushing into bed with the next man we meet, but I don't need a man to meet my needs. All I ever wanted before this was a happy marriage and home with a couple of children. And there's nothing I can do to have that now." She pressed her fingers to the bridge of her nose. "I don't even know why I'm telling you this. It was a simple question about family."

His cheeks reddened and his eyes strained with pity. "If it helps keep things even, I've never touched a woman."

A short laugh blew through her lips and she gripped the hem of her jacket, trying to settle her racing heart. "Does that make you a respectable person or an inexperienced one?"

His brow twisted into a quizzical expression. "It's by choice."

"Well, the tabloids make you Pyron men out to be voyeuristic animals with warped, insatiable appetites."

His eyes pressed down into thin, black slits as his lips twisted into a rope of comic suspicion, and his nostrils flared. "And you know what the tabloids say about sables. I think most of us just want to live a quiet life and raise a family."

"But it's true that you all expect sex after a simple kiss."

"Simple? That kiss is how we pledge the rest of our lives to the person we love. It's no more simple for us than sex is casual."

"So, you see it as a vow of marriage?"

"Yes." His expression was sincere and his tone calm. "It's the first act toward a sexual relationship, of marriage for life. It's making a promise of more to come, and we intend to follow through quickly to show that we don't want to leave any chance for it to be broken or left unfulfilled."

"I had no idea you regarded marriage so highly. Why don't more of you get married before a Kobalt judge instead of making it seem like you're breeding freely in the streets and forests?"

"I think we would, if we could afford it. But we're taxed on every child we produce, and the moment we're unable to pay up, we're castrated. So we join together the way our Sky Father married his first two children, and it seems to hold better than state licenses."

He was right. Ambrosia cleared her throat. "I know plenty of people who pay the judge for a divorce every time they have an opportunity for a better marriage. I never understood how it was any different than a sable sleeping around. Somehow a person's social class guarantees a one way ticket to respect or infamy."

They ambled along the water's edge, and insects flung themselves through the grass along the walk. Her shoulder brushed his, and she moved back. He smelled of sage and lavender, and the silken moonlight traced his nose and lips. His jaw looked smooth and freshly shaven.

He walked a little closer.

"So how many rumors about the Sable Academy are true?"

The memories tumbled in, driving a bitter laugh from her throat. "Where do I even start?"

"The beginning."

She drew a shaky breath. "Our first week. . ." The memories brought emotions tearing through her and she stared, glassy-eyed, at the path ahead.

"Maybe I shouldn't have asked." Disrel's voice broke through the turbulence and calmed the storm.

"It's fine." She clenched her hands and forced a trained smile, the one she'd learned how to wear to hide her emotions when something hurt. "We were all between seven and nine, hopelessly homesick, pouring our tears into the pillows and bedsheets of our bunks. The den mothers brought in a crate of kittens and bunnies and let us each pick one out and name it. We fed and cuddled our pets until we were hopelessly attached. Then the den mothers ordered us to kill and eat them. Hysteria reigned for hours, but they wouldn't serve food to a single one of us until every cadet in the barracks had obeyed. Some broke sooner and pressured the others. It was our first lesson on the dangers of emotional attachment. We were told to drop our dreams of lasting friendship, of motherhood and family, because we had been chosen to be killers for the security of the empire. Then we settled down for a few years of education, a boarding school unlike any other." She slowed under a lamppost, quaking at every flashing memory.

"That's horrible."

She shook hair from her eyes and pressed her lips. "It doesn't bother me. I'm grateful for how it's made me stronger. There are far worse things I could have told you. Rumors? Our breasts aren't removed. Most of us are just too fit to have any. We're not given serums or enhancements or growth hormones, just a good diet and natural supplements. Most of us are taller than five-eight because we had that potential when we were chosen. We're selected on perceived genetics, the likelihood that we will grow to be as strong as men. We're not mutilated, sterilized, or abused to make us mean. Frankly, we're just tired of being treated like scum, and after years of it, we have no tolerance for impudence. Abortions are mandatory. Our team of physicians is always ready to help us return to health and our patrols. The things that are true—we lose our family names to be called sables."

"Do you remember your family's name?"

"Vaxaldin. But our identity is in our sablehood. We are one, not individuals. And any sable who becomes Sable Queen renounces her given name for the title."

Disrel looked at her gently, empathy seeping through his gaze. "Hm. There's so much love in the name a mother gives her child."

Ambrosia shrugged. "I've been shown that even her love can't last forever. But as for other things, we receive a very high education and hone our combat skills throughout life. Our sable family is our only family by the time we graduate, and the cadets who fail to graduate are"—she fished for palatable words—"treated very badly. I know of only one who succeeded in running away during my years as a cadet."

His long eyelashes shielded his eyes, but she caught a glimmer of pain in the shape of his mouth.

"The Abysmal," he muttered, his nostrils flaring.

Her jaw quivered. "How do you know about that?"

No sable ever spoke of the unmentionable horror captured runaways suffered, not even among themselves.

"I knew someone who escaped the academy years before we were born," Disrel said.

She frowned. "How did you know this person?"

"She helped me and my sister many times when we were young. And then she showed me her scars." He shifted back into walking. "Is there anything else you've always wondered about Pyrons?"

Her cheeks tingled when he looked at her. She fished for a question that might save her from those memories she kept locked away. "Do you actually believe that using furniture with legs drains your cosmic connection to your sky deity?"

He threw back his head and rubbed his eyes. "Ha. That's a good one. The tradition of floor seating reminds us that no one is better than the rest or entitled to respect. The only one worthy of a throne is our Sky Father. And since our ancestors used to wander all over the place, furniture like that was easier to pack in a wagon."

The aristocracy often sat on high chairs, sometimes to the point of ridiculousness. They often had to use stools if the heels of their shoes weren't tall enough.

"Does smoke bathing actually give you superhuman strength? Or is it the effect of inhaling the incense?"

His even row of teeth gleamed at her in the moonlight. "I don't know about that one. The Howlers may use opium, but that would only deaden pain. The smoke bath is supposed to represent a cleansing spirit reaching the part of our bodies that are made up of light. Water can only clean the outer flesh."

She wandered over to a bench and settled down to ponder his strange words. Kobalt people cared little for things that couldn't be seen or touched. The physical reality was all that mattered. Some believed in ghosts, but not as human spirits unwilling to break up and dissipate. They regarded them as creations of unstable minds, hallucinations of lunatics and drunkards. And when people infused Pyron folklore with this idea, they believed that if they were touched by a ghost, they would become sick and die. There was plenty of proof of people on the brink of insanity who saw ghosts and claimed to have been chased and touched, falling ill or insane and dying soon after, sometimes from what appeared to be suicide.

Disrel eased down on the opposite end of the seat. A deep ombre of orange and dusky blue domed their world. A crane flapped its way over the rocks and settled on the shore to preen. Ambrosia relaxed against the backrest and sighed, pondering his words. But the backrest provided little resistance, and the world leaned as the bench crumbled, pitching and groaning like a dying animal. Disrel scrambled to sit forward, then fell aside on his shoulder. Ambrosia sprawled in the wreckage, burning with anger, suppressing curses while Disrel turned his head and moaned as he wrestled a rotten board from the small of his back. The board crumbled in his fist.

"Well, there's another reason Pyrons don't use Kobalt furniture." He chucked the splinters and then sputtered as the breeze tossed them back into his face.

Laughter blasted from Ambrosia's mouth as she replayed the scenario in her head, Disrel reaching forward and flailing, the groaning cry of the wood as if the bench had said *Faaare-theee weeell* before collapsing into pieces. And each time was funnier than the last. She heard a piercing squeal and clasped her hands over her mouth. Was that her? Tourmal's Sable Commander lying on her back in a park by the water, cackling like a flustered hen? Hot tears streaked from the corners of her eyes. She wiped them, and Disrel's hand hovered, ready to help her up. She took it, and they both leaned over the bench, looking for a hope of piecing it back together again. But it was a loss.

"Well, it served its last star-crossed couple tonight." Disrel punted a board. "Think you're too good for either of us, don't you? Salty old bench." He plucked up pieces and tossed them into the waves. "We'll show you. Grow some barnacles."

Ambrosia buckled over, stumbling breathlessly and dropping a splintering piece of wood from her limp fingers. Her bones melted with this strange pleasure, and her sides ached. When was the last time she had shared a good laugh with anyone as looney as this Pyron? She wiped her eyes and groaned out the last bits of laughter that threatened to tear her sides.

He rubbed the small of his back. "Are you okay?"

"Yes, I'm fine."

"There's another bench down that way."

"No." She sank down into the grassy knoll, patting the ground. "This is a beautiful spot."

A pair of gulls winged a low path over the surface of the water. Tourmal was nothing like Selen, but it was starting to show her its own subtle beauty. Disrel lay down on his side an arm's reach away and twirled the lacy head of a bright blue beach flower between his fingers, one graceful leg bent out to the side and the other stretched straight ahead. He picked more of the flowers around where he lay and braided their stems. For a little while, the world seemed at rest, content to let the two of them exist side by side. A breeze whispered around them, stirring the grass and blowing strands of hair across Ambrosia's cheeks, pulling a healing sigh from her nose.

Disrel jerked up. "I think I saw a firebeetle."

"Really? It's too early for them."

"They're always early in Tourmal." He pointed. "Ah. I saw another one."

"Where?"

"There." He scootched closer and aimed his finger toward a clump of reeds along the water.

A vibrant flash of yellow popped over the reeds, drawing her eyes and disappearing before she could focus on it. Two more flashes teased her peripheral, and suddenly the waterfront was blooming with repartees of synchronized light. Disrel leaned alongside her, with his arm and shoulder a little behind her, smiling at the show, seemingly unaware of how close they were. She felt his warmth and could just make out the steady beat of his heart. She watched his chest rising and falling for a moment, then stole a glance at his face, never imagining a Pyron could be so comfortable around her. Why didn't he seem to fear her?

He slid away without awkwardness, wrapped his arms around his knees, and stared into the rolling waters.

She snapped a twig in her hands. "I'm curious to know why you sport a Kobalt haircut."

His arched one eyebrow. "To fit in, get a job, survive."

"Do your people shame you for that?"

"Some would. Our hair is a personal expression of strength, purpose, and tribal unity. There is a language to the different patterns that allows the weaver to express the beautiful things they see in you, especially when they include colored strands. Warriors would receive a braid unique to their skyname on their heads, which is what caused the fear of our braids and blessings."

"How long has it been since yours was long enough to braid?"

"Three years," he said. "But there were other times I took a Kobalt cut for a while."

"What about your sister?"

"She keeps hers long. And I braid it for her when I can. The ritual of braiding is a gift. It's unifying, like eating or praying together."

Ambrosia hugged her knees and stared off into the water. Braids were only practical to sables for keeping hair tidy underneath a helmet. They meant nothing. How strange that he had humbled himself by removing his canvas of cultural praise. She'd witnessed many Pyron men dragged into the prisons after a bloody uprising, their braids flinging about their shoulders as they struggled. She'd heard their enraged cries as that glory was shorn away. Shaving a Pyron's head was one sure way to render him a weak and ineffective fighter, to crush his pride and spirit, shame him and his people as conquered.

"I always thought that cutting your hair would remove the power of your skyname."

"No. The state believed the braiding and name to be tied together because of the warriors wearing their skynames in their braids. I think it started as a ceremonial thing. The elder would braid the name upon the head of the blessed so others could look and immediately recognize their gift and the good things someone else saw in them, and honor and appreciate them for that."

"Like a crown of compliments."

His lips pulled into a smile. "Yes."

A cynical smile twisted her face. If this were a Kobalt tradition, there could be no crown of blessing for a sable's head. "So, how do you put a name or any meaning into a braid? Couldn't there only be a handful of possible patterns?"

"It's easier to understand when you see it. If you don't mind me touching your hair, I'll see what I can come up with." He sat up and extended a bright blue beach flower.

Her hands fluttered through the grass. "Oh. That's not why I asked. I was hoping you could—"

"I promise it'll make sense."

She accepted the flower, a mixture of curiosity and apprehension churning through her chest. Was it treasonous to allow him to do this? He didn't seem dangerous, though his heroism on the train had shown her that she had underestimated him once already. She studied him, drawing from her intuition and feeling that he meant her no harm. After all, she was the one who had asked him out, lured him out here alone. Would she be able to take his work apart before returning to her barracks and facing her sables? He only wanted to show her something too difficult to explain. She could stop him before he finished.

"The undercut doesn't leave you much to work with." She jerked at the pins that held her hair in a tight coil and shook her head. "The Sable Queen sets this uniform, and it makes my head look like a monkey's butt."

He chuckled, raking his fingers over her ears and against her scalp. "Don't worry. It will still look nice."

Ambrosia rolled her shoulders, unaccustomed to a man's hands anywhere near her neck. He shook out a few tangles and used one of the pins to make parts. His fingers moved with precision and confidence, twisting tiny strands with a dexterity few men possessed. They flashed in her periphery, sweeping hair from her temples. They were neither short nor lanky, nor bony or fleshy, just strong and creative, with clean, clear nails. They bundled and separated, reserving strands of hair around her shoulders for later use.

A warmth swelled through her, lulling her into memories of steaming elderberry pies bubbling on the sill, of churning goat milk butter, of the crackling hearth and Father's deep voice rumbling stories in her ear while he held her wrapped against his chest, of her brother's glass pen scratching out arithmetic on paper, of the crinkle of straw and the crunch of snow underfoot and the pattering of rain on a slate roof. She strained to focus, but all the stresses of the past month sloughed from her in tingling waves. She felt vulnerable under his touch, but oddly, she didn't feel the least bit unsafe.

While he worked, Disrel explained, "Lateral braids are for fortitude and determination, and upright ones honor, faith, and meekness. Diagonals are for ambidextrous skill and adaptability, a sharp mind and good humor, optimism, and charity."

His hands scraped along the edges, tucking and tugging, twisting and looping without faltering, each motion as natural and swift as a grandmother's crochet needles.

"The number of strands and the color of threads speak of position in a tribe: unmarried girls, brides, mothers, elders. The size and tightness of the weave can talk about rowdy or gentle natures, strength of self-will, or suppleness of character. There is no one trait better than another. We're all just parts of a whole, balancing, receiving where we lack."

The rolling waves along the shore melded together, and her shoulders sank and her eyes closed. Her speech was mellow and unhurried. "Would you always braid the same thing upon a friend's head?"

"Not always. People grow and change, and there is always another fine quality that we didn't have room for in the last braiding."

His hand left her head a moment too long, and she jerked awake in time to see it drop around her shoulder and lay the borrowed pin among the others in her open hand. These were the hands of a skynmaker, a man acquainted with fine materials and accustomed to detail. Despite Callon's vile intentions, the dress he'd given her had been the finest garment she had ever worn. These hands were innocent of the part they had played in condemning her, and still, they'd wrenched her from the burning car in repentance.

She glanced back at him. "Have you found work in your new home?"

"I do odd jobs."

"Was skynmaking something you always wanted to do with your life?"

"No. I'm not sure what I'd like to do. I just took that job because I needed it."

Her head bobbed against the tension as he worked the length of her hair, then floated away to a respectful distance when he finished. She patted over her head, remembering how she used to weave flower crowns as a child while running down the slopes with her goats.

"Thank you."

He nodded pleasantly and stared off across the water. A blue light flashed atop an oblique structure on the opposite shore, like a spitting candle on a top-heavy layer cake.

Ambrosia slid the beach flower he'd given her into her hair. "That trading house is the oddest-looking building in Tourmal."

"I know. I lived there before they built it."

"What was there before?"

"Just us. Some tents. A big flat area with a drain for carrying waste into the bay."

"Us?"

"Pyrons. Strays. My sister and I were strays for a while. It was kind of an old dump or something until they developed it."

The buildings on the opposite side of the bay dimmed, and the surface of the bay turned a smoky white. It was raining on the opposite shore, but it seemed too distant to matter. A few minutes later, the roaring grew louder and the brightness spread on the water as raindrops crushed the surface. The leaves overhead clattered and warm drops pelted Ambrosia's body. She jumped up and pulled her jacket over her head. Disrel laughed out something about unexpected blessings as they raced down the walk. The entire park was a grayed-out world of eerie beauty. Disrel hammered up the steps but waited at the gate for her. When she caught up, they rushed across the bricked street for the porch on the nearest sable barracks. Ambrosia swung herself up by one pillar and leaned, soggy and dripping, breathless and panting, laughing raggedly. Great drops tumbled from Disrel's brow and the tip of his nose. He shook his head, flinging water.

"Agh! You're drowning me."

He grinned out from under a tangled web of black streaking down into his eyes and leaned on the other pillar. Just beyond him, underneath the next barrack's porch, a flash of brown snatched her attention, a hawk settling in the eaves, folding its wings. In the opposite crevice a white dove hunkered. Halos rode the streetlamps along every drive. The shape of buildings intensified and faded through the shrouds of driving rain and sheets of water rolled along the walks under the lashing wind. Cyclists turned on their high beams and slowed around the bends to avoid hydroplaning. Disrel's corecycle was just a sad gray blob by the distant curb.

He folded his arms. "I don't see this letting up for a while. The wind is blowing from the eastern shore."

A once-stray Pyron could never be wrong about the weather.

She patted the side of her head. "Well, it was fun catching up."

"Yeah. It was nice getting to know you better." He scratched his jaw and stared at his bike as if working up the nerve to run through the rain. Then he looked at her steadily, as if trying to memorize her, his dark eyes moving from one point on her face to another. "I guess this is goodbye, then."

"I guess so." She scrambled inside for an excuse to meet up again and found nothing.

He pulled his keystone from his pocket and bounced it in his palm. "Alright, then. Have a good night, Commander."

"Goodnight." Did she even need an excuse? She needed to know more about Pyrons and why he treated her so well. That was reason enough.

He cast a crooked smile and pushed off into the rain, head down, arms swinging, fading with each step.

Ambrosia clung to the pillar. "Disrel?"

"Yes, my lady?" He stopped and turned, black hair streaking down his brow, shoulders squared and face lifted as if the rain was nonexistent.

"Do you have access to a relay there?"

"I think so."

"Would you like to keep in touch? Or maybe hang out again sometime?"

"Sure." His response was immediate and upbeat.

"My schedule changes a lot. So just ask for the Tourmal Command Center, Sable Barracks Three, Sable Commander's desk."

He smiled and backed toward his corecycle. "Duly noted. I'll see you around. Goodnight."

He mounted the corecycle and donned his helmet. The corecycle illuminated, casting a halo about itself in the sheets of rain. Disrel turned it from the curb and cast a farewell wave before rolling off into the bleak jungle of stone and steel.

Ambrosia tugged at her hair a little, longing for a mirror, afraid of what her sables would assume. But the braids were all so many and so intricate that she risked tangling a hopeless mat. He had spent so much time on it, her hair deserved a few minutes of praise in the mirror. What compliments or curses had he weaved there? Could she understand them as he'd promised? She threw her jacket up over her head and pushed through the barrack's door.

Phaedra's eyes pounced from the pages of a splayed book like two golden lionesses. Ulyia's lips snarled over a sugar cookie clamped between her teeth, a sort of impish, prying grin. Crumbs tumbled into the bowl she cradled in her lap, bare knees splayed into the cushions of a plump armchair.

"Did you do it? How was it? What's he like?"

Phaedra slapped at Ulyia with the book from her reclined position on the adjacent couch and pulled her robe more tightly around her breasts. "Shhh! It's only twenty-two hundred hours."

Ambrosia tugged the jacket hard over the sides of her head. "If you must know, we sat and talked."

Phaedra's eyes dove back into the pages of her book, and Ulyia munched.

"Oh." Crumbs plinked down the sides of the bowl. "Maybe next time?"

Phaedra threw a pillow at her comrade. "That's her business. Now pass the cookies."

"I just want to know what a Pyron man is like."

"Then go find your own, foxy."

"My business has been closed since Brody." Ulyia flipped through a magazine on the armrest, devouring page after page of suntanned Kobalt torsos with skyns delicately clinging to the ends of Adonis lines.

"Why do you think she went out with an ashrat? They behave better because they know if they make one wrong move they're dead." Phaedra pressed a cookie to her lips and faded back into her read.

Ulyia tossed her magazine back onto the center table among a slew of other cheap tabloid literature. A sinister-eyed man consumed one cover like a leering monster, his braids dripping like tentacles around his neck. Blurbs summarized articles within. *Pyron genetics linked to emergence and spread of new diseases, experts say. Pandemic likely.* Another cover showed a Pyron clinging to a high windowsill like an ape, peering at the shadows of a couple making love. *Ten unbelievable things Pyron men do at night. Pyron's sky deity: an intolerant, racist myth.* An even more ridiculous news piece portrayed a gaunt Pyron leaping atop a bed in the nude, prolific body hair giving him an animal appearance, growling over a woman helplessly clutching her bed sheets to her throat. The woman's husband writhed in a puddle of blood on the floor in the foreground. *Rodents and Pyrons: Common ancestor? Delusional disorder linked to Pyron sympathy. Everything you need to know about Braids and Birthrights.* Another cover spilled over with anthropomorphic rats wearing Pyron faces, greedily devouring food from the plates of Kobalt children.

Ambrosia jerked from the recreation room and stole up the stairs to her quarters. She pulled the wet jacket from her head, leaned on the washroom sink, and gazed numbly into the mirror. A crown of blue beach flowers sprouted along the deep red braids that swept down the sides of her head, framed in delicate loops of smaller braids that laced over and under and converged together at the nape of her neck. But the plaits seemed only a frame for the visage of a Selenite mountain girl.

His fingers had reached into her soul and sculpted its likeness into her hair. This was herself—her truest self. Not a lost mountain girl in a flower crown. It had brought out something in her eyes, a piece of her soul that had been tucked away in her deepest, innermost parts for years. How had he seen her? Were those black eyes magical, soul-reading probes? Or was it a coincidence? Was she only seeing what she knew was deep down, and he had only ignorantly helped her to see it?

The portrait smudged and streaked, and she caught her nose and mouth in her hand, trying to hold back the boiling floodwaters of pain. She wiped the tears and tore at the braids. The plaits tumbled apart from the bottom and crumbled under her wrathful fingers. Bruised flower petals and stems fluttered in the sink, stinking like noxious weeds. She could not allow this awkward feeling to creep in. Fondness was that little white rabbit she had pulled from the basket, that innocent bunny she had fed and stroked and hugged, whose soft, clean fur had absorbed her tears for home. It had brought a glimmer of joy and a basket of sorrow. One morsel of peace was not worth a plate of pain. Love was pain, because loss shadowed it like a vulture.

Her fingers jerked and caught in the strands, tangling the smallest weaves. She would be undoing this all night. How had it only taken him just shy of an hour? She would have to hide some of these strands, pretend she had braided them herself. But all she had managed to do was mar the picture he had woven there, spin his compliments into curses. *Let it be*. A tangled head was more fitting for a sable anyhow. She drew a robe around her shoulders and slumped upon her bed, clutching one lonely beach flower that had come out unscathed. She could sit with Disrel, talk with him, laugh with him, let him salve her heart for a brief season, but eventually she would have to crush him along with the rest of his people. It was her duty to her emperor, her honor to the state. She was a sable first, Ambrosia second.

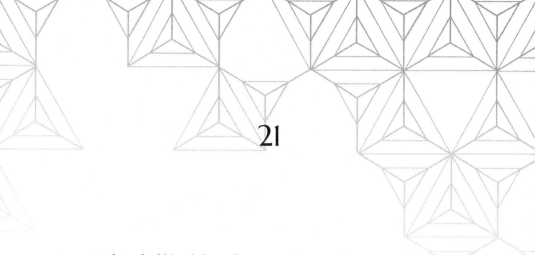

21

Disrel cinched Tygo's bearish torso and twisted. Tygo caught the inside of Disrel's thigh and tested his balance. Sweat rained on the wrestling mat, and it squealed under gripping toes and heels. The air was humid and metallic. Disrel's hands slipped across bare skin, digging for a better hold. Tygo gave an inch and Disrel brought him down to the mat, but not before one sinewy bronze arm caught his neck and swept it into a guillotine choke. An unforgiving elbow mashed his shoulder, and the air yellowed. Disrel wove an arm through Tygo's elbow to the mat and rolled, opening the choke, slipping free and grappling with Tygo from his mount, but Tygo's legs wrapped and rolled him, locking his shoulder as he wrenched his arm straight back. Disrel groaned through his teeth against the sawtooth blade raking through his joints and hammered Tygo's leg in surrender. Tygo released and stretched out, pressing a towel to his bald head.

Mored hunched in his armchair in the corner, his pen scratching over a scorepad. "Tygo, twelve. Disrel . . . five."

Tygo dragged the towel over his face. "What happened to your grit, man? Where's your thirst for blood?"

Disrel sat back, chest working, brow dripping. Every inch of him ached. His temples throbbed. "I keep looking into my next strike, don't I?"

"Your blind swings were pretty deadly. But you've been regressing ever since that train accident. Did it shake you up?"

"I'm fine. Just got a lot on my mind."

"Focus is key. You gotta clear your mind before you come in here or you'll get it cleared with a knockout."

Mored's steely eye raked him. "Care to share what's eating at you?"

Disrel reached down into his backpack and pulled up a crumpled magazine. "Found this on the return train. Page three." He laid it in Mored's hand.

Alta swept into the room bearing a sweating pitcher and a tray of cups and laid them on the table next to Mored's armchair. Disrel thanked her and poured a drink. He handed it off to Tygo, then poured his own and lifted it to his lips.

A white card tumbled from the bunched pages into Mored's lap. He scooped it up and turned it over in his fingers. "This isn't the pass we gave you."

Disrel reached for the card, fire flushing through his face, but Mored evaded, giving it a closer look.

"Sable Commander Ambrosia? Why did the Skynhound write you a pass for Tourmal?"

Disrel raked his neck. His cup clunked down on the table a little harder than he'd meant it to. He couldn't lie in front of Alta.

"She wanted to follow up with some questions—about the incident."

"What do you mean? She wants to meet with you?" Mored's tone darkened.

"It was for her report. Because I saved her life or something."

"Like she needs you to help her with her homework. You already met with her, didn't you?"

Disrel huffed and faced Mored. "We hit it off on the train and she asked if I wanted to hang out."

Mored gored him with a look and whacked the table with the magazine. "Are you insane? You're dating the Skynhound?"

Alta set the pitcher down. "No! Disrel, dearheart, no. This is not wise."

"It was just one date."

"Was, huh?"

His hands dove into his pockets. "I can study her up close, glean information."

"Ah! *Study*. Yes. So just how close are you going to study her exactly?"

Concerned faces pinned him from all sides. He set his hands on his hips and pulled a tight breath. "We both know it can't go anywhere. And I don't even like her."

"Who said you like her?" The armchair squeaked and rattled under the spitting Kobalt. "You know what kind of Pyron dates a sable? A severely addled one! What do you think the Skynhound—let alone any sable—could ever want with a Pyron? You think she isn't going to start noticing that you're a lot like her renegade? Start putting the pieces together? You'll slip up. She'll sit you down to a picnic and bat her eyes, and before you can swallow the first bite—whack! You've got a red collar."

Disrel's skin crawled at the scathing rebuttal.

Alta laid a hand on his shoulder. "Please think this through. The Skynhound's sole purpose is to destroy you."

He backed from her reach. "I know the risks."

Mored pushed up from his chair, muttering salty words. Alta's hand planted into Disrel's chest, and her eyes counseled him to keep the peace.

His chest thundered. "She's not what you think she is."

"She's a highly trained killer." Mored stabbed the air with his finger. "The moment you forget that, you lose."

"She's a young woman with a heart like any other."

"That's exactly why the most elite fighting unit in the Kobalt empire is female: They don't have to be stronger than soldiers to win a fight. They're shrewd. Beguiling. They prey upon men's hearts. One attractive sable can single-handedly defeat the Tourmaline Renegade before the entire Kobalt military has a chance at him." Mored threw the pass at Disrel's feet and snapped the crumpled magazine from the table. "There's nothing wrong with pitying her for being kidnapped from the cradle, but you'll never fix her or save her. If you ever saw one whose heart grew back from some sliver or seed that escaped cauterization, she was hanging on a pole."

"I believe in Thelis." Disrel's jaw clenched and heat blasted through his nose.

"You started this fight for Pyron. Think of your own people and don't try to be the Skynhound's savior. Now Cinnabar has made himself the Emperor–General of the military, and increased your bounty by one hundred and twenty thousand credits. The repairs to the Tourmal–Pyron rail are almost complete, and your headhunter is just waiting for you to drop her another clue. Don't forget that the next time you're 'just hanging out' with her." He snapped the pages open and glared down at an article.

Alta stepped up, her eyes dewy and glistening. "Thelis is strong in you, Disrel. You have an inclination to fix what is broken, to nurture and heal what is wounded. I have seen others who, like you, thought they had more than enough balm for the broken hearts, and they spent everything pouring themselves down bottomless drains and never filling them up. They did not realize the cost of such reckless love. Remember the fable of the lily? The only way to get the healing balm is to crush it. Understand?"

He stared at the floor and clenched his jaw. Crush Ambrosia to heal her? That made no sense.

After a minute, Mored grunted. "Tygo, remember when Hamil told us about Project Dust? He was dead on it. That lab has been perfecting a gas that weakens the pulmonary system, making those who have recently breathed it more susceptible to the virus they've been developing, more likely to die from it. Just imagine how fast Pyron would go, all crammed together like that." He snapped his fingers.

Disrel paced a circle, cracking his knuckles. What sort of evil possessed men to engineer diseases? Wasn't the need for steel and arrows unholy enough?

Mored tapped the page. "Maybe you could sabotage the climate-controlled nurseries."

"Some might survive. And I'd have to disengage the alarms. It's risky."

"You're clearly an expert risk-taker," Mored muttered.

Disrel bit his tongue, more concerned with the news than engaging Mored's irritability.

Tygo hung the towel over his head. Alta poured another cup of water. The grind of turning minds set fire to the air.

"I'd have to destroy all the research, the recipes, the cultures. Every shard, so they can't even find a piece to clone from."

Mored scratched his chin, and his brow lifted. "Tygo, do we still have that corruptor we purchased last year? Would you fetch it for me?"

Tygo jumped up and left the room.

Mored eased back down into his armchair and turned through the magazine. "You don't have any prior obligations with the Skynhound, do you? She won't notice you're missing about the same time the Tourmaline Renegade shows up in Euclase?"

"No."

"At least you won't have to worry about accidentally killing her while she's climbing on your neck. One of my connections sold us a little device that can scramble and destroy organisms by emitting a powerful frequency that shatters cell walls like glass."

A wry smile twisted Disrel's lips. "Like an EMP bomb? That's cute."

"Ha! You have no idea just how cute. Plant it in the lab, and it will turn every living cell and virus in the facility to jelly in minutes. I'm going to set it to give you time to retreat. Get as far away from the lab as possible. The seller warned me the sound is so disorienting that anyone caught within range will walk himself in circles until he dies."

Disrel crammed a fistful of protein bars into his backpack and jerked on the drawstrings. He checked his forged ID and papers before tucking them into his pocket, and divided a makeup kit into a variety of inconspicuous containers in case his bag was searched. Voss's chesty laughter and Doni's dramatic outbursts rang through the vent in the floor. It seemed they were visiting every other evening now. Disrel reasoned he could afford to miss another party.

A knock sounded on the bedroom door.

"Come in," Disrel said.

Koti popped through. "We're almost ready to start." He wilted a little. "Oh. You're leaving."

Disrel shrugged the backpack on his shoulders and buckled it. "Yeah. I just came back to pack some supplies."

"I hope they're paying you well for all these last-minute errands. You take big risks every time you go out wearing Kobalt face."

Disrel squeezed past. "If I can hack the Pyron sector, I can go anywhere."

"You do make a convincing Kobalt. Maybe you should work for me. Then you wouldn't miss fun times like tonight."

He forced a laugh. "Thanks. But I'm not cut out for a desk job. I don't care what it pays."

Koti scratched at his nose and followed down the hall. "I've never seen you packed so heavy. Is your night job sending you somewhere or can't you tell me?"

Disrel turned on the stairs. "It's just for a day or two. But there's a chance I'll be gone longer, so tell Solla four or five days."

Koti tilted his head with a scolding eye.

"I need to sneak out of here without her—you know. . ."

He folded his arms. "You can't afford to gamble like that."

Disrel forced a laugh. "What do you think I do? I'll be back. I just don't want her worrying."

"Right. Right." Koti bobbed his head. "You're probably just painting the side of a new warehouse tonight. And Solla will be so irrationally worried that you have to slip past her."

Disrel clenched his jaw and looked away. He hated lying to people, even when he hadn't directly lied. It was all the same. Having to mince his words and twist meanings was not who he was, not who he wanted to be.

"Disrel. You can't just sneak out. You're missing her birthday party."

He groaned as his heart plummeted. He'd never missed any of Solla's birthdays, and no matter how destitute they had been, he'd always arranged something special for her.

Koti punched his shoulder and held him at arm's length. "Look. You be honest with her, and we'll take good care of her while you're gone. Just stay safe out there, my friend."

Disrel fell into Koti's embrace. *My friend*. When was the last time he had heard that from a Kobalt? *Friend*. Koti patted his back in parting, and they continued down the stairs.

A tinsel banner swung through the kitchen and string lights spiraled up the pillar that separated it from the living area. Solla halted mid-twirl and stared numbly.

"Where are you going? You just got home. You can't leave."

Doni and Voss slowed their movements as they strung the last line of tinsel.

Disrel rubbed his jaw. "I'm sorry, Solla. Something came up at work today. But maybe we can celebrate when I get back."

She pressed forward, eyes brimming. "Tomorrow? We can save leftovers for you and have a two-day celebration."

Disrel rubbed the back of his neck, feeling Doni's judgmental glances. Why couldn't Solla just grow up and understand the dangers in the world around her?

"I'll be gone a few days." He opened his arms up, welcoming her in for a hug.

Solla's lips puckered as she averted her gaze. If he could take her to the Pyron sector and show her the horrors others her age were enduring and the birthdays they were unable to celebrate. . . . He wiggled his fingers, beckoning her in and forcing a smile.

She moved back and folded her arms.

"Come on, Solla. Don't be like that."

"Don't be like what? You're only ever here to eat and sleep. All you care about is your job. What good is money to us, anyway? We can't buy anything with it, can't travel anywhere without getting arrested. Why can't you see that spending our last moments together is more important?"

His arms dropped. If she only knew. Now he looked horrible in front of his friends.

"Solla, the truth is . . ." He bowed his head and bit his tongue, throwing Koti a helpless glance. The truth was hard.

"You're still running with that gang, aren't you?"

"There's no gang. There never was."

Her eyes were hard little balls of burning metal. "You're a liar."

He sighed. "I'm done here. I've got a train to catch." He shrugged the pack farther up his shoulders and made for the back door.

Koti followed all the way out into the stable.

"Disrel. Stop just a minute."

"That's what I was telling you about, Koti. Now she has Voss and Doni thinking I'm just like the posters say—some greedy, money-grubbing ashrat who couldn't care less that it's his sister's nineteenth birthday. Give it five minutes. She'll be crying and bellyaching about how I never loved her." He planted his leg over the corecycle and kicked the stand back.

Koti's hand came down on the handlebar. "It's okay. I know. It was never about money, and you don't need to pay me anything for your time here. I've been counseling her some evenings. She was too young to comprehend the death of her parents, and every time she senses you're too distant, she fears you're going to abandon her, and it triggers the vomiting."

Disrel pushed his helmet on. "That's her attempt at control."

"Maybe. Think how early she lost her mother, and then her father so soon after. And with the world the way it is, don't we all want a little more control? All you did was reinforce her fears. She kicked, you left. You did exactly what she expected you to do."

The corecycle purred to life as he rocked it backward with his toes. "Well, I hate to leave you to clean up the mess, but I don't really have a choice about leaving."

Koti murdered a string of Pyron words as he waved him off.

Disrel halted the bike. "What?"

"May your Sky Father watch over you." Koti laughed. "I'll keep working at it. Solla's a fantastic teacher. I'm just a poor student."

Disrel returned the Pyron blessing, and Koti gave a thumbs up. Then Disrel rode the corecycle down the winding dirt lane, his skyn reflecting the effulgent glow of the sunset.

Behemoth trunks and gnarled boughs wrapped the porches of Selenite Station and its terminals in grandfatherly embraces, disjointing the mossy pavement stones and wrinkling the sidewalks. An eclectic scattering of people waited in the terminals with their bags, some taking up as much room as they needed on vintage benches, the artwork long rubbed down to a dull embossment. Country folk ambled around the scored pillars, their hats and bare heads bathed in rainbows showering from the stained skylight murals in the roofs. A score of children splashed their hands in a singing fountain before the ticket counter, and dropped crumbs in for the metallic and mottled koi lurking among the rocks. Disrel pocketed his ticket and ducked into a communication booth. He lifted the receiver and pressed his hand to the pad. The operator's voice mumbled groggily over the line.

"Connect me with Tourmal Command Center, Sable Barracks Three, please. Sable Commander's line."

Laughter warbled through the speaker before the line popped. A female voice grated in a habitual monotone: "Sable Barracks Three. How may I help you?"

"Sable Commander's line please."

"Official or personal?"

"Personal."

"She's on duty. Leave a message?"

"Sure."

"Fire when ready."

Disrel's hand slipped in and out of his pocket. He had expected her to be on duty. What would jar him more, hearing her voice or leaving his for her to hear later?

"Hey, Ambrosia, it's Disrel." A bright square poster gleamed on the wall at his elbow. *Have you seen him? Report all Tourmaline Renegade sightings to the Tourmal Command Center. Keep the empire's children safe.* The Tourmaline Renegade's masked bust glared back, arms folded, blades protruding from both hands with blood wetting their gleaming edges. The artists were pushing their liberty of late. Mored's criticisms echoed through his mind. What was he doing with a sable anyway? She would never divulge military secrets or plans. Solla deserved what little time he had more than any other woman.

"Is that all?" the raucous monotone bellowed in his ear.

"Hey, Ambrosia, I'm sorry we had to end things a little early last time. If you still want to hang out, we could grab drinks, or go for a drive, or even just crush another bench. The pass you gave me is good for a month. I don't know if you did that intentionally or not, but yeah, I really enjoyed getting to know you and I hope to see you again." He fussed with the receiver. "See you around. Bye."

Disrel hung up and stumbled from the booth on shaking limbs. All Mored could do was throw a hissy fit. This was his fight, his choice, and he would risk another date for the good of the uprising, for Pyron's freedom. That first date had exceeded his expectations. The Skynhound was not so frightening. She was still a woman at heart, with complex human emotions and a past. She had been warm, tolerant, inquisitive, open, even letting him braid her hair. They had set aside their differences for a few hours just to enjoy the stillness and peace they allowed to exist there at the water's edge. It was no miracle. They had created that moment together. What if one impossible friendship could change the world, spark a love that would catch fire and start a revolution in the hearts of thousands? And maybe it wouldn't last much longer. After another date or two, she might lose interest, or they might part ways after a harsh disagreement. Maybe it wouldn't even matter after tonight. If he was caught in Euclase, nothing on this earth would be more significant than where he would find his next breath, his next moment without pain.

Disrel boarded his train and took a seat, wedging his overstuffed bag between his legs. The captain breathed out information about the trip over the intercom, and the doors hissed shut. The train glided into motion and the journey began.

Disrel closed his eyes and mulled over his itinerary. He was prepared to spend several days on the streets or attempt to walk the hundreds of miles back through the wilderness should the military shut off transportation and close the border in and out of Euclase. If he faced capture, he might have the chance to wash his face and hair and turn his skyn to its default white. Then, they might throw him in the Pyron sector where he'd have at least a slim chance of escape. Disrel trained his mind on positive thoughts. He'd slip in and out, and then enjoy a quiet train ride right back into Selen. He'd be back tomorrow evening at the latest, maybe just in time to have some leftover cake and put a smile on Solla's face.

The carriage lights dimmed and reading lamps popped on here and there. Passengers curled up with blankets and books. The car hummed and clacked rhythmically over the joints in the rail creating a lulling ambience. Brown paper rustled and tangy odors of a cheesy, garlic sourdough toastie bread wafted down the aisle. Disrel swallowed hard and slid down in his seat, hugging his stomach with one arm. It was only a few hours to Euclase. He would wait a little to eat and go on that strength through the night.

A wall of dark timberline rushed past his window, and a single star danced in a sea of indigo. His knees squeezed his helmet resting on top of his pack. Just below it in a deep pocket lay the corruptor device, some black-market sorcery designed by a fanatic who probably sold all of his weapons to the highest bidder—no remorse, no discretion. How could Mored afford such weapons, all his corecycles and tools? Were they donations from his secret army? Or was he also supplying that same army, the network of contacts, the silent others who came and went like shadows in the night? Except for the time some had witnessed his blessing, Disrel had never seen more than eight in one place, and all were masked except Tygo, who served as Mored's eyes, ears, hands, and feet in the world above. Just how vast was Mored's army? Did they exist in every sector throughout the empire? Perhaps only Mored knew, and the Pyron sentries who watched the tunnels and gates. Did they even know their leader as Mored, or by various aliases? Or only through agents like Tygo? Perhaps they did not even know of a headquarters in the haunted Selenite subway that had been Mored and Alta's home for the last fifteen years.

Disrel pulled a magazine from the seat pocket and dialed up his reading light. He pulled his hand over the words on the cover in sections, more so on words less frequently used that he hadn't yet committed to memory. *Kobalt Ghost or Pyron Rogue?* The liddicoatite tourmaline shone from the renegade's skyn as he straddled the corecycle, foot planted on the arena floor, dark helmet turned defiantly at the imperial dais. Last month's news paired with fresh speculation. He opened the magazine and worked at deciphering the subheadings below the pictures to see if the articles might be worth the effort of reading.

Pyron quality of life improves after relocation to the new sector. Soldiers tossed supplies from a wagon. Dozens of thin arms stretched upward to catch the falling bundles of material, food, and utensils. *Tourmaline Renegade delays Pyron access to free land by hijacking train.*

Disrel's fingertips burned as he crumpled the magazine in a tight grip. Who believed this garbage? Did the regime care so much about Pyron's welfare that they would forcibly round up thousands and force them into a walled swampland much too small to sustain them?

Segregation of Kobalt and Pyron society necessary for peace, as Pyron insurgents spill blood. The artist's rendition depicted a massive, brute-shouldered Howler gripping a woman by the throat and waving his hatchet high overhead.

Deathmatch games held at Execution Square to relieve overcrowded prisons.

Factcheck: Empire has no intention of exterminating Pyrons once sectored.

Public opinion: Lord Cinnabar declared the people's emperor!

Disrel flipped the page and scanned on. *Compliance is the purest patriotism. Citizens honored for turning in local Pyrons for deportation.* A list of names spilled down the page.

His Supremacy increases reward for the capture of the Tourmaline Renegade to a lucrative two hundred and ten thousand credits. Alpha Vogin still at large for six hundred thousand more.

Page after page brimmed with conflicting headlines, doublespeak, and denial. They would never openly admit their truest intentions, but the comics, the art, and the public sentiment said it all: Pyrons weren't wanted. They were dangerous, unpatriotic, water in the blood of Kobalt veins. They were unsightly, barbaric, and strange. The governors, judges, officials, and all other heads of every Kobalt sector knew deep down of the nebulous plot to exterminate every last Pyron from the empire. Each contributed a cog to the great machine with their local laws and enforcements.

Disrel stuffed the magazine back in the seat pocket. Old news spun on the same old loom of propaganda. They wouldn't be reporting how the Tourmaline Renegade had halted the slaughter of two hundred old men outside the east Pyron wall and sent the soldiers scattering while their guard posts smoldered, or even how he had stopped the forced marches of hostage Pyrons in different areas of Tourmal. No. They couldn't, because the moment they reported on those things, they admitted their sinister intent. They admitted that death was lurking for Pyron behind the high cement walls, lurking on law books and in laboratory vials and in the rusty center of Execution Square. Death waited on every side, salivating for Pyron blood, and the blood of anyone, Kobalt or outlander, who dared oppose its right to rape Pyron life and breath from the earth.

Disrel leaned his head against the window and shut his eyes. When might he be able to sleep again, undisturbed, unroused by the threat of arrest and imprisonment, by the fear that he would wake and be the last Pyron on earth, with no one left to save? This fear bristled at his back more than any other. The burning sense of duty kept him returning to the old subway to grapple with Tygo and plan out his next move under Mored's guidance. Each time Tygo defeated him with a new move, Disrel got right back up. Each time multiple opponents leaped into the training ring, Disrel gave more. The risks of being caught, beaten, tortured, and executed were never as intimidating as Pyron's imminent extinction. As long as he was breathing, the extermination of Pyron would never be easy or cheap.

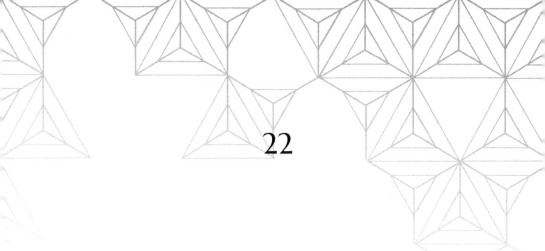

22

The train car rocked under the movements of passengers grabbing their belongings and shuffling for the doors. Bells tolled and voices ground over the intercom. Disrel blinked away the fog, yawned, and stretched in his seat. He sat a while, forgetting his Kobalt disguise, waiting to be among the last to disembark. A lower-class man paused in the aisle and offered his space. After a moment's confusion, Disrel nodded his thanks and scooted out with his bag, hastening through the station, past soldiers and security, beyond all the same wanted posters and headlines, and out into the wide blue streets of Euclase.

Euclase was the sector of bridges and arches spanning numerous streams and lakes. Its shores teemed with decadent marble homes and balconied resorts, offering splendor and delicacies as seasonal retreats for the wealthy. Euclase had extradited Pyrons before any other sector, cleansing its streets and waterfronts to "keep life beautiful." Graffiti marred the slogan on the welcome sign outside the terminal, superimposing "hearts" over "life" with Pyron symbolism worked into the characters. A crew of men ambled around the sign with tools in hand, preparing to take it down and load it onto a wagon for replacement.

Luxury corecycles with lavish sidecars cruised down the streets. Gated estates and illuminated home fronts boasted of the peace and comfort that was only possible when Pyrons were removed from the picture. Which of these upper-class Euclasians could have ever imagined the Tourmaline Renegade paying their sector a visit on a night as still as this?

Disrel walked several miles and crossed a waterway bridge. The crest offered a clear view over the trees on the opposite shore and the wall of the laboratory spanning the river's edge. The facility vaulted into the sky with architectural bravado. Smaller hive-like buildings squatted on the lawn behind it. Along the river, flatboats sat end to end, some loaded with mounds of minerals, others empty, waiting to return to the mines and the mountains.

Disrel stooped in the darkness between the bridge and wall, running his plan through his mind once more, forward and backward. He could not afford to miss a single step. His eyes worked the streets and foliage for any sign of military presence or ground security. He set his helmet on his head and cinched the chinstrap, then replaced his skyn's chip with the Tourmaline chip. Darkness swallowed him up from head to toe. With a sprint and a bound, he caught the upper edge of the wall and hauled himself over. The lush grass hissed under his boots on the other side. The expansive lawn was a spectral plain of silver and blue. No security vehicles flashed their lights on any corner of the grounds. But even dressed in the color of night, he might not cross the open acreage without being seen. He went down on all fours and crawled, and suddenly all of those miles of lizard walking made sense. Pride came before a fall, but a renegade at peace with his animal side would conquer.

At the building's edge, he noted a series of vents vulnerably positioned in the shadows. His entrance. He pulled a small toolkit from his pack and worked one of the grates open, then he pulled a harness from his pack and buckled it around his thighs and waist, checking each clip twice. He latched one end of his cable to the edge and the other to his harness, swung a leg over, and dropped into the blast of parched air. His torch dangled from his belt, illuminating crowns of rivets throughout the conduit. The pipe thundered under an accidental blow from his heel. His boots struck bottom, and he unlatched from the cable. The torch light illuminated three branches, all large enough to crawl through. Disrel slid on his knees and shuffled his hands, counting vague distances as steps and struggling to avoid the haunting nightmares of being trapped in a dark metal box, starving and suffocating, while soldiers dragged Father off in chains. Wind hammered his helmet and rattled the walls, carrying with it the ashy odors of an old ventilator laboring to circulate air through the building and keep equipment cool.

Some time and distance later, slits of light signaled the end of the tortuous journey. A wire-framed filter barred access to the grate. He fished a cutter from his belt, cut the filter from its frame, and hammered the grate open. Finally, he slid out onto the lab floor and raised his visor.

The room stretched for a mile like an underground metropolis, with glossy countertops undergirded by hundreds of unlabeled drawers. Shelves above were lined with a myriad of glass vessels and wire racks gripping glasses by their fluted necks. Scales and baskets and microscopes marked each workstation, neon tape ruled the flooring like the lines of a roadway, and tracks for transporting heavy equipment traced the ceiling. Sheets of tinted glass partitioned offices. Overall, the room was bland, sterile, and unwelcoming.

Disrel walked the cold aisles until he came upon long, glass-covered beds with rotating shelves lined with clear dishes. Each dish contained a splat of green, blue, or yellow goo, the food and host cells for the colonies of microbial cultures—and these viral nurseries were soon to be coffins. A wide window spanned the entire length of the adjacent wall, and behind it were boxes of shavings and pulp, each with a little door at the back. Disrel moved to the glass and walked its length. The shavings bucked and tossed, and a scaly pink serpent dragged along the inside just before a fuzzy white head with burning red eyes and a quivering nose pressed against the glass. Rats. Hundreds of white rats. Dozens in each box, dogpiled in the corners, squirming over and under one another for comfort and protection, crammed like Pyrons waiting their turn to die. Ashrats. Ashrats for the sooty complexion they earned from laboring in the work camps and mines. Ashrats for the way their population had burgeoned freely before the Pyron family taxes. Ashrats for the way their strays huddled in the sewers and grubbed for food in the dumpsters.

Disrel pulled the corruptor device from his pack, climbed a countertop, and mounted it with a wire to a ceiling track running over the aisle.

A glass sign gleamed where the track took a turn: Medical Library. A blue arrow pointed straight down a wide aisle to a black door hovering on a faraway wall. Its armored face forbade entrance to the uninitiated, and lights backlit a keypad of three buttons. A clock hung directly overhead, the sun dipped down behind the horizon and the moon risen to the current hour. Disrel pulled a rolling chair over, carefully stood upon it, and examined the side of the clock. He grabbed a ring of hex keys from his pack, found one that fit, and rolled the time forward. The safe door ticked several times. Disarmed. It was time for work. The lab was open. The keypad brightened.

Tygo and Astros had briefed him on a variety of safes, but those three brass buttons were still terribly intimidating. The passcode might require that all three be hit at once for a single input, or even just two minus the middle, or two on the left or two on the right. And then there was the possibility that the input required just one button: left, middle, or right. Alternatively, safes like these sometimes required up to nine inputs. Disrel fidgeted before the panel then strolled through workspaces, opening drawers and cabinets in search of posted notes scribbled by forgetful scientists. The clock whirred as the sun struck the horizon. He returned to the panel. If the time of day armed and disarmed the safe, perhaps the key also changed with the time of day. Eight hundred hours. How to register eight hundred hours with three buttons? Was it an addition? If he hit just one button, did it matter if it was left, middle, or right? He attempted a sequence that added up to eight. Something groaned inside the safe, but nothing moved. He repeated the sequence, attempting different buttons. The panel groaned. Two, two, two, and two. It groaned again. How many more entries before it denied him access? Three. One. Three. One. An alarm screamed. *Thunder.*

Disrel scrambled over the buttons, attempting sequence after sequence and trying not to forget which ones he had already used. He slammed his fist against the door and turned. The glass sign that had directed him to this safe was just a smoky sliver on the ceiling, but its letters pixelated the slim profile like a pattern, each grouping being three or less. He memorized the sequence and turned back to the keypad. Three. Three. Two left. One left. Two spaced. A click. The bolt slammed. Silence. He threw his weight against the door, revealing a plain black face lined with a hundred buttons and narrow ports, and a panel of scientific jargon indexing the library. Disrel mashed a button and the related port spit out a glass coin, engraved on one side and housing a crystal data chip on its surface. He pushed another button, and another almost identical coin pressed through a slit. Data chips. Each one could contain the life's work of a hundred scientists. Which one contained Pyron's nemesis? What if more than one held that information? What if these also contained cures and knowledge that virtuous physicians needed? Disrel's mind swam with the moral dilemma. For once, the Kobalt news headers might get it right. He retrieved two more chips and studied them in his palm.

The lab echoed with the sounds of a door finding rest in its steel frame. Disrel slammed his hand over the rows of buttons and plucked the chips as they appeared. He dumped them on a counter and tore through his bag, procuring a small cylinder, double sealed. Careful not to touch the inner surfaces with even his gloved hands, he pried the lids open. The world wouldn't crumble into the dark ages over one laboratory catastrophe. The knowledge of cures were well established, shared with other, smaller labs. This sinister research was recent, local, and hopefully irreplaceable. He speared each data chip with a pair of tweezers and lowered them into the vat of acid. Five. Six. Ten. One splashed droplet would end his life. His heart slapped back and forth, popping in his ears. He counted the chips as they swam in the honey-colored liquid. The world had reduced to this moment, this vat, and these chips. Fifty. Seventy. Eighty. The acid threatened the lip of the jar under the displacement. Some nearby space echoed with deliberate boot steps. Three more. An astringent blue torchlight strobed through a glass door at the other end of the metropolis. The acid hissed and boiled against the lip of the container. Disrel dropped the last coin into the bath, grabbed up his pack, and hustled back through the lab, following the track on the ceiling.

A military voice barked, "Hey, Sarge. I think somebody's in there."

Disrel climbed up on a counter and twisted the pin from the side of the corruptor. Then he bounded down and ran the aisles, flinging the glass lids off each unit. The corruptor gurgled to life. Militant voices spewed out orders to sweep the lab. Footsteps echoed and beams of jarring blue light swept the expanse. Disrel flew through the labyrinth like a dark shadow, his boots squeaking on the polished flooring, his breathing heavy and loud within his helmet. A security guard rounded the corner with his light and swung. Disrel went down on his knees, sliding past, staggering up and rushing on.

"He's coming right to you!"

A beacon of searing blue light barred the next intersection. Disrel caught the arm of a machine and planted his feet into a guard's chest, bowling him back. The open vent was in sight. He skimmed a roundabout path to the wall, dove through the hole, and snapped the grate back into place. The grating dissonance of the corruptor continued rising in pitch and severity. Disrel scooted back through the conduit on his butt, then hesitated. What if the guards disarmed the device? The blue lights whirled away from the vent. The guards walked the closest aisle several times, shouting orders at each other that gradually devolved into incoherent babbling as the corruptor's countdown reached zero and its tone began its torture of all living things.

A spark jumped along the conduit. Then another. And another. But they were intangible, ethereal, like rivers of black diamonds sparkling through the air. The rivets danced before Disrel's eyes, and he blinked back tears and clawed at his ears, trying to strike the bees from them. Angelic lights popped in his peripheral in colors he could not name, colors he was sure he had never seen before, but colors so familiar that alien names danced on the tip of his tongue. His stomach churned as he wrestled with a caustic, repulsive turning in his spirit. How many steps out? Was it two lefts and a right or three rights and one left? He gnashed his teeth and punched the conduit. The hypnotizing scream was so frenzied and bizarre that he grappled with a feral desire to run as hard and as fast as he could in whichever direction he could go, to butt his head agains the metal walls until he broke through. He shimmied backward through the duct, his nerves and flesh rattled by the resonance. The voices of ghosts droned rabid rhymes, some words Pyron, some Kobalt, some impossibilities for the human throat. The conduit was a cathedral ringing with a demon-tongued choir and the black crypt pinched like a straw, threatening to crush his head and squeeze him down into an infinitesimal particle.

Disrel gasped and arched his back and locked his shaking arms and knees into the sides of this womb of death. Every time he exhaled, a breeze from hell blew into his face, cramping and stagnating his lungs. And then he paused, trying to figure out who he was and what he was doing in this dark, frightening space. He could hardly remember ever seeing another face or anything outside of the metal curve his gloved hands and knees were pressed into. The only thing he was certain of at that moment was that he didn't want to be found crumbling and stinking in the walls. And that he would be if he didn't force himself to breathe and move forward. He scooted on three limbs, clawing at his neck and turning the helmet clasp over and over without progress. Something thwacked against his helmet, and he seized it in an attempt to fight it. The cable. His lifeline to the outside world. He jerked it taut, pressed his boots and back into the walls, and hauled himself upward, hand over hand, until he spilled over the edge of the vent and flopped onto the gravel, limp, shivering, buzzing from skull to ankle. The eerie droning consumed the night air, broken only by a sharp *bang* and residual crackling sounds in the sky above.

The ground tinkled and plinked with silvery snow. A sheet of glass disintegrated some yards away, and Disrel instinctively drew a hand over his helmet. A weight descended on his back and a crimson arm wrapped around his neck and hauled on him, wrenching his head to the side.

Every muscle in his body reacted with equal parts training and desperation. He rolled his attacker, locked his legs around a neck, wrenched an arm, and wrested a blade from the tortured hand. A female scream tore through the night: a Euclasian sable. Disrel slammed his heel down into her helmet visor before rolling free. As he came up, a jolting blow radiated through his abdomen, and a long shaft withdrew before jabbing again. He trapped it and delivered a crushing kick, turning its blunt end back into a plated torso. The first sable came up, and he cracked the polearm over her shoulder before hurling it away and bolting across the open ground. His pack flopped on his back and his harness jangled around his hips. The silver grass squealed around his boots. The stone fence barred the way, daring him to make the leap. He had trained for moments like this. No sable could outrun him without a corecycle. He could go for miles before tiring—

Shunk! A bolt thudded into the earth a few yards up. Another hissed its death wish at his heels. A sable, riding a corecycle, zipped along the fence, threatening to overtake him. Disrel leaped and set his toes into the bricks, rocketing up the sheer incline, catching hold of the ledge and pulling himself up. Lightning struck his back, and he loosed a mangled cry before he tumbled over on his face, writhing and gasping plugs of air. This was not the way to go. Not shot in the back like a coward.

Gradually, air flowed more freely, and he considered the bolt hadn't punctured a lung. But even if it had only pierced flesh, he'd never be able to make it back to Koti's without seeing a physician. The pain lessened as he flexed his shoulders, and he pushed up and stumbled for the bridge.

The sable's corecycle skidded in the mud at the canal's edge and came shooting up the bank from behind the wall. She twirled a grapple on a line overhead, meant for either one or both of his ankles. He ran closer to the low cement wall on the edge of the bridge. The murky water churned below. Riding the current downstream was his only hope of escape. Better to leap into the unknown—face the riptides and the rocks and whatever else lurked in Euclasian rivers at night—than to face a sable.

The grapple hissed around his left ankle and cinched, jerking his foot out from under him. His hands slapped down on the cement wall and his helmet crunched against the stone. The sable slammed into him, boots and fists. He rolled onto his back and landed two crushing kicks to her ribs before pulling her leg out from under her. She pulled away choking, streaks of deep red hair falling forward in her helmet. Her eyes vowed to kill without remorse.

Disrel drew his blade and aimed it at her face.

"I thought a commander stays in her sector."

The sable crouched and eyed her corecycle, leaning just behind him.

"You know one sable from another, renegade?"

He eased back. "It's hard to forget a head as red as yours."

"What did you steal?"

"Nothing yet. But I am going to take your corecycle." He swung his leg over the seat and toed forward.

"You won't get far." She jerked on his ankle cord, threatening to drag him off the seat. Her end was anchored to her duty belt, tying them both into a deathmatch. "Do you want to make it back to Tourmal dead or alive? Cinnabar has no preference, and neither do I."

The two Euclasian sables trotted around the wall by the water's edge with their crossbows ready.

Disrel pulled forward, dragging Ambrosia along the pavement on her butt. She snapped the release and rolled as bursts of blue lightning strobed the air. Ambrosia stood and peered at the lab through a shielding hand. Thunder rumbled. Then all of Euclase burst into daylight, as bright as a midday sun.

Disrel whipped the corecycle around and sped back across the bridge, the flying end of his ankle cord cracking like a whip on the pavement. A white halo puffed from the lab, billowing eddies of vaporous clouds in its wake, and the ground swelled with a running burst of energy. The Euclasian sables spilled in the grass behind the wall and curled face down. Disrel jerked Ambrosia's arm. "Get on!"

She clawed at his helmet as the bike rolled by.

"Save it! Get on!"

The moment her weight hit the seat, Disrel mashed the throttle and they cleared the bridge. The shock wave blasted through the street, punching breath from his body, and the corecycle lurched and drifted, tires squealing, as the ground rocked. A scorching cloud washed over them, hazing the world. Ambrosia pounded his back and screamed for more speed, and in return Disrel ramped a dead intersection and aimed for a tunnel. The fiery heat and toxic fumes billowed and boiled and licked around them like flaming racehorses. The black tunnel swallowed them, and the corecycle's mirrors showed the smoke coiling and foaming in the tunnel's mouth like a raging monster. A short, curved edge embedded itself between Disrel's throat and his helmet, forcing his chin up.

"I ought to cut your throat right here!"

He trapped the knife to his chest, torqued it from her grip, and flung it away. At the tunnel's belly, Ambrosia's arms folded around his neck and pulled him off the throttle. The bike wobbled and swerved and turned over, sending them both zipping over the pavement with her still locked around his neck.

"You're a monster! Do you know how many innocent lives you just claimed? That explosion must have leveled three square miles of city!"

Sparks leaped from his harness loops. "It wasn't part of the plan. Something must have caught fire."

They ground to a stop against a concrete divider, and yellow clouds gathered inside the helmet.

"Murderer," Ambrosia spat.

Disrel grabbed her boot and jammed his elbow into her leg. The second she released, he twisted, mounting her and smashing her helmet against the pavement.

"You knew what those gasses were for. You knew about the virus they had in that lab. How many times did you stand by while my people were experimented on like rats and slaughtered like sheep?"

Her eyes probed his dark visor. "If it's all my fault, why didn't you let me cook on that bridge?"

He searched her duty belt and shrugged. "Moral obligations. Now, I'd appreciate you cutting this cable from my leg so we can get on with our night. Bondage really isn't my thing."

"I'm morally obligated to kill you."

"So I freed a few hundred Pyrons and accidentally blew up a death factory. Help me understand the morality behind killing me."

"Your actions spark insurrection and chaos, undermining the authority and wisdom of His Supremacy. I will not rest until you're d—"

"Careful. Sleep deprivation leads to insanity." He rummaged around her belt and stripped a key from its magnet, then twirled the thin barrel in the grapple's socket and backed the cable until it slipped from his boot.

Ambrosia bucked and squirmed. "You won't get away with your crimes. I will see you drowning in your own blood for what you did to all these innocent people."

"Sorry I can't be more of a pleasure." He jumped free of her and marched back toward the fallen corecycle. "I'm sure we'll run into each other again and you'll have another opportunity to gore me."

She scrambled up and rushed him, kicking out. He caught her leg and tossed her back onto the pavement.

"I don't want to hurt you." He righted the bike, lifted the medical kit from behind the seat, and set it on the ground. "And you should probably check on your sables."

He mounted the corecycle and soared from the tunnel. The other side of the river was lightly windswept. The buildings on the waterfront gaped like soulless skulls. Sirens wailed and bells chimed, the alleys rang with the barking of dogs, and pillars of smoke towered in the streets. The freeway was a lonesome strip of ink, the trees charred, withered skeletons. His heart beat like a funerary drum, mourning the chaos and destruction in his wake. Ash and debris rained down and he wiped his glove across his visor. He had to get beyond the border before the military swept in and closed the roads.

But what had gone wrong? How had a frequency sparked an explosion of this magnitude? How many people had died in the blast? How many more would suffer for weeks and months the devastating losses of property, homes, pets, and peace? This was not the way of the Tourmaline Renegade, but the newscasters would relish it. It was not enough to stand and say, "I'm sorry. This wasn't supposed to happen." Mored had warned him. Innocent people would suffer in his wake. Innocent people would die at his hand. Somehow, he was supposed to justify this as the price of Pyron's freedom.

At the border, a string of military lights strobed the darkness. A checkpoint. Disrel turned off the road and worked through the forest and up into the bald-peaked mountains that made up the greater part of Dolom. He rode along the timberline and stopped on a barren flat overlooking the wilderness. It was too difficult and torturous a journey to make it back in a single night, with multiple borders to cross, and he ached from head to toe. His shoulders slumped as the adrenaline washed from him. After a long minute of reflection, he pulled his helmet from his head.

A sharp, goring pain snagged through his back. The crossbolt. How had he not punctured some organ in all that running and scuffling? He dropped the pack from his shoulders and reached back, feeling for a hole, a shaft, blood. But his skyn was unbroken. He turned the pack around and opened it up, slipping his finger through a hole on one side and catching hold of a heavy lump. Several supplies came up as one, skewered together by the bolt that should have taken his life. He reverenced them a moment before easing back against the rocky slope and rummaging in his pack for his lantern. He turned the wheel so that the light was just bright enough, but still too soft to be spotted by aircraft in the area, then unlatched the front of his skyn and peeled it down from his shoulders, his thumbs testing the gouge the sable's polearm had left in his armor. A bruise radiated through his abdominals. He pulled a jar of salve from his pack and rubbed it into his wounds, some of them from kicks, punches, and falls that he hardly remembered. Then he pulled the renegade chip out and drew the white skyn back around his shoulders.

A breeze meandered through the conifers, whispering sylvan melodies of peace and comfort. Disrel lifted his eyes to heaven, offering a silent prayer of gratitude and a plea for forgiveness. Iridescent sprays of stars spangled the sky in numbers and colors he had never thought possible. There was no night sky like this in Tourmal. The eyes of the tiger seemed trained upon him with the watchful gaze of a judicious mentor. They burned so fervently, he could always spot them, even from under a streetlamp in Tourmal. Surely his blessing had preserved him, not like a magical spell but like a seal of promise that he would be able to fulfill his purpose, his vow. All the close scrapes he had endured on the streets through the years came flooding back into his mind, assuring him that his Sky Father had preserved him for this moment.

He drank water from a small bottle and ate an energy bar and strips of dried meat while his mind wandered like a mountain sprite from tree to rock to distant precipices. Hoary, blue forests clothed the rolling silvery slopes and valleys. There must have been many nights like this one over hundreds of years with the sky tiger looking down on Pyron tribes traveling through these valleys. How many of his ancestors had migrated through this very pass? How many Pyron warriors might have stood on this flat and prayed to the Eternal Spirit? Had his great-grandmother walked these forests as a young woman? Or had his great-great-grandfather hunted a deer on this mountain? It seemed for just a moment that a graceful woman in white stood at the edge of the wood, her black hair hanging down her back, but the breeze blew, and it was only the moonlight raining upon a bush. If only the souls in heaven could step out upon the earth again to reenact their moments in this very spot for him to witness.

A primal whoop rang down the slope of a neighboring mountain and was answered by a similar, distant call. Disrel pulled his knees up to his chest. How did Father's eyes look upon him now that he had committed an act of terrorism? The world, doubtless, looked altogether less hostile, less critical, even less serious from way up above, from a body that could not be put to death by piercing or lashing, or starvation or heat or cold. But from down here, one had to do drastic things sometimes to survive, things that maybe weren't right but felt right in the moment. Father was surely so much wiser where he stood now, with Mother in his arms again. Perhaps he would not judge his son too harshly for his earthly perspectives, but have the same immeasurable patience and forgiveness and love of the Sky Father.

A mournful howl echoed between the mountains, stirring his native soul. Why was Ambrosia in Euclase? Why had she been in the vicinity of the lab at that exact moment? Had they been expecting him? Was she on to him? If she ever connected him with the Tourmaline Renegade, he would be forced to kill her to escape. He shuddered. Maybe Mored was right. It was already too hard not to go soft on her. The moment he had recognized her, his fist had softened, his fight slackened, and his every movement was checked with the fear that she would recognize him by his voice or his stature. How was she the same woman he had sat with at the water's edge just a few nights ago? Was her gentler side a mask and the aggressive, bloodthirsty Skynhound her real face? Every tangle with the Skynhound was a scrape with death. How much easier this fight would be if she had been executed.

Wolves chorused around the flat. Disrel scooted the lantern closer and eased his head down on his pack, closing his eyes for a moment until a subtle feeling prodded him to open them. One of the silver-headed rocks at the edge of the flat swelled and moved a little to the right. Disrel lifted his head. There could not have been so many rocks there before. Or were his eyes playing tricks on him? Two more rocks moved, and a third drew closer, its mossy edges bristling. Disrel bolted upright, drawing his knife and brightening his lantern. There were ears. Wide, pointed ears and tufts at each side. Three sets on one side, two ahead, and five scattered out along the other edge. The rocks grew faces, grizzly wolfish faces with bright muzzles and patterned foreheads. Their dull, empty eyes stared beyond him as though he was the specter and they were the living. They closed in dreamily, without a sound, walking upright like men, with naked hatchets swinging at their sides. Howlers.

"What do you want?" Disrel broke the silence forcefully. "I have no quarrel with Howlers." As if they had somehow missed his white skyn, he tried to placate them with his native tongue. A blow from a hatchet through armor was still a hammer-stroke, crushing bone and pulping muscle. There was no way he could fight off this many at once.

A snow-white wolf pointed his ax. "The more you wash your stripes, Kyreasheluhn, the bolder they shine."

Disrel's heart hammered out a syncopated rhythm. "I don't understand your riddle."

"Must we be so plain when we both know who you are?"

"How do you know my name?"

"I know a lot more than your name, Disrel. Or would you rather I called you the Tourmaline Renegade?" The man sat on Disrel's corecycle and toyed with its handles. His blood-streaked wolf pelt only broadened his neck and shoulders into a beastly silhouette.

"You're not answering my question."

"Who doesn't know of the Tourmaline Renegade? You're already worth more than every other rogue in the empire, besides myself."

"Who are you?"

The snow wolf threw up his hands and looked at his pack with bewilderment. A dark, stubbled jaw protruded from under the bright snout. "Don't you recognize me from my posters? I am the Alpha. Alpha Vogin."

"I thought you haunted Selen."

"Oh, we're on our way back to reclaim the territory, now that the Skynhound is preoccupied in Tourmal. But when the Tourmaline Renegade beds down on our mountain, how could we miss this opportunity to talk with him?"

Howler hatchets usually did most of the talking. Several of the rogues moved closer, bushy tails dripping limply between their legs from the full-length capes belted around their waists, the forepaws of the wolf-skins tied together around their necks in a macabre embrace. Every Howler was one with their skin, caring for it like they cared for their own body. It was more than a symbol of their brotherhood. It was a talisman of vigor, imparting animal strength to human flesh.

"Then talk," Disrel said.

Vogin lifted his head. Dark tribal patterns swirled and flanked his face from cheek to chin to temple. His rough lips curled. "Right down to business then. We are here to take you into our pack."

"That's quite an offer. But I prefer to work on my own, respectfully."

The tattooed face dipped. "I don't think you heard me. We are here to take you into our pack."

"You don't want me in your pack. We may fight for the same freedom, but not the same way."

"What is your way, Tiger?"

"Thelis."

Laughter rippled through the pack, and Vogin pushed off the corecycle, swinging his ax. "Thelis? It is our way too. When has a Howler ever denied the spirit of Pyron? Thelis is the fire in our blood, the power behind everything we do."

"Thelis isn't cracking open the heads of innocent people and setting fire to homes."

His body felt like a numb shell, floating around his burning spirit as he knew they could kill him for his words.

Vogin's tongue dug into his cheek. "Innocent people? Anyone who stands in the way of Pyron freedom is a lance in the flesh of Pyron. They must be cut out, surgically removed, and thrown into the fire. This is the ultimate Thelis for our people. Why do you despise the bloody hands of the surgeon? There is pain. There is blood. But in the end, there is wellness and life."

"There are two who need healing. Not just Pyron. And sometimes shrapnel is best left where it lies or you do more harm and kill the patient."

"Where are your teeth, tiger? Or are you just a kitten in Cinnabar's lap, scratching his hand for crushing your people?"

"Your way has only bred hate for Pyron."

Vogin raised his hatchet and thumbed its edge. "And your way is to wear the skyn of a Kobalt officer who slaughtered Pyrons for years in his work camp?"

Disrel narrowed his eyes in confusion.

"Ah, I see Mored hasn't told you. It would be a shame if he lost you before he could use you. He must be so proud to see his skyn back in the game. I wonder how he lives with the guilt, all that Pyron blood on his hands, all the backs he shredded. How do you think he met Alta? He became infatuated with one of his prisoners, and it turned him into a hypocrite. Ask him about how he played the part of Commander Mored by day and Tourmaline Renegade by night. Ask him how he sent Alta to a secret home and paid her frequent romantic visits while her people suffered. Ask why the sadism at his camp never ceased. He was never in the fight for Pyron. He's in it for himself. For power. For greed. Why do you think he told you the skyn was cursed? He was warning you of his past without confessing."

Disrel clenched his jaw as fire flushed through his veins. "If what you say is true, Alta wouldn't love him."

"She tolerates him. He corrupted her into thinking that he is her savior and his Kob army will free her people. But what has he done in the last twenty years besides accumulate power and wealth for himself?" The snowy wolf turned away. "Now that we know what you mean to Mored, let's discuss what a tiger like you means to us. The state thinks they killed all of you, but here you are. Alive. Strong. The last? One of the last? Who knows. It was the Pyron tigers and their elders who first resisted imperial rule, who tried to unite the tribes when our freedom was being stripped away. That is why your tribe was surrounded and massacred. And they thought they got every last one of you. Have you ever seen Cinnabar up close? That scar he cakes over with foundation and hides under a beard? He earned that in a duel with a tiger warrior that his father arranged to prove Kobalt superiority. I was there, leaning on my mother's breast when the elder prophesied that his downfall would begin and end the same way." He laid a hand on Disrel's shoulder. "With you on our side, Pyron's freedom is not far off."

Disrel backed out from under his grip.

Vogin's dark eyes twinkled with a sinister light. "But you must prove yourself by spilling Kobalt blood. Preferably Mored's. Koti's will also suffice."

Disrel's heart thundered. "How do you know about Koti?"

The hatchet swung back and forth. "The same way I know about Voss, Doni, and your sister. Everything you tell Mored, I hear."

"Then why haven't you already killed Mored?"

"I would've killed him years ago. But he keeps his network so close to the bone that we had to work hard to earn his trust, gain access to all his resources and information. Just when we snatched up the last piece of the puzzle"—Vogin wiped the edge of his hatchet against his leg—"you came along and Alta revealed you for who you really were. We decided fate would be better served by having the Tourmaline Renegade slay the Tourmaline Renegade before donning his wolf-skin and running with the pack."

"You're a terrorist."

"I'm your brother. And I'm giving you a chance to redeem yourself, baptize yourself back into the tribe by blood. You have three days to cut a Kob throat, starting from the moment you enter Koti's home. Your choice: Koti's life or Mored's. Breathe a word of this to anyone and you will lose everyone you love in an hour, including Solla. And I'll make you watch."

The pack melted into the forest as quickly and as silently as they had come. Virtue drained from Disrel's heart, and when they were gone he slumped down onto the flat and rubbed his face. How many of these fanatics had killed their own family members before taking up a wolf-skin? How he hated Howlers. If not for knowing that they would have gone on to slay Solla and his friends, he would have fought them right here until he was a crimson pulp on the stone. Three days. Which life was worth all the others combined? If he killed Koti, they might make him kill Mored soon after anyway, and then Tygo and Astros. They'd waited for the men to train him until he was actually skilled enough to take on the veterans. And once he wore the wolf-skin, there would be no end to the carnage. If the Howlers were watching Koti's house, how could any of his friends hope to escape in secret? And if he did nothing, they would leave him alive to suffer the horror of his friends' corpses axed open on the ground around him.

And Solla. Oh, God.

Not Solla.

23

Ambrosia's bright and decisive voice rang through the receiver. "Hey, Disrel. Sorry I'm just now responding, I was out of sector on a special assignment. But I've got evenings off all this week. So, drinks sound fun. Just swing by the command center office when you feel like hanging out. I've told them I'm expecting you, so nobody should give you any trouble. Okay. See you soon. Bye."

What a deceptively sweet voice. How was this even the same girl? Did a sable's training fragment her personality, create a monster that could surface on command?

"Operator? Replay the message, please."

"Replays cost one credit."

Disrel slammed the receiver in its port and left the booth. As if it cost them anything to replay information on a chip. He mounted his bike and took the quiet roads through the hills. What if he didn't return to Koti's house? How much did Vogin esteem his own word? If he never returned, would the death clock simply never start ticking above the heads of his friends? Where else could he go? If he hermited in the forest of a remote sector, the Tourmaline Renegade resigned from the fight. Solla would crumble in his abandonment. And what if the Howlers showed up and dealt their wrath for his desertion? What good would running do? There had to be a way to foil their carnage. A bloody knife could coax a wolf to lick up its own blood, but whose blood would serve as bait upon the knife? It could only be his own . . . or could he turn them on each other? It was as if Vogin had strapped an explosive to his chest, one that could only be safely disarmed by taking a friend's life. And if not, it would detonate, taking all of his friends with him.

He weaved down the dirt lane to Koti's grand home, dreading his first steps through the door. Three days was not enough time. Generous on the devil's part, but hardly enough time to stab a friend in the back. He pulled the helmet from his head and laid his hand on the back door. The last time he had faced it, Solla's birthday celebration had been starting and she had questioned his love for her. But there was no question.

The door snapped back, and Koti's smiling face burst into the frame. His arms wrapped Disrel's neck and hauled him across the threshold.

"The cat is back! Solla!"

Footsteps pounded on the upper level and a door slammed.

Disrel winced. "Only a few days late. What did I miss?"

Koti held him at arm's length. "I think I worried more than Solla did. Man, soldiers have been crawling everywhere. Have you seen the news? This lab in Euclase exploded and destroyed miles of infrastructure. People as far away as Uvarov claim they heard the explosion, and the Howlers have taken credit for it as an attack on the aristocracy."

Solla thundered down the stairs, flew into his arms, and buried her face in his chest. "Rel! Rel! You're alive. You came back." Her words choked as she squeezed him. "It's really you. Oh, my goodness, Rel!"

"Hey, it was only a couple days."

"I couldn't stop thinking you'd been caught and executed. And I prayed so hard you'd come back. I'm sorry I didn't hug you before you left. You don't even have to get me anything for my birthday. I'm just glad you're back."

He combed his fingers through her hair. He'd prayed for that chance just as hard, only now Howler eyes watched this once safe haven and the death clock had begun its countdown. He pushed Solla back and a silvery band flashed on her wrist.

He seized her hand to study the delicate bracelet. Two stones set in the crossed ends. "Where'd you get this?"

Koti averted his gaze.

Solla pulled from his grip and clutched it to her chest. "It was a birthday gift."

Disrel's eyes narrowed on the bracelet. It must have been worth hundreds of credits. He moved into the kitchen, rubbing his stomach. "So, tell me about the party."

"It was good. We played pantomimes and I got wrapped in a flatbread blanket and tossed in the air. And Doni gave me some oil pencils and a journal, and Voss gave me some candy and fizzy drinks. And Koti also gave me a lap harp."

Koti almost rolled around the pillar.

"I see." Disrel rummaged in the cold box for leftovers.

Solla wilted a little and covered the bracelet with her hand. "Will you be home tonight?"

His shoulders drooped. "I can't, Solla. I've got something really important to take care of."

She glanced at Koti. "Maybe later, then? Can you ask for a day off so we can at least celebrate your safe return?"

He set a plate of food in the warmer and raked his hair. "Sure. I'll ask."

Now was the worst time to make promises. His entire visit with Mored would be consumed with feeling out the Howler situation and trying to make a decision. If he took Mored's life, Solla would never know. If he took Koti's, Solla would never face or trust him again. But then, Koti would be a far easier kill than Mored. Killing Mored involved taking down Tygo and Astros and facing Alta. Disrel paused in mid-reach for a cup, surprised that he was even considering the two options, sickened to his core. He frowned and cursed the Howlers inwardly for forcing his mind into this vile channel. There had to be another option.

Solla moved toward the stairs. "Thank you so much, Rel. Let me know when you're free. I'll be upstairs practicing my harp."

Her delicate hand slid up the banister, carrying the silver band along her arm. Disrel drummed the countertop, waiting for the sound of her bedroom door. The moment it latched, he turned to Koti.

"You spent too much on her."

"It was nothing."

"Nothing?" All the years he had barely afforded her some trinket for her birthday and it meant everything, and here some Kobalt was smothering her with nothings. Soon she would be prancing around the house like an aristocrat.

"Sure. I'd do the same for you. When's your birthday?"

"I don't know. I just want to live in peace. Can your money buy that?"

Koti's eyes squirmed on the floor. "I just had a really hard time finding something."

"Doni and Voss didn't. If we ever have to run, a bracelet like that will get her killed faster than we could pawn it. Isn't it enough that you share your home and your food? You're putting your life at risk just letting us stay here. Doni's life. Your whole family."

Koti straightened. "If I could have bought her one day of safety in the world out there, I would've. What happened?"

Disrel hid his face. If he and Solla could only pay Miss Mazilyn a visit now, wouldn't she set out the finest flatware and prepare the best food for them? It was wayward Pyrons who were ripping kindred hearts out of Kobalt chests, and here he was growing bitter and wallowing in the mire of hopelessness. It was as if the Howlers' touch had infected him with their hateful virus.

"Train out was good. Locked borders kept me away. I don't want to talk about it."

"But you're not yourself."

Disrel straightened his shoulders and whipped his food from the warmer. "You haven't known me long enough."

Koti backed off with a shrug. "I thought I did. Even Solla knows there's something different about you. You have this look. I don't know. Something's different."

A chef's knife lay benignly on the marble countertop. His mind clutched it and faced Koti. What sort of dread would he have to witness on his friend's face if he faced him like a man? What sort of added guilt would he have to carry if he attacked him from behind? Would Koti's cries haunt him if he could not drain his life in merciful seconds and was forced to plunge the knife across his neck more than once, even more than twice? How would he hide it from Solla? Koti's blood, his limp body? What would happen when Doni and Voss came to visit? He'd have to murder them too before they reported it to the police. When he ran off with the Howlers, where would Solla stay?

"See, there it is again. In your eyes. What were you thinking?"

Disrel plodded to the table with his plate and dropped into a chair.

"It's like you've seen a monster. You go pale, shifty. You didn't even react when I told you about the lab, and that was the saddest look I've ever seen you give your sister. She was so happy to see you. How could you not give her a smile? I've known you long enough to know that's not you."

Disrel forked through the steaming food, but his stomach's readiness was ambiguous. Was this hunger or nausea? What if he choked and died over this plate of food? Would the Howlers still rain death upon his loves? Three days wasn't enough time to decide. There had to be another way to alert Mored to the threat—or should he even trust Mored? What if Vogin was right? When Disrel confronted him about his past, what would Mored say?

Koti sat across the table and opened an old newsposter. He paused upon a photograph of the Tourmaline Renegade riding through the arena with an unidentifiable Pyron girl clinging to his back, her face buried in his shoulder.

"Solla has a copy of this one framed in her bedroom. She asked me for the frame."

Disrel forced himself to swallow another bite. Perhaps his appetite was as unpredictable as Solla's. He didn't often get to relax and enjoy a meal without thinking it might be his last.

"You don't seem the least bit jealous that she's found another hero."

He mashed at his food. "I've never been her hero."

"You should hear her talk. Do you ever ask yourself why the Tourmaline Renegade chose your sister out of all those other people?"

He shrugged. "He saved all of them, didn't he?"

"What if they'd continued chopping heads? He had room for just one on the back of that bike. Why did he pick her?"

"Maybe he thought she was cute. Grabbed the last girl in line."

Koti closed the newsposter and shoved it across the table. The iconic photograph of the renegade throwing his weight down on the flag chain sat front and center on the cover.

"Or maybe it was the threat of losing someone he loved that drove him to take such an enormous risk."

Disrel squeezed his fork more tightly as he wiped his mouth on a napkin, keeping his gaze averted.

Koti lowered his voice. "What man on this green earth risks his life to save strangers, do good out of some pure heart? We're all broken creatures motivated by personal gain, the things that make life better for ourselves. I study human behavior, primal motivations, for a living. And heroes like the Tourmaline Renegade don't do what they do or seek glory out of some deep-seated need to help people they don't know. There's something in it for the hero. Something more than having his picture on headlines and billboards. Solla thinks he chose her above all the others because he's this amazing guy who just wants to help others and she got lucky. And I won't crush that dream. She deserves a beautiful dream like that. But you and I both know the reason he did what he did."

Disrel leaned back and laced his hands over the top of his head. "It had to be guilt. All those people were being falsely condemned."

"It's a lot easier to give guilt a free ride on our shoulders than to dive headlong into a pit of death to try to make something right. You took Solla because she was the most precious thing in the entire world to you, and you couldn't live without her."

Disrel's charging heart forced him to draw several quick breaths. "Solla can't know. She can't."

"She'll never know. I swear." Koti held his hands open on the table and his rich blue eyes bled sincerity. "Your secret dies with me. Now just seemed like the right time to tell you in case you needed someone to talk to."

Disrel pressed his fists to the sides of his head. "How long have you known?"

"A while. I was suspicious from day one. And little by little, I started noticing things, confirmations. You're gone a lot. Your interest in the news. The timing of everything."

His stomach flipped. If Koti could see through him, could Ambrosia?

"I don't know what went wrong," he sighed heavily. "I went to knock out a virus, some records, just the cultures inside the lab so they couldn't poison my people. And now hundreds are dead because of me. And hundreds more are going to live with burns and shrapnel, some crippled the rest of their lives."

"I'm sorry. I cannot imagine carrying that."

"I just wish I'd stayed for Solla's party, found some other way."

A languid, doleful melody wafted from above: single, tender, repentant notes. He couldn't remember the last time he'd heard harp strings, but they were undeniably healing.

Koti fidgeted with the newsposter. "You know, we don't remember heroes for their regrets and mistakes."

"That doesn't make it any easier. Now I'm nothing more than a terrorist and a murderer."

Koti's eyes poured sympathy as the dulcet strings continued their soothing.

"Solla's always loved the harp. Did she tell you?" Disrel said at length.

"She did."

"For her birthday one year, I found some wire and wood in a dumpster and tried to make one for her. It was just a board with screws in it."

Koti cracked a smile. "She told me that too."

Disrel picked at his food, his mind turning circles around the Howler threats. If he crossed them, they'd reveal his identity to the regime. Even if he could get every one of his friends on a train to some faraway haven, the entire empire would have his name and his face, and he'd be forced to live in a hole like Mored for the rest of his life, held in check until the Howlers descended and pulped him with their hatchets. There was no running. There was no hiding. He had to join them, or die. In one equation, he could save himself, and maybe Solla and Alta, though they'd all be doomed to live among the Howlers. In the other equation, everyone died.

Koti leaned in with a furrowed brow. "Is there something else bothering you?"

"No. I'll be okay. I've already had a few days to process what happened."

"Well, if you need anything, just let me know."

"Thanks," Disrel said. But there was no feeling behind it.

"I've got your back. I'm ready to die for you and your people if it comes down to it."

Disrel dropped his gaze, pained by the twisted irony Koti could not see.

Disrel parked his corecycle in the silo and walked through the tunnel to the concourses below. A mortal orange emanated from the stained-glass ceilings, and the walls echoed his steps like sheets of ice. A sentry wandered out from behind a pillar as if only to make his presence known. Disrel slowed his steps until the man disappeared back into the shadows. In all of his visits and time spent training within these tunnels, he'd never seen a sentry. They knew he was no intruder, and now he knew they were no friends.

He ascended the stairs, and a compact and sharp-nosed Pyron bumped into him in passing, then glanced back with a gleam in his eye. Disrel averted his gaze and marched on. Wasn't that the same man that had bound him in that street drain? He would not be intimidated. He was no fool. Murdering one friend wouldn't save the others from Howler savagery. He had made his choice: It was better to lie among the ashes of the world he had tried to save and the people he had tried to help than to walk upon them alone with a friend's blood on his hands.

Disrel entered the cafeteria, descended the stairs, and knocked on the chipped gray door. A medley of savory, spicy odors sifted through the cracks. And sweet potato rolls. Oh, those buttery sweet potato rolls must have just come out of the oven.

"Come in."

The hinges groaned. Mored hunched over his plate at the dining table, his fingers locked around the handle of a coffee cup. Alta pressed a cloth napkin to her lips and rose from her chair.

"Disrel! You look starved. Come, sit. Fill a plate and tell us all about your trip."

The lemony papered walls put sunlight into the cavernous home, and a vase of fresh flowers ornamented the center of the table. Disrel settled into a chair as Alta set a clean plate in front of him.

Mored sipped his coffee. "It's not your fault." His other hand scraped over an open newsposter. An apocalyptic photograph consumed an entire page—twisted metal, blown-out windows, scorched trees, warped signposts.

"Did you know this would happen?" Disrel said.

"No. Absolutely not. I wouldn't have let you go in there if I'd thought there was any risk of blowing up even half the lab, even a quarter of it. They must've had a gas leak, some combustive chemicals. It's as if they had a bomb in there already and the corruptor deteriorated a safety seal and set it off. Still, it was only supposed to render organic matter inert. Not trigger a chain reaction."

"Black market technology can't be trusted to do what it's advertised to do." Alta said, setting a thickly layered cherry and chocolate trifle on the table and laying a handsome scoop onto Disrel's plate. "It's good to start with dessert once in a while."

"I can't ask the seller, now can I?" Mored said wryly. "It would link the incident right back to us."

Disrel forced a smile and pretended to dig in. "Well, there's no virus now. No scents or shoe prints or dropped tools. It's a clean scene . . . for a mile in all directions."

Mored wiped his mouth, his stormy eyes deep in the paper. "How did you cover all those hundreds of miles back? Any trouble crossing borders?"

"I stole a military corecycle in Euclase and took it through the wilderness. Then I dumped it in a pond a few miles from the train station." He spooned through his trifle. "I never realized how beautiful and primitive Dolom is. Heard lots of wolves. Real spooky the way their sounds echo between the mountains."

Mored continued scanning the poster. "Hmm-hmm."

Alta touched her husband's shoulder. "Their songs are hauntingly beautiful, aren't they?"

"What?" Mored threw his attention on Disrel. "You heard owls?"

"Wolves. Must have been a pack of them singing in the forest all night."

Mored's eyes slitted as he grunted.

Disrel laid his spoon in his trifle and scooped a fistful of walnuts from a porcelain boat. He dropped them on the table and began arranging the pieces. "I wish I could wash all the blood from my hands and move on. But there is no neutral ground. I know you told me innocent people will get hurt, but I just wasn't expecting it to be like this." The walnuts trailed across the table in Kobalt lettering.

Mored's face melted, and his coffee mug shook as it fell from his lips.

Alta covered her mouth and stared, glassy-eyed.

Disrel swept the walnuts together and rearranged them into another word. Mored fussed with his napkin and wiped beads of sweat from his forehead.

Alta pulled herself together. "Do you have time for more trifle?" She didn't even move for the bowl.

Disrel sprinkled the walnuts on his untouched dessert. "I've got an errand to run in Tourmal tonight. I'll be back in three days, at sunset. Kind of want to let things settle down and get my head together."

Mored dabbed his temples. "We can plan your next move while the empire is still reeling."

"I'm not sure what to do next," Disrel admitted. "It's not even safe where Solla and I are staying. The police could do a house to house search any time."

Alta laid a hand on his shoulder. "Remember who you are, Kyreasheluhn. Surrender to Thelis and let It use you."

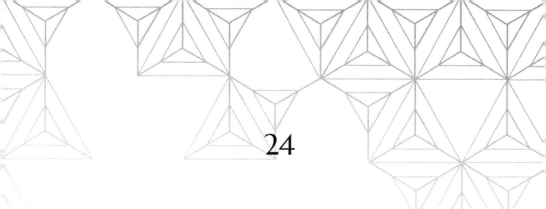

24

The Tourmal Command Center's facade grinned like a skull. Disrel wandered through the sliding doors and down the gaping throat, his nose tingling at the metallic odors emanating from the dark stone walls and floors. The lofty ceilings and towering pillars created wide, empty spaces that served no other purpose than to boast Kobalt authority. The lobby desk sprawled down the length of the room, lit by hanging rods suspended on cables mounted somewhere up in the black recesses above. Bucket seats lined the inner edge. Just behind the desk, a garishly illustrated magazine clasped in tawny, sun-spotted hands glided down, and a pair of dour eyes caked with deep azure flashed over the top, marking him the way a leopard marks a runt piglet. Her wiry gray hair was pulled prudishly against her pointed head and into a tiny knot, and dark freckles covered her weathered skin from decades out in the elements. She sniffed at him as if she had just seen something forbidden or occult.

"Are you lost, Pyron? Or did you come here to turn yourself in?" Her voice grated like steel on pavement.

"I'm here to see the Commander. Sable Commander Ambrosia." He flashed his pass.

"For?"

"A casual date." He raked the back of his neck.

Her nostrils flared as she threw back her head and cackled. "You fool. Get out of here while you still have a running start."

"It's not a joke."

"Really? Then tell me why a nice hunk of Pyron flesh would take a fancy in the Selenite Skynhound? You think being her pet will keep her from eating you when hunting season rolls around?"

His ears burned as her caustic gaze ate into him, and he turned back the way he had come.

She slapped the magazine against the counter. "I dated a few Pyron men some years ago just for the hell of doing something taboo. Every time I killed one, I'd sell his parts as fetishes." Her pointed teeth glistened, and the blue around her eyes shimmered like scales.

How many serial killers made up the sable ranks? Or was she just mocking him?

"Fortunately for you, I can't touch what belongs to my superior. Wait outside. I'll let her know you're here."

"Thank you." Disrel wedged his pass back into his pocket and left the building on putty legs. Sables. They were like a box of acid-stuffed chocolates, some clearly lethal, some mildly warped, others full of a sour hard candy that glued one's teeth together. He rubbed his shoulders as he turned about on the low porch, regretting that he had dared to come at all. What good would another up-close look at his headhunter do once the Tourmaline Renegade had lost his identity to a wolf-skin? He ought to be thinking of a way to save Solla, Koti, and as many of the others as he could.

Disrel turned toward the polished exterior of the building, licked his fingers, and teased his widow's peak until it parted cleanly to the side. A nice hunk of flesh. Would Ambrosia have ever agreed to hang out if he had been anything less than an attractive piece of muscle?

"Hey, stranger. You got my message," a familiar voice crackled.

Disrel tumbled against the wall, heart marching like a military band. "Is now a bad time?"

"Now is perfect. I was just going up for a jump." She swept past, boot soles clacking on the pavement stones, hips swinging. A dozen straps and buckles swayed from her elbows. "How are you with heights?"

"Six foot is overrated. I've always been happy as a five-eleven."

A smirk cracked her lips. "Let me rephrase that. How do you feel about your happy five-eleven falling some fifteen thousand feet?"

He shrugged. "I'm game. But I've heard the ground has hard feelings."

Amusement leached from her eyes as she shook her head. "I want to show you the view from one of my favorite places in Tourmal. We'll wingsuit down to the bay bridge and tandem parachute the landing. Sound fun?"

"And what if we miss the bridge?"

Her eyes gleamed. "You can swim, can't you?"

The metal aircraft squatted like a sick crow on the octagonal airfield behind the barracks, its black wings drooping at its sides. Disrel pulled a harness over his skyn, fussing with the straps as he imagined taking a three-mile nosedive. He had danced with death too often lately. Hadn't the first Tourmaline Renegade's end come about in a skydive over this same bay?

A young sable approached from the opposite end of the field and cast a purple smile in their direction before sidling around the back of the aircraft with Ambrosia. Hushed tones wafted around the tailfins.

"Why didn't you warn me he was hot?"

Harness buckles clinked together in the commander's hands. "You told me you only wanted to hear about the cute ones."

"He's got a nice mixture of both. I'd drag him into bed just to see what he's got."

Heat flushed through Disrel's chest. Sables spoke so freely about their intentions that even their compliments had a dangerous edge. Whispers continued back and forth, and then the comrade released a coarse laugh.

"He could take it. He's Pyron. Just look at him. Such a lamb, just waiting for his lion. Hey, if things don't work out—"

"We'll see how tonight goes." Ambrosia waltzed up from behind. "Arms out."

A light canvas wingsuit slipped around his shoulders. She came around front and helped him step into it and work the harness clips through the openings and secure them. He stole glances at her face, hoping his helmet and visor wouldn't remind her of the Tourmaline Renegade. He wanted to prove to these sables that he was no submissive, but he couldn't afford behaving in a way that would mark him as threatening. He had to feign a little weakness to deflect suspicion. Ambrosia's hands tugged on the harness at his hips, chest, and shoulders, slipping in and under to check the tightness. Her touch was devoid of both malice and affection. It was platonic, methodical, yet invested in his safety. When everything was in place, he closed the front of the wingsuit.

"Where's my parachute?"

"I'll stick with you for an easy hookup when it's time. You just enjoy spreading your wings for the first time." Her lips pulled sideways as she held his gaze. "Ready to fly?"

"Like a day-old duckling. What happens if we fail to connect?"

"That won't happen. But in case it would, flare over the water to slow down. As soon as you touch down, pull this buckle and give this band a sharp tug, then get out of the suit as fast as you can. Tread water or swim to shore." She averted her eyes and tugged once more on the connector straps that crossed his chest before turning and mounting the aircraft by its wing. He followed and crouched at her side. The craft hummed to life and its humped body lifted from the ground, and then he gripped a handlebar as the ground fell away foot by foot. The scent of freedom filled his nose as the barracks shrank and the arena walls grew squat and insignificant. The spires and columns of Tourmal's tallest structures mingled and converged in a slow dance. Neon lights, holoposters, burning windows, and beacons peppered the dark jungle, and corecycles ran the roadways like glowing ants. He glanced over at Ambrosia and instantly she evaded, her gaze plunging to the earth.

"What do you think?"

"It's breathtaking. I wish everyone could experience this."

It was just like the miniature cities and villages he'd seen at fairs and markets and longed to play with as a child. Even now, it all seemed only an arm's reach away, a dreamy oil landscape of twilight blue-greens and purples, with buildings he might pluck up like game pieces or lift the roofs to peek inside. What must it be like to be God and look down on the earth and pity the people who drowned in ponds that looked like puddles, or to see men struggling against their brothers and envying the foolish toys they had made? Even an unsurpassed feat of architecture like Tourmal's bay bridge was just a lucid thread of light spanning an indefinite abyss.

High over the water, the pilot slowed the craft. Ambrosia stood and turned with a competitive glint in her eye.

"Ready to dive?"

Disrel clutched the bar and pushed up. "Die?"

"Dive!"

"Yeah?"

She advanced to the side of the aircraft just behind the wing. "Okay. You first."

"But you've got the parachute."

"Because I can catch up to you. I can't just hang around out there waiting for you to work up the nerve. Now jump."

He bounced up and down on his feet, uncertain, and she gave him a sarcastic stare. He retreated a step from the edge. What an easy way to kill the Tourmaline Renegade. She took him by the harness and drew him back toward the edge with gentle insistence.

"Come. On the count. Five . . . four . . . three—"

She arched a brow, eyes twinkling, and for a second he forgot they were standing on the edge. She tumbled forward, still gripping his harness. Every muscle seized as his feet left the rigid comfort of the aircraft. She dropped away and his wingsuit popped and the wind drummed over his stomach, whistling around his visor. A wild, carefree *whoop* leaped from his chest. She crowed back and soared in close, tumbling through several stunts with ease. He lined up with her until their chests were almost touching and gave her a roguish stare.

"You've got some time, fledgling. See if you can get over the city and skim between some buildings. I'll stick close and turn you back when it's time." She planted her hands into his chest and pushed him away.

He wobbled his limbs, gaining a feel for maneuvering and control, and swung wide around a hive of apartment complexes on the waterfront. The buildings and streets below were a haphazard grid of blocks and lights, a prison for the earthbound. He swooped upon one of Tourmal's tallest structures and glimpsed a dark falcon, a reflection of himself in the rippling glass. Spires passed just under his stomach like the polearms of a marching army. He whirled left and right, turning half circles around the glowing pillars full of eyes. Ambrosia darted in and out of his peripheral, hovering like a mother bird.

"Time to head back," she signed.

They turned toward the bay and its bridge. Fishing vessels bobbed like bath toys in the wharfs below and fisher birds took to the wing. Six dark stone towers divided the bridge evenly, cables spraying like neon rainbows on either side of each. Ambrosia hovered and caught hold of him. The harness straps tugged and tightened and then her weight hit his back, jerking him into an upright position. A bright canopy ballooned overhead. The central bridge tower continued to sweep closer and closer and Ambrosia tugged on the parachute ropes until they were lined up with the length of the tower. A puff of wind blew them off center, and Disrel's feet lined up with the neon cables. In a moment, they were careening back over the centerline.

"Feet up. Get ready to slide."

Disrel fought to lift his legs, but every ounce of his instinct wanted them down to catch him. They skimmed along the illuminated top of the tower, the parachute flaring as the stone rushed under his butt. The naked edge of the tower drew closer and their wingsuits hissed against the stone. Mere feet from the edge, they ground to a halt and tumbled over, laughing sighs of relief. Ambrosia unlatched the parachute and it dripped down the side of the tower. Disrel pushed himself back from the edge.

"That was crazy. We almost went over."

"You're a little heavier than I'm used to. Hold on, we're still attached."

The city twinkled like a geode, with spires crowned and haloed in bands of purple mist. Ambrosia pulled the parachute back together and dropped her harness on top of it, sighing.

"So, what do you think?"

Disrel removed his helmet and sat forward on crossed legs. "Would totally do it again."

"What about the view?"

Her cheeks and chin were silver apples, and her lips were soft and receptive. Her eyes narrowed upon the panorama with pleasure, and she sat poised, a spectral beauty caught between dimensions. She waved a swath of hair from her forehead and looked over.

Disrel grunted into his fist and torqued his head toward the shore. "It's incredible."

"It's my favorite spot in Tourmal, the one place where I can come for a few minutes of peace and clarity. Where I can just be myself."

"It's not hard to see why it's your favorite. Thanks for sharing it with me."

She tucked her chin and rolled her lips. Mahogany strands undulated around her head. "Sorry about what happened at the base. I hope my sable didn't make you feel like a piece of meat."

He shrugged and rubbed his knee.

"What Pyron man doesn't get that? I'm used to it."

"You never get used to it."

He hesitated, stealing a glance and pondering her tone. She wasn't speaking for him. There was a hint of pain etched in the corners of her eyes. "So, how do you see me?"

Her expression stiffened as her nostrils flared. "Don't think that you can change me. A sable's training rips her heart out. I'm no different than any other."

He leaned over just an inch, resting on his hands spread out behind him. "I don't know. I think they left a sliver of yours behind."

"No." She swallowed a painful memory and tossed her head. "I used to hold on to that hope until I was transferred here. Then I realized death is the only door to my prison. What you think is a glimmer of kindness or goodness in me is just the ghost of a girl who died at the Sable Academy."

Her fingers brushed his, then jerked away. Her lips drooped as her eyes widened in panic, and she scooted away. "Sorry. That was an accident."

A warm tingling spread through his chest at the unexpected touch, and he shrugged. "I don't mind. We were closer in the parachute harness."

Her eyelids fluttered. "That was different. We had to. I didn't ask you to come along as an excuse to get close. And I just didn't want you to think I—to think maybe—never mind."

He scratched at his chest. "Well, it was an interesting test of trust. It took every ounce of commitment to take that plunge. Maybe everyone should fall out of the sky before they fall in love."

A smile flickered in the corner of her mouth. "Falling in love has much higher risks."

"True. Trust issues, a broken heart, financial ruin. That's harder to live with than jumping without a parachute."

Her eyes slitted and her face bent between a laugh and a grimace. Disbelief clung to her lips. "Okay, maybe there are some sables who would've let you hit the ground for a laugh, but—" A soft sigh popped from her throat. "I wouldn't hurt you unless I had orders to."

"That's comforting. But if you ever change your mind, just remember to toss the bouquet off my casket and throw it into the crowd to see who's next."

She snorted and squeezed a hand under her nose. "You're crazy."

He feigned irritation, rolling his eyes. "Now you're starting to sound like my therapist."

"Oh, stop." She cackled and rolled back, holding her sides.

"I can't. They tried to put me on sanity a while back, but I refused to take it. The pills were too hard to swallow, and they made me cry. So now I self-medicate with laughter."

She slapped at his shoulder and quivered. "Disrel!"

He'd never seen a sable puddle before, and just lay back next to her, lacing his fingers across his stomach and drinking in her bright laughter. The night sky flashed with crisp stars, like diamonds on the boughs of a celestial tree, ripe for the picking. How far away were Mother and Father actually? Or did time run differently in realms beyond this world? Ambrosia's laughter faded, and her sides stopped quivering.

Disrel tapped his dangling heels against the side of the tower as his eyes wandered all over the starry heavens. "The cityscape is nice. But I like this view a little better."

"Why?"

"It's more peaceful. Tourmal's streets have hunger and pain and death. When I look up, I find hope."

"So it's your favorite view in the world?"

"No."

"Then what is?"

He turned his head and looked deep into her eyes, emerald and sparkling. There was no more pleasing, healing shade of green in the world found anywhere but in these eyes. Warmth crashed through his stomach and he drew closer to those neighboring windows to better see the soul peeping through them. To draw her out. Her gaze searched his entire face, innocently waiting for the answer to fall from his lips, and then the light of revelation evaporated her wonder and she jerked her head back toward the night. His eyes must have said everything. They had hugged every curve of her face, embraced what he saw within her too intensely, too intimately. He hadn't wanted the conversation to ever go there. But she'd asked.

The awkwardness clung to him like a wet blanket, stifling the air. He twiddled his thumbs, waiting for it to pass, for her to say something or throw him from the tower. He hadn't expected to feel like this, not on a second date, not with death looming two sunsets out, not for any Kobalt woman, certainly not for a sable, and especially not for the Skynhound. But he spent every moment around her relishing the challenge and the risk of being caught stealing glances. Every swing of her hip and turn of her shoulder was poetry in motion, her breasts were delicate mounds of feminine beauty, her neck was elegant, a clean path that led right to the little space behind her ears bordered in coils of deep red. But above all that, her bubbling laughter intoxicated his mind and her addictive smile made him high. It was too genuine to be murderous. It was approving, accepting, welcoming.

"Did you like your braids?"

"Yes." It came out rigid, like maybe she hadn't actually appreciated them.

Stars peeped through a cloud, like a myriad of angelic eyes peering around curtains to see if this love was possible. But where were the eyes of the helpers, the strong ones? Could those in heaven see the innocent lives that fell under Howler axes? Could they cry tears for them?

How many Howlers walked Tourmal's streets in disguise? Or in wolf-skin? Roaming packs didn't even bother to hide themselves, cruising with tails trailing from the backs of their corecycles in broad daylight. If the military police were too afraid to touch them while the sun shone, what could one man do to save his friends after sunset?

"If you only had three days left to live, what would you do?"

She pressed her lips and contemplated. "There's too much. Within or without the bounds of military regulations?"

"Without."

"I'd probably destroy my uniform, put on a plain skyn, and just enjoy being treated like a normal person."

"And what do normal people do that you would want to do?" Disrel said.

"Have healthy relationships. Fall in love. Get married. Raise a family. Live a life surrounded by that family. Three days isn't enough time to experience those things, though." She paused, her mouth bunching to one side. "But since you asked, what about you?"

"I don't know. I kind of already spend every day thinking it might be my last."

"You wouldn't want to go anywhere special? Or try some foreign food?" she said.

"Sure. I want to experience everything life has to offer. But I don't think I would regret missing out on those things in my sky home."

"Well, if you could have one wish, what would you wish for?"

"Easy. I'd wish to see my mother and father again and just talk with them for an hour. In the flesh, where I could hug them and hold them, and Solla could be with us too. If it was allowed, I'd wish for my grandparents and uncles and aunts to be included in the reunion because I don't really remember any of them."

"But if you died, you'd see them when they came to take you to your sky home."

Their eyes locked.

"Do you actually believe that?" Disrel asked.

Her eyelashes fluttered over her cheeks. "I don't know. It seems like a good thing to believe, though."

"It puts ploam in any heart that believes that."

"Ploam?"

"Peace."

"I've learned a few Pyron words over the years. Insults mostly, from prisoners." She rattled off twelve Pyron words and short phrases, mutilating each of them by wrong stress placement, not holding certain sounds out long enough, and improper resonation.

Disrel shook his head and grunted. "Those are so obscene I don't even want to correct them."

She snorted. "I know. It's nice to hear something like ploam for once, even if it is a treacherous and heretical language."

Disrel turned his head and scraped his hand over his sandpapery jaw. How could he argue? The root of the Pyron tongue revered the Creating Spirit over all men, including the Kobalt emperor, but any emperor who considered himself divine could only see the Pyron language as promoting treasonous thoughts, and any who dared to speak it as denying him his due worship. It was impossible to even reference the emperor or any man as the first subject of a thought, without preceding it with "if my Sky Father wills it," or "the Great Spirit's will be done" and completely undermining the emperor's absolute authority.

He asked, "Is that why your people always use Pyron words for playing Hang-Sable?"

Her gaze petrified to the waters below, and he pressed his lips with regret. The breeze whispered around them, and a syncopated heartbeat thrummed his ears. Or was that other rhythm her heart? She thrust back from the edge and stuffed the parachute into its sack.

Disrel scooted back. "I'm sorry, Ambrosia. That wasn't funny."

"Forget it. Want to go get those drinks now? It's only a two-mile walk down the bridge, and then Ulyia will take us back to the base." She lifted a plate in the stonework and hauled out two cables. "Here. Clip this to your harness and rappel down. Race you to the bottom."

She dropped over the edge and faded into the blackness. Disrel pinched his lips, raked his hair, and turned a circle. If he'd only thought that through a little more, he wouldn't have killed the whole evening. He clipped his helmet to his waist and eased his weight out over the edge.

At the bottom, Ambrosia stood with her back turned, portions of her un-zipped wingsuit flapping from her elbows and knees. Disrel unclipped and re-leased the cable, and it shot skyward, feeding back into its chamber. The waves lapped at the columns below, spraying mist onto the pedestrian walk that edged the bridge. Corecycles rushed in packs like bursts of lightning. He inched around for a peek at her face, hoping not to find murderous thoughts lingering there. A sable's wrath was insidious. Maybe she wouldn't cut his throat and dump him into the bay. Maybe she would lead him back into the city to string him up on a lamppost to die like a sable.

"Ambrosia, I—"

She turned and shrugged the parachute pack higher. "What's it like in the Pyron sector?" She started walking.

His throat tightened. "Do my feelings really matter in the face of the state?"

"They matter to me." Her eyes flashed over at him. "I only saw it once when the population was just a few hundred and the first buildings were being constructed."

"It's nothing like that now. People are cramped, starving, sick. There's skit and carcasses in the streets, rats, gangs, drugs. Kobalt soldiers come there just to take advantage of our women. Those who are better off live in shipping containers with their animals."

Her eyes scored the sidewalk as her pace quickened. "But your people have more opportunities there. Instead of being homeless on our streets, they have permanent homes."

"And some, like me, lost a nice apartment and a good job."

"Could you not help your own people? Take your skills and knowledge, provide employment and teach them to live better, cleaner lives?"

"We weren't always like this. Decades of unfair laws pushed us into poverty. I would love to help my people make our sector a beautiful place, but we know that's not its design."

Her gaze was almost apologetic. "Maybe things could change for the better, once all of your people are settled in their new home."

He squeezed a fistful of wingsuit. Did she really believe that? Or was she testing him, fishing for clues of an uprising, his beliefs about the renegade? It hardly mattered. Once he was part of Vogin's pack, he couldn't see her anymore. Once they found out, they'd make him kill her. He had to break it off tonight.

"We've been forced to make ourselves smaller, take up less space, for as long as I can remember. Tomorrow the state might take away our right to breathe."

"And if that happens, will you fight back?"

He felt her eyes on him and cleared the lump from his throat, choosing his next words carefully. "If I did, would you try to stop me?"

An excruciating silence, in which the two of them seemed content to leave both questions unanswered. She walked a little more closely by his side. "I have to ask why you're wasting your time hanging out with me when you could be looking for a wife among your own people."

"I'm not looking for a wife right now."

"Any reason?"

"Just not ready."

"Fair enough. But if you were, what would you look for in a woman?"

He shrugged. "I suppose I want someone who isn't afraid to try new things, who is confident and full of life. I always hope I'll find someone who will be more patient than me, help me think things through. Someone who will speak her mind and always be perfectly honest with me about her feelings, and will help me teach our children Pyron ways and the Pyron tongue but also be open to practicing some of the Kobalt customs that are good. And I want her to be strong, ready to face whatever comes when times are hard. Like the kind of woman who is capable of killing me, but chooses to respect and love me."

"And what does this wonder woman look like?"

"She's beautiful—naturally—with a big, gorgeous smile. And just tall enough that I can kiss her forehead without bending over." He hesitated. "What about you?"

"If it was even possible for me to marry, I'd try to find a man who loves to talk and laugh, and is comfortable sharing his feelings, and loves working with his hands and maybe has a few talents. I'd hope he had a loving family that would welcome me in. But mostly, I just want someone willing to overlook my past and love me for who I am, someone who isn't afraid of the things I've done, someone I don't have to hide my truest self from. Someone I can fully trust, and be open and honest with. Someone..."

"Who will love you unconditionally." Disrel said.

Her steps faltered and as she caught his gaze, her lips parted with wonder, like she was seeing for the very first time the person she was describing. Then she shook herself. "I know. It's asking too much."

"I don't think so." He took a half step toward her, reclaiming her gaze. How could he ask her to trust him? How could he ever tell her that she deserved so much more than she expected? A man who could make love to her daily?

She whipped her attention toward the shore and huffed. "We should keep moving."

They started walking again, and her eyes ran up and down his chest as she stole a sideways glance.

Just off the end of the bridge, a squat stone-and-brick booth glowed and gleamed under a circle of sweet gum trees. The pungent odors of coffee and cinnamon beckoned to passersby. Tables and benches hugged the trunks and corners and cobbled walks, and geese and ducks huddled in the shadows, each with one bright orange foot planted in the sand. Ambrosia stood back and studied the menu.

"Every time I come here I get a coffee and an ice cream. I've always wanted to try their hot cocoa and cinnamon rolls, but I never can break away from what I know I love."

A large bearded man stared Disrel down from the window as if daring him to approach. Disrel shoved his hands deeper into his pockets and tried to focus on the menu. He wasn't particular. He'd never spent his money on things like this before, so any one item would make his night. When he noticed Ambrosia hanging back, swinging between choices, Disrel wandered over to the counter and slapped down an ample number of credits.

"Get my lady a coffee and a hot cocoa, and a cinnamon roll and an ice cream, please. Ice cream in a coffee for me."

The Kobalt's heavy eyes scowled as he shoved the credits off the counter. "Sign says 'no ashrats.' But I always have to tell you because you're too stupid to read."

Disrel picked his credits out of the stones and sifted the dirt through his fingers. Then he slapped the money back on the counter with an easy smile. "Maybe you should try serving a Pyron sometime. It could be fun."

The man slammed the counter with his fists.

Ambrosia pushed Disrel back from the window, hissing. "What are you doing? I was going to order so we wouldn't have this problem."

"But this one's on me. Please." He whispered back.

"You can't afford this. And he won't let you."

"Yes, he will. He can see we're together. What difference does it make who hands him the money?"

The vendor jerked the windows shut. "No difference at all. I don't serve sables who date ashrats either."

Ambrosia's brow darkened, and Disrel wondered why the man didn't fear her. A sable could arrest or kill a citizen without warrant. He turned uneasily between her and the counter. The vendor stood with his back to the window, hunched over his dough, slapping it and rolling it like a rebellious putty. The strains of a classical band in stereo trickled through the vents above. Disrel set his knuckles to the window and rapped.

"Disrel. We should leave." Ambrosia backed into the shadows.

Disrel rapped again. Louder. Louder.

"Just leave him alone. We're not wanted here."

He set both fists to the window and drummed out a snappy rhythm. The vendor whirled, hands covered in flour and butter, eyes popping like arcing bolts of electricity. His fat lips snarled. "Beat it, ashrat."

Disrel cupped a hand to his ear and strained.

"I said get lost before I have you arrested."

Disrel leaned closer, hand still cupped to his ear. "Sorry. I'm hard of hearing. Can you?" He motioned at the glass between them.

The big Kobalt clawed the service window open and bellowed, "I said, go find a sewer before I have you thrown in prison for vandalizing my business!"

Disrel slapped the credits down on the counter. "Can we get two coffees, one hot cocoa, one cinnamon roll, and two ice creams? Second ice cream in my coffee, please. Thank you."

A look of perplexity and defeat clouded the business owner's face. He stared numbly at the coins and his stubbly neck pudged under his bulbous chin.

Disrel leaned in casually, fully aware that he was close enough for the angry man to drag him over the counter and throttle him. "Mind if I tell you your favorite joke?"

A scowl darkened his eyes. "How would you know?"

"Easy. It would have to be a cinnamon pun."

A strange light danced in the vendor's eyes as he sputtered.

"Is it ignorance or apathy that's brought our people to this?"

The vendor's shoulders bounced. "I don't know, and I don't really care."

"Ah!" Disrel pointed a finger at the man and gave him a knowing look.

An explosive gust of air burst from the man's chest and he covered it with a sputtering cough. "You know, I don't understand why all of you Pyrons got fired from your jobs a couple weeks ago. It's crazy, because you didn't do anything."

Disrel groaned inside and traced the counter with his finger. Was that the best racist joke the poor man knew? "What's the difference between black, morbid, and brutal humor?"

The vendor grunted half-heartedly.

"Black humor: Five Pyrons in one trash can. Morbid humor: One Pyron in five trash cans. Brutal humor: Five cans of trash in one Pyron."

The vendor wheezed and turned red in the face.

Disrel spread his hands and watched the vendor with intense sobriety. "Good thing the trash doesn't return every time you throw it out."

The vendor jiggled like a jar of jelly and smacked clouds of flour from his hands.

"At least the sector will pick you up off my sidewalk for free, you crazy dog. I've never met a Pyron as funny as you. What's your name?"

"Disrel."

The vendor studied him and wiped a guilty smile off his face, as if for the first time, feeling shame. "Why does your friend look like Tourmal's Sable Commander?"

"Because she is."

"Get out of here. The Selenite Skynhound? What does she see in you?"

"Honestly, I don't know. Maybe she thinks I'm funny."

His wide lips twisted. "Well, you'd better not run out of jokes too soon or she'll be fleshing your carcass for a laugh. I thought Pyrons didn't like coffee and cinnamon anyway."

"We spice most of our meats with those. But she told me that cinnamon was better on bread than lamb shanks, and that you have the best coffee and cinnamon buns in Tourmal. I hope I didn't drive hours to be disappointed."

"You didn't." The vendor scraped up the money, counted out Disrel's change into his hand, and turned into his booth.

Ambrosia wandered over to a lopsided table and sat down. She buried her fingers into the side of her head and scratched.

The vendor began assembling a tray and dispensing drinks. "Why are you so well-spoken? I catch no trace of an accent."

"I grew up here."

"But your people are so clannish. Why don't you act more Pyron? And no braids?"

"A Kobalt lady raised me when my parents died and I was a stray. I had the best of both worlds."

"Both worlds?" He handed the tray through the window. "Well, it's going to take more than stand up comedy to bring this world a peaceful millennium. But you're the most tolerable Pyron I've met, I'll give you that. Enjoy the food. And good luck with her."

Disrel took the tray and went over to Ambrosia. She seemed melancholy, unamused by what had just transpired. He scooted the tray in front of her and eased onto the opposite bench. Her eyes moved over all the items in their pretty paper boats.

"How did you do that?"

Disrel pulled his coffee from the tray and pushed the floating blob of ice cream down into it with his spoon. "Do what?"

She gestured at the tray of food. "This! How'd you get him to like you?"

Disrel clamped the spoon between his lips. "How could he not? He's a nice guy. I don't have any reason not to like him."

She stared hard. "He called you an ashrat." She whispered the word like she'd never used it before. "You didn't even flinch or scowl or . . . nothing. There's just this—this—*thing* about you. You're different. You just hang out with your enemies like they're your best friends."

Even he couldn't explain why he couldn't hate the man, why he could only pity him for his fear. "Try the cinnamon roll."

A smile rushed over her face as she opened the paper and pulled out the steaming pastry. "You shouldn't have gotten me all of this. The roll is big enough for three people. I'll waste your money if I can't finish it."

He tucked a guilty smile behind the rim of his cup. "I'll finish whatever you can't handle."

Her lips closed delicately around a corner of the roll and she moaned at its gooey goodness. "Wow. Now I'll be ordering for two every time I pass here."

Ducks waded down into the water for a moonlight swim. Insects thrummed in the reeds along the shore and waves lapped against the rocks in singsong rhythms.

Disrel scrubbed his thumbnail into the splintering surface of the table. "That was pretty horrible, what happened in Euclase."

Her eyes lit on him like she knew, like she dared him to continue pretending he wasn't the renegade she hunted. She took another bite of the roll and wiped her fingers on a napkin, chewing methodically. At last, she swallowed. "It could have been much worse."

"Do you think it was intentional?"

"I don't know. If the Tourmaline Renegade had wanted to take lives, he would've struck in the daytime. But he was after something else."

"The Tourmaline Renegade?" He sipped his coffee like nothing ever surprised him. "I didn't read that anywhere. I guess the papers they let into Pyron are censored."

She picked at the roll. "I almost had him."

"You were there?"

"I was on a special assignment, training a team of Euclasian sables near the lab when we found out it had been breached."

The pressure fizzled out of Disrel's chest. She had no idea. "What do you think he was after?"

"I can't render those details."

"I understand. And when you capture him?" He scratched the back of his head.

"I'm not going to waste time taking him in. I'm going to kill him."

Coffee pushed up in his chest like a molten plug, and he covered his mouth and squeezed it down. "Hmm. Quickly or—"

"I know he's one of your people and—" She set the roll down and sat back. "Maybe we should talk about something else."

He pricked the lip of his cup with his fingernails. "I know you want justice and peace as much as I do, Ambrosia. Your heart is noble. But after all I've been through in my own life, I struggle to believe the state has good intentions for my people."

Her eyes dared to deny it, and fell again. "We've only been working to empty the prisons and remove troublemakers, insurgents, and gangs from among your people. Once they're dead, Cinnabar will see the good that remains in Pyrons, like you, and let you live in peace in your own sector. I don't think honest men like you have anything to worry about."

He pinched his lips and breathed down into the cup. Any response would only devolve into an argument. What was the point anyway? He'd be a Howler two nights from now. She would not cry if he was locked in a deathmatch at Execution Square for breaking some petty law. He would be one of those troublemakers and insurgents who needed to be purged.

"I really enjoy your friendship, Disrel. I've never had anything like this with a man before. Just being able to sit and talk and enjoy time together without any expectation that I share my body . . . It's wonderful."

He squeezed out a smile. "I'm enjoying every minute of it too."

She picked tiny pieces off the mutilated roll, dropping them onto the napkin one by one. "How do you say 'friend' in Pyron?"

"Oali. Oalit. When we call someone a friend, we're calling them a sister or a brother."

"What would you call me?"

"Dul oali. My sister," he said.

"Dul oalit?"

His core trembled as the phrase "my brother" tumbled from her lips, and they repeated it back and forth until her tonality drew closer to his. Satisfied, she sat back a little. "How do I refer to myself?"

"As a sable?"

"As me. I. Like, I am or I will."

"Zo."

"And how do you say 'you'?"

"Yem," Disrel said.

"Me and you?"

"Zo cy yem."

A smile crept through her face as she repeated it, and she returned to picking at the roll. "Can you teach me a phrase?"

"Any phrase?"

"Sure. Something useful that I might need to use often if I visit your sector."

He wiped his mouth and gave it some thought. "Zo-e habiha."

She repeated it studiously until her pronunciation was decent, but the back and forth made them sound like two nasally gargling geese. "Okay. What does it mean?"

He rubbed at his skipping heart. "I'm sorry." Her smile drooped as she frisked him with a look. He bowed over the table and raked his neck. "It's the phrase I use the most anyway."

Her lips softened and pulled to one side, and she sighed.

"What are you thinking now?" he asked.

"It's nothing."

"I see." He watched her, unable to imagine a woman was ever thinking about nothing at all.

"Well... maybe I was hoping for the chance to tandem parachute with you again."

"Oh. Well, we don't have to be in the air to do that. I'm still wearing my harness." He tugged one of the clips up from his lap.

She laughed, and his knee bounced wildly under the table as his heart thrilled.

"I'm just saying we don't have to risk our lives tumbling through space for an excuse to get close. There's a little room on my bench."

Her eyes wrinkled. She extended the mutilated cinnamon roll to his lips, and he bit down into a plump pillow of sweet, sticky goodness. The spicy aroma struck his nose, and he licked his lips. A part of him had already eased onto her bench and laid an arm around her shoulder, yearning to be closer. And the other part of him was rooted to his own cold, lonely seat just opposite, sulking in the reality of his hypocrisy, the guilt of betrayal to his people in this desire to love her, the knowledge that a serious relationship between a sable and a Pyron was laughably impossible. When they parted ways for the night, he would go back to being the renegade, and she the Skynhound. Was there some place on the earth where they could both stay this way forever? The goodness in her was dim, chained to circumstance, but it was there. Yet flipping a sable's moral compass on its head would only condemn her to a sable's cross, and even if she could come to love him deeply, she would feel betrayed when she discovered that the face beneath that mask was the face of her lover, and turn and slay them both for the lie.

Ambrosia remained where she sat while he finished the roll and the last of her ice cream. Then they sat in the quiet until two sables drove up on bikes, handed Ambrosia the key to one, asked how the flight had gone, and left together on the other.

Once back at the base, Disrel waited at the curb by his bike while Ambrosia tucked the gear into storage. It was impossible to believe the evening was already over, and he fiddled with the keystone in his pocket. Just one more glance at her beautiful face and his life might be full. Was there some way to touch her without offending her? It wouldn't be odd to break it off here. They'd only agreed to a casual date or two on the train, and now that agreement had been fulfilled. Could he just thank her for the two best evenings of his life and part ways? Or would he have to tell her she'd never see him again, not like this. And what if they met again, him in his wolf-skin, carrying his hatchet? Or what if the next time she saw him he sat behind prison glass, a Pyron insurgent awaiting execution?

Ambrosia approached from across the cobbled square, her lithe form snatching his breath with every graceful step, and she stopped just in front of him, sincerity plain in her features.

"It's probably too much for you to come hang out again tomorrow evening, driving all those hours. Want me to come to Pyron?"

He squeezed the keystone in his pocket. "No. Don't. I mean, there's more to do in Tourmal. And Pyron is crowded. I don't mind the drive. It's not like I have a—"

A fresh feeling of worthlessness flooded through him. What would any woman want with a jobless, homeless man like him? What had happened to that sense of normalcy, that quiet life with a routine and a paycheck? His life had been turned on its head in the course of a day, and this time with Ambrosia was the only bit of normalcy he had now. How could he let that go?

"Does it bother you for me to see where you live?"

"Maybe I'm just surprised you want another date, that you seem to like hanging out with a bum like me."

She pushed a lock of mulberry hair from her eyes. "You remember that gown you pulled from the rack when I was touring your skynshop? I wore it to a military ball." Her eyes dropped to the left as she rolled her lips and jittered. "It was the most beautiful, comfortable skyn I'd ever worn in all my life. I didn't know it was possible for a piece of clothing to be anything more than just comfortable or confidence-boosting. But that thing almost destroyed me."

His chest tightened. "Does that mean you loved it or—?"

A deep pain haunted her eyes as she swallowed hard. "I hated it. It was nothing more than a treacherous gift from the general to trap me into being a stepstool in his ascent to power. Every day since his execution, I've thought about destroying it."

"And what's stopping you?"

Her eyes locked with his. "You."

He traced a finger down his nose. "I don't understand."

"I was going to wrap it around Callon's neck during his execution. But you saving my life on the train made me hang on to it. It's probably stupid, but it feels like it would be worse luck to destroy something so perfectly made by such a"—she tossed her head and collected herself—"such a good man."

"When I made it, I didn't know it would be worn by a future friend." His hand flopped out of his pocket. "If you ever decide to put it on again, I'd love to see you in it."

She stepped a little closer, slipping her hand into his palm and lacing her fingers through his. The fit was perfect, like their hands had been carved from the same piece and belonged eternally clasped together. A soft smile flitted across her lips and he returned it, awkwardly, wanting to brush his thumb over the back of her hand but not finding the strength to move, wanting to tighten his grip and never let her go. He searched her eyes, drinking in every glimmer of emotion and storing it away to decipher later. Rivers of energy tumbled from his stomach and down his legs as she squeezed his hand before slipping away.

"I'll consider it." She said pleasantly. "Tomorrow? Same time?"

"Sure."

"Goodnight, Disrel. Be safe out there."

He tottered numbly on the curb and his foot swung a half circle. "Thanks, Ambrosia. Goodnight."

Her form glistened as she passed under the lamp posts along the path to her barracks, head down, hands wedged in her pockets, legs pumping like she was fleeing a stalker. She ascended the steps to the barracks porch, stole a glance over her shoulder, and ducked through the sliding doors.

Disrel blew a heavy sigh and shook himself. He flexed his burning hand and stared at his palm. Her touch was fading, but an imprint seared him just under his ribs on the left side. Had she meant to touch him that deeply? Mored was right. Even now, he might just lie back and love her while she ripped his heart from his chest. But it didn't even matter now. He straddled his bike, pulled his helmet from the barrel, and buckled the chinstrap. In just two days, Howler hatchets would do the same. Nothing would remain for the Skynhound to relish. He'd be a hollow soul, a shell of a man, drinking Kobalt blood to keep Vogin's pack from drinking his own.

25

Cinnabar strolled along the panoramic windows that illuminated the imperial dining hall, caressing the leaves and stems of the bedded plants and potted trees and tipping a pitcher into the soil at intervals. He plucked withering leaves and flowers and tossed them into a basket on the floor.

"You see how beautiful it becomes when the imperfect ones are discarded? This is the necessary sacrifice for beauty, for purity, and for the health of the entire vine."

The twenty military and political heads present around the aquarium dining table stared each other down like a huddle of peckish walruses. This was their first time meeting together since assuming the offices left empty by Callon and his supporters. The Sable Queen's glossy black lips pulled to one side as her glowing blue eyes meandered up and down the table, mocking. Every time her vulturous gaze landed upon one of the men, he would bow his head and clear his throat, or sneak a scratch under his stiff collar. The only position that had not changed hands was the Lieutenant General's. Tharik leaned back in his chair and gnawed on his knuckles. He had only narrowly escaped death by leaping in to defend Cinnabar the moment the tables turned against Callon, thinking that the position of military general would be his in Callon's demise just as easily as in his success. But Cinnabar had reserved the rank of military general for himself, and the uniform amplified his austerity. Cinnabar reached deeper into the flowering bed and jerked up a weed by the roots. A deep orange band hugged the girth of his bicep, marking his continued grief and mourning for his daughter.

"The Euclasian security administration reported that they turned up the charred remains of a Howler, along with his hatchet and blistered wolf-skin, directly under the research floor where the units containing the treatment for Pyron's drinking water were being stored. So either the Tourmaline Renegade was collaborating with the Howlers in this attack, or he himself is one of them."

Ambrosia rubbed her thighs and followed a yellow tang poking in and out of the reef by her feet. The Tourmaline Renegade was no Howler. A Howler would've killed her without hesitation and taken the medical kit with him with no thought for two injured sables. No Howler would've admitted that destroying the lab wasn't part of the plan with a tearful waver in his voice. But what good would it do to prove the renegade wasn't a Howler? He was still an enemy of the state. Cinnabar wanted him dead. The Sable Queen wanted her Skynhound to catch and torture him. Those glowing blue eyes landed on her cheek, and Ambrosia shuddered.

Cinnabar cast a handful of browned flowers into the basket at his feet. "The destruction of the Euclasian laboratory has set us back by months in our plans for peace across the empire. We need an alternative course of action. Something affordable and efficient."

Sharp eyes crisscrossed the table.

Cinnabar's hand hovered over a florid vine. "Would you prefer I go around the table by name?"

A chorus of throat-clearing resounded, and someone mumbled something about a vaccine that rendered the subject infertile.

"And suffer them another one hundred years? We tried that a decade ago and what did it do? I need a plan that will see their numbers cut in half by the end of this year."

Several of the officers and council members raised their voices in turn, suggesting macabre methods for thinning Pyron's population. The words rolled from their tongues like cursed monastic chants, sweetened only by the preceding names of respect and deference they paid their emperor. Ambrosia's stomach boiled.

Now was the worst time to petition Cinnabar for an expansion of Pyron's walls. When the sector was first established, the state had announced it as a gift to Pyron for peace, and many Pyrons had moved willingly, enticed by the free land and opportunity to keep peace with their Kobalt neighbors.

The Sable Queen leaned over and whispered. "Something is bothering you, my sable."

"It's nothing, my Queen. I simply prefer being out on patrol."

She nodded. "Just think, if you had apprehended your renegade in Euclase we could be downstairs working with him right now."

Ambrosia's blood chilled as a caustic fear raked its talons across her heart.

The Sable Queen rolled her chair closer. "That did not excite you like I expected it to."

Ambrosia shook herself. "I—I'm sorry, my Queen. My mind flew back to Euclase." She checked herself, then leaned in toward her superior. "Please forgive me if I bring the renegade to you dead. He is a desperate fighter and won't surrender himself as long as he is breathing."

"You are skillful and strong, Commander. I know you can bring him to me alive." The Sable Queen said. "What is the name of your Pyron lover?"

The queen rarely asked a question to which she didn't already know the answer. Ambrosia swallowed a brick. "Disrel."

"Disrel." She tapped her narrow chin and repeated the name as though it were a drop of honey on her tongue. "Callon described him as one of those Pyrons who obtained citizenship, who tries to blend with our culture, speaks our language fluently, and even contributes to society by working a job."

"But he is no lover, my Queen. Just a man I am using to my advantage, to better understand how Pyrons think and behave, because the Tourmaline Renegade is one of them, fluent in our language and somewhat Kobalt in his ways."

"Hmmm." Her lips bunched as her frosty eyes nipped some of the men sitting around the table. "Then you would have no trouble killing him if I asked you to?"

"There would be no question." Her voice cracked above a whisper, drawing the attention of the officers sitting nearest.

Their eyes danced with dread between queen and commander, as though the Sable Queen's inquiry was leaching like an unpleasant aftertaste in their minds, giving sense to the commander's response, and each was sure that he was the man being discussed. One by one, they squirmed under the queen's gaze before swiveling their chairs back toward the front of the room, some clearing their throats and others scratching at their necks.

Ambrosia rubbed her hands down her legs. "He means nothing more to me than any other ashrat, except that his willingness to teach me about his people has helped me to get into the Tourmaline Renegade's mind when I face him. For that, I need him alive a while longer."

"Hmmm. A while longer then." The Sable Queen sat back and leaned on her elbow, rubbing her fingers together as though she were sprinkling the sands of time.

Ambrosia melted into the chair and released a silent sigh. Her hands trembled in her lap, cupped around an invisible little white rabbit. The Sable Queen had looked just like her old den mother, commanding Ambrosia to strangle the life out of the innocent creature she had loved.

Cinnabar came to the head of the table and leaned on the back of his chair.

"Perhaps none of you heard me clearly. I'm no longer interested in keeping Pyron numbers in check. We could execute every renegade and insurrectionist today, and before we had finished, Pyron women would have given birth to tomorrow's terrorists. We'll forever waste our energy and resources trying to domesticate these people. They need to be wiped out. Give me something that looks so benign that no one can say who sent the last Pyron to his grave."

Lieutenant General Tharik pried his knuckles out from between his teeth and twitched upright in his chair. "Supremacy, many of the people behind those walls are sick and malnourished and desperate for help. And if you'll forgive me for quoting a Pyron proverb: There is a fine gray line between a healing tonic and a poisoned drink." He pulled a small envelope from his pocket and laid it on the table. "Build healthcare clinics at each of Pyron's gates and let the sick see our physicians for free. No one will be alarmed because this compilation of medicinal remedies has two parts—an actual cure for common, minor ailments, and a delayed reaction. The patient appears to benefit for a few days. He goes off and tells his friends that he feels like a new man, and that they should also go see the doctors at the gates. Several months later, he is dead. And who can prove it wasn't because he contracted a second illness or died of unknown causes? They'll come like sheep to the slaughter. What Pyron can afford to turn down free treatment?"

Mumbling conversation died the moment Ambrosia's shadow tumbled into the rec room of barracks three. Off-duty sables sprawled about, consuming garish literature and kelp chips.

"As you were, ladies."

The women tucked their eyes like a bunch of guilty schoolgirls, peeking up now and then. Cygnus resumed rubbing an oilcloth down the rails of her crossbow. "How did the meeting go?"

"Better than expected. The Tourmaline Renegade wasn't the only terrorist involved. They found a Howler carcass in the rubble."

"Ek." Cygnus leaned like she wanted to spit. No sable had qualms about shooting a Howler on sight. Anyone standing around in wolf-skin or with a lupine tail dangling from his backside deserved to be put to death where he stood, no questions asked. It was better that way. Every time one was captured and imprisoned for execution, his pack retaliated with a bloody rampage on innocent civilians.

"We'll be moving forward under Cinnabar's new directive next week: Operation Soapstone. He's keeping a medical codex card in his personal library to copy and distribute to volunteer physicians, who will be offering their services freely at each of Pyron's gates. They'll be reimbursed from Cinnabar's purse, with taxpayer credits of course, so we're to keep security tight around all state buildings and offices until further notice."

Phaedra stopped picking her nose and glanced up from her book. "Maybe get us a list of these physicians so we can all avoid them and live."

Lory pushed a needle through a tea towel she was cross-stitching. "Has anyone gotten to try the new Vindicator TA? I heard it reloads one point five seconds faster and has better accuracy with charged rounds."

Mixed reactions rounded the room, some sables preferring the standard-issue crossbows they were accustomed to. Neris moved from the kitchenette to the couch and knocked her comrade's legs from the seat.

"I carried one during Callon's execution. Didn't get to fire it though. It had an attachment, so I didn't have to clip the shoulder strap to the butt and it wasn't knocking into my breasts all the time."

"Did you see how prickled the Sable Queen got when Cinnabar had to leave early and ordered Callon's throat cut?"

"Yes." Neris rolled her eyes and groaned. "It was hardly three hours. I could've listened to him swear at us all day long."

Lori whisked the needle from the tea towel. "It was the tears for me. I've never relished a grown man's tears more."

"He tried to get Cinnabar to order us to shoot him so he wouldn't have to suffer." Neris plunged a kelp chip into the dip.

Cygnus laid her crossbow aside. "Anyone want to try the new Pluton Plate on Broad Street this week? The fried shrimp dish on their menu looks like it's to die for."

Ulyia rounded the corner of the rec room door in full dress, froze at the sight of Ambrosia, and retreated. Eyes and noses dove back into books, magazines, and crafts, Cygnus's question instantly forgotten. There was angst flowing from the others. They knew something. Why wasn't Ulyia relaxing with her comrades? And if she had somewhere else to be, why did she not want her commander to see her leaving? Ambrosia moved for the back door.

"Is your Pyron friend coming by again tonight, Commander?" Cygnus bounced in her chair like a child desperate for attention.

"Yes. In a couple hours."

"Oooh—oooh—oooh." She twisted her shoulders up and down and winked. "What are you planning on doing with him this time?"

"I might sit him down in the Sable Queen's chair and ask some questions."

Cygnus wilted with a slack mouth and stunned expression. The other women's gazes jerked sideways and a kelp chip sprinkled to the floor in shards.

Ambrosia moved to the den Ulyia shared with two other comrades and found her sitting on her bed, staring into space with a washed-out expression.

"Ulyia, is everything okay?"

"It's fine." She stared down at her hands and picked at a nail. "I'm just tired. Haven't been sleeping well."

"Since Brody's execution?" Ambrosia could never forget the look of betrayal on Ulyia's face when she'd seen her handsome lieutenant standing piteously at the general's side while she stood at the foot of her cross.

"It has nothing to do with Brody." Ulyia sighed, and looked away as if doubting her own words.

"Then what's troubling you?"

Her eyes traced the edges of the room and she rubbed the calf of her boot. Her lips looked like raw pie crusts. "Your Pyron. He's never once asked you for sex, has he?"

"No. Why would he? That keeps you awake at night?"

"No. I just think it's crazy how you actually found a man worth respecting. And he's Pyron. Not one of ours, a flaming Pyron." Her hard eyes punched at

Ambrosia. "How can you sleep knowing there's nothing you can do to keep him from being killed with the rest of them?"

Her tongue turned to leather. She hadn't been sleeping well since she met Disrel. But she couldn't let the others overhear that. "I've learned to never get attached to people, to things."

The corner of Ulyia's mouth drew into a bitter smile, then faded. "Huh. They taught us well." Her eyes fixed on the corner of the room with a faraway look, as if remembering their years at the academy. "Why is he so attached to you, then? If I'm not offering sex, men disappear faster than I can say my name."

Ambrosia bit her lip and looked away. "I honestly don't know, Ulyia. I guess we just enjoy being friends."

Ulyia shook her head. "There's no such thing. Not without benefits."

Ambrosia crossed her arms and tipped her head against the doorframe. "Are you unsure about meeting up with someone tonight?"

Ulyia shook her head. "I'm done." She mulled a moment, her eyes chasing thoughts around the room. "Do you remember Ilake?"

"No."

"We met during my second year of service. I'd never seen a more attractive man in all my life. His voice was hypnotic. His eyes were golden. His skin was perfect. *He* was perfect. He made me feel like his world. Coaxed me into going home with him and made my first time unforgettable in the best way. And then, he disappeared." Her brow lifted, but her gaze remained transfixed, lost in a well of bitterness. "I still don't know why he left. I stayed true to him for about a year, waiting for him to return. There were eight others after that. I thought each one would be the last. I thought we had something real. After the fifth one, I had no more boundaries. And by the time I met Brody . . ." She shrugged. "Love was just a game. Now, it's a game with a price that is too high for me to play anymore."

A sick feeling crept through Ambrosia's stomach. "Did someone hurt you? You know we'll back you up."

"He's dead now. It doesn't matter. It has everything to do with him, and nothing to do with him." She bowed her head and pressed her fingers to the bridge of her nose.

Ambrosia stepped inside and shut the door behind her. "Is there anything I can do to help?"

"Are you asking as my commander or my friend?"

"Whichever one you need me to be right now."

"You're the best friend I could ever ask for in this miserable life, but there's nothing you can do."

"Try me, Ulyia."

Her gaze connected with Ambrosia's. "I'm pregnant."

A chill swept through her. Ulyia pregnant? She'd tried to leave the barracks to see the physician, tried to have it ended before Ambrosia found out. "I'm sorry." The words fell out unbidden. There was no proper response to such hopeless news.

"With a traitor's child. I'm almost positive it's Brody's. I took a pill right after because the condom tore. It shouldn't have happened. But you know my scragged luck. When you're the one girl in your entire village chosen for sablehood, you can't expect anything different. You can't expect everything else in your life to go right."

Her comrade's voice droned like a distant echo in a tunnel. Not even sure it was Brody's? Perception of past, present, and future flowed the way time flows in dreams, all the possibilities and variables like a rainbow of colors mixing into the muddiest gray.

"How long have you known?"

"Since yesterday. Phaedra knows. Neris and Lory know. Serilda might've figured it out on her own. I tested again this morning just to be sure before I went in. I didn't expect you to get back from the meeting so early. I didn't want to bother you with a problem I brought on myself."

"Bother me? It's my duty." Sable Commanders were responsible for reporting pregnancies as early as possible. The farther along a sable was, the more time off she would need to recover from the termination.

Ulyia's mouth quivered. "This isn't my first. A year ago, I thought I ate some tainted food. I didn't know I was pregnant until—" She pulled a shaky breath and wiped her hands down her legs. "Until I—I had it in the toilet. *Her*. I had her in the toilet. I'm sure she was a girl. That's just how I felt when I looked at her. She had fingers. Toes. A nose. A face. She fit right inside my hand." Ulyia stared at her palm, tracing with her finger. "I had no idea she existed inside me until that moment, but there was this flood of emotions. I wanted to know who her father was. I wanted to know her. My mind was full of possibilities and loss and grief. I wanted her to survive by some miracle so I could give her to someone to care for, but at the same time, I wanted to be that someone that kept her forever. I knew it was only hormones making me feel that way, and that I'd get over it in time. So I avoided giving her a name, or thinking of her as anything more than an accident—a bit of menstrual tissue that happened to take shape. For years before that, I thought I wouldn't have been bothered to terminate a pregnancy. I'd been mentally preparing myself to have to, sooner or later. So I flushed and kept my secret."

She looked up, agony heavy on her face. "I don't know why, but I always think of her as Clari. I sometimes have dreams of raising her, of holding her. And now that I'm pregnant again, I realize that what I felt when I first saw Clari wasn't just hormones. It was love. Ambrosia"—a tear streaked down Ulyia's cheek—"I didn't know what love felt like until that moment. I'd never felt something that strong before. And now, just knowing I have another innocent life inside me, just like Clari—how am I supposed to kill that love—traitor's child or not? Think of your Pyron. Could you do it?" Her face broke with grief, but she glared at Ambrosia with a warrior's gaze.

Ambrosia's heart skipped. A sable's child had no right to life, no more than Pyrons had anymore. "I'm so sorry, Ulyia. I wish there was something I could do."

There was. But it was risky and the rec room was like a grave, every ear trained on this conversation. Ulyia's eyes ached at her torturous visions on the dorm wall. It was a blank canvas to Ambrosia's eyes, but even blank canvases held endless possibilities.

Ulyia shrugged and wiped her nose. "It's early enough that the physician will probably just give me some pills. I'll know not to look this time. I'll pretend it's menstruation. Flush and move on."

Ambrosia lowered her voice. "So let's pretend its father is Brody. Once high-ranking military officer, now dead traitor. And let's imagine that you had a middle-class profession and a home and could afford to raise the child on your own. What would you do?"

"What's the point? We're property of the state. The medical team could pull every tooth in my head if they thought I'd be better off without them."

"I'm asking as your friend. Would you abort it? Keep it? Or put it up for adoption?"

"I don't know." Ulyia looked into her open hands. "It deserves a chance to live. It shouldn't suffer because of its father's choices or mine."

Ambrosia drew a steadying breath. "When we served in Selen, Commander Geiya sent Sable Tenli on a special assignment out of sector, close to the border. Remember how she never returned?"

"They're still hunting her."

"Commander Geiya said something to me right before I transferred out: 'Nothing is impossible for the ones you love. Nothing is stronger than your love for the future you have conceived.'" She watched her friend, letting the words sink in. "Tenli was pregnant."

Ulyia stared numbly at Ambrosia, understanding that her commander was offering to give her the same chance. "This is why I didn't want you to know. We don't have that option."

"I'll find a way," Ambrosia whispered, her heart racing. "Trust me."

Ulyia rocked in place, shaking her head. "I watched Callon drown in his own blood on a cross that was mine a few days before. I can't face that again. I can't let you put yourself in that kind of danger for me."

"I'd give my life for you on a battlefield, Ulyia. This is no different. There are families willing to hide you and help you start a new life under a different name. And there are plenty of people who would gladly adopt the child."

"I don't want any of this for my life. I just want it all to go away."

"Then you know you'll regret this beyond the help of any medicine or alcohol. With all the riots there are plenty of ways we can fake a death. We'll find a charred body, something. Please, just promise me you'll take some time to think about it. I may be your commander, but I'm still your friend to my last breath. Knock on my door at three in the morning if you need to. We'll think of some way."

Ulyia sniffed and stared hard into the corner of the room, shaking her head. "You're so close to the Sable Queen. And if you can just get there, I know you'll change the way things are for us, change the way the world sees us. The only way I can let this child go is for that hope."

Ambrosia tucked her chin and rolled her lips. "Never sacrifice a child on a hope, Sable. I have enough power as commander to give you your best chance to escape with your child and make a new life."

"And when they've caught me and you have to watch me hang?"

Ambrosia closed her eyes, shutting out the image that flared up in her mind. She loved Ulyia more than any unborn child, but she could lose her either way—to the guilt of abortion or to a failed escape. "If we don't sacrifice for what we want, what we want will become the sacrifice. Please, promise me you'll think about it."

Ulyia wiped her nose. "I'll give it a few days."

"A week at least."

"Alright. A week."

Ambrosia reached forward and hugged her friend. Ulyia was stiff and empty, and when she pulled back, she avoided eye contact, pain haunting her face. She knew Ambrosia didn't have a reason to send her anywhere near a bordering nation. And with some of her comrades aware of her condition, it would be difficult to wait for an opportunity.

Ambrosia left Ulyia and passed through the rec room on her way to her quarters. Phaedra looked up knowingly from her book. Now it was clear they'd all been talking about Ulyia's pregnancy when Ambrosia had first entered the room. The small talk had been a cover, as if they were all afraid their commander would find out. Ambrosia decided it was better not to say anything about her conversation with Ulyia. She could trust Phaedra to fill her in on the dynamic between the other sables concerning the issue. They probably felt no need to say anything because sables saw the physicians on their off-duty hours, usually speaking of the pregnancy only once it was terminated.

Ambrosia retired to her quarters. She stepped out onto her balcony and leaned on the railing. The world out there moved at a frenzied pace, blind to a sable's pain, overwhelmed with its own. Time had to smile on Ulyia. The only sure redemption for a sable was that someone died in her place so she could run free. Without a body to fake her death, Ulyia would be on the fugitive list, hunted for years and at the mercy of others. Citizens risked prison time and being stripped of rights for harboring runaway sables, and it took months for the hairs of a sable's undercut nape to grow out to a length that would allow them to blend with the free population. They had to try to enter society under a different name, forge an ID that could trick the state into issuing them a valid copy when it came to renew it. Depending upon their age, they were often suspiciously single, without a husband, connections, family, or friends, and having to hide their faces behind layers of makeup meant they only fit in around circuses and nightclubs, making it even more difficult for them to merge back into any respectable part of society. A sable might successfully run from one bondage into another, and state hunters mocked how deserters were too stupid to run anywhere other than straight to a life of prostitution, but it was only because those in the business of prostitution—both whoremasters and self-employed women—were more willing to offer a deserting sable help in exchange for favors. Ambrosia could only hope that the universe would part the seas and blaze straight paths for Ulyia, and land her among good people.

The day was old and dying. Evening light gilded everything it touched, a fiery orange haze that crowned the precipices of the Tourmaline cityscape. What if tomorrow never came? What if this evening was the last day of all days? If an entire world could suddenly stop turning around its sun, nothing mattered. What caused time to continue, giving the condemned—and sables—false hopes? If there was no reality beyond this brutal existence, what did anything matter—good or evil? What was the point of being born at all? What power decided that one life should begin and another should end?

Ulyia's child mattered nothing to anyone but Ulyia. Perhaps it was new life that kept a sun rising upon a world, and a rising sun that kept life blooming from the soil of that same world. Perhaps life was as dependent upon unconditional love as that love was on life coming forth. Or maybe death was like the night, a respite between miraculous sunrises and brushes with inexplicable love. Unless the Pyron stories were true, and there was a life beyond the grave, every breath, every dawn was a false hope. Vanity.

Ambrosia wandered back into her quarters and pulled the silver gown from its hangar. She laid it upon her bed and stroked the shimmering bodice.

"You'd have no trouble killing him if I asked you to?"

"There would be no question."

"Hmmm. A while longer then."

Time worked against them all. And there was no one who could die in Disrel's place.

Ambrosia shed her uniform and slipped into the silver skyn. She strapped a blade to her thigh, pulled her hair down around her shoulders, and descended to the rec room.

Lucid eyes peeked from all corners. Ulyia lay across the couch with her head on a pillow, biting her fingernails like it was a necessary but loathsome chore. She froze, her mouth going slack. They all knew the dress as Callon's treacherous gift, and its presence summoned his ghost. Ambrosia made it to the barracks door, and a whisper trailed her.

"That's just creepy."

She paused with her hand on the pull bar as Neris's impish eyes buried themselves in a game board.

Ambrosia closed her eyes and gathered herself with a slow breath. They didn't have to understand. This was for Disrel, and for her own healing. She whipped the door open and marched across the base, her garment flashing like a flame.

26

Disrel paced by the curb, his white skyn gleaming like fine gold in the evening light. A smile budded on his face when he lifted his head, and a laugh escaped his lips as he spread his hands, his fingers twitching as if he longed to touch her.

"Wow. I didn't think you'd actually . . . Hm!" He swallowed hard, caught her hand, and rubbed it with his thumb. "It's incredible. More beautiful. Not just the dress, I mean you. Because you've always been beautiful, but together. . . Wow." He bowed his head and cleared his throat, then knit his brow and dared another look. "Did you find the hidden pocket? It should be right about—" He reached out and grabbed a fistful of material at her waist, then retreated, his cheeks turning a shade of market tomatoes as he stepped back.

A laugh rolled from Ambrosia's chest as she caught his free hand before he could escape. She wanted him closer, wanted him to touch her. "No. I never knew it had a pocket. Where is it?"

"Between the supports built into the waist. It's for small valuables like cards and credits."

Ambrosia ran her fingers along the waist of the dress.

"Go against the grain. Up, then down."

She swept her fingers up her waist and caught nothing.

"I'm not finding anything."

"Go slowly."

She kept trying, feeling no difference or seam in the fabric. "It's well hidden." She laughed. "Show me."

He set his hand over hers and guided it up the slope of her waist until her fingers caught a lip of fabric. She pushed her hand down into the silky pocket.

"Ah! It's genius."

His lips thinned into a modest smile and his black diamond eyes flashed up and down, peeking out from under those full, dark lashes. "It's perfect." His gaze flooded with fondness—desire—like he wanted to pull her into himself and never let go. He turned away, clearing his throat and rubbing his chin.

Ambrosia felt like the sun had disappeared behind a stormy cloud bank. She wanted more of his touch, more of the desire burning in his eyes. But it wasn't fair to ask him to love her. It only put his life in more danger. She brushed a hand down her hip. "I don't know when I'll ever wear this again. But if and when I do, I'll certainly make use of that pocket. What do you say to walking the mall this evening and doing whatever we find?"

"Yeah, whatever." His brow furrowed.

"You don't like that idea?"

"The mall is good." He looked at her. "I'm happy to be wherever you are."

"Actually, that's a bad idea. I'm so overdressed. I'll change back into uniform. It'll only take a minute."

His hand struck out and hovered over hers, like he wanted to have it again but restrained himself at the last second. "Please. Please don't. I love watching you move in it. I mean—" his eyes ducked to the pavement.

Ambrosia's cheeks ached as she smiled broadly. "Guilty as charged, Pyron."

He knit his brow and smiled. "Is admiration a crime?"

"Between a sable and a Pyron, I'm told it's a heinous one." Her tone betrayed her sadness.

He dipped his head as his eyes searched hers. "Please. Don't reduce this to a sable–Pyron moment. We can be so much more than what the world sees in us."

Us. His words touched her heart and forced her to look away. Love between a sable and a Pryon was not forbidden. It was just ridiculous. Impossible. The state made them predator and prey. The public saw them as unvirtuous and undesirable. But what did he see in her beyond a deadly risk?

"Anyway." His eyes glinted. "What is my punishment for admiring?"

She snorted in good humor. "Why do you ask?"

"To know if I can afford to become a repeat offender."

"If I let you off the hook once, you'll expect mercy every time. I can't afford that." She tucked her hair back and shot him a playful look. "Come on, the evening isn't waiting."

They started the six-block walk to Tourmal Mall, pretending not to notice each other stealing glances. Cyclists and pedestrians slowed and stared. Some cast insults at Disrel, some at the both of them. Dressed as she was, Ambrosia passed as a citizen, but what sort of citizen would walk with a Pyron in public at evening time, clothed in luxury? Only a prostitute or a sable. She felt like every passerby knew the truth. Her silver skyn flashed like liquid diamonds from collar to voluminous hem as they strode through the mall gate and down the east wing, rivers of people flowing from shop to shop with their bundles of goods and clouds of grease and grill smoke gathering in the lofty ceilings and marrying in the crossings. They walked to a quiet street and paused before a restaurant.

Disrel had never tasted Kobalt clos, so Ambrosia ordered and they sat on a bench in the shadow of a pillar, sharing the flaky squares of spiced and powdered dough filled with gooey custard and watching a heron spear for koi in the grand pool at the center of the atrium, surrounded by lanky broad-leafed trees. Each time the heron missed, he would sidle around the edge, hunched over like a gargoyle to try again. Doves bobbed circles on the plaza floor, pecking up crumbs left in the wake of grazing pedestrians, and in the corner a blue tabby crouched, tail twitching, gray eyes darting from bird to bird, struggling to choose one. All had come together to eat, some to eat other hungry creatures. The tabby sprang from her crouch and the doves thundered into the air. The cat's paws sent one into a tailspin, but failed to bring it down; and she glared at the corners of the plaza, as if blaming the passing humans for her failure. She sat, licking her paw and flicking her tail, as though the dove was of no importance. The heron's head came up with a flashing orange tail flailing madly between his beak. His head bobbed once as he tried to reorient the snack, but a mall worker dashed in from one of the wings with a broom and hurled it like a javelin. The heron gave one big flap of his wings, scooting out through the wide arch with his catch before the broom hit the water. The worker stamped his foot and leaned over the pool to retrieve his tool, pitched forward, and went under. He splashed up and hauled himself out with the broom in hand, shook water from his shoes, and marched back to his cleaning cart.

Ambrosia shook with laughter, but Disrel sat with his arms folded, eyes glazed. He'd missed it all. He hadn't reached for a pastry square in several minutes.

"Rel?"

His eyes widened on her.

"I'm sorry. Should I not call you that?"

"Why did you call me that?"

"It just came out. I didn't mean—"

"My sister calls me that."

"Then I won't use it."

"No. It's fine. Call me whatever you want. I really don't care. I just didn't expect you to call me something other than Pyron, or, you know, my actual name."

She wiped a lock of hair from the corner of her mouth. "I don't know why it came out like that. You seem down tonight."

He raked at his neck and huffed. "Yeah. Sorry about that."

She turned toward him and scooted back an inch. "Is something wrong? You were so happy earlier."

"I don't want tonight to ever end." He rubbed his hands together between his legs. "I was just thinking this could be the last time we see each other like this. We never know what tomorrow will be like. And I hate the thought of losing your friendship."

Every point on his face stood out to her: His sculpted throat. His firm chin. The clean edges of his jaw. Those lovely cheekbones. The definition of his lips, and their color, like the flesh of figs. The unobtrusive pleasantness of his nose and brow ridge. The enveloping darkness of those eyes, drawing her to trust him.

She wiped her hands down her hips as guilt riddled her heart. His warm, gracious manner of speaking always set her stomach to fluttering, and when he looked at her and spoke his feelings, his voice took on a smoky edge that sent her spinning. How could he look at her this way and not be afraid? Had her queen given the order, she would be the one wishing the night to never end so she didn't have to sacrifice him to spare her own life a little longer. The blade in its sheath burned against her thigh. Her mind rehearsed the motions, fueled by her training. A quick lift of his chin and a slash across the jugular. Merciful. Almost painless. If she covered his eyes, he would never even see it coming. And then he would slump over as his life drained. Those dark black eyes would mist over and close, and those lips would seal against her, and the bench would be empty.

A knot wadded in her stomach and pushed into her throat. Hot waves crashed through her eyes. She shot to her feet and stumbled over to the pool, forcing the doves to part and wing their way back to the rafters in droves. The water lapped with the eddies of koi fins as they surfaced, hoping for crumbs. One fat tear rolled and rippled the water. He had touched something, like the hand of a physician palpating a wound with the best of intentions. And though the touch hurt, she didn't hate him for it. Hate was familiar. Apathy was comfortable. But this other feeling sent her heart racing and made her want to wrap herself up in his arms and lose herself there.

His presence warmed the air around her, and his shadow fell into the pool as he moved up beside her. "Was it something I said?"

Her breath cinched, and she kept her eyes on the fish, waiting for the strength to speak. "Listen. If you ever get sick, don't go see the Kobalt physicians at the gates."

He leaned in and peered at her eyes. "Why?"

"Just trust me. They're not there to help your people."

Something in his eyes moved for her before he turned back toward the pool with a sigh. Words choked up in her throat like two armies converging on the field of battle. "I—I suppose I've betrayed my feelings."

"That you don't want to see my people die?"

She shook her head, trying to shake the words loose and keep the tears back. "Only because of you, Rel."

"You did it again, Cherry." A flirtatious light sparked through his eyes, snaring her heart again.

"Cherry?" Her frown failed to dampen her amusement. "Now you're picking on my hair."

"I like your hair and I like cherries, Honeybee."

"Stop it." She pushed on his shoulder and wiped a hand over her smile. Her stomach fuzzed and milled with warmth. "If you're going to start name calling, I'll get rough. *Dimples*."

He arched a brow. "You call that rough? I don't even have dimples."

"And I'm not a honeybee."

"Then what would you like me to call you?"

"I don't know. I like hearing my given name."

"Well you need to give me something, because you've called me Rel twice now."

"And why must our relationship be tit for tat?"

His smile widened and he shrugged. "If it's fit for the sable it's fit for the Pyron."

She crossed her arms over her chest. "Then tell me what honeybee means to you."

"It's from a book I read growing up. An evil enchantress took a little girl from her family as a debt collection and changed her into a honeybee. The honeybee made friends with a tiger she passed on her flight to and from the flower fields. And one day the little honeybee got caught in a spider's web."

Ambrosia recognized the story. She had read it many times in the library at the academy and it had inspired her to dream of impossible friendships.

"Well, if you call me Honeybee, I'm going to call you Bun."

"Fair enough."

She buried her eyes in the dark waters again. Bun was short for Bunzer, the little white rabbit she had fallen in love with at the academy, and strangled the life from days later.

Disrel's gaze wandered as he set a hand on his chin. "Hmm. I'd wager the architect must've had dancing on his mind when he laid the floor of this mall. The tiles are just about the right size for a Dahneetsa, see? The deep red tiles could mark the first step, and the blue tiles the run, the white marble for the spin, the yellow for the back steps, green on the crossover and switch, and the black ones help make the reverse."

Her gaze swept the floor and then leaped to his face. How had he noticed such a thing? "Why would anyone make a mall floor for dancing?"

"I don't know. Let's see if it works." He reached for her hand and searched her face.

"Oh, gods, we'll look ridiculous."

"The lighting is perfect here. And that skyn only looks ridiculous when it's not dancing." He backed, pulling her along by the hand gently.

"Really? How would you know?"

"Because I made it." He took her other hand into his palm and squared his toes on a rusty granite slab.

"How do you know the Dahneetsa?"

"The same way I know how to read, write, and speak your language. One very special Kobalt lady." He guided her right into the first step, and as they came together the brush against his straight stomach stole her breath.

"I have to warn you: I have two left feet. I'm always stepping on toes."

"I'm glad I'm not the only one." He stared down hard. "I hope I'm remembering correctly."

"No. Wrong way." They fell out of step and reunited around a black tile.

He laughed. "I learned it only because Miss Mazilyn insisted. I couldn't imagine when a Pyron boy might ever need to know this." His smile was warm, naturally wide and pleasant, with even teeth.

"Well, here you are."

"With you. And you're with me." His anthracite eyes glimmered with unabashed joy. The warmth of his hand on her waist kept her heart jumping as he guided her along with confidence. "It doesn't feel so stupid now. White tile."

She spun under his lead, and the atrium walls and canopies turned in a blur of color. The garment hems pulled around her legs, flashing like a million fiery diamonds.

"Wow," he breathed, slowing as they reached the black square.

The floor was perfect for this dance. She knew the next steps, but did he? Ambrosia switched her momentum from following and pushed closer. He caught her, supporting her waist through the dip and drawing her back up as easily as if he had practiced it a hundred times before. She felt his breath warm the skin of her throat as he leaned in close, gazing intently into her face, eyes twinkling with a sort of wonder or fascination. Then he released her, danced across the floor, and paused, hand outstretched, waiting. A dulcet melody wafted through the plaza from somewhere high above, and Ambrosia turned through her solo steps, scanning the corners of the hall for the minstrel as she twirled. Disrel's intense gaze arrested her once again as she landed clumsily on his chest.

"I suddenly can't remember the next steps," he said.

"There aren't any more. You just go around again from the first."

He swayed right back onto a red tile without missing a beat. The woody melody sang on, the ghostly minstrel bleeding out his heart upon the strings. Ambrosia clutched Disrel's bicep and drank in his face. Either he was not as clumsy as he had let on, or he had given her feet wings. She'd never danced a Dahneetsa as smooth as this one. Perhaps it was the dress, at home in the arms of its designer, in the hands that had lovingly pieced it together and tailored its edges. Now those same hands were giving it a life of joy and beauty in the most unusual of places. At the last step, he planted his legs upon two black tiles and bowed his forehead against hers. The silver hems wrapped around his legs, and she surrendered her gaze to his. Whatever this was, it was intoxicating. His eyes moved between hers, twinkling with mirth one moment, tender with feeling the next, and his hands remained still and firm on her waist, yet gentle enough to let her go the moment she chose to pull away. And then Ambrosia knew: as long as he held her, she could never lose him, because he wasn't hers to let go of. She was his.

Whistles and applause cracked through the atrium. Ambrosia blinked, shuddering from Disrel's hold and looking past him. In all three wings, shoppers stood with bags on their arms, clapping and cheering. A fiddler perched on the railing of an open balcony just above the food court, twirling his bow and striking the strings for an encore. The crowd might be pleased, but some killjoy had probably gone to call for soldiers. Disrel smiled at the ground and laughed, his cheeks reddening before he looked up at her again.

Ambrosia pulled away and darted for a wing. Disrel clung to her hand and stumbled after, bubbling about the dress. How stupid was she, to have let Tourmal see her dancing with a Pyron? If someone recognized her and word got back, it would be a death sentence for him. She could not protect this lamb forever. He was one of thousands in the slaughtering pen, waiting his turn—but she would buy him every minute she could afford.

Dark drapes framed a low opening in the wall. She scooted in and slid along a bench, and Disrel stumbled in right after, knocking his head on the low door, hissing, then laughing at his injury. They fussed around on the seat, catching breaths and checking in on each other. A deep voice serenaded from just overhead, and they jumped.

"Welcome, sweethearts. Look at the red dot on the wall in front of you. Cozy up. Smile. Wait for the flash on the count of three."

Ambrosia clawed at the curtain. "Wait, wait, wait, we don't want a photo. We just need a quiet place."

"The kissing booth is located in the west wing. Three."

"Stop!" Panic surged in her chest. "We're not paying for a photo."

Disrel arrested her in a side-hug, blocking the exit and giving her shoulder a little squeeze. "He's already counting. Just smile."

"Two."

"I'm gonna die." She wilted against his chest.

"Don't tell me you forgot our parachute!" He grinned shamelessly into her eyes.

"Parachute? What?" She pitched forward, laughing.

"One."

Light strobed the dark booth, and Disrel's hand tried to pull her straight. His cheek glanced off hers a moment, and stars burned all around them long after the flashing stopped. They groped for the curtain and there was a thunk and a groan. Disrel ducked again, holding the top of his head as he moved through the opening. Ambrosia held on to a loose fold in his skyn, blinking away stars and scanning the mall street.

"Let's find some other corner."

"Your photos." A man as bald and round as an egg pressed two large sheets of photo stock into her hands. "That will be two credits."

Ambrosia glared through a yellow afterimage. "I said we didn't want photos."

Disrel reached around her and pressed them into the vendor's palm. "Thanks for serving us, sir."

Egg man rubbed the credits together, his jaw hanging. "Agh, filthy Pyron." He glowered and tottered back around the corner, wiping the credits on his sleeve and grumbling.

Ambrosia meandered away from the booth with the photo sheets dangling from her hand. Disrel pulled at one and chuckled. He sat alone in the first two, with only a crown of her red hair peeking from the bottom corner. The next row captured her grimacing laughter, eyes squeezed into slits, mouth pulled, fingers coiled around her cheeks like she was shrieking at the loss of her true love. Disrel's head was tilted into hers, his smile raw and wide, adoring eyes drinking in her mirth. The camera had caught it all, frame by frame.

He laughed. "You look like you're in pain."

"And you look like you're enjoying it." She flicked the sheet at his chest.

"Wait. What about the second sheet? Here's one with your eyes open."

At the bottom of the second, four beautiful pictures. Each one captured the perfect moment where they were looking into each other's eyes and smiling. Disrel laid the sheet on a cutting table and cut the photos out. He pushed two into her hand.

"For memory's sake, of good times and good friendship."

She raked a lock of hair from her eyes. "Thanks."

He glanced down the opposite wing. "So... do you think they run the kissing booth the same way?"

"Huh. Already thinking of marriage, Pyron?" She gave him a teasing smile, only to hide her true feelings. She couldn't let him feel how badly she wanted to sweep in and lace her arms around his neck, press her lips against his and kiss him.

How easily he seemed to forget that she was a disgraceful woman, that she was in a position of power over his people.

"It was an innocent curiosity."

They walked on, and a minute later their steps synced, and she only wanted to walk closer to his side. It didn't matter where they were going. The halls and streets served only them and the occasional shopper walking alone. Disrel's hands swung easily at his sides, one clutching his photos, the other empty. She slipped her fingers between his and held on without checking for a reaction. She could always feel when he was looking.

He cleared his throat. "So, where to?"

"Wherever our feet may take us. Isn't that the Pyron way?"

"Yes. Yes, it is." He closed his fingers around her hand and drew it closer to his thigh.

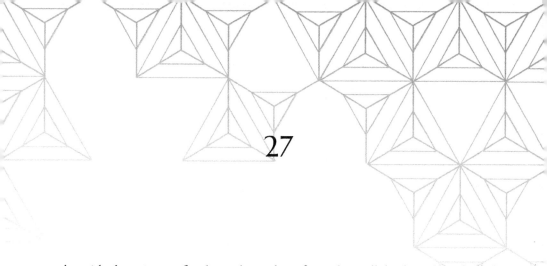

27

T he looming curfew hour drove them from the mall, back to the safety of the base, where they talked under a lamppost for an hour longer. Disrel carefully pocketed his photos next to his pass, while Ambrosia clung a little more tightly to his hand, her gown a prismatic river under the light.

"I'm going to be busy the next few weeks," she said. "I'll relay a message in a few days when I know what my free time looks like in the evenings."

His brow pinched as he bobbed his head. "Please do." There was no way to tell her. He'd savored every glance, every moment, every touch. Three dates with the Skynhound, all better than he could have ever dreamed. He rubbed his thumb over the back of her hand, feeling the roughness of her knuckles from fighting.

She pulled from his grasp. "Goodnight, Rel. Be safe out there."

"That was quite a dance we shared, wasn't it?"

"Yes, it was." They had already talked about the dance.

His heart jackhammered through the passing seconds as he scrambled for anything to stall her. Five more minutes. Would she spare him ten? "And the Clos was amazing. Did we leave our trash on the bench?"

She cocked her head and smiled. "I guess we did. Oops. Well, I've only got five hours before tomorrow's shift."

He shuffled a step closer. "Thanks for wearing the gown tonight. I mean, instead of a uniform."

"Goodnight, Lamb."

He started at the unexpected endearment. "Goodnight, Honeybee."

She cast one more smile over her shoulder and scampered off to her quarters.

His hand hung empty and cold at his side and he flexed his fingers. When the barracks door closed behind her, he turned toward his bike and sighed, remembering the warmth of her touch on his bicep, the scent of her skin and hair, warm and luxurious, like vanilla and black currants and cinnamon. At least he had a keepsake now, a stack of imperfect photos of Tourmal's Sable Commander, the merciless Skynhound, conquered by laughter. He pulled the cards from his pocket and brushed his thumb over her cheek. Knowing this had come to an end made him miss her already.

Movement in the shadowy corner of the Command Center's porch caught his eye: a gray apparition with fat horns sprouting from its head. It trailed into the light, a dark snout and two dead eyes. A human hand swelled from its side, a single digit pointing skyward.

Disrel's blood boiled as he spat through his teeth: "I'm working on it. You gave me until sundown tomorrow."

"Your time is running out, tiger. Disappoint the Alpha and we'll all be at Eight Silkspar Trail the moment the sun drops below the Selenite ridge. Be waiting for us with a cooling corpse. And if not, we will find you."

The Howler turned and slunk off across the street and into the darkness. Disrel's fists tingled until he released them, realizing he had crushed the photos in his fear and anger. Fingernail prints burned in his palms, and through one photo, a white, jagged line ran through his and Ambrosia's faces. He sighed in frustration as he lifted his eyes to the night sky. Only a handful of stars were visible through Tourmal's city lights. Had his vow been heard? Would Father ever answer? Or was a prayer only a one-way message? Why had Father bothered to do it at all if he never received anything? Disrel blinked, searching deep into the abyss, and his lips moved breathlessly.

"Please, if you can hear me, Father told me I can trust you to walk me through fires. These Howlers aren't the Pyron the world needs. We need Thelis with skin on it. A living, breathing Thelis the world can touch and feel. I need strength.

Take all of me and do with me what you will, for my people's sake, for Solla, for my friends . . . and for Ambrosia."

The stars twinkled, and a breeze whistled through the streets, whipping trash and leaves along the curb. The prayer seemed to drip upon his face like something he had thrown toward heaven and in his humanity had not enough strength to cast it far enough. He sighed, threw a leg over the corecycle, and plucked his keystone from his pocket. Less than twenty-four hours remained, and he needed to endure another long sleepless night listening to Solla snore in the next room, blissfully ignorant of the danger. Maybe he would pace the basement tonight, or sit out on the porch to escape the looming fantasies of how easy it would be to murder Koti in his sleep. But he didn't even have the will to do it when it was easiest, when Koti would never see it coming and Solla was out of the way.

Last night, Disrel had laid in bed, eyes open, his mind racing, each train of thought carrying him down endless paths that all led to the same outcome: bloodshed and loss. Distraught, he sat up with his qorzan blade in hand, and peered at the sunset burning through the window, confused because the wall clock's orbs were deep into the hemisphere of night. His heart pounded with dread, knowing that the Howlers were late and would arrive at any moment. He was out of time. He looked down at his naked flesh and touched the dashed circle inked upon his chest over his heart, marking the place where the Howlers would cut to remove the organ and replace it with a wolf's heart. Solla stood in the doorway between their rooms, her eyes rusted by bloody tears.

"Rel is dead," she said to him, much too calmly, as if he were someone else. "I can show you his body." She motioned through the door where she stood and he looked in to see Koti sleeping on Solla's mattress. Disrel wandered closer, confused, as Koti's features morphed into his own likeness, and he saw a man who was supposed to be him, but wasn't. He was different somehow, as if he were him from another decade, or another lifetime.

"He's been dead for three days now, and if you don't cut his throat, you will die," Solla said from the doorway. "It's the only way to wake him up and save yourself. And if you don't, then we will all die."

The burning sunset faded like a vapor from the window, and the world outside was drenched in an infinite darkness. Then came the sounds of wolves running circles around the house and howling, and the air was charged with the presence of a great evil that slowed Disrel's every movement and made it painful.

"See, now you're dying just like he did," Solla said. "You have to wake him up before it's too late."

Disrel looked at the still form lying on the mattress as the sounds of paws thumping on the grass outside the room grew louder and louder. His every will to move was stunted by the oppressive weight in the air. The wolves were hurling their bodies into the door. In a moment they would break inside and devour everything. Disrel laid the knife upon the neck of the strange man in the bed, and just before he made the cut, the shaggy paws of a wolf crossed around his mouth and pushed him forward against the sleeping dead man in the bed. They came nose to nose and the dead man's empty white eyes flew open and sucked him in. Disrel tumbled over and over down a dark shaft through coiling flames, the wolf pelt's hairy limbs strangling him like a noose, the gaping jaws gnawing on his head, devouring him from behind. Its boiling canine breath sucked him up and into its dark belly, and his soul filled its eyes.

And then he was the wolf, falling through the black fire, clutching the jagged hole in his chest and howling for mercy. When had they taken his heart? How was he living without it? Infinite pain radiated through his chest from where his heart should have been, shattering his bones as it moved throughout his body. And then he struck an abysmal bottom and woke, drenched in sweat, chest heaving, feet numb, bound up in a blanket on the floor next to his mattress.

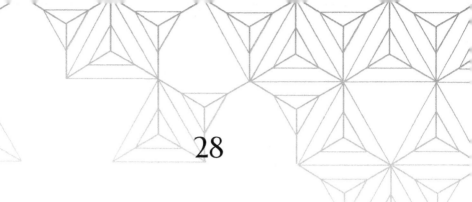

28

Disrel paced his dark bedroom, rubbing his eyes and muttering through spent ideas that offered no promising outcomes. He sat on his mattress, propped his elbows on his knees, and raked his fingers through his hair. A vise wrapped his head, some invisible hand massaging his mind into silence when he needed it to be its sharpest. He'd thought of everything—outlandish things like planting a bomb in the house just to take out the entire pack—but even the most viable idea could only end with him and Solla being shot down by police or taken to the Pyron sector.

He collapsed on the mattress, spread his arms above his head, and listened to the silence. Was it almost dawn? Or just after midnight? He twisted and turned through the waking eternity until at last his head found his pillow, and he stared into the starless abyss. Maybe he needed to stand outside on the deck to hear heaven's answer. But then why hadn't heaven answered the last two nights, when he had wandered outside for fresh air? He sighed and shut his eyes and stroked his fingers over his stomach.

His mind wandered through a forest of hopelessness until a warm, golden glow dawned in his shut-eye world and moved through the sea of whirling phosphenes. He followed it across his field of vision as it grew brighter, closer, and every hair on his body pinned. *Disrel.* His heart jumped. It was as if the sound of his name had been translated by a resonance to some deeper part of himself, capable of hearing without ears. His scalp tingled, coupled with the sense that someone else was in the room, and his eyes flew open. Instead of moving for the blade he kept under his mattress, his hand lay numb at his side. Halfway between himself and the wall, the closed-eye hallucination remained, vivid and liquid golden fire, folding and unfolding itself simultaneously like a four-dimensional rhombus. The low furniture and wall hangings caught the light and cast shadows as it floated closer.

Disrel's breath vaporized as he trembled, straining to move. His throat worked for a cry, but even his tongue was a useless lump. His eyes were prisoners to the light, unwilling to shut it out, as the whirling vision hovered like a sentient nurse, a living eye, an intelligent and self-aware being fully interested and invested in every part of him. Was it Mother or Father, or some other ancestor with a message? He strained to speak to it, but his breath was locked by some invisible hand. A sharp tail, like a thread, spun from the bottom of the light and aimed itself at his heart. It dripped down and spread out over his naked chest where it sparkled and flashed like fireworks, shimmering and boiling into his skin, absorbing, emanating, tumbling heat down into his stomach and bones. Words flooded his mind as vivid and clear as if spoken directly into his ear: *Sacrifice. Thelis. Love.*

The light above drained little by little, concentrating and milling about under his breastbone, scouring him like fire. He tipped his head back and sucked in a breath, still unable to cry out, trapped in an eternity. His only sense of passing time was the movement of the fire, waning as it threaded out, emptying itself into him until every last drop of it had vanished under his skin.

Strength returned and Disrel shot up, snapping his hand to his chest and scratching. His flesh was a little brighter in the center. He quivered and panted, trying to make sense of the experience. Was it another crazy dream? He wiped his hand down the side of his face. No. He was awake. But maybe he had only just woke up. Had it all happened in an instant? Or had he endured countless millennia under that spell? Peace enveloped his mind like a mother's arms, and he closed his eyes and let his head fall forward, content to surrender his spirit if it was his time to go.

The exuberant twittering of birds brought his eyes open, and he lifted his head from his pillow and stared at his chest. The bright spot was gone. He couldn't remember falling asleep nor imagine how long he had slept. But he still had his heart beating in his chest and twelve hours to make a decision.

The third day slogged by. He checked the clock, every hour, every quarter, every minute. Sometimes three times a minute. Time was sprinting and still dragging its feet. Disrel got up and paced the ground floor, trying to find an excuse to drop by and see Mored without being confronted by the treacherous sentries. Surely Mored had been planning the last couple of days, as secretly as he could with Howler eyes watching his every move. Disrel couldn't imagine the veteran letting death come so easily.

He picked at breakfast, nibbled through lunch, and waited for Koti to return from the clinic in the evening. The simplest of tasks triggered the strongest feeling that he had stood in that exact spot and made those same movements some unnamable times past. He had lived out this day before, or dreamed it, but how was it supposed to end? Or could he rewrite the ending? Even a few hours after lunch, what little he had choked down soured in his stomach.

Disrel shadowed Solla for most of the day, even following her absentmindedly to the restroom on one occasion. She gave him a wary look as she settled back on the couch with the book she was reading. A minute later, she glared up at him.

"Rel?"

Disrel paused in the center of the living area. "Hm?"

"I'm trying to read."

"I see."

"Can you please do it somewhere else?"

"Do what?"

"Pace and snap your fingers?"

"Oh. Sorry." He sat in an armchair across from her, rubbing his thighs and looking around the room, feeling listless. After several minutes of silence, he asked: "Is it any good?"

Solla nodded, but her eyes never left the page.

"What's it about?"

"Two people who hate each other and then fall in love."

Disrel wrinkled his nose. "How can they fall in love if they hate each other?"

"They learn to like each other."

Disrel reflected for a moment. "Why did they hate each other?"

"Because the guy thinks he's better than the girl." Solla closed the book and got up, moving into the kitchen where she poured herself a glass of milk and gathered two freshly baked cookies on a plate.

Disrel scratched his head. "But why does he think he's better than her?"

"Because he's a royal idiot with a lot of humble pie to eat," she said.

"Sounds boring."

"Well, unlike you, I'm not bored." Solla cast him a smirk and took her book and food upstairs to continue reading.

Disrel got up and paced the living area. He stood in front of the picture window, looking out at the back of Koti's property for some time longer. The next he knew, he was in the upstairs hall, rapping lightly on Solla's bedroom door. She groaned in response.

"Solla?" He said timidly.

"I'm at the best part." She sounded a little exasperated. "What do you want?"

"Nothing." Disrel's brow knit and he rubbed his eyes before putting his hands on his hips and biting his lip.

"Then why are you knocking?"

"I don't know. Bored, I guess."

"You aren't going to sweep the basement or organize the linen closets again?"

Disrel sighed and turned away, but before he could leave, the door opened and Solla was smiling. "Alright, rain cloud. Out with it. What do you want?"

Disrel pushed both hands into his pockets and shrugged. "To spend time with you."

"That's not a little bit weird after months of caginess." She kept her body tightly wedged between the door and its frame. "What's the password?"

"Password?" He frowned at her.

Solla's smile grew bigger, into one he couldn't help but return. His lips lifted a touch.

"Ehhh . . . not quite there yet." She poked her fingers rapidly at his stomach, catching him off guard and tickling. He chortled, arresting her hands and pinning them together.

"Hey. Go easy, you little jumping cactus."

"Try again." She laughed as she grinned up at him and he couldn't stop the smile that spread across his face. "Correct password," she said, moving aside. "Come on in."

Disrel settled down on a floor cushion and tried to forget for just a minute that their lives were going to change catastrophically at sunset. He had so much he wanted to tell her. But how could he make her understand he had no other choice, no other option that guaranteed her life would be spared? How she would hate him for buying her life with Koti's blood. Especially when it was a life neither one of them wanted to live. It would warp her. She would be forced to live in a secluded Howler camp, constantly on the move, surrounded by and compelled to serve terrorists. And he would be one of those terrorists under Alpha Vogin's leadership.

"What's eating at you?" Solla asked, giving him her full attention.

"I'm just trying to figure something out."

"Maybe I can help."

He rubbed a hand over his mouth and shook his head.

Solla huffed. "Let me guess, another secret you can't share with your only living relative?"

Disrel sighed heavily, keeping his gaze averted while his mind turned through all the things he wanted to tell Solla, but couldn't.

After a long minute, Solla returned to her book, and Disrel returned to jittering, though he took the time to watch Solla, engrossed in the fantasy, and appreciate her. She noticed, glancing up from her book.

"Why are you looking at me like that?"

"Like what?"

"Like that. The way you're looking at me now."

"I'm not looking at you any sort of way. I'm just sitting here. Quietly. Being myself. You know, spending time with you." He raked at his stubbled jaw. "Isn't that what you want? You complain when I have to go away. And when I'm here, you get upset that I'm pestering you."

"You're not acting like yourself. And I don't mind you being here, except that it feels like you're not really here. Don't you have *anything* better to do than stare at me like a disturbed person?"

Disrel pushed up to his feet, more out of annoyance with himself than at her. He couldn't be upset with Solla, not in the slightest. He was the one having to premeditate murder to save her. "I'll be sweeping the basement." He said before closing the door softly behind himself.

Disrel stood in the middle of the basement's main room, wiping his sweating palms against his legs and dreading the only avenue he had left. Without an ample supply of weapons, resisting the Howlers was suicide. He might kill one before they killed him and slaughtered all the others. And in that equation, he lost Alta and Solla as well. By leaving Mored, Tygo, and Astros alive to fight, they might kill several Howlers before losing their lives. Koti, Doni, and Voss had no hope of self-defense. They didn't even have an idea of what was coming. The only sensible thing to do was to ensure that the Howlers would leave Alta and Solla alive. To take one life to save two.

Several hours had passed since he'd left Solla to finish her book, and Disrel found himself back in front of her bedroom door. The dulcet sounds of harp strings wafted through, and he bowed his head and listened for a moment, gathering his thoughts. She was advancing well for one who was teaching herself. Disrel raised his fist, letting it hover over the door while he fought the rising lump in his throat, working up the nerve to speak. What excuse could he make to give her a hug? How could he let her know he loved her without actually saying it? Should he really expect to get any farther with it than he had the last time he'd entered her room? He released the breath he was holding and turned away, sliding down the wall next to the door. He leaned his head back and let the honest timbres bathe his spirit. But even that soothing couldn't wash away the knowing that she had every right in the world to want to disembowel him and stomp on his guts. If only they had more time to talk about anything and everything.

The front door opened and Disrel shut his eyes, suppressing a groan. Koti was home. He wanted to stop time until he could figure out another way. He forced his feet to move toward the stairs, to intercept Koti before Solla realized he was home.

Koti set his work bag down in the hall and piddled around the living room, picking up drinking glasses and resetting throw pillows. "Hey, Disrel. How are you?"

Disrel leaned on the corner by the basement door. "Well enough. How was work?"

"Excellent. I observed five more clients and added their experiences to my report on predicting human choices in time-sensitive, high-pressure scenarios and the effects of regret on future rationalizations. A few more months until it's submitted to the *Journal of Experimental Psychology* for peer review."

Koti's voice fuzzed as Disrel contemplated his proximity to the basement door. The knife was behind the couch cushion downstairs. Solla was occupied.

"Hey, something's up with the hot pool today."

Koti's hands stopped mid-animation. "Pardon?"

"The water is a funny color and smells off."

"That's odd." Koti went straight down into the basement. Disrel followed, latching the door behind him. Clouds of steam cloaked the ceiling.

"Who closed the vent?" Koti moved to the glass and pulled a lever. He moved to the edge of the pool and set his hands on his hips. "So, it looks fine to me. I smell nothing unusual."

Disrel dipped his hand into the couch's backrest and took hold of the knife. Its handle tingled in his slippery palms. His heart pounded like a festival drum in his ears and the corners of the room shook and darkened. His breath echoed inside his chest and the floor lay a mile below his shoes. With all the dead in Euclase hanging on his soul, what was one more? The Tourmaline Renegade was damned, no longer the savior he had set out to be. This was the only way to save Solla. And life among the Howlers' wives and daughters in the wilderness was still a life among people like herself.

Koti took a step forward. "Do you feel alright? You look sick."

Disrel released the knife but kept his hands buried, ashamed, disgusted with himself. "I'm sorry, Koti." Did he sound like that? Raspy. Stained. He had to force every word from his chest. "I'm really, really sorry."

"Did you take drugs? Why are your eyes dull?"

"You've been like a brother to me, Koti. And I just— I'm sorry."

"Disrel, what? Sorry for what? It's okay if you broke something. Just tell me what you did so we can fix it."

Disrel felt caught, like Koti could see the knife, like the confession had already been made. "I shouldn't have called you down here. We're out of time. My hand is being forced and I don't know what else to do."

"Forced to what?"

"Choose between friends."

Koti sighed and relaxed. "Okay. Well, this isn't too difficult. Have a seat on the couch. Is this about Doni? She's a gorgeous lady so I completely understand how you might feel uneasy about approaching her. But you know, she's had an eye for you from the start, and even though she's my sister, I really don't mind if—"

Disrel frowned. "I had to choose you, Koti."

"Me?" Koti's face colored. "Over Doni?"

"Over everyone. You were the only feasible option. For Solla's sake. And if I don't, they'll do it anyway. At sunset."

"Do what anyway? This isn't about Doni? Who is coming at sunset?"

Disrel stared down at the couch, unable to move his hands, urging himself to take up the knife again. After a long struggle he shook his head. "I can't do this. I'm not a killer, Koti. I swear I'm not a killer."

"Okay. Okay, calm down. Take a seat and breathe. What can't you do?"

"I'd sooner cut their livers out for even forcing my hand," Disrel growled to himself.

"Disrel, who and what are you talking about? Wait. Let's keep this simple, one question at a time. Look at me. Who is coming at sunset?"

He fought the urge to wretch by taking a deep breath. "Howlers."

"Sable's cross no. Howlers?" Koti stooped, eyes popping.

"They found me on a mountain on my way back from Euclase. They knew who I was. Said I had to kill you to save Doni and Voss and Solla and others. I'm so sorry, Koti. I would've taken Solla and left, but they only would've come here and killed you to punish me. I couldn't even kill myself to save you or I swear I would've."

"Spirits and thunder! I'm calling the police."

"And when they discover you've been sheltering not only Pyrons but the Tourmaline Renegade? We all lose in this, Koti."

Koti snapped his finger and muttered something out of character. He turned about, rubbing his hands over his head.

"Best-case scenario, you, Doni, and Voss go to prison for life after Solla and I are publicly executed," Disrel continued, not bothering to mention that Mored, Alta, Tygo, and Voss would likely be turned in and executed as well. "Worst-case scenario, I try to take down as many as I can before they kill us all. There is no equation without an insane amount of bloodshed."

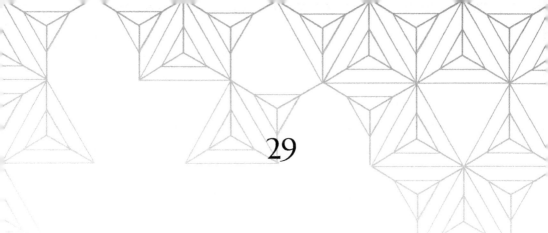

29

The front door boomed under three decisive blows. Disrel and Koti locked eyes, and Disrel felt another wave of deja vu before all of the color drained from Koti's face.

"Do they knock?" Koti said.

"They said sunset."

"Could be the mail."

"Yeah. Could be."

There was an awkward pause as they listened for another knock. Koti wiped his face.

"Yep. Probably just the delivery man is all it was. Really no one else it could be that I can think of."

Koti was clearly disturbed. Disrel glanced at the basement door. There was still an hour or two until sunset, and if it were only Doni or Voss, or even the police, they would've knocked again. But if the Howlers were early, he was going with the worst-case scenario, and the only blood on Disrel's hands would be their own.

Disrel pulled the knife up from behind the couch cushion and studied its edge. At the sight of it, Koti jerked back, stumbling into the pool as the pieces of their conversation slammed together in his mind.

"Koti, I'm sorry. We've got two hours. I'll figure something out," Disrel said, withering with the guilt of entertaining betrayal as he had. The moment oozed with familiarity, pressuring him to ascend and check the door. But if it was Howlers, their lives all ended the moment he opened it.

It was time.

He trudged up the steps and pressed through the basement door with the knife in hand. Koti's soggy, squelching steps followed at a distance. Disrel peeked through the foyer window at the porch and sidewalk. An unassuming wooden crate sat in the shadow of a great fern.

Koti crept closer. "Is anyone there?"

"Just a box."

"A bomb?"

"No. They want me alive. But you'll have to go out and get it."

Koti pointed at himself.

"Whoever left it is gone."

Koti checked the perimeter himself before poking his head through the front door. He dragged the crate into the home like it was contraband. Nails sealed the lid.

"There's nothing on it. No return address. No postage. Nothing."

Disrel jogged to the stable, retrieved a crowbar, and pried the top off the box. The interior was perfectly packed, with a crossbow lying through the center, its multiple prods compacted like spines on a prehistoric fish. A recurve bow nestled alongside it, hovering over a sheath full of arrows, darts, and a canvas pouch of black qorzan throwing blades. Racks of smoke grenades were stacked in all four corners.

Koti's hands trembled over the weapons. "What the actual hex. Do they want us to fight back?"

Disrel sighed deeply and leaned back on his haunches, his shoulders sagging. Simultaneously, his heart leaped with joy and he wanted to pump both fists into the air and shout praises to heaven. Mored had come through. The crate didn't guarantee that all would survive, but they had hope now. They had a fighting chance. "It's from a friend."

"What sort of friends do you have?"

Disrel laid a hand on Koti's shoulder. "Truly irreplaceable ones. Now let's get this to the basement before Solla sees it."

They shuffled down the basement steps, and Koti grunted under his end. "This isn't exactly life insurance for any of us."

"I know." Disrel set his end on the basement floor behind the couch. "We might all die tonight, but not without making it cost them more than they want to pay. You make sure Solla doesn't come down here. I need to think."

Koti rubbed his temples. "So do I. I haven't shot a bow since secondary academy. And never at anyone."

Disrel pulled the sheath up and counted his arrows and then the darts and the smoke grenades. He pulled the crossbow to his shoulder and peered through the sights, laid the equipment on the floor, and adjusted the shoulder strap to the bow. When he looked up, Koti was gone. A while later, there was another knocking at the door, followed by the familiar voices of Doni and Voss echoing in the living area above, mingling with Koti and Solla's responses. They had come over for supper and games as usual, but they were in no more danger than if they had stayed home. In a way, they were safer all together. When Disrel looked up from his munitions spread again, a russett glow was settled over the room and hot pool, transforming the waters into a bloodbath.

Disrel paced a circle around the box, considering his vantage points. The Howlers didn't know the lay of Koti's house, and with the help of his friends, they could turn the nightmare against their tormentors. He shut the vent to the basement, adjusted the crossbow around his shoulder, and ascended the stairs. Just as he pushed on the basement door, the casual conversation turned to chaos. Solla was white as a sheet, turning slow circles and pulling at her hair. Doni rocked and wrung her hands. Voss clawed for the door, with Koti clinging to his belt and sliding over the tile. The moment they saw Disrel, they converged on him, screaming their agonies. Spittle peppered his face.

Voss seized his arm. "Why did you lead them here? I cannot be here! Do you know what they do to people like me? What quarrel do they have with you?"

"They chose me to run in their pack and marked all of you," Disrel said, forcing his breath even. "But they'll only touch you over my dead body. We've got only a few minutes to smoke this place up and make it impossible for them to find their way. Lay stuff out on the floor, every trip hazard you can find. Move furniture, empty cupboards. Shut the blinds. Then get to the safe room. I'll be on the balcony with the bow trained on the front door. If they climb in through the upstairs bedrooms, I'll have a clean shot. If they come through the basement door, I'll have a decent shot. Koti, I'm sorry. But I'm going to get blood on your carpet."

Koti jerked a chair from the kitchen table and tossed it. "I'd love to be able to replace it."

Voss tugged on Disrel. "Are you a warrior? How can the five of us even hope to hold off a pack of Howlers when they kill trained and armored soldiers all the time?"

"I don't know. If it doesn't offend you to pray to Pyron's God, then pray."

Voss tottered away, running his hands over his closely shaved head.

They closed blinds, locked doors and windows, and dragged furniture in, strewing it throughout the main area. Disrel transferred the weapons to the balcony and draped blankets over the railings. It was the perfect vantage point for covering all three doors at once. He ventured downstairs with the racks of grenades and spaced them throughout the ground level, hoping it would last, that the Howlers would not be late. Thick green smoke consumed the spacious ceilings and coiled around the balcony. The friends packed themselves into the pantry, clutching kitchen utensils for weapons and baking sheets for shields, choosing to huddle together for support and forgoing the safe room to be closer to Disrel. Koti laid furniture on the stairs, locking him into position. He reached over the barrier and shook Disrel's hand before retreating to the pantry with the others. Their pitched whispers settled, and the smoke grenades belched their mildly irritating fumes high into the air. Disrel tied a rag around his face to filter the air and help him breathe. The stench might hang around for weeks, but what did that matter if the occupants were dead? He loaded three bolts onto the rails and three into the reloading chambers. Every shot had to count.

A vicious blow sounded against the front door, like a sledgehammer on steel. Wild howls and yips chorused outside. Everything they did was designed to induce terror. The howl was death crowing its victory over a life. Disrel trained the crossbow between two pieces of furniture and peered down the sights. Here they were, assaulting the front door as if he didn't have a fresh carcass for them. They wanted a bloody corpse. He'd give them a bloody corpse. The first one through the door would make a fine cadaver. The front door rattled and vibrated in its frame. Disrel caressed the trigger. He might wait to pop off a shot, wait until they all stood there blinking in the clouds.

Smoke whirled as the door smashed into the wall. A pair of fuzzy ears hesitated in the opening. Snouts poked in, testing the green clouds, and four dark tails turned around in the foyer. Hatchets sliced through the dense screen, stiring the air in tepid currents. The howls died away, and for one eerie moment, the house felt haunted. Disrel centered the crosshairs on a Howler's chest where the paws tied together.

Pthunk!

A choked cry as the wolf sank below the foaming sea.

Pthunk! Pthank!

Another fell, and the third clutched his leg and tumbled out onto the porch. A fresh chorus of howls rose on the lawn and more ears and tails flooded into the clouded kitchen. Their yips rang and their hatchets hissed. Disrel swung the bar and snapped it back, reloading the crossbow.

Pthwak!

He dropped behind the covered railing as a hatchet whirled overhead and glanced off the column at his back. He pushed his front half in-line with the stairs and squeezed off another bolt.

Pthunk!

The Howler gurgled and slid down the foyer wall.

Thwang! The next one through the door staggered back out, shrieking.

Two timber wolves started up the stairs. Disrel tossed the crossbow aside and drew up a fist of throwing knives. One. Two. Three. The timber wolves slumped onto the furniture, kicking and moaning. Eight more milled about the kitchen and living area. Howls echoed through the open basement door. Disrel notched an arrow to his bowstring and leaned over the balcony, dropping a long shaft down on a red wolf. The arrow thudded into the carpet and a knife clattered off the bow, inches from his fist. A mottled wolf bounded through the bedroom door and hurtled down the length of the balcony. Disrel slapped the bowstring and drove a shaft straight into his stomach. The Howler swooned over the railing and tumbled onto the floor below.

Four took up chairs for shields and assaulted the stairs. Disrel's arrows clattered off the metal frames. As they reached the landing, he kicked them down into a heap, notched an arrow to the string, and planted it right into the pile. He reached for another, but a boot stamped into his back, pushing him down the steps onto the writhing heap of limbs and fur. Arms fell around his neck and shoulders, tearing away his bow and scabbard. They yanked him to his feet, twisting both arms behind his back. A white wolf towered in the black doorway, thick arms folded across a human chest. His tattoo cluttered jaw warped as he swept in, shoved one hand around Disrel's throat, and pulled him forward.

"Lying slug-shafted Kob-slagger." Vogin's Pyron scalded like acid. "I'll shank your sable-kissing trunk with my ax, you freckling half-bred traitor. Kyreasheluhn. *Kyreasheluhn.* No!" He spat right into Disrel's face. "Iii-ut-azuimeno-pujcs!"

A cry broke through the walls at the sound of the name that roughly translated to "sow swine kept for beastiality." Two black wolves jerked the pantry door open and smacked the knives away with their hatchets. Tears streamed from Doni's eyes as she stumbled out, clutching her hand. Solla twisted and jerked under a Howler's grip on her braid.

"Pyrons don't talk like that! How dare you insult my brother. Shame on you all."

Voss and Koti's attempts at throwing fists earned them both a vicious return of blows. The Howlers hauled them into the living area, threw them up against the wall, and yipped while brandishing their hatchets.

Vogin released Disrel's neck. "Tonight there will be four less obstacles standing in the way of Pyron's freedom."

"You're no different than the tyrant you want to see kneeling at Pyron feet." The words gushed from Disrel's chest. "Soaking the land in the blood of your brothers and raping Kobalt girls won't bring down the walls and heal the land. You know there is no freedom outside of Thelis, but you know you don't have an ounce of It in you."

The dark circles around Vogin's sunken eyes deepened. "Don't preach Thelis to me, skunk. It's a Pyron fantasy, a legend, an inspirational mantra. Life taught me the hard way. Our Sky Father expects us to live up to our blood, to recognize our place and position as sons of God and put under our hatchets any and all who will not serve us." He pulled a stone from his pocket and turned it before his nose. "It looks a lot like the mark on the Tourmaline Renegade's chest, doesn't it?" He smacked it down on the kitchen counter. "The true test of Thelis was in old times, for the elder to require the warrior to raise a stone bearing its symbol using only the invisible power of Thelis itself. It was to be raised up before the entire tribe as proof of its power, but was this ever actually achieved? Alta was smart enough to not waste time with it the day she blessed you. So here's your chance to prove yourself." He sauntered around, shoulders back, hands held wide. "Raise the stone even an inch and we'll put down our hatchets and love will be the Howler's creed. We'll lay our lives down in the ditch for our . . ." He looked at Koti, Doni, and Voss and enunciated the words like they were poison: "Kobalt brethren."

The pack leaned about the dismantled living room, twirling and catching their weapons. Their invasive stream had stopped. There were twelve, besides Vogin and the two that held him. Five capes of fur sprawled lifelessly in different corners of the open rooms, soaking up blood. The others were missing, likely outside groaning on the lawn.

Disrel glared between Vogin and the stone.

The white wolf leaned on a corner and folded his arms. "Who am I to question the sovereign timing of Thelis? We've only just arrived. We're in no hurry. I'll give you a few minutes to conjure its power."

Disrel set his eyes on the stone and focused. Heartbeats boomed in his ears. A man had no more power to command Thelis to work for him than to command his own body to resurrect from the grave.

"Come on. It's only a light stone. It weighed in at three ounces earlier today. Surely that's not too much for Thelis."

Cruel laughter echoed through the house, followed by jeering. The faces of his friends and sister poured their desperate hopes and expectations. They believed for him, but the stone remained. He fixed his mind and heart on it. Vogin could not be right. Thelis was no fantasy. All were unworthy of it, but all were required to bear its light in their hearts.

One tattooed half of Vogin's face smeared into a taunting smile. "Disrel, Disrel, Disrel. Thelis can't save you anymore than it will save Pyron. That's why we take our fate into our own hands. And our hands must only get heavier. What happened in Euclase was just a foretaste of what's to come."

He twisted toward Vogin. "You blew up the lab."

"You just now figured that out? It's not enough to foil the devices they create to destroy us. We must destroy them with their own devices."

The Howlers turned Solla, Koti, Voss, and Doni toward the wall and stood by with weapons in hand. They pulled Disrel closer and pressed his head to the pillar to watch. Doni sobbed uncontrollably; Voss beat out a prayer in his native tongue. The crossbow went up on the black wolf's shoulder, training at the back of Koti's head.

"Wait." Vogin raised a hand and moved around Solla, looking her over like she was a stock animal. "This is your sister? You never told me how beautiful she was. And so young."

Disrel ground his teeth.

"She'll make a fine concubine for our worthy warriors."

"Touch her and you die," Disrel growled, shoving with his shoulders. His assailants tightened their grip and kicked his shins until he buckled in their arms.

A slow smile crept across Vogin's face as he noted Disrel's pain. "I want you to live to see your twenty-something nieces and nephews running around the camp, to see how willing and happy your sister will be in helping us resurrect the tribe of the tiger." Vogin motioned to two of his men, who plucked Solla from the wall and carried her bodily toward the door. She kicked and screamed. Disrel twisted against the pillar.

Koti jumped off the wall and struck out with his fists, and a Howler slammed him across the face with the flat of his ax. Koti collapsed. Disrel's heart burned like a crucible, radiating fire through his chest and out through his limbs. He kicked into the Howler's knees, escaping the arm locks, bowing forward, and hurling a wolf-skin over his head. He launched the Howler in his other hand into the one holding Solla.

Darkness dropped like a theater curtain, leaving only a straight and narrow channel of vision. Carpet raked and tile squeaked under boot soles. Voss's prayer was the suffering of ten thousand souls, a tear slid down Solla's cheek, and Doni's heartbeat was a dissonant, driving rhythm. Every detail was acutely familiar, every second passing at a lethargic, dreamlike pace. A hatchet head struck the tile and bounced, booming every time it struck down. All twelve Howlers glowed on some internal map, blazing red points on an ethereal field, and every sound, odor, and texture under Disrel's fingers translated into a vivid mental image.

His hands plunged into the cape of a red wolf, and the Howler crunched against the stone wall. He lit into another cape, and a bushy tail sailed overhead. His heel buried into something soft. Bone crunched. The walls shook. Two knives found their way into his hands and then sailed off into the smoke. Howls of agony echoed their results. A grizzled mask drew to his breast and torqued between his hands with a rich snap before dropping to the floor. Dank metallic odors flooded his nose. A hatchet fell down by his shoulder, and he spun the handle in a wide arc, wrestling it from its wielder and pushing back.

Bone splintered and strands of muscle frayed and popped like threads of twine. Blood plinked upon the kitchen tile. The darkness filled with raucous gasps and wails. Sparks whirled like fireflies between coupling ax heads, and their edges boiled with iridescent colors.

Disrel wrested an enemy hatchet from a Howler grip and shoved a white wolf with his shoulder, pushing him into the wall. He caught his opponent by the wrist, pinning his hand to the surface as he rotated the ax head and struck. There was a terrible crunch and the leathery fingers arched like talons. The hand shivered and drooped, sliding down with the white wolf, tattooed throat working, mouth reaching for air. The white wolf's empty eyes and bloody snout lifted to heaven. There was a dry gasp, a rasping choke, and a piercing howl. Alpha Vogin clutched his broken hand to his chest and sank to one side. The black scores on his face raged. The map was empty now, the darkness receding. A hatchet head moved against Vogin's throat, and a strange voice rasped:

"The only hands worthy of judging are scarred by the brethren, and they render mercy to the merciful and judgment to those who judge. Thelis is the sacrifice of self—not others. Without this truth, you will never be worthy of fighting among Pyron warriors. Raise your hand against my people again and I'll finish you. Now get out."

Vogin scrambled along the floor like a legless varmint, belly and elbows dragging. A limping Howler helped him rise at the door and hobble into the darkness. Another stopped feigning dead and peeled himself off the floor, pressing his fur to his gushing head and stumbling after.

Disrel turned about like a man delirious in the desert. Porous crimson splotches smeared the walls. Mangled, fur-draped bodies littered the floor from the kitchen to the basement door. A hulking figure draped the back of the couch like a werewolf caught between moons, not fully beast, not fully human. A salty metal taste buzzed Disrel's tongue, and he wiped his lips with the back of his hand. His cheek was wet, his face sticky, a crusty feeling creeping upon its corners. Two young women knelt in the corner, clinging to each other and avoiding his gaze. A blond man stared like one who had looked upon a forbidden art and been frozen in time as punishment, and a black-skinned man wriggled in the corner, eyes clamped shut, still praying out loud. Disrel's gaze ventured in search of a familiar face, and he remembered Mored. Alta. He adjusted his grip on the hatchet and marched for the back door. How many Howlers had stormed the subway? Could he get there in time to stop them?

Disrel plunged the keystone into the corecycle and rocked it back from the stable. The blond man staggered against the door frame and reached out, shouting something about a helmet and being caught wearing blue. Disrel pushed off and rocketed down the drive, his fingers clamping the hatchet to the handlebars. The night air whipped his hair and stung his eyes and crusted the scabs on his face. He ground over the earthen roads and ramped off the hills, skidded around the bend and soared onto the paved roadway. He did not plan or contemplate. The fire burned deep inside, smoldering in every vein, licking at his bones. Its tendrils danced in his eyes, leading his gaze. His mind was fixed on his destination like a hawk on a sparrow.

There were Howlers ahead. Some distant map sat dark in the back of his mind's eye, with little red blotches coursing over it, drawing him. He rode into the secret access to the subway and the elevator began its descent. When it opened, he sailed through the tunnel and into the silo. Mored's corecycles sat in their usual places, but there were others, parked askew, rimmed with polished bone, decorated with tails and skulls. Disrel leaped from the bike and tore through the station on foot. His chest hummed and the hatchet nodded in his hand, a wicked extension of his arm fueled by his devouring stride through the concourse.

A Howler's carcass hugged the steps like an awkward lover, ears and snout mangled and bloody. Another lay facedown at the bottom. Disrel turned him over; two bolts protruded from his torso. He was supple and warm, but lifeless. Disrel crossed the concourse, watching the shadows, his spine running with static. He pushed on the eatery doors, where three more wolves sprawled on the floor, fletchings budding from their bleeding furs. A clatter in the kitchen slowed his steps, and he sidled along the bar. There was a whimper and an agonized hiss as a shining flesh-colored ball moved just below the counter line. Disrel aimed the hatchet and pulled into the open. Tygo's mouth gaped and his hand cradled a shaft protruding low in his neck.

"Eight." Tygo rasped. "Down in the house. Get the bow. Go the back way." He motioned to a crossbow some feet away. Three fresh bolts lay in the dust around it.

Disrel jumped to it and loaded all three strings. Tygo shuddered and struggled to pull himself up with his good arm.

"No." Disrel kicked a dark blade across the floor. "Wait here in case they run."

He turned and sprinted from the kitchen, through the concourse toward the railway. It might already be too late to save Mored and Alta, but even so, the Howlers would not escape him.

Disrel jumped down into the tunnel and ran, shoes crunching over the loose stone. Rats parted before his footfalls in hissing volleys. He laid the crossbow across his back and kept the hatchet in hand, then caught hold of a pipe and swung his body upward, catching the gaping mouth of an overhead air duct that vented the rail tunnel. The hatchet's head spur bit down into the metal and he heaved himself into the pipe. Memories of Euclase swelled like monsters to oppose him, but he shook himself and shuffled on. He had seen the route from both ends, but never traveled its length. It could not be too much farther to the outlet near Mored's bedroom.

Disrel smacked into a wall and palpated for a handle. A little push and light sifted through a crevice. He turned and kicked, and the cover flew open, spitting him out into a darkened hall. At the far end was the welcoming golden glow of the living area and its lemony wallpaper. Disrel slipped the hatchet into the loop on his thigh and shouldered the crossbow, then minced down the hall like a trained soldier, peering through the sights. Taunts and threats chorused in the kitchen. Eight striped backs stood between the dining and living area, bushy tails dangling between clad human buttocks.

Mored lay prone, clinging to Alta's hand as she knelt by him with her other hand clamped to his head. A crimson river coursed from underneath his gray hair and wept over his dignified brow.

Disrel trained the crossbow on the nearest Howler. "None of you wanted the glory of spilling the blood of elders all to himself? I smell cowardice."

All eight timber wolves turned and bristled.

The bow's arms twitched as the shafts twirled from their chambers, fletchings and strings smoking. A Howler hatchet recoiled for the throw.

Pthunk!

Three timber wolves stooped to the floor.

Disrel hurled the crossbow, stunting the next recoiling hatchet and drawing his own from his thigh. "All who hope to live must leave now."

Three of the five attacked. Disrel's hatchet buried into a shoulder with a crispy chomp, and a Howler hatchet crunched into the outer corner of the hall, inches from his nose. He dropped, grabbing skyn and pushing upward, hurling the Howler into the main area. The flying wolf yowled as two whirling hatchets glanced off his body. The third hatchet grazed Disrel's arm, spraying blood. A fourth descended at his head, gripped by a hand. Disrel slammed into the wall, arresting the Howler's arm and driving the ax head into a thigh. He bowled the gasping thug into the others who lay groveling on the floor and moved out into the open, snatching up Mored's writing desk. The fifth Howler twirled his hatchet with a murderous smile. Disrel caught the hatchet in the belly of the desk and turned its legs on his next attacker. Another wicked head sliced into the wood just an inch from his forehead. He twisted the table, trapping the Howler's arm and torquing it. A splitting wail echoed the tearing of a wrist, and the hatchet thunked on the floor. The table clattered to the ground and Disrel's elbows dug into cheeks and throats. He trapped a neck with the hatchet handle and plunged his knee into an open crotch while punching the hatchet head into the Howler's jaw.

The timber wolves tumbled and sprawled, crawling on their stomachs for the door. Their tails painted swaths of red on the tile. The Howler with the hatchet lodged in his shoulder slumped over against the wall, his eyes glazing from blood loss.

Disrel towered over the groaning men. He hauled on a tail, strangling the man with his own headdress as he dragged him to the door.

"Go back to whatever cave you live in and humble yourselves before God. Don't let me catch one of your cowardly tails anywhere near civilization again."

He held the door open and prodded them through with his gaze. Their faces acknowledged the hatchet in his grip, pleading for mercy as they passed. At the last, he let the door swing shut. The eighth Howler was slumped over, dead.

Disrel staggered a few steps back toward the kitchen, his mind blurring again. What was this place? Who was he? Who was the Pyron elder with ashen lips and frizzy hair, staring at him like she had seen a ghost?

Disrel blinked and shook his head. Alta. Mored struggled to rise, clutching a tea towel to his bleeding head. Disrel noted the ghastly weapon in his fist and cast it to the floor. It thundered end to end on the tile, chipping the stone.

"No. No. No, no, no, no."

He stumbled down the dark hall, pushing off the walls and falling against the open vent, clutching it with rusty fingers. A dark mirror on the adjacent wall revealed the very monster he fled: blood and gore pasted from his temples to his chin. His brow was sooty. Clumps of fur clung to his skyn and hair. His arm throbbed. He turned and collapsed into the corner. The Howler's carcass was a framed trophy of macabre splendor in the light at the other end of the hall. Disrel drew his knees up and buried his head in his arms as warped sobs wrung from his strangled chest. Then a white-robed angel sailed down the hall and bowed over him.

"Disrel, are you okay? Are you hurt?"

He rocked his head back and forth as tears spilled out. "Get back, please. I'm not safe."

Her hand touched him. "Disrel, it's—"

"I don't want to hurt you. Get back!" He pushed into the corner, tucking his head deeper into his arms.

Alta stroked his head, and little by little, clarity returned.

"Are you wounded?"

He tried to force his breathing into a steady rhythm. "How many did I kill?"

"Is your sister okay? And your friends? Why did you come for us?"

He wiped his face and sputtered. Emotions washed through him like rising tides. "Tygo is—Tygo is out there. Hurt. Bolt in the neck. Alive. Was when I came in. I didn't see Astros." He sucked air through his teeth. "It was like fire, all over, devouring me. Blood. Everywhere. And in my hands—" His hand trembled as a growl leaped from him. "Get back! You can't see me like this."

She took his hand. "Hush, little lamb. Fear has nowhere to roost under love's roof. Come sit at the table and have some tea to settle your mind."

For a second, there was Mother looking out through Alta's face, calling him her little lamb like she used to when tucking him into bed, or when he was sick.

"Please. I can't let you see me like this."

"I don't mind what I've seen. Come. It's alright."

She took his hand gently and he hobbled to his feet, shivering, following her down the hall and back into the light. He collapsed in a seat at the table. Mored leaned in a chair just opposite, squeezing an ice pack to the side of his head. His gray eyes approved as he clapped a stained hand onto Disrel's shoulder.

After a long moment, he said: "Were you able to save your friends?"

Disrel pressed his hands to his lips and nodded, squeezing his eyes shut against the images of Howlers falling and blood spraying.

Alta raced about, filling tea strainers with leaves, spinning the glass tops from jars and spooning powders. Steaming water tinkled down into teacups, and then she returned with a loaded tea tray and set a cup before him. His tea was four shades darker than hers or Mored's.

"What is it?"

"Medicinal tea. I made yours a little stronger than ours." She bent over and picked at the loose flap of skyn glistening near his elbow.

He jerked away from the stinging. "It's just a scratch."

The laceration stretched down the bicep and widened when he bent his arm. Blood pooled and dribbled onto the table.

Alta sat and raised her cup to her lips. "It's the right temperature. Drink up."

He'd so often sat around this table in the quiet after the long hours of training, sipping tea with Mored and Alta. But Mored's head seemed misshapen, a purple lump rising off the corner, and a break in the skin that was still flowing with blood. And the stiffening corpse in the corner, the gouges in the walls and blood on the floor made the space so unfamiliar.

Disrel drank, coughed, and pushed the cup away, shaking his head. "Ugh! What did you put in this? It bites and smells like onion grass."

Alta pushed it back toward him. "All good things. Drink it up. You don't want your scratch to give you a blood infection."

He puckered and eyed the tea, working up the nerve to bring it to his lips again. It was like seaweed and turpentine with a touch of moldy dish rags. Usually the tea Alta served was delightful. This was pure medicine. He bobbed the cup in front of his lips, then gulped it down and pressed his fist to his mouth, shuddering as his stomach turned. Alta left her tea and busied herself with pulling small objects from different drawers and cupboards and setting them in a pot of boiling water. Disrel's mind wandered circles as he drummed his thumbs on the lip of his empty teacup.

"Could Thelis ever be an actual, visible fire? Does It put off heat?"

Alta's eyes grew three sizes as she fussed with cleaning and gluing Mored's head wound. "Why do you ask such a question?"

"Because I saw something I can't explain."

"Well, some things require no explanation. They are personal revelations for the heart. Some are born with a greater potential or predisposition toward developing a strong Thelis. I believe you are one of those people, and if you continue to surrender yourself to it, you will do great things."

He balled his fists. The corners of the room doubled. "Vogin said something about a test warriors of old were given. He wanted me to raise a little stone using the power of Thelis. I couldn't do it. I failed."

Alta offered a look of pity and said something fuzzy. He sighed as his eyelids drooped.

A touch landed on his shoulder. "Are you sure you aren't wounded? You must have bruises. Did you get hit on the head?" She stroked his hair and poked at his sleeve.

He cradled his injured arm defensively. "No. I'm fine. I need to check on Solla. Help Koti clean up." He tried to stand, but his watery legs dropped him right back into the chair.

"I'm sure they're fine. Why don't you lie on the couch for a few minutes?"

"I'll just sit here until the tea settles." He slumped farther and farther down, his head nodding between his hands pressed against his temples. Dreams flashed along the buttery walls and the items at the center of the table drifted in and out of focus. Why was he so tired? He'd actually slept a little before dawn.

Alta's hand fell on his shoulder again. "Disrel, I don't mind if you lie down on the couch."

"Huh? But Tygo needs help."

"I'll check on Tygo."

"I need to go back. Solla and Koti." Every word slurred from his thick, lumpy tongue.

"You're much too tired to drive. Just take a short nap. I'll wake you in fifteen minutes."

The couch did look inviting. Disrel pulled himself up, wandered over, flopped down, and pulled a pillow under his head. A moment later, the golden warmth of the room lifted away.

30

Disrel buried his cheek deeper into the pillow as odors of savory and spices made his nose tingle. A groan roused him, and he batted one eye open. A tawny head gleamed an arm's reach away, nestled in a pile of pillows. A dark quilt was tucked around Tygo's bearded chin and rose and fell with his breathing. Disrel pushed against the blue blanket that bound him, ignoring his pain, drawing a deep breath and surveying the golden room. The dead Howler was gone, but the red stain on the wall and floor marked where he had lain. Disrel's arm was stiff and aching, and his left side was naked from the neck to the stomach. A cloth bandage covered his elbow. Little by little, memories of what had brought him to the subway returned, followed by emotions that didn't fit the current atmosphere.

Alta stood at the stove, ladling a deep brown liquid into bowls. She shuffled over with a tray and roused Tygo, propping him up with pillows.

"Here. Try to eat it all."

Tygo groaned, and the blanket tumbled down from his neck. His upper quarter was wrapped to the throat in a bandage that held a dressing to his neck and shoulders. A dark spot on his left trapezius revealed the location of his wound. He thanked her and laid the bowl in his lap.

Disrel clutched his garment around his shoulder and fought to push his wrapped arm through the sleeve. "What did you do to my arm?"

She pushed a bowl of soup at him. "I treated your arm and now you need strength."

Disrel shoved the blanket away. "I'm not hungry. I need to leave."

"I've been listening to your stomach groaning for the last hour, so you're not leaving without eating every drop."

"You said you'd wake me in fifteen minutes!"

"And I did. I woke you, stitched up your arm, and you fell right back asleep."

"How long have I been sleeping?"

"Six hours before getting up to use the toilet. And then four hours since then."

Disrel dropped the sleeve and eased his back into the couch, struggling to recall ever waking to relieve himself and wondering how he had managed to walk there and back. Half of his upper body had been disrobed, and he knew the longest scar on his back stretched to the middle of his left shoulder blade. Alta couldn't have missed it. She disappeared down the hall with the last bowl of soup.

Tygo spooned down several bites and passed a rueful smile. "You came awake just long enough to pull your arm out of the sleeve. Then you were out again for all that sewing. Compared to the rest of us, you came out with little more than a scratch."

He turned the spoon through the soup. "They weren't expecting me. How many got out alive?"

"One dropped dead in the concourse. Another in the silo next to his bike. I doubt the others made it very far."

The spicy broth warmed his entire body. "Alta poisoned your tea, too?"

Tygo chuckled. "And I asked her for a little extra knockout power. Not a chance I wanted to feel that bolt coming out. She told me how it went down in here while she was stitching on you, but it's a little fuzzy." He swallowed another bite and stared into the bowl. "Mind if I ask how you got those pretty pink stripes?"

"It's nothing exciting. How'd it go before I got here?"

"The hardest part was not letting on we knew while they skulked around here the last two days. It was two moles, sentries who betrayed us. As soon as they put on those furs, I started moving, hitting as silently as I could where I found them. Worked my way to the kitchen and waited for my comrades to make their way back. Nobody did, so I did the only thing I could and fired as their tails crossed the threshold. Took a bolt. I thought they'd bust my head." Tygo's mouth drew and his fingers gripped the bowl.

"Did Astros—?"

Tygo shook his head and wiped a tear before it could fall. "It's me and you, by some grace I cannot fathom. Astros fought well. Hard. He—" Tygo wiped his face again and there was a lengthy pause. Then he took a deep breath. "There's a lot I wish I still had the chance to learn from him. He's the reason they forgot about finishing me. And"—he snorted back snot—"Alta's a hero. She's nursed and cooked and cleaned while we sleep and groan. Pyron will owe its freedom to her, and you, when it's all over."

"They know I'm the renegade. It's only a matter of time before one of them cashes in on my bounty for revenge." He stared down into the murky soup. "And yours. And Mored's."

Tygo grimaced.

Disrel peered into the veteran's eyes. "Does knowing that you've taken lives make you feel like a monster some days?"

He wiped a tawny hand across his bearded chin. "Only because I've done worse things to people instead of protecting my friends. The man who cut you down from the ropes in the marketplace is not the same Tygo that once walked those streets. But if I must face my past someday, I'll be ready to reckon with it. Redemption has a place for all of us, I like to think."

Disrel swallowed a long draught of soup. "Except sables, apparently."

Tygo's brow bounced. "Yeah. If they do ever turn good, it probably only happens in some deep room of pain, where they're torn apart and then birthed back into the sunlight just so the world can spit on them while they die in shame." Pain coursed through his eyes and his tone dripped with pity. "They're kidnapped and forced into that life before they even know what life is about. They almost took my daughter once. Tore my heart from my chest when they grabbed her. And then the Sable Queen spotted our neighbor's little girl, a redhead, and took her instead. My heart broke for my neighbor, because I had already felt that pain while the queen was leading my daughter from the house. They say it's only one in every hundred girls, and you think yours is safe, that it'll never happen to you." Tygo sighed. "A good number of them don't survive training. If only we valued our women the way Pyron values theirs."

"Where is your daughter now?"

"Married, somewhere, with children. Fiercely loyal to the state."

"I'm sorry."

"They'll see the light someday. At least, I'm praying so."

They finished their soup in silence.

Disrel rose from the couch and ventured down the hall, clutching the left half of his garment around his neck, his bandaged arm protruding from the opening. He moved into the open doorway to Alta and Mored's bedroom. Alta sat on her side of the bed, holding her husband's hand. The space of years between them was now so much more apparent.

Mored turned his dim eyes toward the door. "Thank you for coming, Disrel. For saving our lives."

"Saving? We're all dead men walking. Once Vogin and the other survivors have patched up their wounds, they'll want revenge. And what better revenge than to reveal my identity, and all that you have here? The Tourmaline Renegade was defeated from the start, all because they saw my face down here in your tunnels. I didn't know what I was up against when I started this." He pulled the black Tourmaline chip from his pocket and pressed it into Mored's hand. "But all I've got left is to run and hide."

Mored pushed the chip back in his direction. "Then run and hide, and take that with you for when you're ready to fight again."

"Fight when? When my people are ashes and they believe me dead?"

"And what do you expect me to do with it?"

"I don't know. Give it to somebody else."

"I gave it to you. You don't work for me. It chose you, you chose It. Remember what you told me the night we met? You said you wanted to fight and die in no other skyn. None of us could've known we were fostering Howlers among the ranks all these years. They came quietly, acting like moderates. Maybe they weren't even Howlers when they joined us. But they dealt their blow, and you dealt yours. I still have contacts in the outside world. Tygo isn't my last man, though he'll certainly always be my most valuable. Besides, while you were resting, we received a message that Cinnabar has come across a data chip containing medical recipes, and he's keeping it in his private library until they can make copies and distribute them to physicians who have volunteered to operate in the Pyron sector." Mored released a weary sigh. "It's a terrible shame there will be no one to steal it and prevent all of those pregnant mothers and suffering infants from receiving those fatal toxins when they go to their enemies for medical help."

Disrel's hand slid down his neck as he turned to the doorframe. This was what Ambrosia had warned him about.

The Tourmaline chip clicked down on the bedside table. "Should anyone decide to stop this evil from happening, this will be right here waiting for him."

Disrel toyed with his bandage and looked to Alta. "How long until I can use my arm?"

"Two weeks. Remove the bandage tomorrow and gently wash with soap and water. Keep it out of the mineral pool or you'll get an infection. Reapply the bandage until the wound scabs, then let it breathe as much as possible, and use a daily moisturizer to prevent scarring. The internal stitches will dissolve but I'll remove the outer ones, unless you break them in a fight. I promise I won't scold you if you break them early." She nodded her approval, knowing he didn't have two weeks to sit around. Cinnabar would have copies of the data chip in a matter of days. Maybe they'd already been made.

His skyn slipped from his fingers, and he jerked it back up his shoulder. Alta lowered her gaze. She had already seen the scars.

Disrel blinked away his humiliation. "I didn't commit any crime. Not a real one. My father took me to an elder in secret to get my blessing when I was seven."

"I didn't assume." She fought back tears. "My hands told me they were undeserved."

"They're not as bad as they look. They only ache a little in the damp cold sometimes."

"Don't ever be ashamed of them, Kyreasheluhn. They're a sign for someone else."

He pinched the fabric under his elbow and scraped the chip from the bedside table.

"I need to get back to my sister. Thank you for mending my arm. And for the soup, which I finished." He looked between Mored and Alta once more and felt gratitude for their lives. "Heaven willing, I'll see you again soon."

Mored closed his eyes and folded his hands across his stomach. "Alta, is that map of the imperial estate still tucked down in the third drawer of the office desk?"

Some minutes later, Disrel forced his stiff arm through the sleeve of his skyn and left the subway on his corecycle. Emergency vehicles blocked the main roads heading east and the military presence was unusually thick, forcing him to take a roundabout path back to Koti's. It was midafternoon when he entered the house through the backdoor.

Most of Koti's furniture had been moved back into place, and piles of dirt and debris sat in tiny mounds around the home. Koti hesitated by the hallway corner with a dustpan and broom in hand.

"You're alive! Oh, man. Where did you run off to?" The ice pack shifted in the bandage tied around his purple jaw.

There were gouges in the plaster and stone, and the ornate wooden railing on the balcony was nicked white in places. "The Howlers were going to kill some other friends of mine. But they're safe now. Some of them. Sorry about the mess. And the blood on the carpet. And the grout."

"Don't worry about the grout. You have a talent for missing parties. I was so worried you'd show up while the police were here bagging up the bodies. They followed a trail of blood and stiffs all the way from the middle of town. Solla hung out in the safe room, so Doni and Voss were the only ones included in the report. I told them a power struggle broke out and they quarreled. The detective bought it. Oh, and the press was here, and all I can say is, Selen is going to be talking about this for years. Three dozen Howlers, stiff and cold in the streets. It's unbelievable. Absolutely unbelievable." Koti stared down at a debris pile, his brow knit. "When you left here, you didn't chase them and . . . finish them off, did you?"

Abstract blotches of rust on the plaster resembled toothed monsters raging at each other. "No. But if any lived to speak of it, they'll turn me in. I owe you so much, Koti, but I think it would be best if Solla and I left."

Koti laid the broom and dustpan against the wall. "Honestly, I feel safer with you around. And where would you go? Here you have privacy and there's very little traffic. Oh, and before I forget—" Koti dug into his pocket and procured the stone that Vogin had challenged Disrel with. He walked over and placed it in Disrel's palm. "I hid it so the police wouldn't confiscate it for evidence. I thought you might want it."

"Thanks." Disrel stared at the pattern within the stone and the way the light played through it. Stones like this one were precious items kept by elders and handed down through generations. Alta had told him that in the past, each tribe kept one on display in a community tent for the people to visit and meditate upon, because they were too rare for each family to have one. Vogin had said the evidence of Thelis was the ability to raise the stone using the power of the mind, but Disrel remembered that Alta had once said the key to raising the stone was to understand Thelis with the heart. And that was not something that could be taught. It was a different journey for each individual. He pocketed it and looked around the room as Koti returned to sweeping.

An aura of death hung in the house like a bad omen. He could not shake the feeling that danger was still lurking nearby. "How's Solla doing?"

"Sleeping. Voss gave her something for her nerves. She ate lunch, and she's keeping food down. Once she finds you're back, I think she'll be alright. Wait until you see her drawings. She's been sketching to stay calm lately."

"Doni and Voss?"

"They went home after breakfast. They're shaken up but thankful to not have a scratch. I lost a tooth and, man, it hurts to talk right now. But I've got too much to say. When you're this grateful to be alive, you can't shut up."

Disrel took the dustpan and broom and swept. "Did they . . . did they say anything about me?"

"None of us knew you could fight like that. You threw those guys like—I can't even think of words to describe it—like they were children. But I don't think they're the least bit suspicious. Not even Solla."

"Thanks." He faltered and spilled a little from the dustpan. "Thanks for moving for Solla when you did. I'm ashamed the Howlers are known as Pyrons, and I'm honored to have Kobalt friends like you."

Eventually, Solla awoke and clung to the banister, watching him through the coiling iron balusters like a child afraid of a stranger. Disrel proffered a welcoming smile from across the room. After a moment, she walked straight to him, slipping her hands around his waist, and turning her head against his chest.

"I knew you'd come back."

He stroked her loose black hair, scented with jasmine from a recent shower.

She buried her face a little deeper. "Thank you for not letting them take me."

Gratitude was so out of place for something so out of the question. He could not live with the pain of ever letting his sister suffer anything against her own will.

"I put a sketch of you on my art wall, right next to the picture of the Tourmaline Renegade. If I ever see him again, I'll tell him what you did. And I know he'll be so impressed he'll want you to work alongside him."

His cheeks warmed, and Koti turned his goofy, knowing smile toward the fryer on the cooktop.

Disrel rocked her in a circle. "Hey, don't exaggerate. I don't need anyone raising the bar higher than I can jump."

After supper and time spent with Solla and Koti in the quiet, Disrel retired to his room and eased down on his mattress. He pulled his skyn from his shoulders and unraveled the bandage into his lap. Deep bruises mottled his flesh and a tight row of dark threads clamped the laceration, doubled from one end to the other. Alta expected him to press on. She anticipated him getting into another fight long before the wound could heal. He ran his fingers through his hair and stared at the sutures. He'd never even felt the ax head, or any other pain during the fight. But now his hands and bones ached like he had spent an hour as Tygo's training bag.

He cleaned the wound with a soft cloth, then pulled the mall photos from their hiding place in his backpack. He caressed Ambrosia's smile with his fingers and gazed at her rich, auburn hair. In a matter of days, she had gone from throwing punches on the train to dancing with him in Tourmal's mall. The challenge of an impossible friendship had lured them both, and now his heart fluttered like a wren in a rain puddle. She was his honeybee, his heart, the gorgeous woman who laughed at random things he said, whose green eyes sparkled at him, whose hands had caressed his. It was hard to remember that she was the decorated Selenite Skynhound, Tourmal's Sable Commander, a sable who had captured and arrested many who had opposed the state, submitting them to justice, and ultimately death.

What did she see in him anyway? Kobalt men were typically six feet tall, tan and robust, muscular without trying, with handsomely large noses and strong jaws that grew full beards. And what Pyron ever hit six feet and wasn't on the scrawny side and wearing a genetically dubious expression on his face?

Was she toying with him? Had she warned him to avoid the physicians at Pyron's gates because she loved him, or did she know his lies, that he wasn't living among his people as he'd said, that he wasn't just an ordinary Pyron? Was this crumb of information bait on a deadly trap set for the Tourmaline Renegade? If he continued to see her, would there come a day when she would smile and kiss him before throwing him to the ground and snapping on the cuffs? Or would she simply cut his throat without a word, out of respect, counting him one more dead Pyron on the pile and letting the world wonder about the mysterious disappearance of the renegade?

He shuddered. Even if she didn't know yet, it was too great a risk. Vogin would betray him. It was only a matter of weeks, maybe even days, until the entire empire knew that he, Disrel of Tourmal, living under Koti Ezwytt-Sygvra's roof at Eight Silkspar Trail, Sector Selen, was the Tourmaline Renegade. Even if she truly loved him, she would no longer once she knew. There was no point in lying to her face on even one more date. He had to devote what little time he had left to his own people, to those men and women trapped behind the concrete walls, at the mercy of the soldier's whips and lust, to the mothers whose only two choices for their sick children were to go to the deadly physicians or to watch their loves fall in the streets untreated.

He pulled the Tourmaline chip from his pocket, laid it over the photo, and rubbed its etched surface. He'd made a promise—free Pyron or die trying. And if it came to death, he would rest with his people, knowing that he had spared no effort. Desperation demanded the sacrifice of everything down to the last breath. But once he was dead, who would act as Pyron's shield? What mortal could end the silent killers of illness and starvation and suicide? Every move the Tourmaline Renegade made seemed only to slow the machine of death, drawing out the agony and suffering. Even striking a tyrant from his throne would never end the hate. The world stood against them: governors, judges, officers, artists, journalists, musicians, laymen.

What could rouse Kobalt from his sleep, make him recognize and embrace his long-lost brother, see Pyron's nakedness and clothe him, see Pyron's hunger and feed him, see Pyron's bondage and set him free of the chains? The golden light of Thelis would have to conquer every heart. It would take a miracle, not a masked mortal.

31

Ambrosia hovered in the doorway of the Tourmal Command Center's mail room, feeling flustered and self-conscious about bothering the secretary again. Had Disrel been arrested? Taken out against the wall and executed? Caught an illness and died? Or was he right now lying feverish and weak on a pallet? Maybe he'd lost his pass and could not leave. Maybe the guards at the gates were refusing to relay his messages.

Thalia peered over the rim of glass that enveloped her squinty eyes. "No word from your Pyron, Commander."

Ambrosia tossed her head and marched into the lobby. "And the arrest log from the Hold?"

"His name isn't on it."

"Any reply from the gates?"

"I sent copies of the last two to all twelve gatehouses and got four replies. I can tell you with their track record over there, that is an excellent response rate."

"Then maybe it's time I go have a look around myself."

Thalia laughed. "Take your oldest pair of boots if you plan on going in. What's so special about this Pyron anyway? You've been in here morning and evening for the last five days."

"I'm keeping my eye on him. That's all."

The secretary pushed her eyepiece up her nose. "Well, if he was mine, I'd keep both on him. He's nice on the eyes. I think I frightened him a little when he came wandering in here the first time."

The secretary's tabloid lay open, and a Howler's grizzly face glared from the page. *Selenite Sensation: Three dozen Howlers found dead in the streets over a stretch of forty miles. Doctor of Psychology Kotizjokohipo Ezwytt-Sygvra, his sister Doniettmeda Ezwytt-Adespalsin, and Doctor of Medicine Voss Biko all testified that the pack turned on itself after a disagreement broke out at Ezwytt-Sygvra's home.*

Odd. Only days before they had assumed responsibility for leveling the Euclasian laboratory. What disagreement was severe enough to make them level their own ranks in a power struggle?

Thalia twirled her ink pen against her lips and smirked. "Anyway, I promise I will notify you the moment we receive any personal message for you or hear anything back on your Disrel. But I wouldn't get your hopes up too high. He's probably ghosted you for a little Pyron girl."

"All the more reason to hunt him down and knock him across the head for lying."

Coils of razor wire crowned the lofty concrete walls that snaked for miles in the dank plain between the lush and snowy Selenite range and the bald, craggy Dolomites. Guard towers pricked the sky at intervals along the wall. The wide gate and its metal doors could've held back a flood. Offices and barracks hugged the barbed levee on either side of the gate, and military vehicles squatted on paved lots nearby.

Ambrosia parked her corecycle by the gate office and dismounted. The guards drifted back into their positions like ducks and straightened their helmets. One coming from the gate office about-faced and marched back inside. Before she even reached the office, a youthful captain broke through the door, straightening his uniform and cap. He met her at the bottom step and popped off a salute.

"Afternoon, Commander. How may I be of service to you at gate twelve today?"

"I'm here for an educational visit, Captain. To have a look around the sector where it pleases me."

He squared his shoulders. "Yes. Definitely. Would you like me to give you a tour of my district? Nothing worth mentioning has happened around here in quite some time. The people are quiet and content, and I can show you our digging crews, and we can take a short walk inside if you'd like."

"I'd like that very much."

They walked through the field to where teams of men bowed in a trench. Their sweaty bodies glistened as they flung soil into heaps with their spades. The dark corners of their eyes bent her way, but their shoulders never broke their rhythm. There were seasoned men in their fifties, strong young men, and even boys in their early teens straining to keep up. Disrel was not among them.

"His Supremacy didn't want the stench of burning or the mess of ashes to carry on the wind, so we now throw the dead into trenches and use the troublemakers to dig them."

"I'm trying to locate a certain Pyron by the name of Disrel. Does it ring any bells?"

"Not a one. We've got about eighty-four thousand per square mile here. And at the rate they drop, it does no good to name them."

"Would a face help?" She pulled one of the mall photos from her pocket, covering half of it with her hand.

The captain rubbed a smile from his fleshy lips. "You could tell me that was the face of the Tourmaline Renegade and it's like you showed me a photo of every ashrat man who has ever walked through this gate. If you want to tell them apart, you look at their backs. About half of them have an entire criminal history tattooed there." He studied her for a moment. "Let me give you a tour of the inside."

They walked back to the gate as the soldiers swung open the heavy metal doors.

"We've paved a little beyond this gate, but you'll still need to watch your step. They're a lot like cattle. Identical, simple, and not very particular where they piss and skit."

The moment they passed the threshold, three soldiers crossed the road, dragging a wiry man by his cuffed wrists. They forced him to hug a light pole and attached his cuffs to a high ring. One soldier stepped back and brought a rawhide flogger down across the man's smooth, ivory skin. The Pyron gasped and turned one sooty eye back at her.

"I didn't do anything! I'm innocent! They just grabbed me from my porch. I swear, I did noth—" A cry splintered his words as he slid against the pole.

Ambrosia's mouth bunched as the lash drew welts. This was not her jurisdiction. She had no authority to stop the beating. No doubt the captain had organized it merely to impress her, knowing that a surprise visit from an Imperial Sable could only lead to a promotion or demotion. "His Supremacy will be very proud of your work here, Captain. I'll be sure to put in a good word for you."

"Much appreciated, Commander. My soldiers are always patrolling these streets and keeping order."

"Good. Now I'll have a look around here on my own."

The captain nodded and cleared his throat. "Certainly. Please let me know if you find room for improvement."

"At the moment, I don't see how you could do any better."

The suffering Pyron moaned as his trembling fingers reached for the sky.

"But if that changes, I'll let you know." She squeezed her thumbs behind her duty belt to steady her stomach, delivered a sharp nod in the captain's direction, and marched down the street. The soil under her boots darkened and the pungent stench of sewage, ammonia, and rotting earth scalded her nose. Tents pitched up against one another in blocks. Campfires smoldered and naked children squatted in the mud, sculpting the putrid earth and poking sticks into the lumps. Mothers stood in the doorways of tents, pressing their squalling infants to their sagging breasts, their wide eyes drinking in the sable and spewing fear.

Ambrosia's eyes narrowed upon the squalid conditions. Kobalt beef cattle were given cleaner stalls than this. How did Disrel come so clean and fresh, smelling of lavender and sage, his garment unspotted? Where did he keep a corecycle among poverty such as this?

A few blocks onward, the tents gave way to more permanent structures, and the streets were paved and drained. Wares dangled from the ceilings of clean, white booths. The vendors hung back, clutching their work to their chests and pulling things from the path of her shadow. Ambrosia scanned every face. Roughly eighty-four thousand per square mile. She could not slog through miles of encampment and hope to find him. A tall, slender man leaned into a post, head bowed, hands working. Shavings rolled and floated around his feet. It looked so much like him. If he would just turn his head . . . Ambrosia peered at his face.

The young man shuddered and dropped the carving block. His eyes flashed and his lips hammered out a string of Pyron oaths. Her heart dropped. It wasn't him. The nose was upturned, and the eyes were too deep.

"Sorry. Uhm—Zo-e, Zo-e habi. Zo-e habiha." She fumbled through the Pyron word several times, aware that her intonation was far from perfect. "I'm looking for someone. Have you seen this man?"

She pulled the photo from her pocket, tapping Disrel's face and repeating his name.

The young man swiped up his block of wood and squinted at the photo. He shrugged and shook his head. Along the tables at his booth sat rows of carved animals, some painted and lifelike, others fun caricatures highlighting the beast's more quizzical features. Each was beautiful and inspiring. This craftsman poured the same love into his talent that Disrel had poured into that dress.

Ambrosia pocketed the photo. "Have you sold? Any?"

The Pyron shook his head. Another curl of wood fluttered to the earth. "Every sun, Zo carve one. All, many suns. Zo here."

Ambrosia didn't have to count. Her eyes took in all three hundred or more pieces standing on the tables. She reached for the purse on her belt and pointed to a row of prancing horses. "May I buy one?"

The young man's brow arched and his eyes illuminated. He propelled himself from the post to the table. "Yes! Yem want which?"

She touched a cremello horse, its features lightly pinked and its body thinly white-washed. It was frozen poetry, muscles defined, every strand of mane and tail in fluid motion.

"How much?"

"Two."

That was hardly enough. Ambrosia drew a twenty-credit coin from her purse and laid it in his hand. "All yours."

His eyes bugged and his lips made a sucking motion as he drew his trembling hand over his nose and mouth. "Stop!" He spun around and grabbed a box from under the table. "Zo promise Zo give first buyer gift."

He procured a small feline figurine, more roughly carved, and set it in her other hand with a broad smile. " Emak-yem! Thank you!"

Her face flushed as she stuttered through several thank yous before turning away and tucking the little cat into her jacket pocket. She would have to carry the horse for some time, but its beauty seemed so worth the effort. If only she knew more Pyron words and could have expressed to the young man just how impressive his work was. Perhaps her purchase had been the greatest compliment he had ever received.

The wind carried the odors of Pyron cuisine, mixing it with human and animal stench. Concrete hotels, three and four stories high, shaded the streets. Men crouched in the open doorways and on steps, leering at every Kobalt passerby and the soldiers patrolling in groups of threes and fours. The atmosphere was subdued, but tense. Laundry crossed the streets in rows and a hunched old man swayed on the back of an ox, singing and punching out a tune on a thumb piano.

His long white beard wisped over his shoulders on both sides and his squinting eyes were buried under tufts of matted white eyebrows.

Ambrosia puzzled at the inconsistencies around her. The sector was like a city, with its wealthy districts and slums scrambled together. The settlements varied in their layout and structure. Some plots were nothing but stretches of mud and tents, others multiple story buildings on cobbled avenues with street restaurants in their basements and ground levels. Others were neat rows of booths with artisan goods. Perhaps these were the marks of different tribes, perhaps even variations within the Pyron culture, now forced to coexist in one cramped area. They had their upper class, their hard-working craftsmen, their beggars, and their troublemakers. Perhaps they had segregation of their own here.

Ambrosia turned down a narrow street and headed toward the settlement that squatted before the adjoining gate. The tall buildings looked nicer, at least from where she stood. That would be the most likely place to find a Pyron prince. The cityscape felt familiar. Perhaps she had seen it in a magazine back when the empire had constructed buildings and given Pyrons materials, hoping to encourage them to move here willingly and develop it themselves. More permanent houses appeared along the way and animals wandered through grassy patches between them. But for all their amenities, the people looked no happier. They scowled from their doorways and pulled their children into the shadows.

A cow lumbered around the corner, kicking up its heels and swinging its dehorned head. A group of youths pursued on foot, swinging ropes in attempts to catch it. Ambrosia retreated into an alcove, and something crunched under her boot. A sooty little face turned upward, ebony eyes squinted into crescents and lips twisted into a pained frown. The child clamored up the sagging steps to its house, heaving forth tears. Ambrosia withdrew, thinking she had stepped on the child's fingers or crushed its foot. But when she looked down, she saw it. The smashed head of a baked clay doll, its tattered white garment stained with mud. The mother rushed from the house, wild eyes punishing the sable from head to toe, and clutched her child's head to her thighs. Ambrosia's heart sank as she squatted by the broken clay doll, fingering through the hopeless mess of shards.

"Would you take her life too?" The mother jabbed her finger at Ambrosia like a knife. "It was all we could bring with us when you people forced us from our home."

The words scalded the back of her neck, and she pushed a pleading hand in the mother's direction.

"Zo-e habiha. Zo-e habiha."

The mother's face melted into a quizzical expression.

Ambrosia held the wooden horse out, motioning to the child to take it. The child pushed a tiny finger into its nose and turned its face against its mother's body. The mother patted the child's back and spoke calm Pyron words. Ambrosia eased toward the steps at a crouch with the beautiful horse fully extended. The child's dirty hands reached out over the breach and seized the horse. A tiny smile turned the sooted lips, pulling a smile from her own face as the child stroked the horse's neck with approval. It would never replace the sentimental void the doll had left, but it would do. The tears had stopped. For now.

Hypocrisy and guilt torqued her heart, and she stood and marched onward. One kindness could not wash Pyron's blood from her hands. Why was she searching for Disrel anyway? If she found him digging graves or tied to a whipping pole, why should she treat him any differently than all the rest of them? Why did he deserve her mercy over the others? She could not rescue these people. A few good deeds would not help her sleep at night when all of Pyron was turned to ashes and compost in this valley. A few kindnesses would never save her lamb from the slaughtering yard.

She paused in a wide food market where droves of people mingled. Her shoulders sagged. What was the point? She could not walk the perimeter of Pyron in a day. What if Disrel was lying sick in the back of a house? She would walk right by and never know to stop and ask. In this market alone, hundreds converged, and their homogenous features made it even more difficult to pick one out of the bunch. Every head was raven, every eye the same color. They were lean and gangly, clad in white skyns. She felt like an outsider observing a cult.

An icy hand clapped down on her wrist and a cloaked form leaned in, lifting its skeletal cheeks up to the sunlight. "There are three you seek. One is masked. The other has unmasked you. And the third you keep close to your heart."

The ancient woman's head was like a dandelion in full seed, and her bony finger tapped the lump in Ambrosia's breast coat pocket. Her eyes were soulless, milky orbs.

Ambrosia jerked out of reach. "What do you want with me, old woman?"

Her dry lips pulled and quivered. "Only to show you the way." She snatched Ambrosia's hand and raked her fingers across her palm, palpating, brushing, all the while chewing on something in her cheek and making noises with her throat. "To find your renegade, you must first lose yourself. And then, my little honey flower, let love find you."

Ambrosia yanked her hand free. "I don't believe in fortunes."

"I'm not reading your fortune, child. I'm making you aware of the paths that lay before you. Guiding you toward the right one. But the choice is yours. What is a life lived without love? Just a dream of death from which there is no waking." She turned, humming and dancing her fingers through the air. "Seven stripes they gave my love, for want of a blessing, for want of a name. Why mark the tiger? Why sharpen his stripes? The Tourmaline Renegade shoulders the shame."

Ambrosia seized the old woman by the shoulder and jerked her around. "Where is the Tourmaline Renegade?"

A crafty smile gleamed through her sunken, wrinkled face. "You weren't listening. Seven stripes they gave my—"

"I don't want riddles. Where does he bed down? What is his name?"

"Ah, his name. Yes. His name is Kyreasheluhn." One bony finger hurled skyward. "You can find him every clear night watching you from heaven. He's also hiding in your pocket there." She winked and turned away, hobbling forward on the metal pipe she used as a cane.

Kyreasheluhn. What a strange Pyron name. Ambrosia tugged the little carved animal from her jacket and turned it over in her fingers. How could a sightless, senile woman know what was in her pocket? What other truth had she dropped? Ambrosia muttered the grandmother's words back to herself as she studied the carving. The features were those of a large cat, but with too short a mane for a lion. Blemishes crossed through the bright, smooth wood, perhaps running too deep to sand out, perhaps the reason the carver had ceased working with it. There were seven pink veins. Maybe that was why the artist had carved a tiger. She clutched it tightly. Why would a Pyron elder want her to find the Tourmaline Renegade? Why would she betray him to a sable?

Her eyes snapped up where she had last seen the woman walking, but she had been swallowed up in the crowd, vanished in the sea of people. Dozens of dark doorways gaped on either side of the street.

Ambrosia released a disgusted sigh and headed back toward gate twelve by way of the wall to avoid retracing her steps. She had no more hope of finding the old woman in that market than she had of finding Disrel in all of Pyron, but there was still always that microscopic chance he was close by and fate would bring them together. Perhaps he had ghosted her, given her up for some more readily available Pyron woman, someone who looked more like himself and understood him like only his own people could. But the last time they'd parted ways, it hardly seemed plausible. He'd been so hesitant to let go of her hand. And when she'd glanced back through the barracks window, he was just standing there, staring into the sky and then at his bike like a homeless man, someone who had lost all hope and will to continue.

She trudged down the streets and alleys, dodging piles of feces, stray animals, wandering children. It had been so easy to turn a blind eye to these people before. But now every graying mother and father looked like someone who could have been Disrel's parent, every child a sibling or relative. It was harder to look at them and not feel something, not feel a little sickening in the stomach, a tug in the heart. It was hard not to imagine Disrel living among them, suffering these cramped and wanting conditions. It was easy to see now how death could actually become a pleasant, beautiful, and desirable release.

Ambrosia stepped out of an alley that ended at the face of the wall, heavily layered with bright graffiti, sometimes overlapping, sometimes varying styles merged end to end where one artist left off and another took up the brush. The mural continued for several hundred feet, and a towering black figure drew her eyes up. It was the Tourmaline Renegade, poised with weapons in hand, his black mirror visor gazing out over the sector. His legs were planted firmly at the bottom of the wall. A young woman crouched there, lapping on globs of paint with a patch of lambswool. The moment she felt herself being watched, she dropped her brush and ran. Ambrosia snared her elbow, halting her, and the girl trembled, whimpering in her native tongue and wringing fistfuls of curly black hair.

Ambrosia pointed at the portrait. "Who is that?"

The artist grimaced and shook her head. "I see picture. Him on newsposters soldiers read."

"Kyreasheluhn?"

The artist blinked away tears. "The sky tiger?"

"Is it a man's name?"

"No mother or father would ever place such a heavy name on their child. Few men could live worthy of it. We choose humble names for our children and let Sky Father name us among the stars. For each, every soul descended from the Spirit Father, there burns a star in the sky, a birthright that shines to us a blessing, a sky name."

Ambrosia released the girl and propped her hands on her hips. She sighed in frustration. Of course the old woman had only been teasing her, laying a false trail. Who would betray the Tourmaline Renegade's true name?

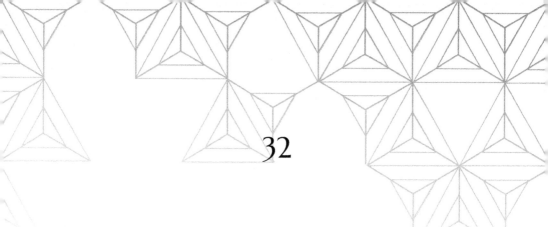

32

The imperial garden glistened with spectral beauty. Shadows deepened and faded. Silver gilded every topiary bush, statue, and verdant alcove. A palace guard strolled along the reflecting pool, spinning his polearm in slow circles, every now and then assuming a martial stance to admire his form in the water.

Disrel crouched in the shadow of a yawning chimeric statue, chalking his hands, counting the windows above him, recalling the layout of the palace's upper floors. He massaged an ache in his left elbow. It had only been a week since his tangle with Vogin, but he couldn't risk waiting another day.

A behemoth cloud spread its jaws and licked the moon down its throat. Disrel set his fingers on a knob overhead, dug his toes into carved accent stones, and climbed to another knob. His wrist strained as he dangled, swinging, gaining momentum for the next handhold. He toed the wall and kicked upward. His gloved fingers grazed the next knob and he fell back on his right arm and dangled a moment. Patches of silver waxed and waned on the side of the palace, threatening to reveal him clinging there in helplessness. He swung again, adjusted his hold, then latched on with his other hand, sucking lungfuls of air, flooding his muscles with oxygen. The window ledge he needed floated many yards to the right and above him, between two smooth pillars and a dry moat. He spent some time just holding on with toes and fingers, dipping his hands into his bag of chalk and searching for nearby holds. Minutes later, he reached a second-floor balcony and scraped over the railing. The giant topiary animals below resembled toys small enough to hold in his hand, and the paved pathways like roads painted on a playmat.

Disrel crouched on all fours in the shadows, panting and gazing through the window and its gauzy drapes at a deep crimson room, glowing like an ember, ornately furnished. As tempting as it was to enter here, there were far too many sables between this room and the library, and once his presence was known, he would be forced to flee. He turned to the polished blue titans that flaunted imperial power and imposed an impassable barrier between a renegade and his goal. Between them, some thirty feet up, the glass-edged balcony jutted, surmountable only by spiders or climbing geckos. If he lost momentum and managed to jump to some safe hold under the ledge, he would dangle there until he fell to the porch below, a fall which he could never hope to walk away from. If he lost his hold and fell straight down the pillar, he was certainly a dead man.

Disrel pumped his fists and flexed his legs. He scrubbed more chalk into his hands, while pulling deep breaths and quieting his mind. Nothing else mattered. Not the chip. Not the sables or the soldiers. Not the waxing light of the moon. Just the climb. These pillars. That balcony. The hours and endless nights of wrestling, lifting, stretching, climbing, crawling, and running were for moments like this. He hadn't put on ten pounds of muscle for any other reason. He sprinted across the wide balcony, hit the stone railing with his feet, and hurled himself toward the second pillar. Hands and feet slapped the stone as he thrust backward, turning and planting his limbs into the body of the opposite column, palms flat, toes flexed. He jumped back to the left pillar, landing higher, then back again, a little higher. There was no looking down, only focusing on gripping and jumping and pushing. Five. Six. Seven. His thighs and calves kindled with heat, and shocks ran like razor wire through the bones in his feet. A saw-toothed pain bit through his left elbow, followed by two pops and a cool flushing. He gritted his teeth and made one desperate leap for the glass balcony.

His left arm extended and another stitch pinged as his hand slipped on the dewy railing. Lightning forked his heart as his right hand clapped the surface. The glass boomed. He glanced down past his swinging legs at the menacing porch, gasped, threw his left hand back up onto the rail, and heaved himself over. He squatted on the balcony, quivering and sucking air, shaking his left hand and flexing his fist. Blood dripped through his sleeve and pattered on the stone. The wound had reopened. If he could get back to Alta tonight, she would restitch it.

He inched to the glass door, planting one foot directly in front of the other and donning his gloves. His curved, blackened blade whispered from its sheath and became a phantom extension of his fist. He leaned upon the door and it rumbled open on its track. Ornately carved wood lined the walls and crowned the ceilings, contrasting with the stone and plaster walls, saturated in frescoes, tapestries, and hanging art. Furniture mingled like circles of friends at a dance, and lamps, turned down low, illuminated the path to the door. Disrel scanned for signs of life, for soldiers, for a body reclining on a couch or nodding over in a chair, and then he closed the door. He brushed his fingers over the threads of a tapestry, appreciating the artist's skill at spinning and weaving the organic old-world fibers by hand. On a pedestal nested in an alcove, a stone head wearing a sarcastic expression mocked him from underneath a Pyron headdress: a stolen relic, the crown of a revered elder of long ago, no doubt murdered. He touched a rusty splatter on the browband, and the gold feathers tinkled and chimed against the stone beads. Did the Kobalt empire hate the Pyron culture, or just the Pyron people? What other relics could be found here? What other treasures had been taken from Pyron homes and families in their displacement and added to the emperor's private collections?

Disrel turned toward the door and reviewed the steps he'd committed to memory. He was only two rooms and a staircase away from the library. He jerked back at a glimmer of movement on the opposite wall and instinctively pushed his blade between himself and the shifter. A pink, tricornered liddicoatite glowed on the far wall, amid the warm threads of light that traced a torso, thighs, and arms. It was the Tourmaline Renegade, straight-stomached and broad-shouldered, expressionless face, silently daring, resisting, fearless. Disrel sighed, turning away from the mirror and stealing into a tranquil blue-green anteroom that seemed to serve no other purpose than to display more treasures and furniture, to impress the emperor's guests with the grandeur of his house and the sheer number of its rooms and decorative themes and aesthetics. None would know that the Tourmaline Renegade was giving himself a private tour in the darkest hours of the morning.

He inched through the double doors and peered down the halls. The expansive home seemed deserted, deathly still, as if they were expecting him, and the trap was about to spring. But the servants would be on the move in less than an hour, hustling to prepare another royal breakfast and dedicate themselves to Cinnabar's morning routine. Disrel ventured out on the grand balcony, sweeping his hand along the immaculate banister. Each baluster was a statuesque column of crystal, and wherever the banister turned, there stood an efflorescent sculpture of polished metals supporting a golden-horned ram's head that knobbed the corner. Glass and agate tiles floored the grand room below and a fountain frolicked in the center, with shimmering golden koi in its silvery waters. The white noise it created was both a blessing and a bane. A flowering array of skylights capped a hexagonal rotunda above.

Disrel mounted the silver banister and slid to the bottom, where the railing sloped into a rampart ram sculpture. He dismounted nimbly and stole along the edges of the wide room, watching for glittering polearms or shifting suits of armor. In the corner opposite the stairs stood the pivotal wooden doors of Cinnabar's library, carved with Kobalt bears fishing the rapids. The grandeur of the room kept snatching his eyes and hurling them aloft. Even in the dark, it sparkled, and the crystal balustrade threw colors under the glow of the wall sconces. What would it look like when sunlight poured through the stained glass and drenched everything in gold? All around the corners of the room, crouched above the crown moldings, were stone carvings of men and beasts in pitched battle, dancing marches, and scenes of frenetic discord. Nightmarish heads glared upon him with monstrous eyes and draconian mouths, gouged into strange mixtures of prideful laughter and divine apathy.

A man like Cinnabar had no comprehension of life on the streets, or life under taxation, or life under the weight of his own laws and dictates. He sat on the clouds of fortune and privilege, ruling like a god. Disrel flicked a gold button on an armored mannequin. What would it have been like to have been born into a noble Kobalt family, birthed upon silk sheets in a house of marble with the ears and eyes of adoring servants trained upon his every need? Life would have been so different. He would be so different. Maybe unable to sympathize with the strays and beggars, the blue-collar workers, even the working middle-class like Koti. What if he had been born in the same class as Koti? Without his mother and father, without Miss Mazilyn, without everything that had ever happened to him, would he be a good man like Koti, or a shortsighted Pyron sympathizer, or just an apathetic, self-absorbed credit pincher, striving to keep his boot heels free of Pyron mud and feces? The dream was hardly tempting. No Pyron was at home behind stone walls. Pyrons wanted the rolling hills and water-fed plains, the stars over their heads, the wind on their backs, and their elders free to speak their minds. But the world had changed, and now the only thing any Pyron wanted was the promise of another day, a land beyond the sector walls, and a place among their Kobalt neighbors.

Disrel set his hand on the doors and pushed, meeting with the rancid smell of tannins and ancient paper. Orbs of light burned like luminaries here and there, hovering their rock bases on tabletops and wall shelves. Three bookcases, wrapped into columns, divided the room into three sections and guided the eyes to fresco murals of constellations, chimeric beasts, and cosmopolitan sceneries on the ceiling. Ancient texts lay under darkened glass, and where the wall lacked a bookcase, there were paintings and valuables on pedestals. It seemed to be more a library of art than books.

Disrel paused before a row of portraits, three generations of emperors and the imperial family. Lord Haddrax had started most of the pain, ruling until a few years after Mother's murder and Father's arrest. He gazed from the frame with savage, ruthless beads of corestone, and his fleshy jowls pulled his mouth into a carpish frown. For decades, schoolchildren and citizens had worshiped this image, and it had never put a good smile into that face. Disrel turned from the wall of portraits, noting a graceful bell organ situated in a glass alcove, overlooking the forested western edge of the palace grounds. Its arms floated like swans over the window seats, and its strings glistened against the bells like diamond-dewed spider silk, waiting for a musician's touch. Next to it, a silver-topped side table was graced with crystalware and a pitcher of hard liquor, half empty. Disrel strolled along the bookcases, glancing over titles on the spines. None of these were books a stray Pyron could have ever read. Reading was a survival necessity, not a pastime, and these were books intelligent men like Koti read for pleasure. The title on one spine glowed a little more than the others. *Euphillem's Anthropology: Our Pyron Brethren.*

Disrel tugged it from the shelf and splayed it open in his hand. Every other page was graced with a full-color print by painters of the past, historians who had documented with the brush instead of the pen or the camera. The portraits of Pyron elders, warriors, mothers, and youths breathed on the paper, their cheeks pink and their eyes glistening. The garments were vivid with blue and crimson set against white and black, and some paintings featured them interacting with and posing beside the early Kobalt settlers.

> *"Less than a week after our arrival to this land beyond the mountains, the natives began making their presence known. They called themselves the Pyr–Eluhn, children of the sky, of the sun, or perhaps, a better translation is, of the burning one. Our throats ever fail to pronounce the delicate sounds the latter half of their name requires, and so we call them Pyrons, for the supernal light they carried with and in themselves wherever they went."*

> *~ Frejjoc the Halite*

Disrel flipped from page to page, perusing the historical scenes and personal accounts that stood out to him.

"The Elders of the tribe that follow the reindeer were the first to greet us and teach us about the native plants and how to use them medicinally. We were greeted like long-lost brethren, regarded as family, and informed of a being rumored to live among the stars that they regard as their Sky Father."

~ Jiblote of Elba

Excerpt from a letter written by Governor Obexus to Lord Governor Qalet at Jeremejev.

"By winter of the same year, it was clear to all that we were stranded in this new world. Less than a day after our plight reached the ears of the nearest Pyron tribe, about twenty-four of their people strode boldly into our midst and presented us with a set of magic stones that provide light and sometimes heat by an unknown and invisible connection. They showed us how the stones lie all around us, in riverbeds and on the hillsides, and how to imbue them with power to levitate objects of incredible size and weight. Fifty of our people were impressed to sit upon a tree trunk that was rolled upon these stones and a Pyron child of about nine years of age was able to push the trunk and its burden of people many yards."

"They regard women strangely, almost as equals, allowing them to sit as Elders to be sought for their counsel and wisdom."

~ Master Sergeant at Arms, Reygali

"When they heard how the governor's daughter suffered mysterious sick spells for years, they brought to us an Elder, in whom there was rumored to dwell a mysterious force they call Thelis. After a simple touch of his hand, the child amended over the space of several hours, and was up again, eating and playing by the end of the day. May posterity never forget Pyron's kindness to us, refugees and vagabonds."

~ author unknown

"Though not one of their men stood as tall or as muscular as any of us, they were just as strong of body, quick of reflex, and capable of mind, and put our best warriors to shame in friendly competitions."

~ Jiblote of Elba

"There is no obvious reason why those from the tribe of the tiger exhibit a greater physical stamina and strength. Their men show an astounding resilience and courage that surpasses that of the other tribes. Most of their legends of heroism and stories of magnificent feats in sports and hunting come from within this small, but indomitable clan."

~ House of Records, 106 Purz Dynasty

Disrel's brow lifted as his chest swelled with pride.

"Generations of intermarriage between Kobalt and Pyron people have proven the dangerous dominance of the Pyron genome. I can only liken their genetic code to a virus that damages the output of the other parent's Kobalt genes in the offspring. Even after four generations of consistent Kobalt breeding, any line which suffered the injection of Pyron genetics will continue to put forth offspring with strong Pyron appearances, lacking diverse colors of the eyes and hair."

~ Silati Veon, Master of the Imperial House of Reproductive Sciences

Disrel's expression darkened beneath his helmet as he studied a portrait of Veon and cast the blame for Pyron suffering on him. There were probably many more men responsible, those who echoed the hate in their own generation. He wished he had the time to sit and see what rebuttals Euphillem might have made against the dangerous rhetoric.

"I predict that in a matter of less than a century, these people will breed our superior traits out of existence. This is not a weakness in our own genetics, but a sign that our bloodlines are pure and must be further guarded from infusion."

~ Silati Veon, Master of the Imperial House of Reproductive Sciences

Disrel flipped to the last page with disgust.

"The technology you see around you today, even the lamplight you will doubtless use to read this book, was a gift from the Pyr–Eluhn people who welcomed us to live among them like family. Without them, our ancestors would have endlessly toiled, and perhaps been conquered by ambitious neighbors more familiar with this land. The Kobalt Empire would never have birthed and entered its golden age. But the real magic of these people and their origins lies in the mysterious force they call Thelis. As they taught us the moment we began to speak each other's languages, carrying the light of Thelis in the heart is what it truly means to be Pyr–Eluhn."

Disrel returned the book and wandered over to the bell organ. He touched a string. It resonated, and the bell warbled. He staunched the bell with a pinch and moved on, passing between a cluster of seating and picking up a small box from a side table. He lifted the lid and swept the velvet interior. A glassy data chip nested in the fabric. He took it to one of the reading tables and pressed it into a slot, then turned up the lamp below. The glass burned with magnified rows of sky-blue characters, strange words like the ones Koti used. They felt sinister. Disrel's eyes raced over instructions until his stomach turned. There were lists of serums with deadly side effects and details for medical administration.

He swiped it from the reading slot and pressed it into a hidden pocket on his side. The neighboring glass was dim, with characters still present. Someone had left a chip in the reading table. He brightened the screen and bowed over it, rolling the sphere next to the glass, scrolling back through yards of text until he reached a heading: *Operation Soapstone: Steps to Purify Kobalt Bloodlines for National Security.* He continued scrolling. *Operation Waterfall: Steps for Cleansing Traitors and Sympathizers From All Sectors.* The next segment outlined various military regiments and their passcodes to buildings and equipment in use. Disrel wrenched the chip from its slot and mashed it down into the pocket with the other. This was the key to Pyron's freedom. The skeleton key, the hellfest that would send Cinnabar's regime to its knees. Mored would know what to do with it. And once distributed, others would have the power to hit the regime where it hurt.

The library brightened.

Disrel twisted, expecting to hear an alarm and see sables flooding through the doors. All remained still, except for a subtle movement on the other side of the room. A pair of ox-sized shoulders shifted as a curly head turned, the whole man rising elegantly from a couch. Cinnabar, wrapped in a damask silk robe with quilted collar and trim, sauntered nearer, touching furniture as he passed. His puffy, reddened eyes bored straight into Disrel's dark visor with renewed vigor. Cinnabar paused at the liquor table and poured the blood red drink into a crystal chalice.

"You finally decided to pay me a visit. I'm tickled." A dark pink scar traced the corner of his bottom lip to the curve of his jaw.

Disrel stepped back, scrambling through escape routes in his head. "You knew I was coming?"

Cinnabar filled a second glass. "Since my daughter's murder, I often experience sleepless nights. So I come here to read. Nothing settles my mind like the subject of ethnic cleansing." He drew up the crystal chalices in his broad, tawny hands and extended one.

Disrel shifted, calculating his exit and listening for footfalls. Just how long had the emperor been watching him before he turned up the lights? Why wasn't he calling for his sables?

"You seemed to be enjoying the book you picked up. Did you learn anything?"

"More than you know." Disrel said, his voice shaking from anger. "Give the people the truth."

Cinnabar set the glasses back on the table. His voice was as deep and fruity as black wine. "I'm doing my best to be civil, renegade. If you hope to die a quick and painless death, you will surrender those data chips."

"I want you to stop murdering my people." Spit showered the visor interior.

A smile turned the emperor's tired face, and he pinched the bridge of his nose. "Murder?"

"Yes. *Murder*. What have we done to deserve extermination?"

"You don't seem to understand that you are my property." Cinnabar leaned back against a chair and folded his arms across his chest. "Look around you. This palace. This empire. These people. All mine. My birthright to rule. And as long as I let Pyron continue, you threaten to convince my people that they belong to a god other than myself. I risk losing control of the population. And what is a god without a people to worship him? Nothing. Nothing at all."

"The people deserve the truth."

Cinnabar chuckled. "Oh, the truth hurts, renegade. Just like you will hurt when I break every bone in your miserable body for what you took from me. Your god is not an eternal spirit. He is flesh. And he lives on in the royal lineage that has ruled this continent since he came to this world. I am of that divine lineage. And every person who is not, Pyron included, are like the cattle: Here to serve us. And as your god, my dislike for Pyron is no more personal than a woman ridding ants from her kitchen, sweeping spiders from her porch, or pulling weeds in her garden. Frankly, I've never even liked the way you ashrats look. You're like an ugly rug in an otherwise perfectly decorated room."

Disrel shook his head in disbelief. "We are *people*."

Cinnabar scratched his scar. "And are all animals just animals? Or would you step on a cockroach without thinking twice? Would you shudder at the thought of eating a dog because it's a wonderful, obedient companion, but never shed a tear for all the pork on your plate? Who hates the lamb, or fish, or fowl that he takes for food or sport? The world is full of many different kinds of people living on different intellectual, emotional, and spiritual levels of consciousness. Some are ever evolving, breeding themselves into a better race. Others are stagnant, bearing hopeless and dangerous genetics and clinging to primal religions that forge defiance against authority."

Disrel shifted closer to the door, hand on his knife. "So that's how you justify it. You think we're animals."

"I don't need to justify anything. I answer to no one, not even your god."

Disrel whipped his knife from its scabbard.

Cinnabar's dark-rimmed eyes gleamed and his nostrils flared as he picked up a chalice and turned it to his lips. His voice had a dangerous edge to it. It rang like a whirling cutlass. "You raised a piece of cloth, stopped a train, blew up a building. Your best efforts only prolong Pyron's miserable existence. You can't save them all."

"If I save just one, I've saved the world."

The library doors blasted open between them as four sables jumped in, lowering their glaives at Disrel's chest and shouting for him to drop his weapon and get down on the ground.

"Then you'd better start with saving yourself, renegade." Cinnabar grinned and sipped the crimson alcohol from the cup he'd offered.

The gleaming head of a glaive pushed closer, menacing his stomach as the sables flanked him. Disrel raised both hands.

"Watch me." He swept under a polearm and twisted it from the sable, flipping her on her back. Clutching both knife and polearm together, he rushed Cinnabar.

The glass of spirits dinged across the top of his helmet and Cinnabar danced around an armchair, catching the glaive in its cushion. Disrel bowled right through the table of crystal ware and hurtled out of the library through the far door. Boots thundered and armor plates clapped syncopated rhythms. Soldiers poured into the great hall, shouting and loading crossbows, taking formation at every exit. Disrel tore up the stairs and down an endless hall and came to a great stained-glass window that entirely filled the end of a wide cul-de-sac.

Thunder. He'd gone the wrong way.

Two doors faced each other. Disrel flew up against one, hammering the handle. Locked. He whirled and collided with the other, also locked, and too stout to kick down. He slammed his blade into its sheath and squared up with the window, his chest heaving, his hands clenching.

Bodies did not break Kobalt glass—Kobalt glass broke bodies.

The soldiers and sables rounded the corner, assuming a double-row formation, lowering their polearms and raising their crossbows.

"It's over, renegade. Surrender or die!"

Disrel's breath roared in his helmet, and sweat lined his upper lip. There were sixteen now, eight of them training crossbows on his chest. "There's a difference?"

Cinnabar towered over them at the back, the head that wielded the jaws of the dragon. "I want him alive."

The soldiers marched forward, weapons glistening like wet teeth.

"Surrender, renegade!"

"Are you kidding me? Where's the fun in that?" Disrel jerked a grenade from his belt and bowled it at them. It spun on the carpet, hissing and spewing smoke before releasing a barrage of pops and flashes of light. Up from his belt, a dark cloud exploded, engulfing him and spraying trails of soot onto the lofty ceiling.

The soldiers fell back with pitched barking and a bolt hissed over Disrel's left shoulder as he crouched. Someone gave the order to fire, and all seven crossbows twanged in rapid succession. Disrel hurled over on his stomach. Three steel bolts stamped into the floor. Eight more punched the grand window, and its myriad segments crunched, screeched, and groaned. The entire window yawned and thundered, and pieces dangled and tumbled from their frames. Eight glaives plunged through the rising cloud.

Disrel rolled up and rushed the compromised window, bracing for impact, setting his feet to strike first. A second volley of heads and shafts whistled and screeched through the glass all around him, and an acidic sting hit his side just as his boot struck the window. Large panes blew outward and crunched from their welds like pieces of hard candy. A massive sheet of crimson chopped down on Disrel's head like a beheading blade, driving him down through the darkness. He bent his knees and could not guess when to brace for impact, when to roll. Leafy boughs hissed and raked around his body, cracking under his weight as he plummeted through them. He struck the ground and crumpled under the crushing remnants that butterflied over his shoulders. Webs of lightning sizzled through his bones and the air reeked of salty iron. He gaped and strained to move while sheets of glass rained and disintegrated upon others pitched on his back.

Cinnabar's voice roared through the blackness.

"He's got my chips! Don't let him escape!"

Stars twirled ellipses around Disrel's head. He groaned and heaved against the rubble, too shaken to consider his wounds as he hobbled out of the window light toward the topiary hedges. Reaching the corecycle was his only hope. Soldiers and sables would flood from the mansion at any moment, and he could not outrun the bolts from their crossbows. Disrel trotted down the garden paths, praying for another cloud to cover the moon while he crossed the great lawn. A grounds patrolman spotted him and pursued, calling for reinforcements. Disrel goaded himself faster, gathering the strength he needed to scale the wall, springing and catching hold of its rough edge. His sutured arm seared under the strain of his weight. He kicked over and scrambled for his corecycle, fishing for his key. He mounted the bike, plunged the keystone into its port, and drove it forward with his feet before the engine even sparked to life. The corecycle lurched and peeled into the black street. Success. Disrel swung his fist at the sky and accelerated until the passing lamps were just a flicker in his helmet visor.

The pursuit was far from over. He had to plan a couple different routes back to base—not Koti's, in case they trailed him—and find somewhere to hunker down and hide if he got blown off course. Police and soldiers would be crawling all over the highways in minutes, conducting traffic stops, arresting anyone remotely suspicious. It was not safe to change his skyn yet. He could not risk a moment of transparency or a brightened visor.

The corecycle swallowed miles of the imperial boulevard, trussed with the boughs of tilted, ancient oaks. He rocketed through intersections, straight for the bay bridge, the least suspect path of escape. The clouds blanketing Execution Square burned, and unusually large, wandering stars pulsed in the dawn's blush. Disrel's neck bristled as blue spotlights swept the streets. Three aircraft headed for the bay bridge. Cyclists merged into drifting packs, congesting as they drew to the waterfront. Brake lights and fog lights pulsed and the lanes dwindled.

Fantastic. Morning rush-hour traffic. All five eastbound lanes on that bridge would be crawling. Mist shrouded the tide-drenched trunks of the black stone titans. The light aircraft swooped down in formation and hovered over traffic, spotlighting cyclists at random. Disrel slowed behind the creeping vehicles, and others pulled up around him. Riders sat back and folded their arms, accustomed to congestion but irritated all the same. Some turned and lifted their helmet visors, checking out the dark-skynned rider in their midst. Disrel hunched his shoulders to conceal the image on his breast.

One rider slapped the barrel of his bike and pointed. "Bro! The slag is that? Am I crazy? Is that the Tourmaline Renegade?"

Another punched the shoulder of the rider next to him and pointed.

Disrel toed backward and torqued the bike around, forging his path against the accumulating traffic at the mouth of the bridge. He weaved in and out down the lanes, roaring through breaks and scraping through tighter sections with inches to spare. He put a deep scratch in the fender of a lime-green bike and the rider pushed him, throwing curses and a punch across his helmet. Disrel sputtered an apology as the rider reeled back at the sight of the renegade skyn. He needed space to find air, somewhere to ramp, somewhere to throw the throttle into flight. The flow broke, and Disrel barreled down the freeway and straight into oncoming traffic. Cyclists burned left and right, shouting at the rogue driver. Collision whistles shrieked and headlights flared, as though he were some drunk driver. His shadow splattered on the roadway, framed in a caustic halo of cold light, and a sable's voice screeched through a trumpet.

"I've got a round trained on your butt, renegade! Surrender or die!"

He gunned the throttle and scooted into the darkness. The spotlight licked over his path, and two thunderbolts punched the pavement. Perhaps they were warning shots, but she might not overshoot the third time.

A nest of lights strobed in the roadway ahead, a barricade of police and military vehicles. Disrel willed every ounce of power from the bike and jumped on the footrests, yanking on the handles. The front wheel and its suspension carriage flipped, blasting its energy at the ground. He hurled his weight down and jumped again, catching a sloped retaining wall, and took to the air like a swallow. The hunched body and drooping wings of a QAV-X shadowed his left, driving him toward the coast. Four pursued from behind at various distances, all vying for a clean shot. Disrel hung low, weaving between the skyscrapers to hide. The aircraft spread out and pushed him away from the buildings, forcing him out over the bay and closing the distance. Disrel's thumb ached against the throttle. He had to shake them and get back over land before they drove him into the water. Had Mored not upgraded his craft after his fall into the bay? Or had Kobalt technology improved this much in the last fifteen years?

Disrel skimmed underneath the bay bridge toward the open sea. Pockets of seawater splunked and erupted under fire. He beat the throttle with the heel of his palm, hoping to unlock some emergency feature, some burst of speed trapped within the bike's engine. He gave the opposite handle a twist as the bike swallowed the altitude like a rocket, squashing him down upon the seat. The vultures rose behind him.

Thunder cracked and rattled his bones. A shower of ash and smoke rained over the glistening waves. They'd brought fireworks to the party. Disrel flew erratically and burned through clouds to cover his taillights. The twinkling lights of Tourmal dimmed on the horizon in a curtain of fog as a QAV-X ripped through the cloud on his wing quarter. Two rounds detonated off his tail, rattling the corecycle's corestone, and he lost altitude. Was the pilot toying with him? Why hadn't they already blown him out of the sky? His heart pounded like a hammer mill and he dreaded the next round that would finish him. At any second he expected a bolt to skewer him through the center of his chest or a charged missile to blow him to pieces.

Five more QAV-Xs glinted against the shrouded cityscape, latecomers bristling with heavy qorzan bolts. They burst through the pink cotton candy, strafing his trajectory with rounds. The missiles whistled and exploded into showers of fire. Each burst stopped Disrel's heart and the heat flashed through his skyn. The corecycle shuddered and lurched and the wheel lights faded. He clung to it help-lessly, diving underneath a passing aircraft as the machine took an explosive bolt to the undercarriage. The shock wave blew him from the seat, and he tumbled, hands straining, legs pedaling. He stretched for the handles of the corecycle, for the faint hope that he could revive its engine. Rushing air battered his helmet and body as if Heaven had once again cast down the Tourmaline Renegade. The corecycle turned wheel over wheel below him in the pearlescent mists. Miles out, the wounded QAV-X spiraled like a leaf in a cyclone, its ejected pilot fighting with the cords of a tangled strip of faulty parachute streaming above.

And between them lay a rocky isle, mocking them both with false promises of refuge. What was this sparsely green shoal in the Gulf of Tourmal? Disrel fought to right himself as the water became more imminent, and wrestled with the knowledge that his end had come.

He had failed.

The force of his fall would break his legs and back, leaving him unable to swim.

Which was easier? Drowning in his helmet or being dragged by sables from the waves to suffer Cinnabar's wrath?

He didn't want to face Ambrosia as a prisoner, feel her hatred, and find that their love had been a lie. The water was growing darker. He had maybe seconds left on this ride to meet death. And there was no getting off. No tangible hope to grasp.

How long until Mored learned of his death?

Would Tygo find a way to tell Solla the truth?

Would Solla understand?

Would she forgive him?

Would she be happy living with Koti in his absence?

Solla needed her birthright.

The foaming waves devoured the corecycle first, and Disrel pushed his heels down and locked his arms around his helmet, streamlining himself and bracing for impact.

He struck down, the gurgling waters crushing his chest and back like jaws of ice, the vortex created by the corecycle sucking him deeper into the murky abyss and pulping his consciousness.

the adventure continues in

BIRTHRIGHT
OF
SCARS

CHOOSING

About the Author

Growing up along the Alabama Gulf Coast, Laurisa Brandt spent her summers playing along the creek behind her home, dreaming of high fantasy adventures and writing them down in spiral notebooks. She once narrowly missed being struck by lightning and later came face to face with the ghost in Uncle John's house.

While working for a therapeutic horseback riding program for people with special needs, she was hired by a Hollywood stunt actor to write a TV pilot episode.

She finds inspiration through her many interests, which include: mixed martial arts, freestyle motocross, horseback archery, and antediluvian archaeology. She lives in rural Pennsylvania with her husband and their adopted Timneh African Grey parrot, Hercules.

You can visit her online at laurisabrandt.com.

Acknowledgments

I really cannot thank my husband enough for tolerating me living in an alternate dimension for about two years and speaking to fictional men he will never meet. Or for all of the evenings he had to spend alone while I stared into my computer screen. And I now believe that if a marriage can survive the writing of a book, it can survive just about anything.

My husband always found so many home-improvement projects and yard chores for me to help him with whenever he saw me typing away at the computer. His dancing in my peripheral and asking questions that would drag my head out of the scene right when inspiration was striking will never be forgotten, but is surely forgiven—mostly due to the surprise bars of chocolate left around my workspace. I'm so grateful for his initiation of the lovely bike rides, picnics, movie-nights, and togetherness. And I do show my appreciation for him as often as I can. I'm just letting the rest of you know this book exists because my husband is a patient, understanding, and loving man. I couldn't ask for a more wonderful person to live my life with.

I would also like to thank my sister, Esther, for alpha-reading the G-rated vomit draft and spurring me on to discover more of Cinnabar through Ambrosia's POV. Who knew this book would ever grow to become an R-rated masterpiece? My appreciation also to Olivia for your patient ear whenever I steered our phone conversations onto the topic of this world and its characters. And of course, a huge thanks to both of you for putting up with text bombardments of character sketches, videos of me flabbergasted at the things my characters were telling me, and my joyful rants of discovery.

To Cassie Sanchez, a huge thanks for your helpful critiques and proofreading. I'm humbled that an author with seven literary awards on her debut novel could have actually enjoyed what I threw down.

To Anusha Muradi, for beta reading the entire book before it became a duology: Your encouragement and feedback lit a fire under me. Thank you for believing in Disrel and Ambrosia's story.

To Maddie Silvers, for your insightful critique of the first half. I wish you the best in your future as an editor.

To Ian Craven: I'm so glad to have you as a critique partner and friend. Your insight and Christian perspective on this work have been invaluable.

To Kyle Ronin and all of my friends who waited so patiently for over a year for this book to become a reality—your presence kept me going. Thanks for sticking around and believing I would get'er done.

To my fantastic editor, thank you for all of your suggestions, support, and patience as I divided this work into a duology. I still can hardly believe how fortunate I was to have found you when I did—and how glad I was to learn you were a Tron fan. I really wouldn't have entrusted this story to anyone else.

To Franziska Stern, thanks for your patience with me through all the little tweaks the covers required. I'm so lucky to have landed such a talented and indemand designer.

My highest praise and appreciation goes to my Lord and Savior, Jesus Christ, for His constant guidance along every step of the way. I owe Him every ounce of my creative energy, and am thankful for His providing hand that allowed me the time and strength to bring this story into this world.

Printed in Great Britain
by Amazon